BABE IN THE WOODS

A Novel

For Elmdea,

with best wishes.

Thanks for your book

Frank DiMarco

Books by Frank DeMarco

Fiction
Messenger: A Sequel to Lost Horizon
Babe in the Woods

Non-fiction
Muddy Tracks: Exploring an Unsuspected Reality
Chasing Smallwood: Talking with the Other Side
The Sphere and the Hologram: Explanations from the Other Side
The Cosmic Internet: Explanations from the Other Side
Hemingway on Hemingway: Afterlife Conversations

BABE IN THE WOODS
A Novel

Frank DeMarco

HOLOGRAM BOOKS
www.hologrambooks.com

For information visit: www.hologrambooks.com

or write:

Hologram Books
112 Brandywine Court
Charlottesville, Virginia 22901

Design by Allen Design Studio

Cover and interior photos by Frank DeMarco

Printed in the United States of America

ISBN 978-0-9820098-1-9

Dedication

To my friends and family, some still living
on this side, some on the other side. In particular,

Dana Redfield (1944-2007)
John J. DeMarco (1940-2007)
Rita Warren (1920-2008)

Acknowledgements

This is the part people usually skip, which is too bad. It takes a lot of help to produce a book.

Sarah Hilfer, for taking care of so many details, and for her ace proof-reading. (Any remaining mistakes are probably mine, stemming from last-minute changes.)

Melynn Allen, of Allen Design Studio, for a crisp professional design, a cheerful can-do attitude, and consistent encouragement.

So many friends and acquaintances with whom I have discussed my and their experiences at Monroe Institute programs over the past 15 years.

Last and certainly NOT least, my cadre of friends who read the first version of this story and provided helpful feedback. Alphabetically,

Barbara Bowen
Robert Clarke
Margaret DeMarco
Paul DeMarco
Nancy Ford
Dave Garland
Sarah Hilfer
John King
Michael Langevin
Ann Martin
Nancy (Scooter) McMoneagle
Louis Meinhardt
Chris Nelson
Paul Rademacher
Linda Rogers
Rich Spees
Rita Warren

Author's Note

The C.T. Merriman Institute of this story, and its programs, surroundings, and underlying assumptions, are all based on The Monroe Institute, which, like the C.T. Merriman Institute, is located in central Virginia. I know the place, the programs, and the nature of the participants as well as I know anything in my life. It was there, as I often say, that my conscious life began at age 46. I owe the place and the people a tremendous debt of gratitude, and this story is my way of acknowledging that debt and of indicating to others something of the wealth of new experience and growth that many people have found there.

However, having said that, I hasten to add that this is a work of *fiction*. It is neither history, nor biography, nor autobiography. My portrait of C.T. Merriman draws on Bob Monroe as I remember him, but is not strictly factual, and is not meant to be. Similarly, Angelo Chiari shares much of my background and characteristics (as did his brother George in my novel *Messenger*) but he is not me. Nor are the other characters, nor the situations, limited to fact. Rather, I took people, places, and situations that I knew, and some that I invented, and shuffled them, working to produce a story that tells a truth that is truer than any mere recounting of facts.

And that's the point, really: telling a truth that is truer than facts. I made up the story, but not out of thin air.

Babe in the Woods is an attempt to show just what it's like to take the first tentative steps toward greater awareness. The practices that I have made part of this story were not necessarily things I learned at Monroe, and certainly weren't all learned in my initial program there! Nonetheless, I have stuck to what I know first-hand. Everything I describe, I or friends have done. In fact, I and others have experienced much more in the way of "psychic" experiences than I dare describe here, for fear of losing credibility with those who do not yet know how much is possible.

The concepts presented here are partly things long known, partly my own way of understanding things, and partly concepts that I now think of as my own mainly because I have used them so long and so profitably. Above all I rank Bruce Moen's concepts of perceiver and interpreter, and his technique of raising energy by remembering a time when you were loved.

CONTENTS

PROLOGUE

Friday Night
March 24, 1995

It was about six when I walked into the newsroom, a typical Friday night in progress. Joe Lampman looked up from his keyboard, saw me, and said, "Well! Back from the dead! How'd it go, Ace?" I grinned at him and made a waffling motion with my hand, and didn't even slow down. A couple of other reporters and I exchanged nods, and then there I was at Charlie Reilly's desk. I'd seen him glance up and register my presence and then go back to whoever's copy he was editing. By the time I sat myself in the chair next to his desk, he had already saved the copy and was giving me the usual – the piercing appraisal, the challenging grin with the sparkle in his eye, the indefinable attitude that made him look like reporters must have looked 50 years earlier. He should have been wearing a battered fedora, cocked back and to one side, maybe with a little feather in the hatband.

"So, Angelo," he said. "We friends again?"

I was biting down on my own grin. "Yeah, you're forgiven, maybe."

"Do we have a story?"

"I do believe we do."

"Do we have a *good* story?"

"Affirmative."

He pursed his lips in that funny way of his, thinking. "Maybe a six-part series? Enough material for that?"

"Ohhh yeah. Plenty of material – if I can get it out."

He shrugged. "If you've got the material, you'll get it out. *That*, I'm not worried about."

I looked at him, startled. I started to say something like, "since when the compliments?" Then I thought, *Charlie's tough, but he's never torn you down. Maybe this is something else you've been missing right along.*

"I take it you haven't been home yet."

"You take it correctly. I thought I'd just stop in here, since it's on the way, more or less."

"Can you tell me something about it, or would you lose the steam, do you think?"

I shrugged. "I've been doing this a long time, Charlie."

He swiveled around to Jack Henderson. "Hey Jack, take over for a few minutes, okay? I'll be down in the cafeteria if you need me." He swiveled back to me, getting to his feet. "Let's go get some coffee. You *do* still drink coffee, right? Haven't given it up and gone natural-foods on us?"

I grinned, mostly at a memory. ("C.T. *smokes?*") "Still with you, Charlie. You're buying, I presume."

"*I'm* buying? After I send you on a full week's junket?" We set off down the hall back toward the elevators. "But, Angelo, you got the scoop on Bowen? Is he the real deal, do you think? And what about Merriman? Did you ever talk to him as a reporter, or did you just go through the program like anybody else?" He made an impatient motion with his hand. "Forget all that, I'll read your story when you file it. What I want to know is," – pressing the elevator button – "what did it do to *you*? Because I'll tell you what, whatever happened down there, I saw it the minute you came in."

The doors opened and we got in. Charlie hit the button for the second floor. "Well?"

I was still hesitating. "It isn't that I mind telling you, Charlie, but there's a lot of threads to it. I don't know how easy it's going to be to separate them all out."

"Start somewhere and see what happens."

"Charlie – last week, what'd you mean when you said this could be my ticket? Why did you say that?"

The doors opened and we walked down the hallway to the cafeteria. "You want it straight, I take it?"

"As usual."

"Yeah, sure. As usual. Okay – you were going stale, Angelo. You'd started settling for just going through the motions." *Well, that's what they said!* He waved me off. "And don't tell me it's because you've been doing this a long time, and you're in your fifties and that's what happens to old firehouse horses, or whatever it is you've been saying lately. The fact of the matter is, I figured, if there was a chance of knocking you out of your rut, I was going to take it."

He thinks of me as a friend. How could I miss that all this time?

"So what happened? You fall in love or something?" Then, startled: "You *did!* Man, and on the paper's dime, that's got to be a first." Cautiously, "Not going to make the home life any easier."

I sighed. "No, it's not."

"Any future in it?"

I shook my head. *("We're not alone, even when we feel alone. I'm going to hold on to that.")*

"Makes it hard."

I nodded. *But better at least to* know *it.*

"Anything else important happen?"

("Angelo, This is *your real life. What's so real about being unable to feel?")*

"Charlie, you're entitled to rub it in for a while, I suppose. You want to let me know when you're done, or should I give you hints?"

He made a conciliatory motion with his hands, as if he were Italian instead of Irish. We got our coffees and sat down.

"I will say this, though," I said. "I'm well aware that the only reason I did the program was because you pushed me. Thanks for doing that."

Again I'd startled Charlie. *It's going to be a shock for everybody I deal with. How have I gone so many years without telling people thank you?*

"So tell me about the program," he said after a minute. "Does Merriman's program deliver the 'extraordinary potential' that it promises? How'd it go?"

CHAPTER ONE

Saturday Evening
March 18, 1995

My first thought was: *What in the world am I doing here and how am I going to last the week?*

I got off the plane in the early evening darkness, walked through the automatic doors and there I was in the Charlottesville airport, finally. Up the escalator, through the empty second-floor lounge, and down the escalator to the main floor, wondering if my van ride to the institute had waited the extra hour, and if not, how I was going to get out there. *I suppose if the rental car agencies are closed, I'll have to call a taxi,* I thought. *A 40-mile taxi ride will make an impressive addition to the tab.*

Wasted anticipation, because as soon as I came out of the secured area through the revolving door, a guy came up and said, "You must be Angelo. I'm Mick. I'm your transportation to the institute, and I've got two of your fellow participants over here," pointing behind him. He was maybe 50, a youngish 50, pretty average looking.

"Yes, I'm Angelo. How did you know?" I wasn't the only man from the plane coming through the door.

Mick smiled. "I can generally tell. Let's get your baggage and get on the road so we can get you some supper." He led the way to the airport's only baggage carousel. "You guys can introduce yourselves. You're going to know each other a little better by the time I bring you back here next week, you might as well start now."

They were Bobby Durant and Roberta Harrison Sellers. Durant was in his 30s probably, and said he was from Shawnee, Kansas. Sellers I figured to be a little older than myself, in her 60s somewhere. She said she was from Kentucky, and immediately described herself as an artist. She said that she and Durant had come in on the same connecting flight from Cincinnati, about an hour earlier.

"I would've gotten here at about the same time you did," I said, "but the airplane driver thought otherwise. Sorry you had to wait."

"Oh, it wasn't a problem," Roberta Harrison Sellers said. "No doubt the universe had a good reason."

Oh my! Here we go.

"Either the universe or USAirways," Mick said. "I keep getting the two confused."

They asked what brought me to the Open Door program, and I was not about to tell them that I was on assignment. "*Extraordinary Potential*," I said, and tried to leave it at that.

"Me too," Bobby Durant said enthusiastically. "The minute I read that book, I *knew* I'd be coming here."

Yeah? The minute I read that book, I thought, "Boy, it's true, there's one born every minute." The book was a bestseller, it was still selling in paperback, and the clerk said it was a classic in its field: I figured there had to be a lot more than one being born every minute.

The drive from the airport to the institute took about an hour and seemed longer. It wasn't just that we were driving in the dark, or that we were driving to a destination I hadn't been to before, both of which always make a drive seem longer. It wasn't even that it was at the end of a long day which came at the end of a somewhat hectic week as I cleared my desk for this. Mostly, it was Bobby Durant and Roberta Harrison Sellers, talking most of the way. I didn't at all mind them talking, but the content of their talk seemed so ungrounded, so impractical, so New Age starry-eyed, that I began to dread the long week to come. They'd already been an hour at the airport together, and hadn't run out of topics. Lucid dreaming and out-of-body experiences and Entry State and Wider Vision, and comparing notes on every book they'd ever read and every workshop they'd ever done. I felt distinctly left out, and very glad of it. And we hadn't even gotten there yet!

❖ 2 ❖

"Merriman Hall," Mick said, turning off the engine. "In short, we're here. Welcome to the training center."

The training center, as the introductory material had made clear, consisted of two buildings. Merriman Hall contained participants' rooms on the upper floor, with kitchen, dining room, and conference room beneath. Edwin Carter Hall housed the institute's offices on its upper floor and an assembly room on the lower floor. (A third building they called "the lab" was not officially a part of the facilities as far as program participants were concerned.)

We climbed down from the van, and Mick opened the back doors and handed us our bags. We trooped into Merriman Hall, and were greeted at the door by a middle aged woman with a big smile and a pleasant voice. "You made it," she said, beaming. "I'm Rebecca, and I've talked to you all on the phone I'm sure." So she had. As registrar, it was her job to answer questions and help people jump through whatever logistical hoops the world put in their way. I noted with amusement that Roberta Harrison Sellers and Bobby Durant greeted her like lifelong friends, hugging warmly. *If Bobby had a tail, he'd be wagging it.*

"Let's get your bags into your rooms, so you can get some supper," Rebecca said. "Everybody else has finished, but the kitchen staff has made up a plate for each of you, and David and Annette are going to hold off tonight's program for a few minutes so that you can actually sit down and eat without having to wolf it down. Mick, would you like to join us?"

"Actually, I will, thanks."

"Then, Angelo and Bobby, if you'll just wait while I show Roberta to her room, I'll be right back to show you yours, and you all can drop off your bags and get some supper, and you can unpack later. Roberta, if you'll just come this way?" They went down the hall, just two or three doors down, Roberta pulling her wheeled luggage behind her.

"You and I are roomies, I see," Bobby Durant said. *Oh swell!* He was reading a room-assignment chart on the bulletin board by the door, a diagram of the physical layout that showed each room, and each bed in each room. Each bed had a participant's name on it. "You've got the bed by the window."

I shrugged. "Makes no difference to me. You can have it if you want."

"Better not," Mick said humorously. "You'll mess up their system." He shook his head, forestalling questions. "You'll see."

❖ 3 ❖

The dining room turned out to be a big corner room containing five six-person tables. The two outside walls were mostly windows. One interior wall was set up as a salad bar and a service bar with cereals, fruits, and a machine dispensing juices. *I sure hope this isn't going to be a vegetarian week!* The other interior wall featured a big steam table, stacks of plates, and a door leading to the kitchen, through which, presently, came a member of the kitchen staff carrying two plates covered in foil. She set them on one of the tables. "Thanks, Jeannie," Rebecca said. The woman nodded, went back through the door, and returned with two more. Against the same wall that held the steam table, I was glad to see a stack of mugs and a coffee maker, with a pot ready brewed.

I walked over and poured myself a mugful and set it down at one of the places at the table.

"And it's after dark," Mick said. "So which is it? Computer programmer, engineer, or Navy?"

"Reporter. You can't be a reporter if you don't drink coffee."

"They teach you that in journalism school, I suppose."

I took off the foil: chicken breast and gravy, with mashed potatoes and overcooked green beans. *Could be worse. Not tofu, anyway.* "I wouldn't know. I never went to J-school. I'm just a displaced liberal arts major."

Bobby Durant said, "I'm sorry, I forgot your name already."

"Angelo Chiari."

"Angelo. Bobby Durant. What kind of reporter are you, Angelo?"

"About fair to middling."

"No, I mean, television, newspapers, magazines, what?"

"Newspaper."

"Oh yeah? Which one?"

"Philadelphia *Inquirer*. Mick, how much time are they going to give us to eat, do you think?"

"Not a whole lot. In fact, here's one of the zookeepers now." He nodded toward the tall, smiling man, maybe in his forties, coming through the outside door.

"Hi," the man said, "I'm David Taylor, and I'm one of your trainers. I'm here to harass you into gulping it all down and not looking around for dessert." He pulled out a chair and sat.

"He'll do it, too," Mick said. "You can see from the look of him that he's a tyrant."

Tyrant or not, I was glad of his timing.

"So David," Roberta Harrison Sellers said, "how much have we missed?"

He smiled at her. "Well, you missed your intake interviews, but we'll work around that. Mainly what you missed was a long, awkward Saturday afternoon."

"Oh, did something happen?"

His shook his head, still smiling. "Only the same thing that happens in every Open Door program. A whole bunch of people from all over the country come together and sit around and make small talk and feel uncomfortable. The usual."

"Small talk!" Bobby Durant apparently put a lot of energy into everything he did. "You mean people come to C.T. Merriman's home turf and they sit around and make *small talk?*"

Mick raised his head innocently. "Yeah, wouldn't you think they could do that at home, instead of coming all that way here?"

David looked like he was enjoying himself. "It doesn't last long. You'll see. In fact, you'll see real soon, if you'll just eat a little faster."

❖ 4 ❖

Mick went home and we walked over to the next building, and so there I was, sitting with 25 strangers (counting the two trainers) in the assembly room that was the bottom floor of Edwin Carter Hall. The wood-paneled room was filled with two dozen comfortable rolling armchairs set at a dozen wooden tables arrayed in ranks like schoolroom desks.

A woman was sitting at the front of the hall, facing the rows of participants. David Taylor went up and sat in the chair next to her. When we three newcomers had found seats, she smiled and said, "So now we're all here.

Welcome, everybody, to the first night of the Merriman Institute's Open Door program. For the three who just arrived, I am Annette Jones and this is David Taylor, and we are going to be your trainers this week.

"Tonight we're going to give you an overview of the week to come. First, the basic practical information you need to function together, like where are the bathrooms and when is it too early in the morning to shower, and so on. Then we will give you a sense of how the days will be structured, just a taste, to orient you. You don't have to remember it all, and you certainly don't have to take notes! Mostly, we want you to relax and let us handle all the details. Your job, for these next few days, is to explore your own potential. We will do everything we can to support you in that. The whole program is designed with just that in mind."

David, coming in smoothly, said, "And since we do have a lot of ground to cover in the next few days, that means we don't have a lot of time to waste in getting to know each other, so we're going to start right now. I know that many of you met this afternoon, and the rest of you met at least a few people at the supper table. Even our latecomers have at least met each other. But now we're going to go right to the next level. We want everybody to pick a partner, and we're going to give you five minutes each to interview each other, and then you're going to introduce each other to the group."

Oh God! I thought. *An encounter group! I'll bet we wind up with group hugs.*

❖ 5 ❖

Ten minutes later, more or less, we proceeded to introduce each other, giving the name first and again at the end, as instructed. I had been a journalist a long time, and I was on assignment. I listened closely to see what kind of people were doing this program. (And if you find the following list a bit overwhelming, think how it was for us! On the one hand, we had faces and general impressions that I can't convey to you, but on the other hand, it seemed impossible that we could immediately get and keep so many people straight in our minds. Nor did we, at first.)

Elizabeth Tyrone, in her thirties somewhere, from, of all places, Elizabeth, New Jersey. I thought, *I think if I were in her fix, I'd move.* Dee West from Laurel, Maryland. Roommates, about the same age, neither one giving much of a clue. Office workers, they each said. *New Age searchers,* I thought. *Seminar hoppers.*

Bobby Durant stood up and gestured toward the man next to him, who looked to be in his seventies, and said, "My partner is John Ellis Sinclair, who is a retired chemical engineer. He's from New Hampshire, and says he's down here mostly to get warm for a week. He's a grandfather six times over and he likes taking pictures of nature and wildlife. He's here because he read C.T.'s book *Extraordinary Potential*, of course. John Sinclair." *Well, I've already got Bobby pegged: tail-wagging true believer. Doesn't have another life and never will have one.*

John Ellis Sinclair stood up. "My friend here likes to be called Bobby. Bobby Durant lives in Shawnee, Kansas, and he's a graduate of Indiana University, where he majored in the environmental sciences. He is self-employed, which is the next best thing to retired, he is unmarried, and he's here because C.T. Merriman's book sparked his curiosity, as I expect it did for most of us. Bobby Durant." I hesitated, trying to sum up Sinclair, not immediately finding a category to put him into. *Old man looking for something he missed along the way,* I finally decided.

Next to stand, somewhat hesitantly, was an attractive young girl – easily the youngest, probably not older than her late twenties. "This is Klaus Bishof," she said of the man sitting beside her. "He is a student of the work of Rudolf Steiner, by profession a reflexologist." *I wonder what that is.* She spoke English musically and well, with accents sometimes slightly misplaced. "Klaus is from Köln, Germany, and he says he is a student and hopes to be a student his whole life, in whatever way he makes his living. And he read the German translation of Mr. Merriman's book. Klaus Bishof." *She's from Spain probably, or somewhere in Latin American. Pretty. This one, we'll have to wait and see.*

Klaus Bishof stood up, dark complected, open and relaxed. "That was Marta Verdura y Rielo, from Lima, Peru. You have already heard that her English is better than my own. She is – " He fired a question in German at a man sitting behind him. "Pursuing," the man said. "She is pursuing her professional degree – her Ph.D. – in psychology. Maria Verdura y Rielo." He sat down and stood up again. "She read the book, but also she has a friend who did Open Door." *Funny, he looks too solid for this kind of thing. I'll have to remember to ask him what a reflexologist does.*

An attractive young woman – in her 40s, maybe, or late 30s – stood up and gestured to the man who was sitting next to her, a man perhaps in his vigorous fifties. With a slight French accent, she said, "This is Francois Arouet, and like me he is French Canadian. He is from Quebec City and he is a priest." *A priest?!* "He is here because he read Mr. Merriman's book. In the French edition. Francois Arouet." *A priest?*

She sat down and Arouet stood up, a big man, of average height but solid with a big smile. His English was fluent with occasional pauses. *A priest. What in the world is he doing here?* "You have just heard from my compatriot, Regina Marie du Plessis. She is from Montreal, where she works as a translator of books. She as well is here because she read Mr. Merriman's book, also in the French. However, she also speaks and reads English and Spanish. Miss du Plessis is unmarried, which seems to me an improbability." He smiled. "Regina Marie du Plessis." *Hard to figure her. She looks pretty solid – stern, even. A professional, clearly. Can't see her and Bobby having much of a conversation. But on the other hand – she's here. Of course, so am I! But I at least have an excuse: I was pushed.*

A young woman stood up. "Selena Juras is undoubtedly known to at least some of you. She lives in Hollywood and is a professional psychic." *Oh God!* (But then, I'd figured they'd *all* be professional psychics!) The woman went on to list some of Selena Juras' better-known clients, and, I noticed, completely forgot to mention why she was at Open Door. *I mean, what could she expect to learn? She's a psychic, right?*

Selena Juras stood up, all shoulder-length blond hair and expensive clothes and careful grooming. Just looking at her, from years of experience interviewing celebrities and newsmakers, I had the sense that she had the potential to be a queen-sized pain in the posterior. *Hollywood psychic!* "This is Toni Shaw, an artist from Vancouver, Canada. She is married and the mother of two. Toni Shaw." *She isn't used to talking much about someone else, and doesn't have much interest in doing so.* I made a mental note to find out more about Toni Shaw sometime during the week.

A man in his forties stood up. "This is Claire Clarke, and she is a psychotherapist from Platt, Texas." *First a priest, then a psychotherapist! What the hell?* "She tells me that she read *Extraordinary Potential* more than ten years ago and never dreamed that she would get to meet C.T. Merriman, let alone do Open Door, and she can't quite believe she's here. I feel a little the same way myself, and I expect we're not the only ones. Claire Clarke."

Claire Clarke stood up. *After her, we're next.* "That was Tony Giordano, who is from Santa Cruz, California." *Huh. Toni and Tony.* "He is an executive in a Silicon Valley start-up, he is married with three children, he likes skiing and parachute diving and he says he has always wanted to go to Antarctica. He read the book, of course, and he tells me that just a few weeks ago he was having one of those conversations where out of the blue somebody started talking about *Extraordinary Potential* and they told him about Open Door, and here he is. Tony Giordano." *Huh! Well, California, it figures, but a computer guy? And what did she mean "one of those conversations"? People laughed like, "oh yeah!"*

Helene Porter stood up. "This is Angelo Chiari, who is a newspaper reporter. He lives in Cherry Hill, New Jersey, he's married with two children, he likes writing – of course – and reading and canoeing and spending time at the ocean. Like most of us, he's here because he read *Extraordinary Potential*." *Not to mention Charlie strong-arming me.* "Angelo Chiari."

I stood up. "This is Helene Porter. She is a psychiatrist from Falls Church, Virginia. She tells me she heard C.T. Merriman speak several years ago, and bought the book at that time, and only recently learned about the Open Door program. She is the mother of two and grandmother of three. Helene Porter." *"I'm here to see what the universe wants me to do next,"* *she had said. And she's a psychiatrist! Maybe Goldwyn was right, anybody who goes to see a psychiatrist ought to have his head examined.*

A man in his fifties stood up, gesturing toward a woman who looked to be in her mid-forties. "This is Edith Fontaine, she's a massage therapist from Santa Barbara, California, describes herself as an average mom and I guess she is, if most moms have had near-death experiences of their own. Like pretty much all of us, I suspect, she read C.T.'s book and then it was just a matter of time until she wound up here. In her case, her own NDE was an incentive, she says, to sort of compare notes. She is the mother of two boys and has two cats. Oh yeah, there's a husband in there too. Edith Fontaine." *I suppose massage therapist is different from what comes to mind. Well, this just keeps getting crazier. I'd have said she was a solid citizen for sure.*

Edith Fontaine stood up. "And that was Jeff Richards, who is a computer analyst from Casper, Wyoming. He likes photography and flying airplanes when he has time and money for them. He describes himself as a searcher, possibly not the only one in the room, and says he hopes to learn more about what's possible and what isn't. Naturally, he's read the book. He is unmarried and says he is wholly owned by his cat, named Jonathan Livingston Seacat. Jeff Richards." *He looks solid, just like she does, but what kind of guy describes himself as a searcher? But then, computer guys are crazy anyway.*

A woman stood up, in her fifties probably, comfortably stout. In a Texas accent she said, "This is Lou Hardin, a security consultant from Big Knob, South Carolina, and he read the book and wanted to learn more. He's married, he has three children, and the way he put it, he has other bad habits as well. Lou Hardin." *Is everybody here a comedian? I used to think that a sense of humor was a sign of mental balance. May have to reconsider that one.*

Hardin stood up, slim, intense, in his forties somewhere. *Lean and hungry look, this guy.* "As you can hear, Dottie Blunt speaks right, not like you Yankees and foreigners. She's from Texas and calls herself an ordinary wife and mother and grandmother, but she's been interested in this kind of thing all her life. C.T.'s book is just one of a long string of books, apparently – I don't see how she had time enough to be a wife and mother, reading all the books she mentioned, but anyway there she is. Dottie Blunt."

Roberta Harrison Sellers stood up and indicated a woman probably in her fifties or early sixties. "This is Jane Mullen, she's from Santa Rosa, California, and she says she's an ordinary wife and mother, and grandmother of three. She has had a lifelong interest in metaphysics, she's been a Rosicrucian all her adult life, and she's a member of the Association for Research and Enlightenment, that's the Edgar Cayce group. She read C.T.'s book years ago and only found out about Open Door recently. Jane Mullen." *Another searcher. All that sincere searching in this room. What is it they're looking for? What's wrong with their lives that they're trying to fix?*

Jane Mullen introduced Roberta Harrison Sellers as being from Lexington, Kentucky, an artist. "She and I are roommates, and so I know that she has a portfolio with her that has some of her drawings, and they really are extraordinary." *And, for sale if anyone is interested.* "Roberta, too, is here because she's had a life-long interest in these things, and of course she read C.T.'s book. Roberta Harrison Sellers."

"This is Katie van Osten, she's from Boulder, Colorado, a mother of two and grandmother of five." *This guy that's introducing her – something different about this one.* "She tells me that after her husband died a few years ago, after a long illness, she found herself with more time to read and think about things that had long interested her, and that led her to C.T.'s book and other things like it. Katie van Osten." *Katie van Osten looks like she's in her seventies or thereabouts. Can't make much more of her at this point.*

"This is Emil Hoffman," she said. "He is 34, and he is a banker, from Geneva, Switzerland." *A banker!? Fluent English. I didn't hear any accent when he was talking.* "He read C.T.'s book in the German edition, and he's here to learn more. Emil Hoffman."

Getting near the end, now.

"This is Sam Andover, from Northern Virginia. A few years ago he retired from the military, and he's been spending his time following his interests, which he says includes screwy stuff like this. He read C.T.'s book, and knows somebody who did an Open Door, and he thought he'd take a look for himself. Sam is unmarried, no family, not even a cat. Sam Andover." *Mid-fifties, you can see he's naturally closed-mouthed. Let's see if he opens up any during the week.*

"This is Andrew St. George, he's from Seattle, Washington, and he is an environmental abatement officer for the state, he tells me." *Another one in his forties or fifties. People here are older than I would have thought. I guess I'm not going to be holding up the upper end of the demographic scale after all.* "He says that he is going to do Inner Voice next month, so I guess he has some interest in all this. Andrew St. George. Oh, and he is unmarried and I neglected to ask if he has any cats."

❖ 6 ❖

Annette stood up. "Is that everybody? Anybody missed? Good. This is David Taylor, he lives in Portland, Oregon, he has a master's degree in psychology and works as a humans relations counselor for an insurance company there. He has been a trainer for – what, David, ten years now? Eleven, that's right. Like many people, he came to his Open Door after reading C.T.'s book and came back for more. Unlike most people, in about three years he became a trainer. He comes out to train a course – usually Open Door – roughly six times a year. You are going to find that he's a lot of fun and he knows a lot. Oh, David is unmarried and is the full-time servant to two cats named Entry State and Wider Vision. So, meet David Taylor." *She got her laughs, in the right places.* She sat down and David stood up again.

"And finally, last and greatest, this is Annette Jones, from Marin County, California. She has been a trainer here for seventeen years. She came originally because a long-time friend did Open Door and wouldn't stop bugging her about it, the sort of behavior we like to encourage." *Got his laugh.* "I'm not positive, but I *think* that Annette liked her experiences in Open Door. In fact, she never did quite find her way back to her previous life. Like so many of us. Annette's other job is being a psychotherapist." *Another one!* "I'm sure that is not so different from being a full-time trainer. She is the mother of two grown children – as you can see she was married at about age six – and is soon to become a grandmother, impossible though that is for some of us to believe. She is one of our busiest trainers, out here practically every other week, it seems. Annette, how many programs did you train last year? Twenty, I think? Yes, twenty. Like I said, nearly every other week. How would you like to have *that* schedule and still keep up a psychotherapist practice? Anyway, I don't know about the patients on the west coast who she is continually abandoning, but the airlines love her and we love her and I know you will love her too. Annette Jones."

Again, applause. And everybody was ready for this to be the end of preliminaries.

"Okay," David said, sitting down, "now we've all gotten a peek behind the curtain at those other people hiding in there. You might want to keep in mind, these next few days, the possibility that there *might just be a reason* why just these particular people showed up for your Open Door." *Or maybe it was just coincidence.* "They might have come sooner, they might have come later, but instead they're here right now. Maybe there's a reason for that. It may be that you will find there is somebody here who is important for you right now. And you might find that you yourself are important to somebody here. It wouldn't be the first time we've seen it happen."

"And we're not necessarily talking about romance," Annette said with a smile. "We've had our share of those, but there *are* other ways of relating."

"Meanwhile," David said, "as promised, here are some ground rules. You will have noticed in the material we sent you, no alcohol, no recreational drugs. What you do in your life isn't our concern, but for this week, we ask that you refrain from both of these activities."

Selena Juras said, "Why? You don't seem to mind if people continue to smoke, or drink caffeine."

"Two reasons. For one thing, we don't want anybody doing anything illegal on the premises so that nobody gets in trouble or gets *us* in trouble. Drugs are illegal, caffeine and nicotine aren't."

"If people recognized what they did to their bodies, they would be."

David waved it aside. "We can argue about it during breaks, if you want to, but this isn't the time or place for it. Alcohol isn't illegal, but we prohibit it, too, along with drugs, for one good reason. You are here to learn to experience subtle states of mind so that you can acquire the knack of moving to those states at will. Drinking alcohol and using recreational drugs will only interfere with the process, so what's the point? And by the same token, this is *not* the time to try to quit smoking, or quit drinking coffee. You are moving into unknown territory this week. You are going to be experiencing things that are very vague, very nebulous. A lot of the time, you aren't going to know *what* you're experiencing, or even if you're experiencing anything at all. The last thing you want is to quit using caffeine or nicotine at the same time. You'd never figure out what's coming from your tape experiences and what's coming from withdrawal symptoms."

He looked around and saw acceptance. "Okay, rule number two. We ask you please, no shoes in the conference room, the room at the bottom of the stairs right off the dining room. If any of you have ever tried to get red Virginia clay out of a white carpet, you'll understand why that rule. In general, you're free to wear shoes anywhere except in the conference room. No shoes in that room, under penalty of death."

"What if we want to go barefoot all the time?" That was Bobby Durant.

"Barefoot, socks, we don't care, indoors and outdoors both if you wish. The only rule is, no shoes in the conference room. But if you're going to go around barefoot outside, take care that you don't track clay onto that rug."

Annette smiled. "And if this group is like the groups that have preceded it, we'll catch at least two of you in there with your shoes on before tomorrow is out."

"That's why I just repeated myself," David said. "Hopefully you'll get the idea. No shoes, okay? Now: What room don't we wear shoes in?"

The big guy from Washington. "Uh – the kitchen?"

David laughed. "Somebody remind me why I do this?"

"Okay," Annette said. "Next rule. The only other rule there is, actually, but it's a big one. For this next week, you're going to give up your dependence on clocks. You're not going to need them, and you'll be amazed at how your perception of time changes when you aren't constantly structuring it by looking at your wrist. David is going to go around with a box. Anybody with a watch, put it in the box."

I was used to living by my watch. "What if we'd rather keep them?" I asked.

Annette shook her head. "No. Really, this is important. Just trust the process. You can get by for this next week without telling yourself what time it is all the time."

"But just practically, how do we – ?"

"I'm coming to that. We're going to get you up in the morning by clanging that very loud bell that you may have noticed in the dining room. Believe me, you can hear it all through the building without any trouble."

David came in. "And in case you happen to be outside, we also ring the cowbell out on the deck – and *that* you can hear for half a mile or more."

"We'll get you up, give you time to shower and dress, and we'll ring it again when breakfast is ready, and whenever we are ready to assemble in the conference room or in Edwin Carter Hall."

David again: "Henry Thoreau asked, 'Can the Valhalla be warmed by steam and go by clock and bell?' Well, assuming this is Valhalla, the answer is, yes, we can."

I shook my head. *What in the world have I gotten myself into? Or rather, what has* Charlie *gotten me into?*

David stood up, holding a cardboard box, and ostentatiously came first to me and held the box in front of me. "Your watch," he said firmly. "Now. Or else." *Oh well.* I unbuckled the watch and dropped it into the box. "You'll live," David said – and proceeded to move around the room, collecting.

"By the way," Annette said, "those of you with alarm clocks and such, we know that you can use them to defeat the purpose of this little arrange-ment, but we'd ask you to stop and think, why would you want to defeat the purpose? You have invested good money and a week of your time – why not let us give you your best chance of obtaining what you came for?" She looked over at me. "Okay, Angelo? Give it a good try?"

I shrugged. "He already stole my watch. You've got me where you want me."

David, from the other side of the room, still collecting watches, piped up, "Oh no we don't, not yet. But we will."

❖ 7 ❖

"Okay," Annette said, "that takes care of housekeeping. Just to recap: Before each tape, we will meet either here or in the conference room. We'll talk about what we're going to do, and you will go up to your units, using the bathroom first. Trust us on this, there is nothing more likely to interrupt a tape experience than a full bladder. It's so easy to prevent, it would be silly not to: We'll remind you but in case we ever forget: *use the bathroom* before each tape.

"Then you go up to your beds, put on your sleep masks, and put on the stereo earphones. You'll be guided from there. Some of you will find that you get very warm during an exercise. Others will find that you get cold, so be sure to have a blanket nearby to pull over you in case you need it. There's really no predicting how any one individual is going to react.

"Now, we know that many of you have come a long way today and you are tired, so the first order of business is for you to get a good night's sleep. From long experience, we know that on the first evening of your first program, few of you are really settled in your bodies. You have had too much to get adjusted to; too many people to meet, and most of you have been too many hours on the road or in the air. The 'real' program starts tomorrow morning; Sunday.

"But we also know that you're curious, and you want to get started. So tonight we will give you just a taste, just one short introductory exercise to get you more or less into the groove, and we won't meet afterwards to debrief. After the tape is finished, you can just go to bed and get some rest and we'll see you in the morning, or you are welcome to come back downstairs. We will put out some munchies in the dining room for those who want to snack and socialize. Okay?" They looked around for questions or comments. "Then off we go, by way of the bathrooms."

❖ **8** ❖

By the time I got to the room, Bobby Durant had already gotten into bed, and put on the earphones and sleep mask. *He can't wait. I wonder: Will he let himself be disappointed when nothing happens?* I lay down atop my covers. *Handy, not to have to worry about shoes.* I wondered if I was going to be bored. *Probably Bobby won't* let *nothing happen. He's so keyed up, he'll imagine something.* Slowly, reluctantly, I put on earphones and sleep mask. *"Whatever they tell you to do,"* Charlie had said, *"do it and see."* I remembered the ready light, pulled the sleep mask up to uncover one eye, reached over and flipped the switch, then lay back again and readjusted the mask.

The earphones were playing music, pleasant enough. I lay there quietly waiting. I imagined Bobby champing at the bit, impatient for the music to end. I smiled, and waited peacefully, daydreaming.

Annette's voice, almost a whisper: "We are still waiting for two more ready lights – ah, thank you, Edith. One more and we'll start." *Edith, so she knew which ready light belongs to whom. Mick said, better not trade beds. I*

wonder: does that mean they can send different signals to different people?
The music continued. "All right, folks, here we go. Relax, have a nice time, and either we'll see you downstairs afterwards for snacks, or we'll see you tomorrow morning."

The music faded out and for the first time I heard the sound I would come to know as pink noise – a sort of snapping, crackling sound, a background continuing hiss, not unpleasant and, after a while, not obtrusive. The pink noise diminished and another sound increased, the sound of rippling water, like a stream over rocks. And over the sound of water, over the pink noise, I heard C.T.'s voice. I would come to know it very well, but this was the first time.

It was a pleasant, soothing voice, easy to listen to, and the message was not what I had expected. "Sink now into a state of pleasant relaxation," the voice said. "Be sure your body is in a relaxed position, with no stress or strain. Follow my voice as I guide you." C.T. then proceeded to run down the entire body, from head to toe, suggesting that the listener relax that particular part of the body. I had no particular objection to relaxing, so I lazily followed along as instructed.

"That's fine," the voice on the tape said. "Take a moment or two to enjoy this state of enhanced relaxation. I will join you shortly." I lay there, pleasantly relaxed, listening to the noise. I thought, *Sooner or later this is going to go woo-woo. "Let's all join with the angels as we proclaim the ineffable wonder of creation."* I thought of Bobby Durant, and smiled, not without compassion, at the thought of him waiting impatiently for something that wasn't going to happen.

After an indeterminate time – I couldn't decide if it had been a long time or not – the voice returned, and began to methodically bring us to take our first steps into a deliberately altered state, and, although I didn't begin to suspect it, the adventure began.

❖ **9** ❖

For much of the tape, I daydreamed. Not expecting anything to happen, I wasn't on edge. Besides, I was tired. The program was an assignment I didn't believe in, and even if I had expected that something might happen, I would not have expected it to happen on the first night, in the first tape. So I listened to C.T.'s instructions, made a halfhearted effort to follow them, and mostly just lay on the bed drowsing.

One thing, they could sell this tape as something people could use to relax.

I came back at one point from wherever I had been, and realized that I had been in a dreamlike state. *If I didn't know I was awake, I'd be sure it was a dream.* Not that it was anything dramatic. No characters, no plot, no action, only a very vivid sense of trees beneath me, as though I were flying silently above the hills surrounding the center. *Weird.* Yet, the experience had been rather pleasant. I tried to drift back into it, to see if I could re-create the picture. But for some reason the very fact that I now had an intent made it harder for me to relax into that same daydreaming state of mind. Then I tried to re-create the picture by brute force, as it were, and found that I couldn't.

I had no particular reason to want to re-create the picture – or so I told himself. Yet I found myself disappointed that I was unable to do so. And then there was C.T.'s voice saying that it was time to reverse the process and return to normal consciousness. *Normal consciousness? Who left normal consciousness?* Still, I wanted to return to the feeling of floating above the ground, and would have liked to have had a chance to try again. *If I had to guess, I'd say I was heading a little north of east.*

"This concludes the first exercise," I heard Annette say softly. "Please remember to turn off your ready lights. For those of you who wish to social-ize downstairs, there will be snacks in the dining room. Those of you who wish to call it a day, have a good night's sleep and we'll see you in the morn-ing." I took off my headphones and sleep mask, and looked over at Bobby Durant across the room, getting off his bed, who shrugged. "Oh well, it was only an intro tape," Bobby said. "Let's go get some munchies."

❖ 10 ❖

"I hate my life," Tony said. I thought, *Well,* there's *a conversation stop-per!* But Tony Giordano went on chomping on peanuts from the paper plate in front of him as though he had said he didn't like Brussels Sprouts.

We were all munching snacks or drinking tea or fruit juice or water, maybe half the class – the half that had come downstairs after the tape. Me, Bobby, Francois the jovial priest from French Canada, and others that I hadn't yet sorted out. They'd straggled down one or two at a time and had clustered around first one table, then two, forming big irregular circles centered more or less on the overflowing bowl of popcorn and the plastic containers of potato chips, peanuts, and some vegetables and dip. I had expected – with a combination of professional interest and dread – that the conversation would center around people's experience of the tape, or their supposed psychic attainments in general – particularly after Selena Juras made her appearance. Instead, the talk had quickly settled into "where are you from again, what do you do, what brought you here" – for of course at this point everybody was finding most of the others still little more than a blur despite the earlier introductions.

"You hate your life?" This was the humorous guy from Washington or Oregon or somewhere who was in environmental protection. "Why don't you change it?"

"Well, it's like Woody Allen said, I considered suicide but with my luck it wouldn't be a permanent solution."

"No, really. Why don't you just change it?"

Giordano almost shrugged. "Family, responsibilities. Not so easy to just rip things up and start again." *Like we couldn't all say that!*

The woman from southern California, the massage therapist. "I'm sorry, I've forgotten your name – Tony, right – what is it you hate, particularly?"

Giordano made a throw-away gesture. "*Most* of it. Earn it, spend it, earn some more. I used to enjoy my work and now it just seems pretty point-less."

The older man *(retired, if I remember right)* asked what Giordano did for a living.

"Well, I *used to be* an engineer, but I don't get to do engineering any more. I'm one of the owners of a software company, one of your basic Sili-con Valley start-ups."

"Doing pretty well?"

"Yeah, pretty well. We had a couple of good products that sort of dug us in. We're making money. I suppose I shouldn't complain. But it's all getting old, you know? After a while, you think, so what?"

"It sounds like you're your own boss," one of the women said quietly. "I'd think *that* part of it would be nice." *She's got that strong west-Texas accent. Dottie something.*

"Oh – " again the impression of a shrug, if not quite the gesture. "Yeah, I suppose. I mean, I've done the cubicle thing, and I'd rather be the squirrel-cage owner than the squirrel, but in a way it's like they say about the pris-oners and the guards: The guards get to go home at night, but they're both spending their lives in jail. How much difference does it make that you're the boss if you're still commuting an hour to work each way?" *Oh, that's right, you're the guy who daydreams about going to Antarctica!*

"It might make a difference in your work-day," Dottie said, still quietly.

A gesture of impatience, or of despair of conveying his point of view. "Sure, I know that. It's different, and certainly I have a lot more money to play with than the people who work for me. But the actual work isn't any more satisfying, it's just different. I'm always flying to Europe or Japan for meetings. Pretty glamorous, right? But actually, what happens is that I fly somewhere and I talk to grumpy foreign businessmen in some airport hotel meeting room, and I fly back the same day and I still have to drive home from the airport. To somebody who spends all day in his cubicle, my life's magic. From the inside, it isn't what it's cracked up to be."

Funny. That's what I've been thinking about reporting. Been thinking it a lot, as a matter of fact. You see your byline on a story once, it's a big deal. You see it several times a week for 20 years, not so big a deal.

Meanwhile at the other table, I was hearing Selena Juras holding forth to her audience – Bobby Durant among others. "So I said, '*How* do you expect me to get to Charlottesville in time to meet my ride if you cancel the flight,' and she says, 'I'm sorry, ma'am, but there's nothing I can do,' and I say, 'Of course there's something you can do, and I expect you to find out what it is, and do it.' I mean, *what* is the point in paying for first class if you can't get service? So then she says – " *She's a celebrity, and she assumes that everyone here thinks she's as important as she does. I suspect she's in for a shock when she realizes how few people here have heard of her, or care. Or maybe I'm wrong and she's a bigger deal than I think.*

"So again, Tony, why not quit?" *Andrew. Andrew something.*

"And do what?"

"Well *I* don't know – but *something* would have to happen!"

Giordano smiled at him. "Yeah, but a lot of the possible somethings, I don't much like the thought of." *Aye, there's the rub. How do you change squirrel cages when you're past 50? And after a certain point you start to think, why bother?*

At the other table I could see that the young woman from Maryland who'd described herself as an office worker – Dee something – had taken the girl from Peru under her wing. There couldn't be that many years between them, but the younger girl was clearly feeling a bit overwhelmed. Of course that gave Dee whatever-her-name-was a comfortable role, too, but still I noted it as a bit of kindness.

The older man again. "I don't know Tony's situation, but I can tell you this much: Wherever you go, you take yourself with you. Whatever it is that you hate about your life now won't change just because you change jobs. If you want something to change, you have to change something inside yourself first, or you'll keep on attracting what you already have."

Now there's *some ungrounded opinion!* I said, "Mr. – ?"

"Sinclair. But call me Ellis, please."

"Ellis, I think I heard that you're retired now, right? What did you used to do for a living?"

"I was an engineer, like Tony here, except I was a chemical engineer, not electrical. In my day, you didn't just go out and start up your own company. I spent my whole career working for the same firm."

"And you found that true, what you said? That changing your situation didn't matter?"

"Unless you change yourself, as I said. How else could it be? Unless you believe in coincidence."

I could feel myself give him a blank look. "Doesn't everybody? Don't you?"

"There's no such thing as coincidence."

"There isn't?"

"Not in my experience." *Huh! That's just the kind of thing I expected to hear this week, but he wouldn't have been the one I'd have picked to come up with it. Isn't that weird?*

At the other table I heard the older woman – Katie I thought her name was – say she was here hoping to make contact with her dead husband!

CHAPTER TWO

Sunday
March 19, 1995

The early morning air was cold on my chest, even through an undershirt and a long-sleeved flannel shirt. Too cold? I felt for that elusive first warning, the little catch in my breathing, the faint rasp behind my breastbone. Nothing. So far, so good. But I had already needed to use my prescription inhaler when I first got out of bed.

I was standing on the long porch looking southward beyond the nearby lawn and trees to the mountains. A little later in the day, as I would learn, the porch would become a refuge for smokers, but it was early enough, long enough before breakfast, that I had it to myself. I spent a few minutes leaning on the chest-high railing, enjoying the warmth of my half-empty coffee mug, thinking of nothing in particular and enjoying the sensation though mostly unaware of it. *Sunday morning. Quiet time.*

Behind me, the door opened and closed, and there beside me was the quiet guy from out west somewhere. Rather than a flannel shirt, he was wearing a jersey. Evidently the March morning felt warm to him. Like me, he had coffee mug in hand.

"Good morning. Is it Angelo? Do I have it right?"

"Right. You're Jeff, I think."

"That's me." A sip of coffee. "It looks like we're the only ones up, although I did hear some rustling around as I was coming down. I had expected to have to fight to get to use the bathroom. An advantage of being an early bird."

"Yeah, plus you get first choice of worms."

Richards smiled into his coffee. "You're not usually up so early?"

"God no! Not in *my* business. I work for a *morning* paper. Sometimes I don't go in till noon."

"Must be nice, get your mornings to yourself. Me, I'm in the office by eight."

"So you see the sunrise on a regular basis, I take it."

"Oh yeah. But I'm in the middle of town." He gestured toward the blue-green hills. "This isn't what I'm used to seeing when I get up."

"Well, me neither. Not a lot of mountains where I live. South Jersey has two kinds of terrain; flat and flatter."

"Well they do say flattery will get you somewhere," Richards said, throwing away the line. After a pause: "It's sort of funny to think of these as mountains, though. At home they'd be foothills, and hardly even that."

"I suppose they *would* look different to you. You're from – Wyoming, was it?"

"That's right. Casper."

"A lot of mountains in Casper?"

"No, not particularly, but I used to live in Sheridan, and before that in a little town near Yellowstone, and there's lots of mountains in both places. Not green like this though."

David Taylor emerged. "Morning, folks," he said over his shoulder, walking to the end of the deck. He clanged the cowbell. "That'll get 'em up," he said, and without pause he returned inside. We heard him clang the inside bell.

We sipped our coffee in comfortable silence, and after a while Richards said, "Did you notice anything funny about your night's sleep?"

I laughed. "I noticed that I was up and dressed before sunrise, if that's what you mean."

"Well, not quite. I mean, it felt like that sleep processor was keeping me awake. It was this annoying presence I couldn't get rid of no matter what I did. Sort of like the government."

I grinned at that. "I turned mine down as far as it would go. The processor, I mean."

"I did too, but it was like I could still hear it even when I couldn't hear it. Finally I just got up, and I was real surprised to see that it was daybreak. I would have guessed two or three in the morning."

I shrugged. "For all we know, it *is* two or three in the morning. Merriman probably rearranges the sunrise just for Open Door."

Richards smiled. "He probably does. It's nice that they have the coffee ready in thermoses for whenever we do get up."

I gave a sort of grunt. "They'd be in trouble if they didn't!"

"Yes they would." Sip. "So you didn't hear the sleep processor?"

"I must have, or I wouldn't be up this early, especially after sitting up so late talking – at least, it *felt* late – but I didn't think so at the time, no."

The door opened and we turned and there was the woman from Texas. "Morning, guys," she said. We made room for her, each of us instinctively moving to place her between us. "Morning, Claire," Richards said, and so I was reminded of her name and was able to echo Richards.

"So how did you two sleep?"

"We were just talking about that," Richards said. "We think we're going to have to destroy the sleep processor."

She smiled, looking out at the mountains. *She looks tired.* "What did you two think of the exercise? Did you get anything out of it?" *Look at him smiling at her. It's like they've been friends for years. Funny, that's how I feel too.*

"*I* sure didn't," Richards said. "I think I fell asleep in the middle of the tape, and I didn't wake up until the end, when I heard C.T. calling us back."

"So, nothing at all?"

"Well, I did go downstairs and raise my consciousness on some potato chips and dip."

I could get to like this guy.

"And – ?" She hesitated, and I helped her out.

"Angelo," I said. "Nothing much. I sort of drifted off. Daydreaming, you know. I'd come back and listen, and then drift off again, three or four times, until finally the tape ended." Of course, *I spent a certain amount of time wondering why I was spending a week here.* "So then I came downstairs to see if anybody was reporting any profound experiences, but mostly people were trying to get the potato chips away from this one guy who was hogging them all."

"Hey, it was a full-time job just to get my fair share."

"You didn't come down after the tape, Claire, so you didn't see it. Two people got their fingers broken. It got pretty ugly."

"I *did* warn them."

"And it's only Sunday morning," Claire said as if to herself. "What's it going to be like after you've done a day's worth of tapes, you two?"

"Oh, we're likely to become downright normal," Richards said.

Later, thinking about it, I would remember that on the very first morning the three of us had come together, naturally and instinctively.

"So," I said, "how about you? Did *you* experience anything?"

Surprisingly, she hesitated. "Maybe." *Maybe, hell! More like "I'm not sure I trust either of you yet."* "It resembled daydreaming, as you said. I had thought that a tape experience would be more definite, I don't know why."

"Either this or that," Richards said, "either normal or special."

"Exactly. You'd think I'd know better after all these years, if only professionally."

"Oh that's right, you're a psychiatrist."

"Psychotherapist. Like Annette."

"I can't ever keep track of the difference between the two," I said.

"We are professionally crazy in different ways." We laughed with her. I said, "Why?"

"Why are we crazy in different ways?"

"Why should being a psychotherapist lead you to expect that whatever happens during a tape would be hard to get a handle on?" *More to the point, why should it lead you to expect anything to happen in the first place?*

"You've never had therapy, I take it."

"No, I haven't. My boss has recommended it, though, several times."

She smiled, a nice smile I thought. "Dealing with matters of the mind and spirit isn't like reading a book, where either the words are there or they aren't there. It's more like looking out at the horizon in twilight, trying to decide if what you see is really there or is an illusion, and if it is there, what is it? New discoveries often come with great subtlety."

"So what was it that maybe happened and maybe didn't?" Again she hesitated. "Or maybe you don't want to talk about it?"

"No, I want to talk about it." *I know you do, or you wouldn't have been asking us what we experienced. You'd be steering us right the other way.* "By itself it wasn't any big deal. I was lying there concentrating on keeping my mind clear, as they suggested, and I kept thinking about how green everything is out here compared to Texas. And then I'd go back to clearing my mind, and then the thought of the green trees kept coming back to me, and then I think I was daydreaming and then all of a sudden I was looking down at the trees from up in the air, like I was flying."

Richards smiled. "One tape and you've had an out-of-body experience."

She laughed with us. "Well, I've never *had* an out-of-body experience, so how would I know? But that isn't what's strange. This wasn't a dream – at least, it felt like I was awake – but if it *were* a dream, and I was examining it professionally, I would be focusing on the content of the dream, and the emotions that the dream aroused. Instead, I have the feeling that what's important here is more the feeling around it than the experience itself. I can't quite grasp it. I can tell you what it isn't, but I can't yet tell you what it is."

Flying over trees? I was startled at the coincidence.

❖ 2 ❖

I was in the middle of writing in my journal when the cowbell clanged again, and so I was among the last to arrive for breakfast. I loaded my tray with scrambled eggs and toast, took a couple of slices of bacon, filled a juice glass with a mixture of orange juice and grapefruit juice, and looked around for a table. Claire Clarke and Jeff Richards were sitting next to each other and the other four places at that table were filled. I set down my tray at the last free spot on the table next to theirs.

"Angelo. Andrew." *That's right, we talked last night. He's the environmental guy.* "And this is Francois." *The priest, yes.* "Marta on your end of the table, Dee next to her, and Katie next to you."

I nodded a general recognition. *Marta is staying close to Dee. For support, maybe. Or maybe they just wound up at the same table.* "That's pretty good. You have everybody's name down already?"

"Not everybody," Andrew said with some complacence. "I'll have 'em by noon, though."

"I'll be right back," I said, and I walked over to the coffee brewing machine, filled a mug, and brought it back to the table.

"So," Andrew said to me after I sat down, "I didn't see you down in the exercise class either."

"Didn't you? I was being real quiet, in the background. You must have missed me."

Andrew laughed. "Yeah, right. You were lost in the crowd of ten."

"Ten? You mean we have *that many* lunatics among us?"

"I take it that physical exercise is not your thing."

"You take it correctly." *Bacon, not tofu burgers. Something to be thankful for.* Tucking into my eggs: "And *I* take it, if your count is right, that I'm not the only sensible one in the crowd."

Andrew took it with the casual good nature that seemed to be his preferred style. "That's well and good, but you're missing out. You heard them say, last night, that physical exercise is the best grounding, and that grounding is the best way to experience altered states."

The older woman next to me – *Katie, Andrew said her name was* – smiled and asked Andrew if the class had induced an altered state. He grinned at her and said, no, he figured it would take till lunch, and for a while we listened as he described the exercise class. *Sounds like stretching exercises, mostly. Loosen people up for a hard day of lying in bed listening to tapes.*

Katie – *social director*, I thought, but I appreciated her talents and inclination – asked Dee if she had been waiting a long time to come to Open Door. Dee smiled and said, no, it was an idea that had come to her only recently.

"But you had a long-time interest in such things?"

"Well, I've read the literature, like most people, and I have attended a couple of weekend meditation workshops." *That's right, she's one of the ones I had pegged as a New Age seminar hopper.*

"Oh, like what?" They traded names for a bit, and Andrew joined in. This was the first time I heard the name Gurdjieff, when Andrew brought him up. None of the other names was familiar to me except that I had heard of Edgar Cayce, though what I knew of him was little enough.

"The trouble is," Dee said finally, "there's so much out there, it would take me a whole lifetime just to know where to start. You've got hundreds of groups, maybe thousands, all claiming that they can show you the way to the truth. But how do you know who to believe?"

"That is the value of a religious tradition," Francois said. "You stand on the shoulders of those who have come before you who care about the same things."

Dee toyed with her food, considering that. "I never thought of it that way. But the trouble is, if you commit yourself to one tradition, you have to go along with everything they think, and I don't know if I could stand having somebody tell me what I had to believe."

Francois didn't seem to be offended by the implied insult, perhaps because it was so clearly unintended. "But you see," he said, "it need not be a strait-jacket. You might think of it as a seat belt. It provides us a firm place to stand, so that we do not need to begin at the beginning as if no one had ever concerned himself with such matters before."

Katie asked Francois if his attending the Open Door didn't conflict with his religious beliefs. Mentally I raised my eyebrows at the question. Francois, though, didn't seem perturbed. "My dear lady, surely you must see that not everyone in religious orders could be so simple as you seem to imagine us. Do we not live in the same world? Do we not all face the problems that life poses? Having faith is not the same thing as thinking that we know the answers. If we could *know*, then it would cease to be a matter of faith, would it not?"

"But I thought – " She hesitated, and Francois smoothed her path. "Please, I hope that you will feel free to say what you mean. You are unlikely to shock me, and you need not try to spare my feelings. I assure you, I will take your words in the spirit you mean them, and will not easily take offense."

"It's just that I'm not used to talking to priests, you know." Another hesitation. "It's hard to know what – Well, I mean, you Catholics have things you have to believe, and – "

"And you do not know where forbidden ground begins," he said. With an expansive gesture: "Dismiss that from your thoughts. I am here, after all, and not cloistered in a monastery. If I could not bear to hear thoughts that may be strange to me, surely I should have stayed away." *Not the kind of conversation I expected to hear in this place – especially over breakfast. But then, I didn't expect bacon, either!*

"Yes. All right. Well, I can't help wondering what you make of the idea of psychic abilities in general. I mean, isn't there some official church teaching about it?"

He nodded as he drank his coffee. "The church attempts to guide the faithful, and so naturally its rulings touch upon all aspects of life. So, one finds prohibitions against fortune-telling, and much of what constitutes psychic investigation. But strictures designed to protect the undeveloped must not be confused with willfully imposed ignorance which would defeat its purpose. *Quod licit jovi non licit bovi.*"

"For those without a classical education," Andrew said, "it's an old Roman maxim that means that things are permitted to Jove – the god Jupiter – that are not necessarily permitted to cattle."

"Very good, my friend. And perhaps you can see the force of the saying. Because dangerous tools are kept from the hands of children does not mean that *everyone* should avoid dangerous tools, or no tool would ever be used: What tool is not dangerous when misused? It is a matter of discretion."

"And the church makes the decisions and makes the rules," Katie said.

He shrugged. "For Catholics it does, yes. And I do not suppose any of you would agree, that we would all be better off if it made them for society at large. That is no longer possible, of course – it hasn't been possible for 500 years, to the extent that it ever was – but remember this. Always, *someone* makes the rules, whether it is the church or economic interests or the mass media. The rules are made well or badly, out of wisdom and knowledge or out of passion and ignorance – but they are made, and they shape our lives, whether we know it or not. All the more thoroughly, in fact, when we do not."

"That's where I am," Dee said thoughtfully, half to herself. "It's so hard to know what's possible, because it's so hard to know what's real. That's one of the things that attracted me to Open Door, they don't have a list of things you're supposed to believe in."

"Personal experience," Andrew said. "Me, too. Just let me find out for myself what works and what doesn't, that's all I ask."

"However," Francois said, "bear in mind, once you know what works, you remain faced with the larger question of what it means."

❖ 3 ❖

It was our first time in the conference room, that we would soon automatically begin to call the debrief room. Unlike the gathering in Carter Hall the night before – and unlike the dining room where we had just had break-fast – here were no padded armchairs on wheels, no tables to sit behind. We sat, in an irregular circle, on the floor, on little canvas and aluminum contraptions called back-jacks, consisting of a seat and a back support.

My somewhat satirical eye found something comical in the vision of two dozen people, most of them more than old enough to know better, ear-nestly sitting in a circle on the floor, all of us barefoot or in socks, our discarded shoes littering the entryway to the room. I made a mental note of the detail; Charlie liked little touches like that.

Annette and David sat – on the floor – in front of a blackboard and a flip chart on a tripod; in front of them, on the floor, note cards. "So," Annette said. "Before we start the day, how was last night's tape? Did any-one experience anything that they would like to talk about?"

"I fell asleep with the headphone on, and I didn't wake up until the mid-dle of the night sometime." *The massage therapist from California. What was her name?*

One of the men – the guy from South Carolina – asked, "How'd you do that with the earphones on?"

"I must have taken them off at some point. When I woke up I wasn't wearing them."

"I fell asleep too," Richards said, "and I didn't wake up until right at the end of the tape, where C.T.'s voice was telling us to return."

I noticed two or three others nodding. "Me too," Bobby Durant piped up. "Is that because the frequencies on the tape changed then?"

Annette smiled. "I don't know. Maybe. Ideally, the frequencies lead you into Entry State at the beginning of the tape, and out of it again at the end. Edith, I can't say why it didn't bring you back. Maybe you took off the earphones in the middle of the tape, and Entry State moved into normal sleep. Nothing wrong with that."

"Nothing, except I missed the experience!"

"Let's talk a little about that," David said. "Sooner or later that always comes up, so we might as well get it out of the way right here. One thing you *don't* have to worry about in this program is missing something. If you're doing a tape and you fall asleep, you're processing it on some level anyway." *Now there's an infallible cover story!* "Lots of things are going to happen this week, and some of them you're going to be conscious of, and some not. Just because you don't remember it, doesn't mean it didn't happen."

"So what *did* happen?"

"Well, Bobby, nobody else can tell you that. If you just stay open to experience, maybe at some point you'll find out."

That was more than I could take. "I don't quite see why we should assume that *anything* happened. People do fall asleep sometimes, right?"

Annette smiled at me. "There's something we call 'clicking out' that is different from falling asleep. Sometimes, you will be in Entry State or some other focus level, and then you will be gone and all of a sudden you will be back, and you won't have any idea where you have been or how long you were gone."

"And that's different from just drifting off?"

"The telltale sign is that you come back when you're being counted back at the end of the tape. If you had merely fallen asleep, you wouldn't necessarily hear the instructions."

Edith said, "So I just went to sleep?"

"Well, it's hard to say. Maybe you just needed to sleep."

"But it doesn't matter, really," David said. "Don't worry about it."

"In every program, we have to remind people to go with the flow," Annette said. "Things take just as long as they take, and they can't be hurried. Sometimes it's Tuesday, even Wednesday, before somebody 'gets it' – but then they get it all in a rush, believe me. By the end of the week everything generally evens out."

She paused. "We want to get started, but did anybody else want to say anything about last night's experience?"

The German – Klaus something – cleared his throat. "I don't know if I should say this. I would not, except I have the feeling that I must." I found myself leaning forward. This seemed a solid guy, not a flake. Someone to take seriously. "Last night I had a picture appear to me."

"A vision?" *Bobby.*

"A vision, yes, a clear picture. It was my body but in front of my body was a skull. The skull was from here to here" – holding one hand at the level of his nipples and the other just below his navel." He looked ill at ease. "I do not know what this may mean, but I felt that I was to mention it, because it is about someone here. Maybe this does not mean anything, I don't know."

There was an embarrassed silence, and then Annette said, "Thank you for being open enough to deliver that message, Klaus. It can be scary to deliver a message when you don't know who you're delivering it to and if it's even a real message or something you're making up."

"That business about 'am I making this up' is going to haunt you through this entire process," David put in. "We might as well warn you now. It is a good thing to listen to that kind of prompting. The difficult thing is to remember to use our judgment, so we don't go off the deep end either."

"That's right," Annette said. "This week is going to be filled with promptings, and it is important that you learn to give them a hearing. Don't just seal them off on the assumption that they are meaningless. And on the other hand, as David says, they won't all be right – but it's important to dare to listen."

Got him off the hook, I thought with approval. *Didn't leave him out there hanging. That was kind.* My life had taught me to value kindness. I appreciated good technique, too.

Then I happened to notice Claire's face, halfway across the circle from me. Either the lighting was bad, or she'd lost all the color in her face, just as if she'd turned white from fear.

❖ 4 ❖

"All right," David said. "Here we go. First a little lecture, then we'll send you off to play." He stood up and turned over the cover sheet of the flip chart. "Here you see the four altered states we're going to be exploring this week: Entry State, Wider Vision, Time Choice, and Interface. You got just a whiff of Entry State last night. We'll spend the rest of today exploring various aspects of it. Monday we move on to Wider Vision, Tuesday to Time Choice, and Wednesday to Interface. Thursday we'll show you how to mix and match according to need."

The guy from Seattle: "And Friday?"

"Friday, Andrew, we shoo you all out of here and let you practice your new skills in the great big outside world."

"In other words you send us out to play in traffic."

David smiled. "Individual mileage may vary." He pointed to the first line of the chart. "Okay, Entry State. Why do we call it that? Because if Open Door is your journey of a thousand miles, Entry State is your single first step. Entry State is how you go through the doorway."

He flipped the page over.

"We don't want to load you down with a lot of theory – we find that theory just gets in the way of your actually *experiencing*, rather than *thinking about*. So we try to give you just enough to orient you. After you have had some experience, we can talk a little bit about what we think it means. All we want to do at this point is to give you enough to get started.

"As you can see from this rather crude cartoon, the person with headphones is lying down with eyes wide open. This is not the way we expect you to do tapes! It's a representation of your situation when you are in Entry State: Your body is asleep, but your mind is wide awake. Some of you may have noticed, in last night's tape, that the quality of your experience felt different. You weren't asleep, but something felt different. And of course if it really is different, you wouldn't know quite how to think about it."

That's like what Claire said. She thought the important thing wasn't the experience, but the feeling around it.

"Keep in mind our ultimate purpose, here. For you to learn how to direct your mind to do what you want, rather than to do whatever the moment suggests, you first need to be able to distinguish between different states of mind that until now you may have taken for granted, and in fact may not even have noticed. Anything new is difficult to perceive, and if it *is* perceived, it's difficult to make sense of. So it is important to get as many distractions as possible out of the way. And what do you suppose the major distraction in our lives is? It's the body.

"The sound frequencies in the Entry State tapes are designed to quiet your body's background noise. For some people, this will mean that their bodies are actually in a sleep state. If someone were to run an EEG on them, the readings would say they were asleep. For others, their bodies will be merely very relaxed, very calm. And the interesting thing is that some people, being so mentally awake, will not realize that their body is asleep. We have had people ready to complain that someone in the room was snoring – only to realize that the snoring was coming from their own body! And at the same time that the body has been tranquilized, Entry State frequencies are also stimulating the mind, so that you can take advantage of the newly quieted environment. Yes, Bobby?"

"Are you going to give us the frequencies for the various focus levels?"

David glanced down at Annette, then said, "No, that would be a distraction."

"I didn't mean specific frequencies by number, I meant how much alpha, how much beta, how much theta and delta."

Annette said, "At some point perhaps we will talk about it, but as David said, it would only be a distraction at this point."

"I was just trying to get a general idea, to orient myself, sort of."

David said, "I don't know how many of you remember E.F. Schumacher, the man who wrote *Small Is Beautiful*, but he once said that it's amazing how much theory you can do without, when you set out to do some real work. We are going to continually come back to this point. You all came here to do some work. Annette and I are here to help you do the work. Anything and everything else is a distraction."

"Well, I just – "

"You're going to have to trust us for a while, Bobby."

Annette said, "Bobby, think of it this way. Suppose we gave you the exact frequency mix for Entry State – what good would it do you? You wouldn't know anything you don't know now, not really. You'd have another bit of data, but so what?" She looked intently at him. "I can see you're not convinced. Trust us."

"All right," David said. "The purpose of this first tape is to give you a good solid grounding in what it feels like to experience Entry State. Last night you got your initial taste, whether or not you consciously recognized it while it was happening. Today we're going to show you how to enter that state at will and re-enter it whenever you wish. It isn't complicated and it isn't difficult. You'll have C.T.'s instructions as you go along: Just follow his lead."

"Now, remember the suggestions we gave you last night," Annette said, smiling warmly. "It's great to go into these experiences in a state of high expectation, but don't overdo it. Maybe something huge will happen right off, but maybe it *won't* – and maybe it *shouldn't*. The flashy things aren't always important, and important things aren't always flashy. Sometimes they aren't even evident. We have sometimes had people leave Open Door very discouraged and depressed, saying that nothing happened to them all week – and then we meet them at another program months later and they tell us that their big breakthrough came on an ordinary day, a week after they returned home. There isn't any schedule for these things. Or perhaps we should say, things have their own schedule."

"Try not to over-expect," David said. "Just *be*, and see what happens. Do the exercise as best you can, and then *be* with whatever happens or doesn't happen."

I was struck with admiration at how well and naturally they worked together.

"You know," David said, "we tell you when you come here that we're not going to feed you dogma or try to make you believe anything except what your own experience leads you to believe. And it's true. But it is also true that you can't do this for as many years as we've done it without learning a few things about the process. So we ask you to just take our word for this, subject to your own later verification. The best way to go into this is with a general sense of expectation, but not with any specific expectations. Leave yourself loose."

"Trust," Annette said. "Trust the process, trust yourselves. We all have our inner guidance, and you probably listen to it more than you realize; it's just a matter of not fighting it so much."

"Sometimes the hardest thing is just getting out of our own way."

"For those of you who aren't yet comfortable with the idea of listening to your guidance, let us suggest this. Try it just for this one tape. Go into the tape experience assuming that whatever happens is just what is supposed to happen. And then *be* with it and see. After all, if it doesn't work out, all you will have lost is a little bit of time."

"Of course, you won't have your watches, so you'll never find out just how *much* time," David said. That got a little laugh, and he topped it by adding, "and in any case you will have had another chance to use the bathroom." *I can see that's going to become a running gag.*

"Remember to consider using the sleep masks that we provided you. You wouldn't think that keeping your eyes closed could be a strain, but it can be, even in a darkened room. You might try using the mask, and then if it bothers you, just slip it up onto your forehead for the rest of the tape, and next time don't use it. But some of you will find that it helps, I think."

"Also, remember, as soon as you are in bed with earphones on, flip the switch to 'ready.' As soon as all the ready lights are on, we'll start the tape."

Annette said, "Okay? Anybody have any questions? All right, ready or not, here we come. Go get 'em, tigers."

"And," David said – dramatic pause, serious face – "don't forget to go to your rooms by way of the bathrooms."

I looked around as people picked themselves up and headed for the tape exercise. Some faces seemed to show a slight apprehension; others, expectation; still others – a few – determination, almost a grim determination.

"Well, here we go again, roomie." Bobby Durant had already kicked off his shoes and lay down on his bed, pulling a blanket over him. He reached over to the wall and flipped the ready light to "on" and put on his sleep mask, leaving it on his forehead while he pulled on his headphones. "Luck," he said, and pulled the sleep mask down over his eyes.

"Yeah, you too," I said, trying to keep the wry amusement out of my voice.

"Give it a fair trial," Charlie had said. *"You're not there to believe it or disbelieve it. Be prepared for it to work."*

"Look, Charlie, I said I'd take the assignment. I'll give it a shot. But there's no use pretending the impossible is going to happen, no matter how many people swear they've seen it. People need to believe, Charlie, you know that. Some people believe in God, some believe in science, some in politics, and some in all this stuff. 'A man's got to believe in something – and I believe I'll have another drink.'"

"W.C. Fields. Very funny. But there's got to be something *people get from going there, or they wouldn't keep going back. Find out what that something is, there's your story. It might be a scam, it might be honest self-delusion, it might be real. Whatever it is, find it."*

"Charlie, can I ask you something? Why is this suddenly such a big deal?"

"What sudden? I've been thinking about it for a while."

"Charlie, don't give me that, okay? Not with your Irish blue eyes giving me the look, you know? Old Mr. Honest and Open, 'what, me hold out on you?'"

"Just get the story, Angelo, okay? Don't write it in your head before you even get on the airplane to go down there. I don't want you digging in your heels and proving a point at the paper's expense."

"Charlie, how long have I worked for you? When have you ever known me to do that?"

"Way too long, and you do it whenever anything comes up that even smells like the word 'psychic,' is when."

"So why send me*? Send one of your thirty-somethings."*

"I don't want a true believer, Angelo. I'm just asking you to remember that you're a reporter, not a crusader for a point of view. I don't want to send a true believer either way. You don't realize it, but this could be a big deal

for you. If you do this story right – the way you can do it when you're on your game – this could be your ticket."

"My ticket to what?"

"Let's just leave it at that for the moment. I don't want to see you again until you bring me back the story, whatever the story turns out to be. Hit the road."

I sighed and pulled on the headphones. I reached over and turned on the light to show that I was ready. *As ready as I'm going to be, anyway.*

❖ 6 ❖

Again the pink noise, again the sounds of a stream running over rocks, again C.T.'s voice leading us through systematic relaxation. Again long periods of daydreaming, as I half-listened to C.T.'s instructions, and half-heartedly tried to follow them. *I wonder if many people sleep through the entire week.*

I was very aware that I was lying on my back but still breathing comfortably. *Remarkable!* For that matter, so far I hadn't felt even a twinge in my lungs even in the early morning air. *I did bring my inhaler, right? Yes, sure, it's in my pants pocket as usual.*

C.T. finished leading us through the relaxation process, and there were a few moments of silence on the tape. *If nothing else I'll get good and rested this week. "Think of it as a vacation, Angelo," Julie had said. "God knows you could use one." And she didn't say it, but she might as well have: "I can use one too, from you." Well, Mom used to talk about "too much together-ness" when she and Dad were getting on each other's nerves. Come to think of it, their "too much togetherness" lasted for decades – and it's starting to look like I'm going to have a shot at breaking their record.*

A flash of something went by, an image or a memory too fast to catch. I realized that it wasn't the first such flash I'd noticed. *I wonder if that happens all the time and usually I don't notice it.*

I got a vivid picture of myself standing on the side porch in the early morning light, talking to Jeff Richards and Claire whatever-her-name-was. *A couple of people to talk to ought to make the week easier to take – assuming they don't go all woo-woo after we've done a few tapes.*

I thought of the fear I'd seen in her face – for, after the fact, it seemed plain that it *had* been fear – and wondered what that was all about. I had a sudden *feeling* about her. *Interesting! If I'm going to start with fantasies, why start with her? Although, she is mighty attractive, and not just physically.*

The tape had been silent for some while now, except for the faint pink-noise background. C.T.'s voice came in and talked us through a procedure designed to embed a key phrase in our minds so that we could return to Entry State whenever we desired. I listened, hardly noticing, and perhaps I did not notice, either, that I did not greet the procedure with my usual impatience and suspicion. It happened more or less while I was elsewhere.

C.T.'s voice sent us off to play – to continue to experience the feel of Entry State, he said. *"The big barrier to experiencing altered states of consciousness is fear,"* Annette had said to us. *"C.T.'s big contribution is that he figured out a way to remove the fear."* Well, I don't know about altered states, but he certainly has made the process enjoyable as far as we've gone.

I thought again of how naturally Jeff Richards and Claire and I had come together. For some reason, I was again thinking of married life as my wife and I were enduring it, and then without transition I was thinking of my desk at the paper, and commuting, and my everyday life that had begun to get so tiresome, thinking I was not so different, in that respect, from Tony Giordano. *I wonder if we'll start swapping complaints about how my wife doesn't understand me. Or worse, how she does!* But it wasn't funny, really. Too long a sacrifice can make a stone of the heart, Yeats said. He knew.

❖ 7 ❖

Annette looked around the room, embracing us in goodwill and support. "Okay! So how do people feel?"

"No big deal," someone said, "I've been to the bathroom before." Carolina twang. *That's Lou Hardin, our wisecracking security consultant. He was wisecracking at the other table last night, too.*

"Merriman bathroom humor," Annette said, laughing with the rest of us. "It is always with us. Other than that, any experiences you *haven't* had before?"

Hardin shook his head. "There was some stuff, but I can't remember most of it, and what I did remember didn't make sense. Probably I was just making it up anyway."

David smiled. "We've heard *that* once or twice over the years, too!"

Helene asked, "In general, do you think that happens a lot, us making things up?"

Annette said, "I don't know, what do you think?"

"But I'm asking what *you* think."

Again Annette's warm smile. "Don't be in a hurry to decide. Remember this is all new territory. Whatever happens, try not to judge it; *be* with it for a while, and see if it clarifies."

"However," David said, "it's true, you're running out of time. If you haven't had an undeniable transcendent experience by the end of the first exercise of the first full day, it may be that there isn't any hope for you, and you ought to pack it in."

That, too, got a laugh. Annette said, "Anybody else?"

Klaus Bishof raised his hand and dropped it, a motion that was almost a wave. "I found it very interesting," he said. His English, though heavily accented, turned out to have few hesitations, though his choice of words was sometimes peculiar. "I found that I wondered to myself who was the person listening to the tape and who was the person who appeared from somewhere else." He paused. "Do I make it clear?"

Since he had addressed himself mostly to Annette, she held the contact. "Say a little more about it."

"Yes. Well, I am lying there, it is very pleasant, and I am attempting to keep my mind blank as we were instructed. But thoughts come in and I must shoo them away." Nods from some of the others sitting in the circle. "Yes, others too, I see. Well, this is not uncommon in meditation practice, I think, distraction."

"It is a skill that has to be learned," David said, "learning to silence mind chatter."

"But I see that when I do keep the mind still, what happens? It is like a voice, but without sound. It wishes to tell me things."

"You are hearing your higher self," Selena Juras put in. "That voice is available to everyone."

David said, smoothly, gently, "Let's hold off on deciding what it is. In general, we find it works better to keep things as open as possible, as long as possible."

"But I have *years* of experience at this!"

"And I am not saying that you are wrong. But it is better for people to come to their own understandings, and anyway – speaking only for myself here – I find that when I hold off for a while on deciding what something is, or what it means, I wind up with a richer, deeper, understanding of it."

"Yes, but if you already know what it means – "

"We are infinite mysteries to each other, and what is true for some of us may not be true for all," David said.

"And anyway," Annette said, "C.T. always says, what we decide for ourselves, we know. What others tell us is only what others tell us. We try hard not to stop people from interpreting their own experience – just as we also try to stop them from drawing conclusions that are too firm, too soon."

Selena subsided, without very good grace, and into the gap came a very quiet voice, apparently hesitant at speaking up in front of this group of still mostly unknown quantities. *Elizabeth Tyrone, our "office worker" from Elizabeth.* "About that voice? Can you – Klaus, is it? I'm not sure I understand what you meant. Can you tell us more about it?"

Klaus made a gesture with his hands. Had he been French, he would have shrugged. "I do not know what to say. It was words in my head. Not a voice, but words, and they are not my words."

"Do you remember what they said?" *Who was that? Woman from Texas. Dotti Blunt.*

"No, I do not remember. I remember only being so surprised that there are words and they are not mine."

Later I'd realize that behind the carefully neutral facades, people (Emil and Helene in particular) were having their first experiences, and were not necessarily happy with what they were experiencing. But on Sunday morning, that realization was a way down the road.

"I'd like to ask a question." *Bobby.* "Where is what Klaus just reported, within the usual parameters of response from an Entry State tape?"

David and Annette looked at him a bit blankly, then David picked up, smoothly as always, asking, "What do you mean by that?"

"If Entry State is a specific mix of frequencies designed to produce a specific mix of brain waves, then I would expect the observed response to fit into a bell curve, and I was wondering where on the curve that would fit, to hear voices."

Unless I'm seriously mistaken, I can see David smothering a laugh under that accepting smile. "That's probably a very good research question, Bobby. I don't know the answer."

"But don't you at least have a generalized conceptual framework?"

"Not me. I mostly concentrate on reminding people to go to the bathroom before tapes."

"All right," Annette said, "you've had your introduction to Entry State, you've encoded the pattern, so now we'll do it again. Yes, Helene?"

"Annette, I still don't quite understand about encoding. How does it work and what is it we're really doing?"

Annette smiled at her. "What we're doing is giving you a way to get into Entry State without having to lie in bed listening to earphones. You know? 'I need to get into Entry State; I'll have to run home and listen to a tape! Or maybe I'll have to run back to the institute and take another program!' How much use would that be? The whole idea here is to acquire the skills and *have* them."

"You might think of these exercises as training wheels," David said. "Once you learn the feel of the various states, and once you've encoded the intent to return to the states, you *have* them; they're part of your everyday repertoire. That's what encoding is all about."

Annette said, "Okay? Good. So let's move into the next tape exercise. This tape is designed to give you an opportunity to have another experience of Entry State. It'll be the same thing again, more or less. C.T. will go through the relaxation procedures, he'll get you to Entry State, you'll embed a suggestion that will help you return there at will, and you'll have another chance to experience, to *learn*, the feel of Entry State energy. For this tape it's okay to have a specific purpose in mind, but if you don't, just enjoy the ride and experience the energy of Entry State. Any questions? Okay then, off we go by way of the bathrooms, and we'll meet down here for debrief when the tape is over."

Again lying on the bed wearing sleep mask and headphones. Again lying there relaxed, daydreaming, pleasantly idling. Whenever C.T.'s voice instructed us to imagine something, I imagined it (more or less), neither expecting nor desiring any particular result. Again, as in the previous tape, I fell into a state of calm acceptance that I found very relaxing. During the encoding process – as I was told to envision numbers or create images – I smiled and followed instructions. *I'm going along with it, Charlie. You won't be able to say I didn't give it a try. But turning into Bobby Durant isn't part of the deal. If something is going to happen, it's going to have to happen to me. I'm not into making stuff up and telling myself it's real.*

C.T.'s voice led us from normal consciousness to Entry State and back again, three times in all, and each time the voice encouraged us to notice the difference in how the two mental states *felt*. I lay there and daydreamed and half-consciously followed instructions.

❖ 10 ❖

"Well, gang?" The group had reassembled in the debrief room and David was looking around at our faces with a clear but indescribable look of satisfaction on his face. For a long moment nobody responded. *Nobody feels like moving. Everybody's feeling too mellow.*

"That was *wonderful!*" Roberta said quietly.

"How do you mean, Roberta?" *Dee West. Didn't say ten words at breakfast.*

"Oh, I was practically out of my body! C.T. counted us in and said 'go experience now' and the next thing I knew he was reeling us back in." *A couple of nods there. Does that mean this makes sense to some people?* "Unfortunately I lost most of what happened while I was out there, but – my goodness!"

The trainers nodded and waited for someone else to speak. Instead, everyone sat tranquilly, enjoying the afterglow of the deep relaxation the tape had provided. After a moment, Annette said, "Can you feel how the group energy has changed? How much more centered you feel?" *Yes, actually, I can. That's a good way to put it.*

"One thing we don't tell you beforehand," David said, smiling broadly: "Once you've begun to experience real consciousness, you can't ever go back to what you were before. Yes, Andrew?"

"I have a question. After the first time C.T. brought us to Entry State, I was sort of floating, you know, and . . ."

❖ 11 ❖

I got into line behind John Ellis Sinclair, followed him to a table, and sat down next to him. Andrew St. George was already there at one end of the table *(Sinclair's roommate, that's right)* and we were shortly joined by Katie van Osten, who took the other end, and Helene, who sat opposite me, and, lastly, by trainer David Taylor who sat opposite Ellis Sinclair. Six at the table, full house.

"So much for Sunday morning," St. George said cheerfully. "A pretty good morning."

"Was it?" Helene asked.

"Oh yes," St. George said comfortably. He tapped his head. "It turns out, I have a whole playroom in here!"

Ellis said, "If I have a playroom, I seem to have mislaid the key. I listen to people's experiences and it is clear that at least some of them are having a great time, but so far I can't see what the excitement is about."

Katie van Osten, our grandmother from Colorado, nodded vigorously. "That's *just* what I was saying to my roommate here" – gesturing toward Helene Porter, to her left. "Either these people have a vivid imagination or I'm getting too old."

"Or both," Ellis said dryly, and they laughed, in the way that elders sometimes laugh at themselves and their predicament. *Well, yes they're in their seventies, but we've got two people in their sixties, and the rest of us aren't exactly spring chickens.* He seemed a bit subdued, almost glum.

David said, "I have noticed that you engineers often have a hard time with this kind of thing at first. But in a way, you guys have the perfect background for this kind of work."

"How so?"

"Hold on a sec until I get some more coffee," I said. As I was getting up, Helene Porter said, "Do you customarily drink coffee nonstop? I don't think I have yet seen you without a mug in your hand, all last night or this morning, except in the debrief room."

"They don't allow coffee in there," I said automatically. *Whoops! Accidentally got a laugh at my own expense.* Standing there with the empty mug in my hand, I said, "Coffee is one of the important things in life. If I could drink it while doing tapes, I know I'd have better experiences." I left on the laugh, but when I came back Helene was still talking about how drinking a lot of coffee couldn't possibly be good for us. Finally David Taylor laughed. "Tell it to C.T. The only time he isn't drinking coffee is when he's eating chocolate mints or smoking cigarettes."

Katie and Helene actually gasped. "C.T. *smokes?*"

David laughed again. "Yes, and I am reliably informed that he occasionally uses bad language. He's just a mountain of vices, that man." *People have these ideas about how other people "should" be, especially famous people they admire.*

"So," Sinclair said, "about engineers?"

"I always like it when we have engineers doing Open Door. In this program, we're used to hearing people say, 'Well, I'm probably making this up, but – ' Happens all the time, because it takes people a while to figure out what they're experiencing. But when I hear somebody say, 'I just don't know how to isolate the noise from the signal,' I think, 'Aha, we're dealing with an engineer, here.' You engineers have a habit of examining your situation and seeing what works and what doesn't work. The problem is, usually you're accustomed to looking outside yourselves for facts, so it sometimes makes it difficult for you to pick up the knack of using that same skill to examine what's going on inside."

Smiling, Sinclair said, "That doesn't sound like me or anybody I know, of course."

"Yes, but on the other hand, in my experience, engineers are a little more open to experimentation, because as a rule they don't care so much about theory, if they can get results."

Sinclair said, "I should think that would apply to anyone."

"No, you'd be surprised. Some people have such strong preconceptions about the way things are that they can't let in anything new. It has to fit into their existing categories, or they disregard it." I resisted the temptation to look over at Selena Juras, holding forth at another table.

"Sounds like the economists Ronald Reagan used to talk about," Sinclair said, "who worried that just because something worked in practice didn't mean it would work in theory."

David laughed. "That's about it. When you already know what's going to happen and what it's going to mean, it's a bit harder for something new to come in through the window."

"Premature clarity," Helene Porter said. "One of the enemies Castaneda talked about."

"A psychiatrist who reads Castaneda," Andrew said. "I'm impressed."

"You'd be surprised what psychiatrists read. C.T.'s book, for one." The others nodded. *That's what brought them here, the promise of expanded consciousness.*

"Do you think that's what is happening to me?"

"I don't know, Mr. Sinclair – "

"Call me Ellis, please. Or John, even, if you prefer. 'Mr. Sinclair' makes me feel even older than I do anyway."

"Ellis. I don't know what's happening to you. Nobody can. Maybe *you* can't know, or can't know yet. Maybe you aren't supposed to."

"All part of the big mystery, eh?"

"Seems to be."

❖ 12 ❖

Bobby opened the door of our room and stuck his head in. "Yo, roomie, we're going to take a walk down to the lake, want to come?"

I was sitting at my desk, writing in my journal. "Who's 'we'?"

"Oh, whoever's interested. Edith and Tony, anyway. Emil, maybe. Maybe Marta – whoever wants to come."

"Yeah, I suppose so. You leaving right this minute?"

"Well, a couple of minutes, after people get their stuff, use the bathroom, you know."

"Go to the lake by way of the bathroom. They going to ring the cowbell first?"

Bobby grinned, said "See you downstairs," and left in his usual hurry.

Little exercise, bright day, why not? I finished my journal entry, stood up and stretched. I automatically checked my pockets for the inhaler, found it where it should be. *If we're all the way out at the lake, I wonder if we'll actually be able to hear that cowbell when it's time to come back. Weird working without a watch.* I put on my shoes and picked up my windbreaker. *Hope this is going to be warm enough.* I opened a drawer in my dresser and took out my knit watch cap *(Overkill, maybe, but maybe not)* and put it in the windbreaker's left pocket.

❖ 13 ❖

Seven people walking down the gravel road toward the little man-made lake. Besides Bobby and me, Tony Giordano, Andrew St. George, Marta from Peru, Toni Shaw, and Edith Fontaine. Andrew seemed to know the way; he led and three of the others walked with him in a little cluster. Tony and Edith and I followed a few feet behind them.

"Tony, I thought of you during that last tape," I said.

He laughed. "Oh yeah? Not a major fantasy, I hope. That could be embarrassing."

I snorted in derision. "I wouldn't get my hopes up if I were you. We've barely met, and anyway I'm a married man." Edith laughed, a quiet little laugh. I said, "Going to be a long week, huh Edith?"

"I'm sure I'll enjoy it," she said. "Like being with a bunch of guys fishing."

Tony said, "Do you do that a lot?" He got another laugh, and settled for that. "So how did I enter into your tape experience, Angelo?"

We walked along in the sunlight, I wondering if I could feel just the beginnings of something stirring. Always hard to describe. Something like a cold damp spot just behind the breastbone. Not quite a problem, but not quite right. Very boringly familiar. I checked my pocket to be sure I had the inhaler, even though I knew I did. *Anyway, so far I'm breathing fine and it's a bright beautiful day and I'm getting paid to goof off here!*

"I was thinking about what you were saying last night about your life. I feel a little that way too. Walking down this road sure beats commuting."

Tony nodded. "Does it not!"

"I'm lucky that way," Edith said. "My office is in my home, so I don't have to commute. I let my clients commute, instead."

"That *is* lucky," Tony said. "I'm out there at six with the other wage-slaves and I'm heading home at six with the other wage-slaves. Six if I'm lucky! The only time I see open highway is when I've been working later than usual, or I'm coming to work earlier than usual."

"I thought you said you were one of the owners of your company, Tony."

"I am. Doesn't mean I can avoid the commute. Wish I could! You too, I suppose, Angelo?"

"I'm sort of between the two of you. I commute, but mostly everybody else is off the road. I usually don't go to work till late morning, and by the time I head on home the rush hour is long over."

"Must be nice," Tony said.

"It has its moments. And if I'm covering a night meeting, city council or something, I usually don't go in till mid-afternoon or something."

"Before I became a massage therapist, I worked in an office in the city, and I came to dread commuting every day. I was very grateful to be able to give that up. Tony, I think you said last night you live in Menlo Park, so your commute must be even worse than mine was in San Diego. And I gather from last night that you're tired of corporate life."

Now, it isn't all that long a way down to the lake – half a mile, maybe – and you wouldn't think that so short a walk would give us time enough to get into deep waters (so to speak) but somehow by the time we left the gravel road and started walking across the field to the lake, Tony and Edith and I were deep into sharing our dissatisfactions with the lives we were leading. It isn't that we were complaining – more like we were thinking aloud, going over and over the questions that puzzled us. Why, having so much that the world esteems, did we find it all so unsatisfying?

Plenty of people didn't get enough to eat, or didn't have a decent place to live. Many people did not have families they supported and were supported by. Many, perhaps, hadn't a soul on earth to care for them or care for. Some didn't have a job. Others had jobs that left them stuck doing meaningless, soul-starving work, working for the bare minimum that would keep them alive. And of course plenty of people would have given anything to have one day of the health and wholeness we took for granted as our due. Even as we talked, I said to myself, *compared with most people, what in the world do you have to complain about?* And this was true, but yet it wasn't the whole story either.

I said, "One thing about being a reporter, you get to get out of the office a lot, you know? I get to poke into other people's lives, and I get to see what cops see, or judges. I do a certain amount of feature stories, whatever I dig up or Charlie – that's my editor – digs up for me. There's always interesting things if you look around. But yeah, a lot of the time lately I notice that I'm thinking it's pretty pointless. But what are you going to do? You have to make a living."

She stayed on it. "What would you do if you *didn't* have to make a living?"

We were getting near the lake, now; I could see it ahead of us. *What would I do?* My mind was a blank. What *would* I do? "I haven't thought about it much. I'm a little old to be changing careers."

"I'm not sure we're ever too old, really. It isn't like our parents' generation. I think it's more a matter of knowing what you *want* to do. As soon as I learned about massage therapy, I realized that this is what I wanted to do. I had to go back to school to do it, and then I had to go out on my own, which was a little scary, but I'm so glad I did! Now I like what I'm doing and I know that I'm really helping people. It's a world of difference from being just another office worker."

"Yeah, but changing careers can't be the magic bullet. You did it, and you like what you're doing now, but even so you're not content."

"No, that's true. It still feels like I'm *missing* something, and I keep hoping to find it."

"That's how I feel, too," Tony said forcefully. "I think, there *must* be more to life than this! I'm a millionaire, at least on paper, and I've got plenty of money coming in all the time. I'm good at what I do. If I sold my company tomorrow I could get another job in a couple of phone calls. In fact, every so often I *do* get phone calls, asking if I'd consider coming over to be the CEO of this or that company. You know what I'm saying? In my own little world, I'm known. I have a reputation. There's no way anybody could say I haven't succeeded. But there's something missing."

"Even with success, your life isn't enough to satisfy you any more."

"That's putting it mildly! I can't even stand it. Maybe I should think about becoming a massage therapist."

"I know you're kidding, but maybe you should."

Tony smiled, dismissing the idea. "What I'd really like to do is go to Antarctica."

"Yeah, you said that last night. What's that all about?"

He shrugged. "I don't know. I've just always had a hankering to go there. I dream about it sometimes."

"Could you make the dream come true if you wanted to?"

Another dismissive gesture. "I don't see how. My wife would kill me, for one thing. And, I have responsibilities. I couldn't just walk off and do what I wanted."

I thought Edith would leave it there, but instead she said, quietly and simply, "Why couldn't you?"

"You think it's easy?"

She said, slowly, "No, I don't think it is easy. But staying where we are isn't necessarily easy either."

Tony looked at her curiously, intently. "You got a message today, didn't you?"

She smiled at him. "Yes, I did, very good. It was in the second tape."

"And you aren't sure what to do with it."

"You should be a trainer. That's right, I am *being* with it, because if I listen to what it is telling me, well, it won't be easy." And for the moment, that was all that she would say about it.

❖ 14 ❖

Toni Shaw let out a long sigh and leaned back against the wooden picnic table. "It feels so *healing* here! It feels like, if I could live my whole life right on this spot I'd be well." Immediately I thought, s*omething serious being said here.*

Andrew was usually quick with a joke or a wisecrack, but not this time. Turning to stand in front of her, looking directly at her, he said with quiet intensity, "Toni, if ever there was a place to expect miracles, it's here at the institute. It's just a matter of your reaching out for it."

I liked Andrew, but I spoke a little more sharply than I realized I would when I opened my mouth. "Andrew, what does *that* mean?" For he had spoken as if he were an expert on the subject of miracles.

He responded to my words and not my tone of voice, "It means what it says. If there's one place in the world where you ought to be able to expect miracles, it's here."

"Why?"

"Because miracles don't come from the *outside*, they come from *within*. We learn to cooperate with the universe, and it lets us do more than when it had to fight tooth and nail even to get our attention."

Oh for –

But Toni said, "So you think I'm not crazy, Andrew?"

"Not at all! You're doing just what you *should* be doing." To Edith and Tony and me, he said, "I don't know if you heard it when we were walking up here, but Toni was telling us that she has a serious health problem, and she's hoping that this week will give her the tools to handle it."

Good luck, I thought. Edith asked, "What condition is that, Toni?"

"It's called interstitial cystitis. IC for short."

"Yes, I have had clients who have had it. They say their attacks are excruciatingly painful."

"Oh God yes. Like pouring acid on an open wound."

Even allowing for possible hyperbole, I winced.

"That's what they've told me. It must make your life difficult – to put it mildly."

"Difficult like you wouldn't believe! It's crippling, sort of like your whole body having a migraine. But there's no point talking about it." I recognized *that* reaction.

"But have you had it for a long time?"

"Nearly ten years now. At that, it's a little bit better, or I wouldn't have been able to come here. There's no way I could have been away from home for a week two years ago."

Ten years of crippling pain? "So what is it?" I asked. "Technically, I mean."

"It's a disease that causes massively painful burning in the entire pelvic region, especially in the bladder. In fact, it's also known as painful bladder syndrome."

"It's a bladder disease?"

"Well, that's what the doctors think. I don't happen to think so, myself. For one thing, it's systemic." She could see that I didn't pick up the inference. "Even though it affects the bladder more than other parts of the body, it *does* affect the other organs. Also, it stems from many factors. I'm not at all convinced it begins with the bladder."

"So where does it come from?"

"There are so *many* theories. Some think it's caused by infection, or *candida*, or allergies, or over-acidity of the body. You want more? A compromised immune system, environmental sensitivity, *chemical* sensitivity, *food* sensitivity . . ."

"Got it. They don't know. So what do *you* think causes it?"

"I think it's probably an auto-immune disease. When my urologist did a biopsy of my bladder wall, it was covered with mast cells, indicating a massive allergic reaction was taking place. And, since it mostly happens to women, probably on some level it's hormone-related. My doctor seems to think it has to do with estrogen and how the by-products of injected hormones in our food supply disrupt normal hormone production."

"Not a bug of some kind?"

"Bacterial infection, you mean? A virus? There's no evidence of either one. And even if an infection is involved somehow, it can't be the whole story, when 95% of the time it strikes women rather than men. About a million women in this country, more or less."

"So what's the cure?"

"There isn't any. In fact, a lot of doctors don't even believe it exists, believe it or not. And, well, they're right, in a sense, in that IC is just a name they made up to categorize certain patterns that have no visible origin or obvious cure. But they know enough to say it is incurable."

"Unbelievable." I couldn't restrain myself. "And you think that doing Open Door is going to help you? How?"

Andrew: "The mind-body connection, of course."

"I don't see that there's any 'of course' about it. Learning to relax is all well and good, but how is it going to cure a disease? Diseases are physical situations; they have physical causes. They can't just be wished away." *And don't I wish they could be!*

Andrew said, "It isn't just relaxation they're going to teach us, you know, it's specific unusual mental states."

"Yeah, I know, but I gather that it's mostly aimed at helping us have out-of-body experiences, or special insights into life."

Bobby said, "A *lot* more than that, roomie! Think of all the stuff C.T. talks about in his book."

Cautiously, feeling like Daniel in the lion's den, I said, "I haven't decided how much of what he said I could take literally and how much was – sort of literary license." *And how much was just general bullshitting.*

Bobby was all but open-mouthed in astonishment. "You think some it was *made up*?"

"Well, don't you think it's possible?"

Marta spoke, the first time I'd heard her speak since the introductions Saturday night. "I think he wrote what he believed. He had certain experiences and he described them. I do not think he was using – taking? – literary license."

"So you think we could all learn to do the things he said he did?"

Toni answered. "I don't know about anyone else, but yes, I do," she said, and I saw Bobby, Marta, Edith, and Andrew nod in agreement. I said, "Tony? Are you with them? What do you think? Is C.T.'s book a sketch of what we can learn to do?"

He hesitated, and as we waited his hesitation stretched out farther. "I don't know," he said finally. "I'm willing to be persuaded, but as of right here and now, I don't know. Maybe it's all true, maybe it's partly true and partly not, maybe it's true for some of us and not for others. I don't know."

"But you're here," Andrew said.

"Oh, I'm willing to be persuaded. In fact, I'd be delighted. And I'm not even saying it isn't true. I just don't have any idea what we're dealing with, or what the limits are, and until I do, I don't know what else I can say but 'I don't know.'"

"Seems like a reasonable position to me," Andrew said. "So Angelo, where are you? Are you a disbeliever? Mostly a disbeliever? Or on the fence, or what?"

I didn't feel like possibly alienating people. "Like I said, Andrew, I don't know yet."

"Well," Toni said, "they tell us we'll either have our experience or we won't, and in either case we don't have to take anything on faith. So I imagine they'd be okay with your attitude toward it. By the end of the week, we ought to know a lot more about what's possible and what isn't."

"Maybe by the end of the week, you'll have a handle on IC," Andrew said. "Let's program for that."

Jesus! I could see the sub-head on the story as though it were already written.

"Believers flock to New Age Mecca
in search of miraculous healings."

Nor would it be untrue – but I could already see that true-believer-ism wasn't the whole story, either. I found myself hoping for positive things to report, for I did like the people, very much. They weren't what I had expected, and neither – so far, anyway! – was the program.

❖ **15** ❖

Back to the debrief room. "Okay," David said after counting heads to be sure he had everybody. "Everybody back in exploration mode after that great afternoon? I'll put it another way, is anybody at all back in normal consciousness?"

"You want to remind us what normal consciousness is?"

"Sure, Andrew, it's what all the other people in this room experience on a regular basis." I watched them smile at each other. *David likes the sparring.* "Normal consciousness is what you can have any time you want it, night or day, and it comes free. But the reason you're paying the institute its exorbitant fee to do Open Door is so that you can learn to experience non-normal consciousness when you want it, and use it for whatever you want to use it for. So – here we go again. Last night we gave you a taste, just so you wouldn't go to bed grumbling. This morning you did two more tapes, and from what we heard in debrief, and again at lunch, it sounds like at least some of you are getting the idea. Now, let me emphasize it one more time, if you did the first two tapes and you didn't have any experiences that seem to you to be in any way unusual, and especially if it seems to you that you just slept through them – *don't let yourself get discouraged.*"

"Easy for you to say," somebody – I didn't catch who – muttered.

"It's easy for me to say because I've had a lot of experience at this. And anyway, it isn't whether it's easy to say or hard, it's whether it's true or false. And I'm telling you, we do know what we're talking about. Just because you feel you haven't gotten anything doesn't mean you aren't building the foundation you need."

Bobby said, "It's sort of hard to figure out the theory there."

Annette looked over at him and said, "You might think of it this way. You are bringing your mind into totally new territory. We like to say that our brains have two complementary functions: One is perception, the other is interpretation. When you perceive something you've seen before, or something similar to what you've seen before, your perceiver passes the perception over to the interpreter, and the interpreter says 'Oh sure, that's a widget, I've seen plenty of widgets.' Or it says, 'Not exactly sure what you've got there, it's sort of like a widget, but not exactly. Call it widget-like.' But when you perceive something that's totally unlike anything you have ever seen before, sometimes your interpreter just throws up its hands and says, 'I give up!' – and as a result, you click out, or you go to sleep, and you come back discouraged. But the next time you perceive the same thing, or something like it, your interpreter is more likely to say, 'Hey, wait a minute, I saw something like that a bit ago. I guess you could say it's very like a whale, in a way.' And sooner or later you've got data to chew on."

"But you see," David cut in smoothly, "no two of you start from the same place. A couple of you may have had experiences that are similar enough that your interpreter is saying, 'Oh sure, that's not all that new.' And others of you have to build the entire floor before you can get to consciously dealing with these things. And most of you are somewhere between these two extremes."

Annette said, "This is probably a good time to put in our commercial for non-comparison and non-judgment."

"Absolutely, and you can see why. You can't judge how well you're doing vis-à-vis anybody else, because you don't know where you're starting from or they're starting from or what kind of obstacles they're going to face, or you or anybody else are going to face before we're through. So it's a waste of time, and a *discouraging* waste of time, to compare yourself to others. Forget about others; just work out your salvation with diligence, as the Buddhists would say."

"I had a funny dream once that sort of makes the point," Annette said. "This was many years ago, when I was new to the path, and I was all anxious about becoming enlightened before next Tuesday. You know." *Judging from the nods, they do!* "So I went to bed one night asking for a dream that would tell me how I was doing, and would tell me how to do better – which in context meant, faster." She smiled. "What do you think I got? I woke up with a mental image of a field of stars. That's all it was, a nighttime sky filled with stars – and the question in my head, 'Who's ahead?'" She laughed with us. "But, you see? We're all like that – until we learn not to be. And I must tell you, once you learn to trust and relax, it gets a lot easier."

"Okay," David said. "So here we go again. This is a free-flow Entry State. You'll hear the usual instructions to help bring you to Entry State, and then you'll be on your own until C.T. comes back on to bring you back."

"Useful to have a specific purpose, doing this tape?"

"Not necessarily, Andrew. Some tapes yes, and we'll tell you. But on this one, if you happen to have a purpose – if something is foremost in your mind for whatever reason – go ahead and pursue it. Otherwise, just go along for the ride, try to be as aware as you can of the *feel* of Entry State, and see where it leads you." He looked around. "Okay? Everybody ready? Let's do it then."

"And wherever it leads you," Annette threw in, "it should be by way of the bathrooms."

❖ 16 ❖

I listened to C.T.'s voice going through the preparation process that was already becoming familiar. *Getting used to it. Well, after all, third tape today. I suppose I should be getting used to it!* "Now proceed to experience Entry State once again," C.T.'s voice said, "and I will call you when it is time to return." *It's funny, last night I just lay and daydreamed because I didn't expect anything to happen. But something did happen, sort of, and maybe you could say something happened in today's two tapes. Might as well stay with what's working.*

C.T.'s voice gave way to silence, or rather to the faint hissing crackling pink noise that was masking the sound of the coded signals, and I lay there daydreaming. After all, they had said that for this tape there was no particular advantage to having a definite purpose. That suited me fine.

[I drifted along.]

So Toni Shaw has her hopes pinned on Entry State? She really thinks that fooling around with different mental states could cure this disease she has. Amazing what people will believe.

[More drifting.]

And Tony Giordano wants out of his life and he doesn't have the slightest idea how to change it. Well, not so surprising, I guess. I don't either. How would I change mine? I had a sudden vivid picture of the people in the newsroom. Not a vision, exactly, not a memory, nor a daydream. More like a thought that came in pictures instead of words. A few dozen people, their eccentricities known to the last detail, but their inner selves a total mystery to me. *Funny, I already know some of these people here better than I know people I've been working with for years.* I thought of Jeff Richards, and how he and I had drifted into conversation – only this morning! *It felt like we'd known each other forever, even though we weren't immediately sure what the other guy's name was.*

[Drifting.]

What was that?! Suddenly I came back to what seemed like normal consciousness from wherever I had been. I had been daydreaming of flying again, floating in the air above the trees. This time I "knew" – how did I know? – that I was floating toward the east. It was as though I had risen straight up from the bed, had gone through the ceiling and the roof, and had floated directly up, then started east. Not that I remembered any of that: The first thing I knew was that I was remembering having watched the trees below as I drifted above them, heading eastward.

Huh! I wonder what that's all about? That's the same thing I imagined last night, flying above the trees. And that's what Claire imagined, too. I've got to remember to ask her if it happened to her again.

After a moment: *And what was her fear all about? If it was fear.* (I said "if" – but I knew.)

[Drifting again.]

So far, so good. Had to use the inhaler walking back from the lake, but that's not too bad. Fairly chilly today.

[Drifting.]

I had a sudden thought – vision? – of two dozen people lying in bed wearing sleep masks and listening to pink noise via earphones. It made me smile.

[Drifting.]

Another image, here and gone again. *What was it?* These things didn't come the way I would have thought. It wasn't like looking at pictures, but it wasn't the same thing as deliberately making them up, either. *How am I going to describe it when I come to write this up? It's more like remembering something. How do you remember something you've never seen?*

A cabin, I think. Not a Daniel Boone log cabin, more like one of those wooden houses people built after the frontier had passed them by and things were a little more settled. I tried to bring the image back but hadn't any luck. I resumed drifting, hoping it would return on its own. *Was that it?* Something. *Hard to tell how much is there and how much is me wanting to make it up.*

More drifting, and then there was C.T.'s voice beginning the re-entry process, calling us back. *Damn,* I thought. *I would have liked to stay with that a little more. Probably I'm just making it up, but still.*

❖ 17 ❖

I had thought I'd talk about it in debrief, but for some reason everybody wanted to talk about their experiences this time. Well, not everybody, but a good half dozen at least. I forget what Regina said, but something she said gave me a sudden strong sense of her, how reserved and French and mystically inclined she was. And of course Selena Juras used up some time trying to tell people what their experiences "meant" although I noticed that I didn't hear her describing any of her own. What with one thing and another, it went on for quite a while (or so it seemed, none of us having wristwatches) and then Annette smoothly gathered the threads into her hands.

"We've been hearing some very encouraging reports, I think you'll agree. Not everybody feels like they've really gotten with the program, I know, but again, patience! You're doing better than you know. Look how far you have come in a day. You had your first tape experience only last night, and now you have had four. After our program tonight we'll do one more, so by the time you go to bed you will have done five tapes all together. If you think you can do that much in one day and be left unchanged, well, all we can say is you're in for a surprise."

"And now we come to the part of the program where nearly everybody has a good experience," David said. "It's time to eat."

"Is it?" Andrew called out. "How do you know, without a watch?"

"Ah, well, that's just the magic that is inherent in being a trainer. Anyway, after supper when we ring the bell again, we will assemble next door in Edwin Carter Hall."

I got to my feet and went over to where Claire was sitting, and said to her, "Talk to you a second before we go eat?" She smiled up at me and used my hand to help pull her to her feet. "I was wondering if you'd say something." Around us, people formed a tide flowing out the bottleneck that was the doorway.

"So you experienced it too?"

She inclined her head. "After you."

Jeff Richards came over and stood with us. I said, "This morning, when you talked about flying over trees, it startled me, because the same thing had happened to me. And this tape it happened again."

"And?"

"'And' what?"

"Was there something else?"

"No, should there be? Oh! I saw what looked like a house, or a cabin or something. At least, I think I did."

She beamed. "And did you see any *people* in your vision, Angelo?"

"People? No, not that I remember. Why, did you?"

"You might say that. I saw two people, a man and a woman. I was one of them, and you were the other. And yes, we were in a little house, I suppose it might have been made of logs. Wooden, anyway. No, I think maybe a little fancier than a log cabin."

"Husband and wife, you think?"

"Well, if not, it's like that spoof country and western title, 'I'll marry you tomorrow, but let's honeymoon tonight.'"

Jeff laughed. "It sounds like your visions are a lot more fun than mine! I figure if I just don't snore too loud it'll be an accomplishment. I didn't realize we had more entertaining options."

"Well don't get your hopes up," I said. "So far she's honeymooning and I haven't even gotten an invitation to the wedding."

But, it's interesting! Whatever it turns out to be, something *is going on.*

❖ 18 ❖

Jeff and Claire and I got into line together, loaded our plates, and sat together, Claire sitting against the wall, at the end of the table, flanked by Jeff and me. While I was getting coffee, Jane, Elizabeth, and Regina joined us. Regina sat at the other end, flanked by Jane, next to me, and Elizabeth, next to Jeff.

This was only our third meal at Open Door – if you don't count the hurried, snatched supper that Bobby and Roberta and I had when we arrived the night before – but already I could see that every meal was more than a meal, because every group of four or five or six that gathered at a table turned into a miniature discussion group. By the time I got back with my coffee, it had already begun.

Elizabeth hadn't said much in debrief sessions, but I had noticed her. An office worker, Dee had called her, introducing her. But I had noticed, or seemed to notice, an intensity about her. As I carefully put down the mug by my plate and sat down to my supper, she was saying, "It's the story of my life, really, and the tapes are just rubbing it in. The closer I look at anything, the more I realize that I don't *know* anything and so I don't know how to judge anything, and so I don't know where to look or even *how* to look! It's like trying to get somewhere without a road map."

Regina nodded. "The Spanish have a saying, I think it is originally by Antonio Machado, that says more or less, 'Traveler, you won't find roads to where you want to go. Roads are made by traveling.'"

Jeff: "In my case, it's more like, roads are made by stumbling."

"Isn't *that* the truth," Jane said. "The whole idea behind Open Door is that we won't be on our own, that the tapes will lead us, but they've just been leading *me* out into the wilderness!"

We laughed. "That's about it," Jeff said. "Of course, there is a little bit of the program left."

"If nothing else, we're getting used to sleeping with earphones on," I said, "not to mention going to the bathroom on command. Surely that's worth something."

Claire paused with her fork in the air and said to me, "*You* can hardly say that nothing's happening, Angelo." To the others she said, "Angelo and I seem to be sharing aspects of the same experiences." *That* sharpened their attention. *When nothing's certain, everything's possible,* I thought. Then I thought, *actually, that's probably exactly the attitude Merriman is trying to encourage here.*

Jane said, "You mean you're sharing each other's thoughts?" *Ready to believe in miracles.*

"No, I don't think you could say that – although, who knows? It's more like we're tuning in to the same TV show. Last night, for instance, we were both flying over the trees outside."

"Not really flying, of course," I said. "More like, an idea of flying, sort of a daydream about flying."

Claire smiled. "Angelo is more cautious than I am. Whatever we were doing, we were doing the same thing without knowing it. Then on this last tape – do you mind if I tell them, Angelo?"

I shook my head. "Go ahead." I was smiling at myself: *I don't believe all this, sure, but I don't mind people thinking I'm linked up with something special happening.*

"I was a few minutes into the tape, waiting for something to happen, and suddenly there I was again, looking down at the trees. It was just like being outside here, but a few hundred feet in the air. It was just what had happened on last night's tape. So I waited to see if anything would happen, but then my attention sort of flickered and instead I was seeing a very old house. If it had been Texas, I would have guessed it was from the 1800s sometime, but out east here I suppose it could have been built a hundred years earlier."

"It was more elaborate than a log cabin, but probably still pre-revolution," I said. "*If* we were seeing the same thing."

Another smile, already an affectionate smile. "Mr. Caution. Yes, *if* we were seeing the same thing. And *if* we were seeing the same thing, *I* saw a man and a woman inside that house, and I have a pretty good idea who they were."

I could see that the women were impressed. "However," I said, "I don't necessarily believe in reincarnation."

"I don't know that I do either," Elizabeth said. "But I do believe in experience. If the two of you are sharing visions, it may not mean you're seeing a past life together, but it must mean *something*."

"Could just be a coincidence," I said.

Jane glanced at me. "Do you believe in coincidence?"

"Sure. Doesn't everybody? Or (thinking of Ellis Sinclair) most people, anyway?"

"I don't know about 'most people', but *I* don't. It seems to me that coincidence is a word that usually means 'I can't figure out what the connections are here, and I can't be bothered to look too hard.'"

"That's an interesting viewpoint," I said politely. "Ellis Sinclair said about the same thing to me. I have to say, it doesn't seem reasonable."

"It depends on how you see reality," Jane said. "If you think reality is individual things bumping into each other, then of course there will be coincidences, just as there will be collisions. In fact, you could say a coincidence *is* a collision. But suppose that we're all part of one great unity, all connected in ways we cannot see. Instead of being like molecules of gas bumping into one another, we'd be more like individual cars in traffic, or – I don't know, maybe like dots in a dot-matrix display." She had to join in the laugh the image produced. "It's only an analogy."

Screwy idea, but I liked the "feel" of her personality. "That's a very interesting thought, abstractly," I said, "but does it feel like the way you experience real life? I can't see how it would play out in the day-to-day world."

Claire said, "It certainly plays out in the world of dreams. We learn to pay attention to *everything* in a dream, because whether or not we can see it at first, everything is connected."

"Yeah, but that's dreams. I'm talking about waking life."

"Maybe the rules aren't any different in waking life," she said. "I'm with Jane on that."

Well, I thought, smiling to myself, *you've got to admit, this place is different!*

❖ 19 ❖

Back to the big comfortable assembly room that was the first floor of Edwin Carter Hall. *The chairs are facing forward again, not like a circle, the way we left them last night. And they're arranged behind rows of tables. We're in for a talk, I suppose.* I took a seat and set down my coffee mug in front of me. Francois, our priest, took the seat next to me, setting a glass of fruit juice on the table.

David was seated at the front of the hall, facing the participants. Annette took a seat at one of the tables toward the rear where she could quietly observe. *David's show, tonight, apparently.*

"Now you've had a day of first-hand experience," he said. "It's one thing to talk about extraordinary potential, but another thing entirely to begin to know first hand what we're talking about. And you've already begun that process." He smiled at us. "You came to be changed, right? To change yourselves? As you're starting to see, you came to the right place. Okay. So how did we get here?"

He proceeded to give us a summary of C.T.'s life. We already knew the bare bones of the story: After all, most of the people in the room had come because they had been captivated by his book. But now David fleshed it out, beginning with Merriman's birth in November, 1919, and his youth spent not far from here, saving his money, building radios from kits, and daydreaming of Escaping Rural Virginia, Seeing the World, and Making Big Money. He told how Merriman had worked his way through four lean years at Virginia Tech, emerging in 1938 with a degree in electrical engineering and, in that late depression year, no steady jobs in sight, and certainly none in his chosen field.

The war delivered him, as it did for so many. He got out of the Navy in July, 1946, and found a job without trouble. By the time the Korean War began, in mid-1950, it was clear that he was in the right field, electronics being a vital part of every weapons system more complicated than a rifle.

"After a while he got tired of working for somebody else," David said, "so in 1958 he quit and started up his own show. Seven years later he spun

off a second corporation. A year after that, he bought a third company out-
right. The country boy was doing all right for himself. Then, in 1966, he
flew down to the Caribbean for a scuba-diving holiday with three businessman friends, and in a few minutes his life changed completely. As most of
you know, a SCUBA diving accident left him without oxygen for nearly
eight minutes, which should have killed him or left him with irreparable
brain damage. His friends got him to the nearest hospital, and C.T. often
says that it was a good thing that he was in the Caribbean, because when he
came back to life the things he was saying might have gotten him a ticket to
a mental ward if he'd been at home.

"In those eight minutes, he had what today we would call a near-death
experience, or NDE, but this was before the day of Raymond Moody's
book, and George Ritchie's, and the other NDE pioneers. In those days
people didn't know much about it, and so if you were out long enough
that you should have sustained mental damage, and you came back talking
about things you'd seen and heard while you were gone, including the grand
plan of your whole life – well, you can imagine.

"Fortunately, C.T. was – is! – no slouch at picking up clues from people's body language. When he realized that people were beginning to look
at him sideways, he shut up fast. He stopped telling people what had happened to him while he was clinically dead, and said he couldn't remember
anything between the time he lost consciousness and the time he awoke to
find that somebody seemed to be determined to break his ribs.

"There wasn't anybody to contradict him. The doctors who checked
him out, and the nurses who cared for him during his brief hospital stay
were not in contact with his personal physician at home – and no doubt
C.T. worked to make sure it stayed that way. The other three men on the trip
hadn't heard him babbling, because by the time he started talking he was
already in the ambulance. And his wife and children were back in the States
and so didn't see him until he returned, a couple of days later than expected
but apparently as well as ever.

"Everybody counted it as a close call with no lasting effects. But within
six months he had sold his interest in the three businesses, including the one
he had founded, and announced that he wanted to retire – at age 47 – to the
rural county in central Virginia where he had grown up. This was all right
with his wife and children, who hadn't seen all that much of him, and probably looked forward to his slowing down.

"But that isn't quite what happened. First came finding a place to live. His family's house had been sold long before, and anyway it wouldn't have suited him now. He had left home poor, and now he was rich. In three weeks of concentrated looking, he bought this property, which was then the Robertson farm, a thousand-acre cattle and hay farm. Before the year was up he had built a house for himself and his wife at the top of the hill, leaving the previous house for the farm's manager, and announced that he was going to build himself a sound laboratory.

"Now, what C.T. knew about brain waves and theories of consciousness you could have put in your hat, as they say. And where he got the idea to electronically simulate certain wave lengths and feed them into the brain via sound, he wasn't saying. It was something he brought back from his NDE, of course, but it would be a long time before he admitted that. In fact, he wasn't saying much, other than vague explanations that amounted to 'it's my money and I can have fun with it however I want to.'"

David proceeded to tell us how C.T. Merriman's explorations led him to write the book *Extraordinary Potential: First-Hand Experiences of Altered States of Consciousness*, and how a string of "coincidences" led to his manuscript being published by a major New York publishing house and becoming a surprise best-seller. He told how many hundred thousand copies C.T.'s book had sold, and how many schools and institutions he had spoken at during his two-month long lecture tour. Out of that income, and the research sponsored by questions posed during that lecture tour, had grown everything around us.

"One thing kept leading to another, and finally he decided to do a series of residential programs. That's when he built these two buildings, and began recruiting trainers. And that's where we are today."

David paused. "As to where we go in the future, really you should talk to C.T. Merriman." A gesture toward the stairs, and we turned around and saw C.T. standing there. It was nicely done.

❖ **20** ❖

He's walking into a room filled with people, most of whom are ready to fall over and die of hero-worship. They've read his book and they've spent time and money to come here in hope that some of his magic might rub off on them. Few of them are used to dealing with famous people, and now – here he is*! He has to know all this. Let's see how he does.*

C.T. stepped down the last step, slowly, and people suddenly realized, "why, he's an old man!" We'd all known his age, of course, but now we were confronted with the effects of his age. He was only the same age as John Ellis Sinclair, more or less, but he looked, walked, and acted ten years older. We took in his slight stoop, and his craggy, ravaged face; we saw that he was dressed in an old, old navy pea-coat – even to the anchors etched into the buttons – and a nondescript beret. We watched him slowly walk the length of the room, nodding here and there to those who eagerly caught his eye. We saw him come to the chair David had been sitting in. He turned around. Standing, he took off the coat and held it out to the side as if to hang it on a hook – and let it drop to the floor. He shrugged and said, "Sometimes it's there," and got a laugh and got another fast, startled redefinition from his audience. "He's a comedian!"

He's got his routine down. Well, he's had innumerable opportunities in the institute's twenty-year history, and there was his lecture tour when his book got published. He's had enough practice.

C.T. sat down in the chair, and now we noticed the end table that David had placed by the chair while we had been watching C.T.'s progress. On the table were a mug of coffee and an ash tray and a pack of cigarettes. (I remembered Katie and Helene's shocked reaction at lunch. "C.T. *smokes?!*") Starting at the first table to his left, he went from face to face asking where they were from. With each response, he nodded, but said nothing, and turned to the next, one by one until he had contacted each person. As he did so, I could feel the group's reaction change again, in effect to something like, "Well, he isn't what he was, but let's be kind to the old man." *Apparently he is too confident to need groupies, too clever to want acolytes, and too private to submit to the demands of the guru role. Yet clearly he enjoys the personal contact, and cherishes his celebrity, especially the fact that these people value his work. So, he's managed to detach himself without alienating his fans, and in almost less time than it takes to tell it. Guru to old man to comedian to old-man-who-is-past-it, in not more than five minutes. Not bad.*

❖ 21 ❖

C.T. lit a cigarette and took a deep thoughtful drag on it. "I know that it is a cliché to say that it's a pleasure to see you all here tonight, but it is true. Truer perhaps than you know. In fact I don't think you can remotely realize *how* true it is for me.

"And before I say anything else, I want to assure you that in Annette and David, you are in very good hands. Perhaps you realize that already. And there are lots of others, some of whom you probably have met – Mick McChesney, for instance – and others that you probably haven't. Putting on these programs is a group effort, and it takes a lot of talented and dedicated people to make it happen. There's Dave Simmons and Harry O'Dell, for instance, who run the lab, and direct our research, and do booth sessions. You'll meet them when we give you a tour of the lab. And Rudy Linder, who does the technical sound work in creating all our new tapes, and others including the cafeteria staff and the cleaning crew – it's a team effort, certainly." Still holding his cigarette, he reached down with his left hand and picked up the mug of coffee. He took a cautious sip, then another, and put it back onto the table.

"If this group is at all similar to past groups that have come here," he said, "most of you are here because something in my book excited you. That is almost always the case. Occasionally, we get a would-be debunker, but we never worry much about that. The urge to debunk often stems from an active concern for the truth, and that is always good. In fact, our main worry is that sometimes debunkers have a big 'aha' experience while here, and they turn into true believers, and then they *really* become a nuisance!"

He chuckled and took a drag from his cigarette. "But mostly, we have been blessed with a steady stream of people like yourselves, people who for one reason or another were led to read my book, and suddenly realized that they were not alone in their conviction that their life could – *and should* – be deeper, more satisfying, more *engaging* than it is." I flashed back to our discussion by the lake. "They come here, as I suppose most of you have come here, in hope that we have developed a foolproof method of giving you reliable access to unusually productive states of consciousness. And, by the way, doesn't it tell you something about our culture, that it describes a controlled, productive state of consciousness as an 'altered' state?" He accompanied our laughter with another chuckle. "But I'm afraid that, if that's why you are here, you may be in for a disappointment. We don't have any such thing. For all we know, it's possible that nobody here in this whole week will experience anything extraordinary."

"Already too late for that!" somebody called out. Andrew St. George.

C.T. smiled. "Well, good. I'm always glad to have at least one satisfied customer. But for the rest of you, I want to be clear. Guarantees in this work are not to be had, and they're not what we're offering. In our experience, we cannot even guarantee that everyone here will attain Entry State, or that they will recognize it if they do." *Same thing Annette and David keep stressing: no guarantees. I thought at first it was just an infallible excuse, but now I'm not so sure.*

"So if anyone came here thinking we had something foolproof, I offer you my apologies for the misunderstanding. If you want to bail out of the program, we will understand. Tomorrow morning, when the office opens, we'll give you your money back and see you on your way with no hard feelings."

He paused. More cigarette, more coffee. "I can make that offer with some confidence, you see, because in 20 years no one has ever taken us up on it.

"Why haven't they? I think because although we can't offer a guarantee, we offer something better. We offer a chance to explore, in a safe environment, guided by people who have themselves gone where they will lead you. And the method of achieving altered states that we offer you is safe. It is safe for the same reason that results cannot be guaranteed: because it is non-invasive, non-intrusive, non-coercive. If you want to resist it, you can. If you don't let your brain follow the frequencies, nothing is going to happen. That's your safety valve. If you get scared or overwhelmed, you can snap out of it at any time, and the only consequence is that you lose whatever experience might have followed. And if you do, so what? There's always another time, as long as you keep trying. Sooner or later, when the time is right, when *you* are right, you're likely to succeed. The only way to fail, as far as we know, is to bail out.

"But on the basis of 20 years of experience with Open Door and other programs, I can predict that the overwhelming majority of you will not bail out and will not want to bail out. In fact – " (another chuckle) "if you are at all like past groups, I predict that the major problem we will have will be at the end of the week, when we have to shoo you out of here with brooms because you don't want to leave!"

❖ 22 ❖

"The future of the institute. Yes, I heard David say I'd talk about it. I'm happy to talk about anything you want to talk about."

C.T. was on his tenth cigarette by now, or nearly. I recognized the symptoms. On the one hand, his body was getting tired from performing in public, and on the other hand, as the questions engaged his interest, his level of mental energy rose. Probably he would have to spend much of the following day doing not much of anything, waiting for his tanks to refill.

He was holding his audience tightly in the web that he and we had been weaving for an hour and a half. "By all means, let's talk about the future," he said, "but let's not confine ourselves to the institute. That's a subject of deep interest to me, as you might imagine. When you put more than 20 years of your life into something, you end up caring deeply about it. But the future I really want to talk about is *your* future. I am an old man, and don't think I don't know it. Every day my body tells me so. When I was a boy, my grandmother used to remind me that what she called the Good Book said that the days of a man are threescore and ten, and last November I turned 76. You might say I am already in danger of overdrawing my account, at least a little."

He brushed away the slight sounds of protest. "Look, there isn't any need for us to pretend. It might be this year, or next year, or ten years from now. It doesn't make any difference. The length of future that I am going to see in this body is pretty well limited. It isn't a tragedy, it isn't a shame, it isn't something to fight against. It's just what is. And do you know what? It is just as it should be. Think of yourselves. Would *you* want to stay trapped in your body after it gets old and ill and you have nothing else you want to do? No! You'll want to trade it in on a new one, with better options and more horsepower and at least a new paint job." He had people smiling, now. "The worst thing that could ever happen to us would be immortal life in one body. Think how many kinds of a trap that would be. One body, one birthplace and one birth-time, one country, one family, one set of beliefs and talents – one window on the world. Period. It would be a terrible deprivation because, you see, we already *have* eternal life. I know this, first-hand. I have seen it, and I tell you, my friends, seeing it takes away your fear of death."

Fear of death. Am I afraid to die? I don't think so – but how can anybody know for sure?

"So, while we're here thinking together, let's not waste time pretending that I have a lot of time left in this body. Let's consider the future. And to do that, we need to consider where it is that we find ourselves.

"Everybody in this room is here on earth because you *wanted* to be here. Everybody anywhere on earth is here because they *wanted* to be here. You don't get here by accident. It isn't a matter of wandering through the wrong door somewhere. Life on earth is a highly valued experience, over *there*.

You can be sure that it isn't handed out lightly, and neither is it undertaken on a whim.

"Now, you might say, 'If that's so why do so many people have miserable lives?' They die of disease or accident or murder, and before that, they are abused in any number of ways. They chase down one dead-end after another, looking for happiness and just wearing themselves out. They find themselves at war, and in poverty, and in neurosis, and they find themselves prey to all the seven deadly sins, both on the committing end and the receiving end. By the way, can anybody here name the seven deadly sins? (I glanced at Francois. He smiled and made no move, nor did I.) No, I thought not. When I was a boy, we were required to learn the whole list of them. Today, people settle for committing them." He smiled through the laugh. "In case you're wondering, they are pride, anger, envy, sloth, gluttony, covetousness, and lust." (Out of the corner of my eye I saw Francois nod, barely.) "Between them, these are all the things that sometimes turn this beautiful earth we live on into hell-on-earth. If anybody can think of one of the ills that flesh is heir to that isn't caused by one or more items on that list, I'll give you a free program.

"But my point is, with all the painful things that happen to us in this life on earth, this is still the place in the universe where it's all happening. Your slot – the life you are leading right now, badly or well – is highly prized on the other side, and if you wanted to trade, there are millions of beings over there who would trade places with you in a heartbeat. You see, our lives aren't what they usually appear to us to be, because neither are *we*. And here we come to the big secret, the only thing I said in my book, I sometimes think, that I know for sure was critical.

"*The secret is in changing your point of view.* When you change that, everything around you changes. That's why we drew you here tonight, as we have drawn so many thousands before you – to help you change your point of view."

He picked up his mug, saw (again) that it was empty, and put it down again. He smiled at us. "One of the major reasons to take on earth life: coffee." He started to talk, then paused, distracted by something only he could see or hear or think.

"You know," he said thoughtfully, slowly, "it occurs to me that you may be thinking that I've forgotten about the question, but I haven't, at all. You asked about the future of the institute, and I said let's talk about the future in general, and for me by now it's a straight-line projection. The future? We have to talk about immortality. Immortality? We have to talk about the purpose of life on earth. The purpose? To understand that, you have to change your viewpoint. By now it's so natural that I forget, sometimes, that the links may not be immediately obvious."

He stubbed out his cigarette. "In the end, you see, it all boils down to definitions. Life only makes sense when you start from the right point of view. If you start from the wrong point of view, it *doesn't* make sense. Nothing simpler. For instance, every one of you sitting in front of me is an individual, yes? Are you certain of it? Of course you are. Everything in your life conspires to make you think so, and you can't imagine yourself *not* being an individual. And I'm not talking about social non-conformity, here. I mean something as basic as, do you feel like you are one person, different from others. And I'd be tremendously surprised if any of you were to say no. It is just one of those things that seem self-evident. But not everything that seems self-evident is true."

A pause for dramatic effect. "Or perhaps a better way of saying it would be, not everything that seems self-evident still looks that way when you look at it from a different point of view. My life has brought me to see everything from a different angle. You might almost say that this is why life has gone to so much trouble to bring us all together here – so that you, too, would begin to see things from a different angle."

Another thoughtful pause. I could see him slowing down now, pacing himself. *He's giving us a gift, talking to us. It's costing him. So he must be getting something out of doing it, as well.* "Let me put it to you as plainly as I can. Your life is a precious gift. You are here on this earth at this time because you knew that the world needs you, and because you know that we are in a once-in-the-life-of-a-species event, and you wanted to be on the playing field for that event, rather than sitting in the stands.

"You see, we are about to finally leave adolescence, and this difficult time we are undergoing is our rite of passage. We humans began the process as children, and we will come out the other end as adults. That, you must admit, is a pretty major change. As I said, a once-in-a-species change, and just as dramatic and difficult for the species as it is for individuals." A pause. "And the secret is this. There *are* no individuals. We start the process thinking of ourselves as limited individuals; we end it knowing that in a very real sense – not at all a metaphor – we are all one."

He looked out at us, looking from one to another, perhaps searching for the one who would understand him. "You know, I have told this to thousands of people over the years, and I don't suppose that one percent of them ever believed me. Not really. Some of them may have thought they did, but not to the extent of changing their way of seeing life. And if your viewpoint doesn't change, what changes?

"We are all individuals, yes, in a way. But in a larger sense, it is truer to say that we are part of one thing. Those of you who are able to achieve transcendent states may perhaps discover this for yourselves. It is a matter of viewpoint. Looked at one way, we are individuals, true enough. But looked at from beyond time and space – from the other side, we say here – we are all one thing. Literally.

"Now, I don't expect you to be able to visualize the reality of it, not without personal experience. So for the moment, take my word for it. But I want to encourage you to imagine this. At the far end of our graduation process – when we are young adults for the first time, you might say – we will be all living our lives here and now, in this physical world, and yet at the same time fully aware that a part of us extends beyond time and space, what the New Agers call 'the higher self' – which isn't a bad description of that part of us, really. That higher self will be a part of our everyday conscious reality."

I couldn't help think how easy it would be to selectively quote him in such a way as to make his talk seem ridiculous.

Again he searched us out. "Can you imagine what that will mean, on a day-to-day basis? To *know* we are immortal? To *know* we are all connected? To know that from a certain point of view it is literally true that we are each part of each other? I tell you, it is going to send a lot of people back to the scriptures, which they will read for the first time with opened eyes. Instead of imagining a lot of rules they think God wants them to follow, they will see descriptions of their new everyday reality."

He paused and nodded at Bobby, who had raised a hand. "C.T., can you tell us how long the process will last, and when it will start?"

C.T. smiled. "No to both questions, but I can say that I've long since given up hope of seeing it in this body." He gave a small shrug. "But on the other hand, who knows? Maybe it won't be a slow process at all. Maybe it will happen all at once. Maybe tonight."

❖ 23 ❖

"All right," David said, back in the debrief room. "You heard it from The Man himself: There's more going on here than just exploring for the fun of it." *Yes, a little more mystical than I would have expected.* "On the other hand – there's nothing wrong with exploring for the fun of it. Last tape of the day, another free-flow Entry State."

"You know the routine by now," Annette said. "Go to your rooms by way of the bathrooms, be sure to turn on your 'ready' lights, and in a few minutes we'll start the tape. Just like last night, we won't debrief the tape, so when it finishes you can either go on to sleep or you can come downstairs and snack and socialize."

David looked around. "All set? Anybody have any problems? Okay, let's do it. We'll see you either after the tape or tomorrow morning, depending on what you decide to do. Off you go, by way of the bathroom."

"Have a good trip," Annette said.

"And if necessary," David said, "you might even have fun."

❖ 24 ❖

It was strange. Not the process – this was the fifth time through the process, the fourth time today, and I would have had to be a slow learner indeed not to have gotten used to it. But – well, what happened? Even after the fact, I couldn't decide.

I had told Charlie that I'd give it the old college try even though I didn't believe in it. But now, after those two experiences that I seemed to be sharing with Claire, I couldn't exactly go into the tape expecting nothing to happen. Now I was half-prepared for something to happen; in fact, I was half-prepared to *expect* something to happen, and maybe something dramatic. It made for a problem. I didn't want to start fooling myself into thinking that something had happened when it hadn't. Yet it would be just as misleading – just as foolish, even – to tell myself that nothing had happened if something *did* happen. For the first time, I went into a tape experience with some anxiety.

I went through C.T.'s initial relaxation exercises as usual, but this time I was unable to really relax. *It was easier when I was just daydreaming.* C.T.'s voice ceased, and I was alone with the pink noise, but this time I found myself continually monitoring, in a sense looking in all directions, looking over my shoulder, ready and waiting to hear unexplained sounds, or see unexpected sights, or experience unfamiliar feelings. *This must be how Bobby feels all the time. And maybe those other people who called themselves searchers.* Things look different when you experience them first-hand!

For what seemed like quite a while, as far as I could tell, nothing was going on. *A little harder, being in a state of expectation, and trying to keep some kind of control over it.* This time, I couldn't just drift – at least, I didn't feel I could, which amounts to the same thing. Instead, I waited, but waited with full attention.

Afterwards, I told myself that what had happened was that I had been waiting in full attention, and this naturally had caused fatigue, and in effect I put myself into a mild hypnotic state and began suggesting things to myself. However, I have to admit, I wasn't really able to convince myself. And even if that's what happened, does it really explain anything?

As best I can recall the sequence, what happened is that I went through the initial routine and a good deal of the free-flow part of the tape in that state of heightened expectation, and nothing at all happened except that I got a little tired and, if truth be told, a little disappointed. And then, when I suppose I'd given up, though I didn't experience it as any kind of conscious decision, I drifted for a minute, and when I was back –

How to say this carefully? *And how in the world would I put this in my stories for Charlie?!*

Here's what I *didn't* experience.

I *didn't* envision myself floating in mid-air, and *didn't* find myself back at that little cabin. (I had half-expected to experience one or the other, or both, and had I experienced either one I was already prepared to doubt it.)

I *didn't* have an out-of-body experience such as C.T. reported, where you forget you're lying on the bed and you experience yourself elsewhere.

I *didn't* lie there and make up a narrative and envision myself in the middle of it. And as far as I can tell neither did my unconscious mind, or if it did I didn't bring back any memory of it.

So what *did* I experience? I'm glad you asked. I drifted, and when I came back (from where?) I realized that I was sort of seeing myself in two places at once. I knew full well where I was. I could feel the earphones and the sleep mask, and the bed underneath me. I knew I could move my hands and feet if I wanted to. And yet – it was as though another me, a more shadowy, less substantial me, was walking down the hallway outside, heading down to the debrief room.

I'm trying to say this carefully. It wasn't as if I was making it happen, yet I wasn't scared or even particularly startled. It wasn't as if I was experiencing it as real, exactly – the real me was on the bed, experiencing this

– but it wasn't exactly imagined either. It wasn't an OBE, or a daydream, or a fantasy, or normal life. It was beyond any category I had for it.

It wasn't particularly exciting, or meaningful. I was half-seeing, half-imagining a more shadowy version of myself walking down the familiar corridor. The only thing was – and I had no idea why – when I came "back," (so to speak) I was in a state of exhilaration. Just as earlier, I felt, *something is happening.* Why that should fill me with exultation I had no idea.

❖ 25 ❖

Wanting to hold on to the *feel* of the experience, whatever it was, I got up from bed before C.T. finished counting us back to a normal state of consciousness, and I was out the door before Bobby had even stirred. *Did I hit the ready light? Yes I did.* Of course, that ready light switch would tell the trainers that I hadn't come back in the normal manner, but so what. I was the first one downstairs. I filled a mug with hot coffee from one of the thermoses and made the mistake of going out on the side porch, intending to spend a few minutes alone.

It was too cold for me to be out there, really, and even the coffee wasn't going to help. I knew it before the door closed behind me. I don't think I took three breaths before I felt that sharp cold fog behind the breastbone. *Dammit.* I went back inside, put down the coffee mug and pulled the inhaler out of my pocket. *Necessary? Or will this go away by itself?* I had been told many times not to overdo it with the inhaler. The question was, would my breathing clear up in a reasonable time without it. If so, it would be better to put up with a few minutes' discomfort than to use the inhaler. "Use it when you need it, Angelo," my doctor told me as he wrote out the prescription, "but *only* when you need it. These things have side-effects." So, I was standing there with inhaler in hand, trying to breathe smoothly, when people started coming downstairs.

"What's going on, Angelo?" Ellis asked. I grimaced and held up the inhaler. It isn't that I was incapable of speaking, but I didn't want to disrupt the rhythm I was trying to re-establish.

He nodded. "Asthma?" I nodded back. "That going to take care of it?" I nodded again. *It will if I have to use it!*

Well, this certainly wasn't what I intended! There I was, the center of attention for the half dozen people who had come downstairs (and more coming every minute). I lasted only a minute or two, then I gave up. *I hate this! Public exhibition!* I pulled the cap off the inhaler and held it up to my mouth. I exhaled fully, put the end of the tube in my mouth, and as I pressed the tube, I inhaled as deeply as I could, and held the breath. Immediately I could feel things loosen, but I held my breath as long as I could. I put it back into my pocket. I was burning mad, and a little humiliated, and very damned tired of it. But I tried not to let my face show any of it. I breathed out. "That's better," I said, just as if it were no big deal.

David came out from the control room where they play the tapes. "Got some excitement here?"

"Just watching Angelo breathe," Andrew said.

"That's one way to pass the time, I suppose."

"There wasn't a lot going on here, with the snacks not out, and all."

I was grateful, in a way, that Andrew was running interference, even while I hated the necessity for it.

David looked carefully at me. "Okay?" The trainers would know I had asthma, of course, from the registration questionnaire.

"Yeah," I said. "Just, an ounce of inhaler is worth a pound of wheezing. Colder outside than you might think."

"I saw you turned off your ready light ahead of time. Were you having problems then?"

"Breathing, you mean? No, I was fine. Just had something I wanted to think about and I was ready to get up."

"Okay," David said, back in scout-leader mode, "the important business of the evening: Snacks. Somebody give me a hand and we'll go see what's in the kitchen."

Claire came up to me. "That's hard on you, isn't it?"

"Asthma, you mean? It wasn't anything much, this time."

"I mean what comes with it. We can talk about it sometime, if you want to. I *am* a medical professional, you know."

"But I'm not having a problem, now."

"The problem I'm talking about isn't your breathing, Angelo, it's just caused by your breathing."

Our eyes met and for the first time I became fully aware of the depth of intelligence and perception behind those lovely brown eyes.

❖ 26 ❖

There must have been a dozen of us more or less crammed in a wildly irregular ring around a table designed for half as many chairs. We all had paper plates and munchies in front of us, and some had drinks.

"We ought to do this after every tape," Andrew said to David, "instead of debriefings."

I shrugged. "This is one time I could have *used* a good debrief."

"Why," Jeff asked. "What happened?"

I looked at David, munching potato chips and sipping lemonade. "David, any reason why I shouldn't talk about something here instead of in debrief tomorrow morning?"

"None that I know of. We're pretty laid back here, if you haven't noticed. Not a lot of rules, once we manage to get your wristwatches away from you. It's just a question of what you're inclined to do. Do you mean, if you talk about it here and now, are you liable to lose the experience?"

"Well, I wasn't thinking about that, exactly, but yeah. Would I?"

He made a sideways motion with his head, somewhere between a shrug and throwing up his hands. "There's no way to know. Everybody's different, so everybody's *experience* is different. People are different from one day to the next, for that matter. By tomorrow night, you won't be reacting the way you do tonight, and I'm pretty willing to bet that you're not reacting tonight the way you would have last night."

"You've got *that* right," I said. "So?"

"So, dealer's choice. It's up to you. What do you *feel* is the right thing for you to be doing?"

I don't know, what do you think? Seems to be their theme song. "Talking about it, I guess. *Something* happened, last tape. Just what, I don't exactly know. And what it means, I don't have a clue."

Jeff: "And this is different from the rest of your life, how?"

I laughed. "It isn't, but I live in hope."

"You going to tell us?"

"Depends on whether I get any of those potato chips."

He pushed the bowl toward me. "I'd like to see that bowl again," he said.

"Soon as I empty it," I said.

Bobby said, "So?"

"Well I was in the free-flow portion of the tape, and I drifted off, and when I came back from wherever I went, I realized that I was sort of out of my body."

"Hey, wow! I wish *I* could say that!"

"No, but Bobby, it isn't that simple. It was like I was seeing myself in two places at once. I was on the bed doing the tape, I knew that much. But at the same time, there was another me walking down the hall going toward the debrief room."

I saw Lou Hardin shrug, and asked him: "What, Lou?" He said, "That isn't how C.T. describes his out-of-body's. Yours sounds more like imagination, to me."

"Wait a minute!" Bobby said in some excitement. "Are you going to just say somebody else's experience didn't happen?"

"I'm not calling him a liar, if that's what you mean, but I think it's fair to say maybe it didn't mean what he thinks it means."

"I didn't *say* what I think it means, for the very good reason that I don't have the slightest idea what it means. I'm just reporting what I experienced."

"What you *think* you experienced."

This threatens him, somehow. "That's all any of have to work with, what we *think* we're experiencing. Even C.T."

"He's got you, Lou," David said. "Nobody really knows what goes on in his own life, as far as I can tell. We just make the best guesses we can as we go along."

"Well, isn't that what I just said?"

Yeah, but David didn't say it in the obnoxious way you did! "Anyway, that's all I know. It wasn't a dream, it wasn't a daydream, and it sure as hell wasn't normal consciousness. It doesn't sound to me like an OBE either, but how would I know? I don't know *what* it was." *Sure left me "up" though! Until the asthma kicked in, anyway.*

"So how do you know it wasn't a daydream, Angelo?"

I sat looking at Edith, maybe frowning a little, as I thought about it. She said, "I don't mean to imply that it was . . ."

"No, I know," I said. "I'm just trying to figure out how to talk about it." *Just talk about it and see what happens, maybe something will come to you.* "I guess I'd have to say that the thing that was the most different was the *way* in which I was experiencing that walk. I don't know exactly how to explain it, but it was different from the way we usually experience things. I mean, it felt different."

"I don't get it," Bobby said.

"I'd be amazed if you could, from just that. But I don't know – Well, the best I can do is to say that in normal life, we experience the world through the senses, right? And it's all definite, very differentiated. Even if we sense smells and sounds at the same time, say, we don't experience them as *blend-*

ed. We pull data from various senses, but they don't all mix up together into one thing, and that's sort of how I was experiencing this."

"I still don't get it."

"Well, I know, but I don't know how else to put it."

"I'm beginning to think you might be a pretty good reporter, Angelo," David said. "You experienced something, and you don't have the slightest idea what it means but you give a very clear description of what it felt like. Very good."

We turned to him. Andrew said, "I take it that you do know, then?"

"It has a familiar ring to it, yes. And if you think I'm going to tell you what it means, you haven't heard how many Merriman trainers it takes to change a light bulb."

"I have, actually," Andrew said. "The answer is, 'I don't know, what do you think?' But how about giving us a clue?"

"I'll give you one clue, and that's all you're going to get out of me. Angelo said we don't experience our senses all blended in with one another, but that isn't quite true. We do when we remember something, or when we imagine it."

"That's what I said," Lou Hardin said complacently. "Imagination."

"I said I'm only going to give one clue, but I'll give you another one. Lou, you're about half right, but no more." And that's all we could get out of him on the subject.

CHAPTER THREE

Monday
March 20, 1995

It never took much. I was enjoying being up drinking hot coffee in the early Spring morning, quite a bit nicer than it would be in South Jersey or Philly, but again it was a little too cold for my lungs. *Don't overuse it, Angelo. It has side-effects.* The wheeze was on the left side this time, a little above the heart. I kept trying to make it smooth out, breathing as slowly and carefully as I could. I can never help thinking, if I breathe slowly enough, I can slide past the place that causes the wheeze. And if I can stop the wheeze, I can stop it from moving on into a full-fledged attack. Or if I can cough just right I can get rid of the obstruction (for that is what it feels like sometimes). Not that any of it works, but it gives me the illusion of having some control over my life. Something other than carrying around The Answer That Also Has Side-Effects.

I did try, but finally I had to give up. Alone on the porch, no one around to see, I put my mug down on the wooden ledge and pulled out the inhaler. I used it and was putting it back into my pocket when the door opened and Claire came out.

We exchanged good mornings.

"I thought you'd be Jeff. In fact, I thought he'd be here before me, he likes getting up early."

"Apparently you do too."

I shook my head. "I don't, actually. Usually I get off to a slow start. But I don't seem to need much sleep here. I don't know what that sleep processor is doing to me, but I intend to sue." *I do like her smile.*

"Other than the sleep processor, though. Are you able to sleep all right?"

Reluctantly: "You mean because of asthma?" She nodded. "It hasn't been a problem."

She touched my arm, lightly. "There's no reason to talk about it unless you want to, but if you do, we can talk any time."

I wasn't under the illusion that she meant that we could talk prescriptions or symptoms. "Thanks," I said.

I had no intention of taking her up on it. She knew it, too. "So," she said, "you said you're married. Is your wife into this kind of thing too? Did she read *Extraordinary Potential?*"

I laughed. "God no! She doesn't read much anyway, but that's about the *last* thing she'd read!"

"Not into this stuff, then."

"Hardly." *Until now, it was one of the few things we still had in common.* "The little bit that has happened to me already would be enough to scare her silly."

"That's something I've noticed over the years, how many couples consist of one who is deeply interested and one who can't stand the idea of it. There must be some dynamic that causes that to happen so often, but I've never been able to figure out what it is."

Keep your big mouth shut, Angelo! But I said it anyway. "Well, actually, if you'll keep this between us two, it isn't really that way in my case. I haven't ever believed in any of this stuff either."

She was amused. "What are you doing here, then?"

"I – " (sorting out my feelings, teetering between impulse and long-ingrained habit) " – uh, I – "

She touched my arm. "None of my business, I know. That's all right."

I relaxed, off the hook. "I'm supposed to look around, see if any of this is for real." I had blurted it out, shocking myself. "I'm here as a reporter; it's for a story. I'm, like, undercover without the melodramatic overtones. I'm not really a believer in this kind of thing."

She was looking at me closely, reading – I realize now – the emotional context around my words.

"I'd appreciate it if you didn't talk about it to anybody. Really I shouldn't have said anything."

"I can see that it would make things difficult if everybody was on guard around you, thinking you were going to record their every word. I won't say anything." I nodded my thanks. "But just out of curiosity, why did you tell *me*?"

"Claire, I don't have the slightest idea. I didn't intend to."

She seemed pleased about something. "I thought maybe you didn't. Well, thank you. I won't tell anybody."

After a minute or so – not uncomfortable, though it should have been – I said, "The funny thing is, I'm starting to get the idea that there's more in this than I had thought. And if so, it's going to play hell with things at home. You aren't a Lutheran, I suppose?"

"Me? No, I'm – well, I was raised Methodist, but it has been a long time since I've been a church-goer."

"Yeah, me too. Well, have you ever heard of the Missouri Synod? It's the most conservative kind of Lutheran there is, and that's my wife. If she were here listening to people, she wouldn't have any doubt at all that this is the work of the devil."

"And now maybe you're moving into the enemy camp."

"Yeah. Well, I'm already in the enemy camp; I'd just be changing enemies. Instead of a common-sense skeptic, I'd be a New Age true believer, just as bad but coming at her from the opposite direction." I barked out a kind of laugh. "It'd be a shock, sure thing."

Then Jeff came out with his coffee, and a couple more people followed him, and we all talked about other things. In a little while, I was annoyed with myself for telling her so much. None of it was anybody's business.

❖ 2 ❖

I could hear it in the conversation at breakfast. Sunday morning had been nervous small talk. By noon it had gotten to be an excited buzz, and more so by supper. *Today, it's different again. Quieter, more intense.*

Emil Hoffman, the Swiss banker, put down his fork to make a statement, in the way that I occasionally had seen Europeans do. *They do it quite un-self-consciously. I suppose it's a cultural thing.* "I do not for certain know that I correctly understand what Mr. Merriman meant by that. I read his book in German, and perhaps it is a fault of the translation. But in the book I understood him to say that the purpose of his work is to provide methods to alter our minds, to – " He paused, not finding the words he wanted. Marta from Peru, sitting next to him, said, "To provide altered states of consciousness."

"Yes, but – " Again a sort of helpless floundering. His English was pretty good, but the kind of things he wanted to talk about required words that weren't prominently featured in ESL courses. He tried again. "What we attempt to do here is to improve control, yes? We wish to tell the mind what to do, where to go, instead of *it* always telling *us*. Yes? This I think is very practical. Useful, I think you say. But last night, Mr. Merriman does not speak of this at all. Instead he speaked – spoke – of things that seemed to me mystical. Perhaps I do not understand correctly?"

Sitting at the table along with Emil and Marta and me were Tony, Claire, and Annette. At Emil's question, naturally we all turned to the authority at the table.

"Don't look at me," Annette said. "You all heard everything I did. What do *you* think it meant?" *How many Merriman trainers does it take to change a light bulb?*

"But you've known C.T. so long, and you work with him," Tony said.

"I didn't hear anything I haven't heard before."

Claire spoke up – quietly, as always, but decisively. "What he said last night was what he said in his book, just carried a little farther. If you remember, in *Extraordinary Potential*, he said that his experiences, and the experiences of others that he had observed, told him that we are much more than we suspect we are."

Emil tried to brush that aside. "He referred to our present inability to control our minds, I think, not to an ability to become something different."

"No, I don't think so," Claire said. "That's a *part* of it, but if all he had to offer was more self-control, or more disciplined awareness – you can get that anywhere."

"Not precisely anywhere," Tony said with a grin.

"No, but you know what I mean. Certainly *I* didn't come here just to learn to exert will-power, and I don't think many other people did either."

"However, to gain the ability to exert discipline over the mind is of great value," Emil insisted.

"I agree with you, and I don't mean to deny it. Discipline over our mind and emotions *is* taught here, clearly. You can't do much in life if you let your thoughts and emotions blow you all over the landscape. But does that mean that's *all* there is?"

Emil was puzzled. "The world is what it is. We are what we are. It is true, we have hidden depths, this I believe. But this is not to say that we live in an unknown world, or that we are in our essentials different from what we know ourselves – from how we experience ourselves. Nor do I think that C.T. intended to report otherwise."

Claire glanced at Annette, but Annette, the faintest of smiles in her eyes, shook her head the tiniest bit, declining to be drawn in. So Claire kept on. "But you see, I think that is *just* what he *was* doing. He was laying down hints, telling us, 'If you go looking in this direction, maybe you'll find something interesting.' He's being careful not to program us, it seems to me, but he doesn't mind throwing out some ideas for anybody who is ready to pursue them."

"But it may be that he is only – how do you say it? – he played with ideas."

"Didn't sound like it to me," Tony said. "I agree with Claire, he was laying down some heavy hints."

Determined, perplexed, insistent: "But what can there be to *find*? What sense makes it – does it make – to look where there can be nothing?"

"Maybe that's the point, Emil. Maybe his experience told him there *is* something, and everything he's done since has been designed to point the way."

Emil of course was not convinced, but subsided, as we do when we see no way forward.

"Pass the salt and pepper, Angelo? Thanks." Tony looked around the table. "So Emil is here to learn greater control over his mind. What's everybody else here for?"

"I'm here to train an Open Door," Annette said, smiling at him. "And to meet some more curious, valuable, fascinating people, as always."

Tony looked at Marta. "I am here to explore," she said. "I do not know what is possible and what is hearsay, so I look."

"Angelo?"

Well, originally I was here to research a hatchet- job, but now I'm not so sure. "Like Marta, I guess. I'm trying to see what's what." Claire didn't let on. "What about you?"

Tony shrugged. "It sounds grandiose, I suppose. But as I read C.T.'s book, I thought, 'He's found a path.' I always thought that wherever it is that we're going, and whatever it is we're supposed to become, there *must* be a path to it. I think he has found it, and if *he* found it, others should be able to find it, and if others can, maybe I can. Claire?"

"Well, Tony, I suppose really I am here only because I had to have done Open Door before I could do Bridging Over next week."

"You have a particular interest in connecting with dead people?"

"The idea interests me, yes." And right there, at some deep level I *knew* something. I couldn't pin the knowing to a rational cause, though, so I automatically, unconsciously, refashioned it. The small part I held onto could be put this way: *Interests you, like hell. Whatever your reason is for doing Bridging Over, it's more than curiosity.*

❖ **3** ❖

"Okay, gang, new horizons. Today we move from Entry State to Wider Visions." David looked around the room. "But before we introduce today's first tape, let's talk about last night's tape. Anybody have anything they want to share?" A pause. "Let me rephrase that. Is anybody awake? No? Angelo, how about you? You want to say something about what you told us last night? You don't have to, of course."

"Well, I don't know," I said. "I don't mind talking about it, but it isn't any big deal, and as I said last night, I don't know what it means. In the middle of the tape I suddenly realized that I was experiencing two different kinds of thing at the same time. I was aware that I was lying on the bed with the earphones on, and at the same time it seemed like there was a sort of shadowy second 'me' that was walking down the hallway. After a little bit something changed and I was just lying there listening to the tape. I'm sure I didn't *consciously,* deliberately make it up, and I'm pretty sure I hadn't been asleep, but that's all I know about it. Maybe I'm making it up at some subconscious level."

"You were out of body," someone said.

"I don't think so," I said. "But I don't know."

David said, "I told Angelo last night, he's a good reporter. The way he reported that experience is a good model of how to approach all this. When we have a new experience, we *don't* necessarily know what it means. We don't have familiar categories to put it into. So it's better, more useful, to keep in mind that we *don't* know than to rush to assume that whatever happened must be this or must be that. Accumulate some experience before you draw too many conclusions. Take your time. There's plenty of time available. Okay. Anybody else? Bobby."

"I keep wondering what combination of frequencies you're using, and I'll tell you why. Any combination you use – say it's a lot of alpha and only a little delta, just for a theoretical example – couldn't it be that some people will be able to respond to that combination because it fits their bran-wave patterns and others won't because it won't be right for their brain-wave patterns? So, doesn't that put us in a one-size-fits-all situation here? What happens to the people it doesn't fit?"

David paused, considering the question. "Well first off, you're right that the mixture of frequencies in these tapes is designed to hit the hump in the bell curve, and so it's not likely to *exactly* hit anybody, and I suppose it may miss one or two people entirely. But if I see where you're going with this, I don't agree that you or anybody else who is having trouble seeing results is wasting their time because of some mismatch between their brain and the frequencies on the tape. For one thing, that's a very rare situation that I have yet to encounter, as far as I know."

"Then how do you explain the fact that I'm not getting *anything* from these tapes? I'm willing to. I'm *eager* to. And I came here *expecting* to. I don't see how my attitude could possibly be any more positive, but here it is Monday and I'm not sure I've even experienced Entry State!"

I thought, *This is not the time for I Don't Know, What Do You Think!* But I needn't have worried, that wasn't where David was going.

"Bobby, we told you up front, everybody gets this at their own rate. And besides, you don't know that you're getting it or you aren't getting it, no matter what it feels like. As long as something is moving at an unconscious level, by definition you won't know it until it becomes conscious."

"So there's nothing I can do?"

Annette said, "Maybe there's nothing you *need to* do, Bobby. Just live in trust, continue to be open to new things, and let the universe unfold at its own pace."

"I've wondered sometimes," Andrew threw in, "how the universe came to be folded in the first place."

"Yeah, it's funny if you're having experiences," Bobby said sourly. There was a moment of uncomfortable silence. "I know how Bobby feels," Katie said quietly. *Oh yes, she's expecting to contact her deceased husband. No need to ask how* that's *going.*

Annette was all sympathy and understanding, and yet firm. "Bobby, Katie, it's always hard when you see others going ahead into the promised land and you feel like you're being left behind. But remember – believe it if you can – nobody here knows or has any way to know who's 'ahead.' Nobody can tell who is the hare and who is the tortoise, and it *doesn't matter.* I know it's hard to hear, but you'll save yourselves lots of useless anguish if you can continue to live in trust that all is well. In our experience – and we've had *a lot* of it – all is well because it's always well." Her warm smile. "Trust. It will be okay. And Bobby, I know this will be hard for you to believe, but knowing the frequencies really wouldn't help. If anything, it would hold you back, because it would set your analytical faculty working overtime. Analysis is not where the treasure is buried."

"Well, okay, I'm taking your word for it. But I sure hope I get to the treasure before it disintegrates."

"You literally never know. It might be next week. It might be this tape."

"And speaking of this tape," David said, "let's talk about the purpose of this first tape, introduction to Wider Vision."

"Yesterday you were introduced to Entry State," Annette said, smoothly picking up from him. "We think of Entry State as a stable, non-threatening altered state that allows you to establish a place to stand. We don't put a lot of definitions on it beyond that. You'll notice that we didn't tell you, 'Now you're going to have this kind of experience.' Instead, we said, 'Go play; go immerse yourself in this mental state so that you know what it feels like and you can return to it whenever you wish.' That isn't quite the way we use Wider Vision, however."

"Wider Vision is a highly focused state," David said. "Where Entry State is floating on clouds, Wider Vision is doing spot-welding with lasers.

Where you could live with Entry State as your default position, you could never do that with Wider Vision, and you wouldn't want to."

"It would be like doing the multiplication tables at high speed, all day long," Annette said.

"So, today we're going to be doing two things at once. We're going to help you implant some familiarity with Wider Vision so that you can return to it at will, just as we did with Entry State, and we're going to show you how to *use* it, in very practical ways. So, this first tape is called Introduction to Wider Vision."

❖ 4 ❖

It was like starting over. After my good luck with the previous couple of tapes I was hoping to experience something worthwhile. In fact, I was half expecting to, so much had my attitude been changing behind my back. Instead, nothing. I followed C.T. as he had us do this and that to encode the Wider Vision state, but when he gave us time to experience the state, nothing special happened. Then, as he had done in the Intro to Entry State tape, he brought us back to normal consciousness – or, in this case, Entry State – and then back up to Wider Vision. He did it three times in all, presumably encoding the state for us, but in none of the intervals he left did I experience anything except drift and, for the first time, impatience. I had begun to get the idea that there was something real here, and now I wanted it. But on this first Monday tape, I didn't get it. What I did get was a fragmentary image or two, nothing that added up to anything. Disappointing.

❖ 5 ❖

The debrief session was miles beyond Sunday morning's. David, smiling as ever, pointed out to us again how much more centered we were. "Yes Ellis?"

This was the first time I could remember John Ellis Sinclair saying anything in a debrief session.

"I found that tape remarkable," he said in his slow, self-assured way. He laughed quietly, mostly to himself. "I thought, 'I'll be damned if I know what's going on here, but I hope it continues.'" He looked around the circle. "After yesterday, I was beginning to think that maybe nothing much was going to happen all week. I thought, maybe I've left it too late in life. Maybe I'm too old."

It struck me that perhaps Sinclair's engineer's mind found it easier to deal with Wider Vision than it had with Entry State. Perhaps Entry State was too reflective, too receptive, for him to easily adjust to, and Wider Vision was closer to mental states he had used all his professional life.

"I can't get over the clarity of it," he was saying. "I thought I was fully prepared for anything that might happen, but I see now that I wasn't, and I'm still not."

"So what did you see?" That was our enthusiastic Bobby. But Annette said, "Wait, Bobby. We're all interested in anything anybody wants to say, but we have to be careful to give each other space." Glancing around, she added, "This isn't just for Bobby, of course. It's important that nobody feel pressured to share their experiences, particularly early on, when the experiences are likely to be tentative, and poorly understood, and often quite private."

"Yes, I see that," Bobby said, nodding. "Sorry."

"Again, it's not just you. It happens all the time. People get carried away wanting to hear other people's experiences."

"And when they get carried away, it's our job to carry them back again," David said. "It's on the list of rules for trainers, along with wristwatches and going to the bathroom."

"So," Annette said, "Ellis, if you'd like to tell us, we're certainly interested, but if you would rather sit with it, that's fine too. It's entirely up to you."

"Oh, I don't mind sharing, as long as everyone understands that I don't necessarily believe that what I saw was true; it's just what I saw. In the middle of the tape, after C.T. left us to experience things, suddenly it was as though I was watching a movie. I saw a man hanged, just like in a western. He was a horse thief, maybe, I don't know, but I had a definite sense that it was in the west somewhere, maybe a hundred years ago, maybe more. I don't mean to imply that this was a full-scale color movie, because it wasn't. I didn't see it in any detail – but I *sort of* saw it. I don't know how else to put it. Maybe it's a bit like what Angelo said last night. I knew that if it was being made up, I wasn't the one making it up. And I knew I wasn't asleep. So what was it?"

"A fantasy, maybe." There went Lou Hardin again. *What's with that guy?*

"For all I know, yes, a fantasy. But I haven't yet mentioned the most curious thing. I experienced this as if I were the man being hanged." He paused, perhaps a bit embarrassed. "And the thing is, for most of my adult life, I've had this problem with my neck. I have two vertebrae out of line, as if they'd been yanked out of place somehow. But they haven't. At least – not in *this* lifetime." He looked around at the rest of us, part of the arc of back-jack chairs he was sitting in. "And if you find this hard to believe, I certainly sympathize. If somebody else were saying it, I don't know if I'd believe it either."

David smiled at him. "You're about as believable as anybody else here, I guess."

"Do you have any idea what that was all about?"

"Not me, I'm a trainer. But between you, me, and the lamppost, I will say that I think that you're on tomorrow's page, perhaps. That happens sometimes. Yes, Regina?"

Andrew said, "Is that all you're going to say about it? Just a teaser and then leave us hanging?"

"That's about it. Go ahead, Regina."

"I do not know if my experience is what should be expected of a Wider Vision exercise, and neither do I know if it is truly a result of the tape or if it is something I imagined." She paused for reassurance, which David provided: "That's a common concern, Regina. We always say, pursue it and with time its meaning will become clear."

"Yes. I have heard this." A pause. "Well. I was standing on a small cliff – a bluff I think you call it – and I was looking out at the ocean far away. It was a beautiful day, everything blue and sunny. It was very – calm, I would say. After, when I told this again to myself to remember, I thought, 'Yes it was so pleasant and calm.' But then I noticed that the ground beneath my feet was going away. It was being sucked down and out, into the ocean, as though by some power vacuum machine. You know – "

"Vacuum cleaner," Bobby said.

"Yes, vacuum cleaner, thank you. And as the ground was being pulled out from under my feet, the bluff was getting lower and lower, until I was down at the level of the ocean." She bit her lip and gazed at the floor as if reluctant to continue. Edith, very softly, said, "And – ?"

"And I looked out at the ocean and I saw the water flowing out along with the land, and it flowed – out and down. I do not remember how you say it in English, the tide going away."

"Ebbed," Andrew said.

"Yes, thank you. Ebbed. The tide ebbed, until I could see almost nothing of the water that had been there, and as it ebbed, it took everything I had been standing on, and I was then standing on the water's edge. Shingle, I think you say?"

"The English do," Ellis said. "We'd say you were standing on the beach, or on the sand."

"Yes? Well – I stood there it seemed a long time and I knew somehow that this moment of *waiting* was the point of my entire life. What that means I do not understand, but I know that this was the point. I am down at the level of the ocean and it is the moment before the waves rush back in as a tidal wave." She smiled, a bit helplessly. "This is what I saw, but does it mean anything?"

"I-don't-know,-what-do-you-think?" Andrew shot out, but David shushed him with a sideways motion of his hand. "It's usually safer to assume that these experiences do mean *something*, Regina," he said, "but the question always is, *what* do they mean? And nobody else can tell you that."

"You might ask yourself," Annette said, "'if this were a dream, how would I interpret it?' If you'd like, I will be glad to walk you through the process the next time we have time."

"Thank you. But, so you do think it is something to put attention to?"

"To pay attention to? Absolutely. It's always safer to assume that something has a meaning than that it doesn't. At least, that's how I work."

Emil hadn't yet said a word in any of the debrief sessions, but something Regina had said had caught his attention. I noticed him looking at her with great intensity, and I wasn't surprised to see him approach her as we got up for our short break before beginning our next briefing.

❖ **6** ❖

The break would be just time enough for a cup of coffee, or a smoke on the side deck for those so inclined, or just a few minutes of quiet time looking out at the low green hills. I filled my mug and followed Sinclair onto the deck. We were the only participants there, at least for the moment.

"So you're not quite too old after all," I said.

He seemed quite pleased. "Possibly I'm not. I was very surprised."

I told him my hunch about engineers and Wider Vision and he was interested. "However, it has been 25 years or more since I was a practicing engineer. Once I got stuck in management jobs, that was the end of play-ing."

"I didn't know you were in management. You had yourself introduced as an engineer."

"Well, that's true enough, and I still like to think of myself that way."

"Didn't you like being in management?"

"Like it?" He took a long thoughtful sip from his mug. "Like it. Well, like most things in life, I suppose, it had its pros and cons. Certainly it was very good for my career. I went much higher than I ever would have as an engineer. But I missed engineering."

"Because – ?"

He paused, thinking how to say it, I guess. "When I was an engineer, if I got stuck on a problem, I could lay it all out and go away and think about it, and when I got back the pieces would still be where I had left them. But once I got involved with managing people, it wasn't like that at all. If I set out the pieces and went away to think about them, by the time I got back all the pieces would have rearranged themselves." He smiled. "Not at all like engineering."

I asked where he had worked, and he named a household word. Call it Metals, Inc., one of the older giants, now international, that had earned a place in America's industrial history.

I made a polite response, and I guess he could see me wondering, and maybe he wanted me to know. I can think of several overlapping reasons why he might have wanted me to. A quiet pride in a solid career, perhaps. A way of modestly blowing his own horn. A simple willingness to satisfy my curiosity. "I have been retired for seven years now," he said quietly, "but by the time I retired, I had spent five years as CEO."

CEO, and here to do an Open Door! Him and Tony Giordano. Priests, psychotherapists, CEO's – I'm going to have to work on retyping my stereo-types.

❖ 7 ❖

"Everybody back? Okay, second tape. Remember we said earlier that we have different uses for Wider Vision than for Entry State? Here comes your first example of Wider Vision as a specialized tool. Annette?"

"Yesterday, after we did the Introduction to Entry State tape, you did free-flows, so that you could experience the state thoroughly and also –

what we didn't tell you – so that if you had any unsuspected internal agendas, they might bubble up into the open.

"Today's a little different. You just had the Intro to Wider Vision tape, but now, instead of moving into a free-flow pattern, we're going to ask you to perform specific, pointed, tasks. That's what Wider Vision is *for* – concentrated, focused attention aimed at pattern recognition and problem-solving. So, this time, once you're firmly into the state, C.T. is going to come back in and tell you when it's time for you to ask three questions of the universe, one at a time. Remember the question, pose the question, listen for the answer, each time."

"Are you going to tell us the questions?"

David shook his head decisively. "No. We're going to give you a couple of minutes to think of your own questions."

"What if we don't *have* any questions?"

"Just ask for help in formulating them, and they'll come. Maybe you'll get a surprise."

"But if they don't?"

"Bobby, just try. If you don't get anything, we'll worry about it then. All right? Everybody have pencil and paper, or pen and journal or whatever? Okay. What three questions would you like answered that you couldn't answer on your own?"

We sat there together hoping to come up with questions. To my surprise, I formulated the first one without any trouble at all. "What is the most important thing for me to be doing here?" *Pretty clearly, this is more than just a news assignment.* A second question formed naturally: "Who are the most important people I should be dealing with?" I thought of Claire, and a third suggested itself immediately thereafter, although I figured this probably wasn't the kind of question I ought to be asking. *I mean, shouldn't I be asking things like "is there a God" or "what's the formula for world peace?"* "Why do I feel so connected to Claire?"

"All right? Everybody finished? Okay, one more minute. Got your questions, Bobby? See, was that so hard? Okay? Good. Now, I know that some of you are thinking, 'I'll ask, but I'll probably get a busy signal!' To this I say, don't worry about it. Guidance on these questions is available, and it is trustworthy; it is only a matter of learning how to ask."

"As David says, the guidance is available. But you can't hear it as long as you're certain it isn't there! And you can't hear it if you aren't listening.

And even if you do hear it, you can't benefit from it if your automatic reaction is to say it can't be true, you must be making it up."

"That's a very natural reaction, and I'd guess that Annette and I have heard people express it, in one form or another, not more than six million times. But just because it's natural doesn't mean its helpful. In fact, it's an obstacle. So try to put it aside."

"That's right. When you do the tape, just *do* the tape, and put aside your reservations until later. You can always go back and second-guess it, but if you miss the experience for fear of getting fooled, what good is that?"

"Just do the tape and stay right with it. Ask the questions – and pay attention to the answers!"

"Which means more than just 'stay awake.' It means, use your wits. Answers don't always come in complete sentences, or even as words. Sometimes they come as images, or as puns, or as knowings. There's no way to predict the form they will come in, so keep your eyes open – and your ears too, and your other senses. There's no telling what will come, or how."

"One last thing, and we'll go," David said. "In my experience, three qualities will improve your chances of getting meaningful and helpful answers. Remember these three words: clarity, intensity, gratitude. Posing your questions with great *clarity* heightens your chances of understanding the nuances of whatever reply you receive. If you aren't sure what you asked, how can you be sure what you were answered? So, clarity. Intensity. Focus your energy on this question while you ask it. If *you* don't care about it, why should the universe? I know that sounds funny, but I don't mean it as a joke. Ask with great intensity. And don't forget gratitude for the fact that you're going to receive an answer. We're not just talking manners here, there's another reason. If you think about it, you don't feel gratitude for what you haven't received. So if you do feel gratitude, it is because you received something. So – feel the gratitude in advance and you enhance your chances of persuading yourself that you're not going to come up dry." He grinned. "Screwy reasoning, huh? But just try it, you might be surprised. Okay? Clarity, intensity, gratitude. Off you go."

"By way of the bathrooms," Annette said.

❖ 8 ❖

"Asking questions of the universe." Expanded awareness, again: the drawing of information from sources not always accessible in normal states of consciousness. *This is starting to sound a lot less screwy. Am I losing it, or – am I maybe getting with the program?*

We go through the intro procedure. *If I was in Wider Vision before, that's where I am again, I guess. At least, it feels the same. Okay, C.T., your show.*

As if on cue, C.T.'s voice: "Now, holding yourself firmly in the state of Wider Vision, a state of expanded awareness, ask the first of your three questions. Ask it firmly, with full expectation that you will receive an answer, the proper answer for *you*. Ask the universe your first question. Ask it now."

What's the most important thing for me to be doing here? Just as the question had come, the answer came. I heard, "In terms of making the experiences happen, just relax and allow it, you've got all Monday and all Tuesday and all Wednesday and all Thursday and then you have Friday and you have the rest of your life, and there's a LOT of time and a lot of experience ahead and plenty of time for it."

Now, in saying that I "heard" this answer, I don't of course mean I heard it with my physical ears. Neither did I "hear" it like a voice inside my head. *I haven't gone completely around the bend yet! If I start hearing voices, maybe.* So in what sense did I "hear" the message? Like so many things in this field of exploration it is much harder to explain than to experience. Perhaps the closest I can come to it is to say that it was like – but note the word "like"! – my knowing something, and putting it into words, and saying the words to myself. That isn't exactly what happened, but that's as close as I have been able to come to explaining.

After we asked our questions and (presumably!) got our answers, an indeterminate amount of time went by, and there was C.T.'s voice again, telling us to ask the second question. I had to stop and think, and then I remembered. *Who are the most important people I should be dealing with?* I heard, "Don't try to force yourself to go to any one or every one. Don't think you need to relate to any particular one. But, if something comes up, deal with things one at a time, one on one. Deal with people honestly and openly and lovingly." The answer did have a flavor of coming from someone other than me. *"Lovingly"? Not a word I'd choose.*

C.T.'s voice returned. Ask the third question.

"Why do I feel so connected to Claire?" This time, instead of a knowing, I saw a picture. It wasn't Technicolor, and it wasn't digitally enhanced. It was blurry, vague, changing – half imagination, half hasty perception. But

I could see the house – more of the house. A modern porch or a one-story structure had been added to the older house I saw before. It was a white house, it seemed like it had a stone foundation, white boards on top. Clapboard or something. I asked how old, and got the feeling that "the house [itself]will tell you how old it is."

And beyond that, I got that it is not far from the institute, and that if I were to look for it, it could be found, and that the way to find it is to drive in the direction I "saw" myself floating in air, and trust intuition to bring me to the right place. I made a mental note: *If I'm ever down here with a car, maybe I'll go poke around, just to see.*

And then a vivid sense of Claire as my wife. The couple married young and she died young, which explained the concern for her I'm feeling and the – well, the love. How else to put it?

❖ 9 ❖

As soon as C.T. counted us back to normal consciousness, I sat up and grabbed my journal, not waiting even to take off my headphones or turn off the ready light. Bobby saw me sketching, and left without saying anything.

I drew a sketch of the house, trying to fix a fleeting memory, and wrote, "An older house – stone foundation, white clapboard, with a more modern structure attached to it – not a shed, more like a family room or breakfast room. It can be found, and 'the house will tell you when it was constructed.'"

As I wrote I became aware of even more. *Clara was my wife, and died young, perhaps in childbirth, and I became a wanderer. His name was John, and after she died he never again felt any attachment to the house or the life he had delighted in. I get the feeling that he left those surroundings and moved on in later years.*

What was most surprising, most startling, actually, is that I realized a natural emotional connection between that life and mine. Later I will think: *Probably that's why it was the first memory to come in.* After his wife died, never again did he really sink roots. Never again did he really commit himself to a person, or a place, or even a way of life – and neither have I, external circumstances to the contrary. The thought came, seemingly on its own: *This is where I lost the ability to fit into a settled scheme of things.* I thought of my home life, and my career, always on the outskirts, always on the margins. Even when I seemed (judging by externals) to fit into a situation, internally really I didn't. Never had. Was used to it. Had always told myself, nothing to be done about it.

I asked myself if I should discuss this with Claire. Would she think I was putting the moves on her? Would she think I was crazy? Or should I talk to her about it, if only to see how she would approach it?

So far had I traveled, so quickly. It was still only Monday morning.

❖ 10 ❖

I saw Annette glance at my face as I entered the debrief room. *She doesn't miss much.* I was nearly the last one down, and there weren't any open seats near Claire. I sat against a wall. She was about a third of the way around the horseshoe of participants. To see her, I would have to crane my head.

David: "Is that everybody?"

Annette, using her pointing finger to count: "Two more. Whose room-mate isn't here yet?"

"Dee isn't here," Elizabeth said.

"Edith," Toni Shaw said.

"Okay, we need to go on. While we're waiting, did anybody have anything happen that they want to talk about?" *Hell of a definition of waiting!* "Bobby."

A little uncharacteristically subdued. "I think I must be doing something wrong, and I wonder if you can set me straight. I'm still not getting anything."

"Well, Bobby, remember, we said these things have their own time. They can't be pushed."

Annette's expression was one of complete sympathy. "I know it can be hard, Bobby – and I'm sure that others of you are experiencing the same thing. You just have to trust the process. If you're willing for things to happen, and you don't insist that they only come one way, sooner or later you *will* get what you need. We have a saying around here, perhaps you've heard it already. People get what they need from Open Door."

"I would have thought I'd get at least *one* answer."

"Perhaps you did and don't yet recognize it. Perhaps it is on its way. All we can say is, trust and be as patient and as open as you can."

"One thing," David said. "It may not have occurred to you – all of you, not just Bobby – but some of your answers are going to come from your fellow participants, or from life in general. They won't all come during a

9 3

tape experience. So, try to stay open to experience in general, not just when you're listening to tapes. Yes, Andrew?"

"What do you do when you ask one question and get the answer to an entirely different question? Does that ever happen?"

"Did it just happen to you?"

"That's sure what it seems like."

"Then, yes, apparently it happens."

Andrew laughed with the rest of us, but he didn't give up. "Yes, but – what sense does that make? I mean, if they're going to tell us whatever they want to tell us, why should we bother figuring out questions to ask them?"

"I think there are a couple of things going on here, Andrew," David said carefully, but quick as thought, Andrew shot back, "What, you're not going to say 'I-don't-know-what-do-you-think?'" This time *he* got the laugh. "You can see why they don't much want to talk to us," David said. "Seriously, we could tell you what various things mean, but suppose we did. In the first place we'd be depriving you of the experience of finding out for yourselves, and in the second place, if you're taking our word for things as you go along, and not checking what we say against your own experience, and we're telling you things that don't happen to be true, where does that leave you? I can give you a hint where it leaves you. It's someplace where you don't have a paddle."

"But maybe our intuition tells us that you're not lying to us."

"Maybe so. But maybe the way we see things isn't the only way to see it. Maybe it's not even the best way. Maybe it's flat wrong. It's as close to an iron-clad rule as we have around here: Don't deprive someone of their experience. What you figure out for yourself is yours. What you're told is just something borrowed. It's a bus stop, not a place to live."

"So about the things that you *are* going to tell us? About my getting an answer to a question I didn't ask?"

"Well, you're not the first person to experience this. We see it a lot. So we have a couple of ideas about what's going on. In the first place, sometimes it's the answer to the question behind the question you thought you were asking. You know, you ask 'How do I get rid of this awful cold,' and what you're really asking is, 'Is there something really wrong with my health?' So sometimes you are getting an answer to your question, and it's up to you to realize it."

Andrew, doubtfully: "I'll look at it, but that doesn't seem to fit the answer I got."

Annette said: "Sometimes we have a hard time reading the language. You know, we've said, these visions seem to follow the same rules as dreams. They use verbal puns, and visual puns, and they use what seem to us to be wild mixtures of various elements that don't make any sense as descriptions of the physical world, but make perfect sense as descriptions of the emotional or mental or energetic world. So sometimes all you can do is sit with it and ask it for greater clarity."

Ain't that the truth! I thought.

"One thing you have to remember," David said. "Language, whether it's English or French or Spanish or what, was designed to reflect the reality of *this* world. Three dimensions, linear time, up and down, and all that. So using language to try to describe the inner world, the world that is not inside time and space, means *mis*-using it. But what else can we do? We have to use something to communicate, and language is one of the few tools we have."

"Somebody in one of our programs said something I like," Annette said. "He said, 'Please don't bite my finger, look where I'm pointing.'"

"He stole that from somewhere," Lou Hardin said. "I've read it."

"Well, whoever he stole it from, I like it. The map is not the territory; don't bite my finger; words are only pointers – the fact that there are lots of ways to say it shows us that it is a limitation that we should keep in mind."

With this tape, they'd evidently hit the jackpot, at least in terms of people willing and anxious to talk about their experience. I did my best, but the input outran my ability to make mental notes. Quiet-as-a-church-mouse Marta had a vision of herself as a buried treasure, and appeared to be entirely innocent of how that sounded to the rest of us. Helene saw herself in a very pleasant, if slightly chilly library room with no doors or windows, and was not upset but was figuratively scratching her head both as to how to get out and as to how she had gotten in there in the first place. Tony, looking a little grim, said that he was driving his Mercedes in a subdivision but kept turning into one street after another that was a dead end. (He was careful to tell us that in real life he didn't have a Mercedes.) I think he had a pretty good guess as to what he was being told.

Roberta Harrison Sellers had a meaningful experience, too, as it turned out, but in this session she was unable to – couldn't bear to – tell anyone about it. We didn't hear about it until quite a bit later when it returned (so to speak) trailing consequences.

And, finally, both Toni and Edith reported receiving messages that at first seemed clear-cut but upon re-examination proved less so. Toni's at first seemed a promise of renewed artistic creativity. Edith's looked to be a prediction of her massage therapy practice expanding and thriving. As it turned out, in both cases, not quite.

That's about all I remembered of that debrief session. Naturally I was focused much more on my own process.

❖ 11 ❖

"Ready to go? Okay, here's our third Wider Vision tape, another free flow."

They'd given us a short break between the end of debriefing tape two and beginning briefing tape three. I'd hoped to talk to Claire, but she wound up talking to Helene Porter and Toni Shaw about something, and I didn't care to interrupt. So I waited until we went back to the debrief room, and made sure to sit next to her. "How about a lunch date?" I said, and she smiled and said sure. I considered taking her hand but I decided that sitting there holding hands would look entirely too much like high school. Besides, she might think I was an idiot, and might be right. So I settled for sitting next to her. It was the weirdest feeling. I was well aware that I hadn't yet known her for two full days yet, and knew almost nothing of who she was or what kind of life she led. At the same time it was as if she and I were long-married lovers. I *know* that it doesn't make sense. You don't need to tell me that. But that's what it felt like.

"As usual," David said, "we're not going to tell you much."

"We've noticed the pattern emerging," Andrew said.

David grinned. "And here we thought we were being so subtle. Oh well. The motto of the firm here, you know, is somewhere between 'We're from the government and we're here to help you,' and 'So long, good luck, you're on your own.' Some people respond better to the first, and others to the second. Your choice. However, as I was saying – "

"Before I was so rudely interrupted."

"Before I was so rudely interrupted – he said it, I didn't – the idea is still for you to have *your* experience, not something we pre-program you to have. So, once again, we give you the tools and you go see what you can see."

"Our approach is 'the bear went over the mountain,'" Annette said. "You remember that the bear went over the mountain to see what he could see. Not much point in telling him what he was going to see, especially since nobody else has ever *been* over the particular mountain he's going to be going over."

Tony said, "Huh? As long as you've been doing this?"

"The mountain isn't the tapes, Tony, and it isn't the program or the trainers. Each of you bring your own mountain to climb, and how can anyone else know what it is?" She smiled at him and gave a sort of helpless shrug.

"We know some of the generic pitfalls, sure," David said, "and those we tell you about."

"But surely after you've had feedback from so many hundreds of program participants – ?"

"Think about it, though. You come here with your distinctive background, your mental habits, your emotional hang-ups, all your strengths and weaknesses. You are a distinct package, and there isn't another one like it. We take two dozen packages just like that, and we run them through Open Door together. Yes, you'll all have certain reactions, more or less. Yes, we can predict that on a given day of the week, a certain percentage of you will probably tend to react like x and such. But what does that tell us really? Just that doing *this* kind of tape after *that* kind of tape seems to work pretty well, but doing it after a different kind of tape doesn't work so well. You see? We can make pragmatic decisions, but we really never know very much about what's going on with you unless you tell us – and *that's* assuming you know! Some of you may, some of you won't. Not by the time the week is over, maybe not for months."

I wondered, later, if they were deliberately not telling us that this tape might be an eye-opener. Maybe they were trying not to raise our expectations. Maybe it was just as they said, that they could never predict when somebody was about to have a life-changing experience. But maybe it was them saying, "Pay no attention to the man behind the curtain."

❖ 12 ❖

It's hard, almost, to remember that I came here a total skeptic. That was all of two days ago. Less, I got here Saturday night. At this rate I'm going to be a total fruitcake by the end of the week.

Lying in the darkness caused by the sleep mask, listening to the crackling hiss as I waited for C.T.'s voice to start me through the rabbit hole again. *How many Merriman trainers does it take to screw up Alice's mind so badly, she stays in Wonderland forever?*

"We don't promise that anyone will have an out-of-body experience this week," they'd said Saturday. "It isn't the kind of thing that can be predicted. There are too many variables." Yet this time, faced with Andrew's direct question, David had waffled. "Maybe," he'd said, and then had denied that that was anything different from what they'd said before.

Pay no attention to the man behind the curtain.

"Free-flow tapes are designed to help you to structure your own experience, rather than having us structure it for you. Go with it."

Go with it. Find the territory on your own, without a road map. And don't forget to leave a trail of bread crumbs, so if you happen to find yourself outside your body, you can get back.

C.T. began leading us through the process of physical relaxation that always preceded a move to an altered state. Very old stuff by now, already a habit. I followed his lead, mechanically, my thoughts elsewhere.

The house can be found, and it will tell you when it was built.

He led our attention down our physical bodies, suggesting that we examine and release potential points of stress or strain, one after another. I found that this can be done with half your attention, or less.

Clara was my wife, and died young, perhaps in childbirth, and I became a wanderer.

He completed the relaxation process, and left an interval of silence, with only the pink noise, crackling away.

His name was John, and after she died he never again felt any attachment to the house or the life he had delighted in.

"Now you are free," C.T.'s voice said. "Free to explore. Free to experience. Free to see how much more you really are."

That's where I lost the ability to fit into a settled scheme of things.

"Go, experience whatever is here for you today in your state of Wider Vision, and I will call you when it is time to return."

Of course, I could be just making this all up.

I lay there amid the pink noise, drifting and daydreaming, and after a minute or two decided to see if I could learn any more about whatever was going on with Clara and John.

❖ 13 ❖

This time when I entered the debrief room, Annette happened to be standing by the entrance, not yet having taken her accustomed place next to David. "Angelo," she said quietly, "your process is your own business and nobody is going to pry, but I want to remind you that if you ever feel you need to talk about things one on one rather than in a group, that's what David and I are here for. You're welcome to talk to either one of us any time."

I nodded, and said, just as quietly. "You've got good eyes. I saw you notice, last time. Thanks." *I'm not sure you're the one I need to discuss it with, though.* I looked around, saw that Claire hadn't come down yet, and lowered myself onto the floor, taking a seat at random. I didn't much feel like talking to anybody, so I opened my journal, but I found I didn't much feel like writing anything, either.

People were filing in. "Yo, roomie," Bobby said.

I looked up at him. "No luck?"

"Not so far." I didn't know what to say. He found a seat near one of the corners.

Jeff levered himself down next to me. "Another day in so-so land," he said, grinning widely.

I could feel him bubbling over. "You had a worthwhile experience, I take it?"

"Might say so."

"Better than potato chips?"

"Well – that's asking a lot, but – maybe. How about you?"

"Oh, – " I didn't know what to say. "It's getting interesting."

"Boy, isn't it!"

Claire gracefully lowered herself into the backjack seat next to me. *All her movements are graceful, even getting down onto the floor.* She smiled at Jeff and me. "Hi guys. Jeff, you're positively radiating."

"Yeah, well, you know, a good nap will do it every time."

"I think he visited the land of eternal potato chips," I said.

"You had an OBE!" she said.

His grin got broader. "Well, it's sort of like Ace Reporter, here, I don't know for sure. But yeah, I think so. Either that or my imagination is better than I thought."

And as it turned out, he wasn't the only one, but again, as before, it would be a while before we heard about some of it.

Jeff didn't usually do a lot of talking in debrief, so when David asked if anybody had anything they'd like to share with the group (we never talked or discussed or argued or described, alas, but nearly always "shared") and Jeff raised a finger, David gave him the nod.

"That was really interesting. Like everybody else has been saying, I don't know if I'm making this up or not, but – well, actually, I *do* know that I wasn't making this one up. I just don't have any framework for it. It was strange enough that I got up before C.T. finished bringing us back, just so I'd have time to make some notes, so I wouldn't forget what I want to ask about, because it was weird."

"Yeah, not like what else has been going on here," Andrew said.

Jeff grinned. "Well, I know! It's like, how do I go farther out than we've already been? But in a way – well, here's what happened. At first I was lying there listening to C.T., sort of daydreaming, you know?" Several people nodded. "And then it's like I must have fallen asleep, because I remember sort of waking up and – no, that's not the way to put it. Let's put it this way, all of a sudden I realized I was running down the street back home, only I wasn't exactly running. I was sort of jumping, long gliding jumps that covered 10 or 20 feet at a time, like an ice skater, only on steroids or something. And I was enjoying this great freedom of movement, this way of running that was almost like flying, when I said, 'Wait a minute, nobody can jump like that, I must be dreaming.' But it didn't *feel* like a dream, it felt real, it's just – I knew it *had to be.* So I thought, 'Well, if this is a dream, I ought to be able to do whatever I can think of' – so I turned a somersault and had my feet stop three inches above the level of the ground. You see? It still felt real, and I knew it couldn't be ordinary waking reality." He grinned. "Well, maybe here at the institute it could, but I mean normally."

"So I thought, 'Holy moley, this must be a lucid dream.' Then I thought, 'Okay, let's say it is, now what?' because I didn't want to knock myself out of it, you know, and I didn't know how long it would last anyway. So I decided I'd run faster than a horse, and in fact I thought about flying but decided not to, and I guess it's a good thing because when I started running I thought, 'Well, it's a dream and I can do what I want to,' so I stuck out my arm and went through the lamp posts as I ran, just for fun, only after about the third lamp post, my arm *hit* it, instead of going through it."

He was looking at Annette and David, going from one to the other, being sure they were still with him.

"As soon as I couldn't go through the lamp post, it was like things changed again, and this is where it gets *really* weird. Suddenly I was in a room and I wasn't dreaming anymore."

Tony asked what he meant by that, and I was glad he did, because I wanted to know too, but didn't want to interrupt.

Jeff frowned, concentrating. "It's like, this was the third time it changed. First I was dreaming, at least I guess that's what it was, then it turned into a lucid dream, if that's what *that* was, and now it was something different from either of those. And it wasn't normal consciousness, either."

Again intently holding Annette and David. "It was something I've never experienced, and I don't really have words for it. It's like I was in a place that's *realer* than this. That's the only way I can put it. And the one thing I'm sure of is, that part wasn't a dream or anything else, I was really there, and it was really real." I could hear the deep sincerity in his voice, and almost a desperation, wanting to be believed but not quite confident that he would be.

"Tell us more about that place, Jeff," Annette suggested.

"It was like a room, with people in it, like they were sitting around a table and I just popped in. I had the impression they were surprised to see me show up, but it wasn't like they didn't understand what had happened. I mean, this wasn't anything new to them, that's the sense I got, it's just that whenever it happened it was surprising, but not amazing, if you understand what I mean. Anyway one of them asked me how long I'd been in a body and I told him, and it's like they were real impressed, like being down here is hard. And I think we said a few other things but that's all I remember, and then I could feel myself losing the energy that had brought me there, and I said to them, 'I can't hold this, I've got to let it go' – and I don't know where *that* came from, because I sure didn't think it out in advance – and then I was back and after a while C.T. brought us out of the exercise."

A couple of people asked questions – what was lucid dreaming, for instance – but none of us really knew what to do with it. And then of course Lou Hardin had to suggest somehow that Jeff had been making it up, or exaggerating for effect. He didn't put it that way, but that's what it amounted to. I thought, not for the first time, *no matter what it is that's reported, he has to cancel it out. It's important to him.*

I leaned over to Jeff – after debrief had gone off in another direction – and quietly said, "*I* thought *I* was having a good day until you had to open your big mouth, Mr. Story-Topper." He grinned and said, equally quietly, "You know what Bob Dylan said, 'I wouldn't worry about it none, them old dreams is only in your head.'"

❖ 14 ❖

"We're the modern additions," Claire said. "You and I."

Naturally the talk around the lunch tables centered on out-of-body experiences. That's the kind of anomalous experience that most people had come for, hoping against hope (or believing beyond doubt) that this was the place if any where they could experience them, and now no fewer than three people had reported having one. Even after debrief, they wanted to hear more. Jeff and Andrew and Edith were still comparing notes and still being questioned. Claire and I, though, had scooped up place mats and silverware and had moved ourselves to one of the little two-person tables by the windows.

"We are the modern additions?" I said. "I don't get it."

"You and I are not Clara and John. Maybe we were once – it feels as if we were – but we're not the same people now. So maybe your vision is showing you that we have this old connection, but it's not that simple."

"It couldn't be just that the old house has been added on to, physically, and they're trying to show me what it looks like?"

"Angelo, I don't know, maybe it's that too. I'm a psychotherapist. I was trained to interpret dreams, and that's how my mind works. I treat visions the same way I treat dreams. When our mind experiences unfamiliar things, it interprets them for us, and then it's up to us to figure out the interpretation. So in a way everything's symbolic."

"You don't think the vision of the house was for real, then?"

"I do – especially since what I remember seeing looks like your sketch. But I don't think we can treat a vision as if it were a photograph, or a memory. It's very likely to have other elements mixed in with it, so that it can do the job of presenting us with the meaning of what it's showing."

"And what about Clara losing the baby, or whatever happened?"

An indefinable expression passed over her face. Something moved behind her eyes, as they say. "I don't think it was a death in childbirth," she said slowly, "but there was something there. I can feel it." She reached her hand over to mine across the little table. "I can feel it in you, too, my love."

And there we were. The tie between us – whatever it was and whatever it meant – had been acknowledged. There could be no going back to pretending that we hadn't felt it. *Getting kind of hard to say it isn't real,* I thought. It would have been hard to do even if my body hadn't been telling me it was *interested.*

Some of it was lust, I suppose. There was *chemistry* between us. We liked each other. I don't know how it is for other people, but for me there is no lust without there first being a liking. I can't imagine wanting to go to bed with someone I didn't like just for the sake of the physical act. I mean – why? So yes, there was some lust. I found her very physically attractive, and I could tell that we responded to each other. But it wasn't all lust, or even mostly. (Mid-fifties is a long way from being a teenager, after all. If you haven't gotten the hormones under some kind of control by then, there is no hope for you.) Mostly, it was a sudden end to loneliness. Well, I can't speak for her. That's what was going on within me.

Julie and I had been married a long, long time – long enough to know that we weren't likely ever to take comfort in each other, or to be able to give it. Instead, our every difference rubbed the raw places. She was religious, I was a skeptic. She believed what she read in the papers, I knew better. She wanted a "normal" suburban life and I wanted – something else, whatever it was. She had an endless list of criticisms of who and what I was, and I had a list for her. After years of conflict, we had come to a sort of weary tolerance, a "staying together for the sake of the kids" tolerance that left us both numb and exhausted. And lonely.

With Claire, I knew already, it was different. This relationship was like coming home. I felt that, regardless of whether we immediately understood each other's ideas, we would always understand where the other was coming from. It was like long-married people when they're *not* incompatible. And, in a way, that's what we were, if this story of John and Clara had any validity. Not that I'd ever believed in reincarnation – or even considered it as a possibility! But it did seem to make emotional sense of this mutual attraction, and these mutual experiences, and I couldn't think what else would. *On the other hand, as she says, we're not the same people now.*

Maybe the thing to do would be to disown the experience, say we were mistaken, call it irrelevant to our present lives. *Forty-eight hours ago, I didn't know she existed. How much obligation can there be?* But on the other hand, the feelings of loss are welling up within me, so strongly that trainers are coming up to me to remind me that if I'm getting into deep waters, they're available to help.

❖ 15 ❖

The lab building was next to Edward Carter Hall. Annette knocked on the door, and it was opened from inside. *That's the first locked door I've seen here*, I thought. "All yours, Dave. We announced the lab tour at lunch-time, and it looks like everybody's here but Claire. I'm going to go take a nap."

The smiling man standing in the doorway looked to be in his fifties, but perhaps his neat brown mustache made him look a little older than his years. "Okay, come on in, folks. My name is Dave Simmons, and I am go-ing to give you the ten-cent tour of the lab, and after I talk to you a little bit about how we got here, I'm going to turn you over to Harry O'Dell, and he'll tell you what he's doing with our new software. Then he'll hand you off to Rudy Linder, who hopefully will get you so excited about the tapes he produces that you will all go out and buy a bunch of them to use at home after the program. So come in."

With the others, I stepped into an entryway, and followed Simmons through a small reception room into another room behind it. One side of the room was dominated by an electronic console, along with a computer and printer, tape racks, and assorted detritus. On the other side of the room was a little desk and chair and guest chair pulled up next to it, looking like any other intake station I'd ever seen.

"Okay, let me start with a little history. You all heard about C.T.'s near-death experience and all that, right? And he came back with the idea that he could produce an altered state of consciousness using sound. So he decided he was going to set up a lab and figure out how to do it. I suppose you know, he had been in electronics, so he had a pretty good idea of where he wanted to start – but knowing where to start isn't the same thing as knowing how to set up a laboratory. He was used to walking into the lab and hitting switches, and if he needed something else he hired somebody to build it. That's what he did when he was in business, and had a lot of money to throw at a prob-lem. Development costs are all tax deductible, and as long as the money's still coming in, who cares how much it costs? But here he was watching costs as much as he could. And that's where I came in.

"Before I came here I learned electronics in the Air Farce." *Jesus,* I thought, *another comedian.* "After that I had twenty years with a certain de-fense contractor – He Who Is To Be Obeyed, if you know Rider Haggard's *She*, or maybe I should say He Who Is Not To Be Named, like the evil-doers in native society. Anyway, as soon as I could, I took retirement and went looking for something fun to do. How I got here is a long story, and I am not going to go into it, but anyway I got here just at the time that C.T. needed someone to put together a sound lab for him."

He made an all-encompassing gesture. "Everything you see here, we built. When I got here, the building had just been constructed, and it was just a shell, all smooth concrete floors, with some wiring and conduit coming down from the ceiling with electrical outlets on it, and a bathroom, and that was it. We put in the interior walls according to C.T.'s basic floor plan – C.T.'s carpenter and a few volunteers, including me, and we soundproofed the room and all that. Then it was up to me to fix it so that you could walk in there and create tapes.

"It was up to me, you see, because that's what I had done at He Whose Name Must Not Be Said. I worked my way up from grunt with a soldering iron to manager of an R & D team, so I knew what we had to do. I knew how to build up the equipment, rack-mount it, interconnect it, and work from one end to the other, to be sure you could generate a tone, see it over here, patch it down, look at it, record it, and mix it. Making tapes is Rudy's bag, not mine, so I'll let him tell you about what he actually does. But he does it on the system that we put together ourselves, basically with off-the-shelf equipment, and I'm proud that I was part of it."

He gestured toward the console. "Now, this monster that you're looking at doesn't have anything to do with developing tapes. This is for communicating with people in the black box in the next room, that I'll show you in a minute. Does everybody here know what I'm talking about when I say the black box? No? Maybe you know it as the booth? The isolation chamber? Still no? Okay, let me say a few words about that, then. This room we're standing in is the control room. Let's go into the other room and we'll take a look at the black box itself."

We moved into a two-story clerestory-lit room lined with shelves, filing cases, and what looked like the accumulated office litter of decades. But what drew the eye was a big black cube, perhaps ten feet on a side, standing on four wooden posts.

"C.T. was trying to find ways to put people into altered states. That meant that he had to figure out a way to monitor them, of course. And that led to the question, how are we going to do it? At first he'd question them at the end of the experiment. 'What did you feel? Was it pleasant or unpleasant? Did anything special happen that you noticed? Unusual physical sensations? Drowsiness?' Like that. But that wasn't very satisfactory. For one thing, what people notice is sometimes quite a bit different from what really happens. For another thing, it's all subjective, and for yet *another* thing, there's no record, no hard data. After a while he wanted to be able to say, like, 'We fed in this mixture of frequencies and it changed their brain-waves this way.' Well, that's easier said than done, especially in the early days.

"The whole thing was a logical development, one thing leading to the next. When he first started playing with this, he had people sit in a chair located between two stereo speakers. He went right away to headphones, and then it didn't take long till he was having people lie down on a bed so that they could relax more. Then he began hooking people up to recording devices, sort of like a lie detector, so that he'd have an electronic record, and if their physiology changed suddenly in a certain direction, he'd know just when it happened, and what frequencies were being played at that time."

"How did he do that?" Ellis asked.

"Nothing fancy. You tape three sensors to the person's right hand, the thumb and first two fingers. One measures changes in skin temperature, another one measures skin potential voltage, and the third measures galvanic skin response. It's pretty basic, as instrumentation goes, but like I say it gave him some kind of record. Well, so then he got to thinking about it and he decided that what he wanted was an environment that would screen out every possible kind of interference. So we made a list – that was C.T., Jim Bowen, me, a couple of others – and we came up with light, sound, temperature changes, electronic interference, and we designed the black box against a list of things we wanted to eliminate. Come around here."

He walked around the box to the opposite side, and climbed three steps to a door. "You'll see, when I open this door, how we got it light-proof." He pulled the door open, leaning away from it slightly, and swung it wide. "We've got four inches of hard foam insulation in this door, and another door inside." He pulled at the handle of the inner door and swung it to the side. You see, the edges of the two doors don't overlap – the outside door is three inches wider, higher and lower than the inside door – and that's done on purpose to keep out light. The insulation in both layers helps keep out sound. To stop stray electronics, we tacked up wire mesh – like wire cloth, only much finer – between the inside and outside walls, which made it into a Faraday cage. When we finished, I turned on a transistor radio and climbed into the box and had them close the doors. When the first door shut, the sound from the radio cut off. The radio was still working, but it wasn't receiving anything."

Elizabeth asked, "Where is the electrical connection between the black box and the control room?"

"When we go back to the control room, look up about eight feet and you'll see something that looks like a rubber hose about a foot across. That carries the electrical wiring, and it's stuffed with foam insulation. So anyway, when we thought we were finished, we thought, what about vibration? Sometimes those big eighteen-wheelers come by on the state road a couple of miles away, and we wondered if that might mess up anything. So we picked up the whole box and put it on posts and embedded the posts in sand. That's why we have to climb these stairs to get in.

"So there we had it. We put a waterbed inside to make it super comfortable, and of course headphones. Then we added a microphone so that the person in the box could talk to us as we went along. When you take a look inside here, look carefully at the ceiling and you'll see the air-exchange vents. We put them as far from the waterbed as we could, so we wouldn't create a breeze. We really did try to eliminate all possible distractions. Now I'm going to go back down from here, and you can come up two or three at a time and have a look inside."

❖ 16 ❖

Harry O'Dell was about the same age and body size as Dave Simmons, maybe a few years younger. Unlike Simmons, he was clean-shaven, and perhaps his body was in better shape. He looked us over with a practiced eye, and seemed to be measuring something invisible.

"As Dave told you, it's my job to monitor our subjects during their black box sessions, but in a way that's almost a minor part of my job. My personal interest is mapping human potential. And we have the tool here to begin to do it." He patted his keyboard.

"A lot of the time we use the black box as a convenient way to interact with someone who is having altered-state experiences at our direction. We can change the inputs from here, and talk to them, and listen to them, and the instrumentation on their fingers gives us an idea of how they are reacting."

"You mean you can read their thoughts?" That, of course, was Bobby.

O'Dell laughed, a curious smothered laugh which, had it been higher pitched, would qualify as a giggle. "No, if we could do that we could make a *lot* of *money* instead of fooling around. We can't read thoughts, and we can't read emotions. But we can infer a couple of things. For one thing, if the skin temperature goes down, it's probably an indicator that the person has tensed up. And if the skin potential voltage and telephonic skin response start moving in opposite directions, it probably means that the subject is experiencing something meaningful. So that's very useful, especially for people who are just learning to recognize unusual mental states. If any of you go on to take Inner Voice, you will get a session in the box as part of the program.

"But as far as I'm concerned, the exciting part is our on-going reverse-engineering project. You know what reverse engineering is? It's where you start with the final result, and break it into its component parts so that you can see how to replicate whatever it is that you're looking at."

"Japanese electronics," Sam Andover said.

"Same principle, yes. Rather than starting from scratch, start from the best you can find, and maybe improve it from there. Well, suppose you have somebody who does energy healing, say. We think it would be nice to be able to teach others how to do it. C.T. always says that if even one person can do something, it is obviously a human ability, and so presumably everybody could learn to do it, if only badly. He is always saying, not everybody can be Mozart, but anybody can learn to play chopsticks. And we know that this kind of thing can be taught, because it *is* taught. Only, the way it usually is taught is that the student is introduced to the theory, and then practices, and remains in the presence of someone who can do it, practicing, until the student stumbles upon the technique, or doesn't.

"Our way is simpler. We record the brain wave patterns of the healer while he is doing healing – or she is – and we produce a tape with those same frequencies, so that the student can *feel* what it feels like from the inside, rather than trying to stumble upon it by external practice. You can see how much more direct an approach this is. So that's how I spend a good deal of my time: researching the literature in the field, researching what else is out there in terms of measuring brain wave patterns, that kind of thing. I also spend a lot of time recording special talents, examining the electronic record of our sessions, and trying to find out which combinations of brain waves seem to be significant."

Tony said, "You can get that kind of result that easily?"

"Oh no. I'm just giving you the conceptual overview. In practice, we try to get several healers in here, and we like to do several sessions with each. That's the only way we can think of to come up with something like an average pattern. And even then, who knows if the healer was really 'on' in a given session? Just because somebody thinks they are doing healing doesn't mean they really are, and just because they think they're 'on' doesn't mean they really are. So we try to build in as much redundancy as we can. We figure, given enough sampling, the noise in the data will cancel out."

"So what kind of things are you trying to learn how to teach besides healing?"

"Oh, lots of things. Any human aptitude is likely to have a characteristic set of brain wave patterns."

"I've used Sharpener quite a bit," Bobby said. "I think it really helped develop my mathematical abilities."

"Well that's one good example," O'Dell said. "We wanted an application that would help people to concentrate and increase their access to computational and conceptual process. We put in a good deal of alpha and delta, to produce a sharpened mental acuity accompanied by physical relaxation – to get the body out of the way, in other words. For that particular application, we did not include theta. We weren't trying to set you off to have anomalous experiences, but to keep you focused on something very near at hand and practical."

"Well, for some of us, mathematics *counts* as an anomalous experience," Jane Mullen said.

O'Dell laughed again. "Be that as it may, that's what we did."

"No beta?" Andrew asked.

"No, no beta. In this context, beta would be more like mental noise than anything else."

"And how did you come up with that idea?"

"We were looking for a product that would have commercial applications. We are continually trying to expand our product line, because as you may know, none of this operation is funded by grants. It's all C.T.'s money, and he likes to see some coming back in as well as always flowing out." A grin. "He mentions this from time to time."

"Does that commercialization concern you at all?" I asked.

"No not really. The way I look at it, that commercialization, if it helps us stay in business, subsidizes me while I look for ways to produce something of value for the whole human race. I've been with C.T. for quite a while now, and I think I can speak for him as well on this. With this technology, we have stumbled on the ultimate teaching tool. Given enough time and imagination and cooperation from talented subjects, we ought to be able to totally transform the range of practical human possibilities." He laughed. "Other than that, we don't think any of this amounts to much."

Rudy Linder was an easy-going guy, he immediately made clear. *An act? A philosophical statement?* He had a low mellow voice, a lazy smile, and from the looks of him, a joke ready to pop out at any moment. Even the extra pounds on his large frame hinted at low-key good nature. *Whoever he is, he isn't Cassius. No lean and hungry look here.*

He was sitting at his console, his chair turned toward his visitors. "So. You've heard Dave and Harry and if you can just get through this last bit, you can go enjoy what's left of your long break. Any questions before we wrap it up?" *They must audition.*

"Okay. Well, you're standing in the sound lab – I guess you know that much, anyway. This is where we mix new tapes. You probably don't know about the kinds of tapes we produce other than the ones you are using in your Open Door, but you'll get a hand-out describing them and telling you how to order them, so I'm not going to talk about them. What I think you'll find more interesting is, what is it we're doing here, and how does this fit in with your program?

"Did Harry talk to you about reverse engineering? Okay, so you got the idea? They find a talented subject, they record their brain waves while they're doing their thing, and then we try to produce a tape that's going to encourage your brain to produce the same frequencies in the same ratios. Sometimes it works like magic, sometimes not so well, and sometimes we never do figure it out for whatever reason."

"I've used your Sharpener tape at home," Bobby said.

"Well, good. Glad to hear it. We aim to please."

I said, "I don't quite have the sense of it. They tape someone doing something special and you just produce another tape with the same frequencies?"

"Well, it isn't really that simple, that's just our shorthand. It goes more like this. First we identify the frequencies and their strength relative to each other. In other words, how much alpha, beta, theta, delta."

"Not gamma?" That was Andrew St. George.

"No, gamma is beyond the range of our equipment. Probably it would be good if we could measure it, but it must not be essential, because we're getting results with what we have. Anyway, once we have the signature, then we have to bring you – the person using the tape – to where your brain begins to operate at those frequencies. If you think about it, we don't know who *you* are, nor where you're going to be starting from, and we don't know

how easily you'll move from whatever point you do start from. So we have
to make a guess at the average person's configuration. We want to start you
from a position near Entry State, that's why the instructions get you to lie
down, relax, and breathe calmly before you start. Then we can amp up the
frequencies until we get you where we want you – at least, we can if you're
willing to follow – and we leave you there for a while and then we bring you
back to a more normal brain wave pattern, less focused.

"That's the theory. The complication in practice is that if we were doing
all that and your ear was following it, your mind would start to analyze it.
So then you wouldn't be relaxing and following the flow, you'd be holding
yourself in analytical mode. Also, if you started to pay too much attention
to the sounds, you'd obviously be paying less attention to the purpose of
the exercise. So to overcome that, we overlay a layer of pink noise – that
whooshing static you hear – and then on top of that, we put C.T.'s voice
with the narrative, suggesting things for you to do." He spread his hands.
"And that's what I do: I mix tapes."

And, later –

Linder laughed. "Well, I'll tell you, if you don't tell C.T. what I said. I
used to have my own sound studio in Charlottesville, about a hundred years
ago, and one day I'm sitting there and I get a call out of the blue from C.T.
Of course I didn't know him then. Would I be interested in doing a little
part-time work in a sound studio down in Nelson County? Things were
slow – it was the middle of February, nothing much happening – so I said
I'd come down on Friday and talk. I figured at least I would check out the
competition. So we meet and have some coffee, and he says, 'Let's go look
at the lab.' And we come over here to this building and I'm expecting a
regular music studio – because I worked with rock bands – and he opens the
door and I thought, 'You're kidding, right?' I'm looking at concrete floors,
regular wallboard ceiling – I mean just the echoes alone! Of course, they
weren't recording live music, they were synthesizing everything, so that
didn't make any difference. But what a first impression!

"So C.T. very proudly says, 'What do you think?' And I'm trying to
think of something safe to say, and I look around and finally I say, 'This is
quite an arrangement.'" He laughed. "I mean, what could you say? So he
shows me the console, obviously very proud of it. And it was pretty fair,
actually. Not top of the line, but not Radio Shark either. I say 'Has all this
stuff been calibrated?' and C.T. makes a motion like 'be my guest' so I sit
down and fool around with it, getting the hang of the signal flow. And after

about two minutes, C.T. says 'You seem to know what you're doing there, let's go get some lunch.' And that was my job interview. He offered me a part-time job making tapes and it wasn't too long before I closed my studio and came here full-time. That was six years ago. All right, now get out of here and enjoy the rest of this lovely spring afternoon."

❖ 18 ❖

Jeff and I found her standing alone on the side porch, nursing a mug of hot tea and staring out at the mountains.

"Missed you," Jeff said. "It was kind of interesting. I think you would have enjoyed it."

She gave us a smile – a wan smile – and said she was sure she would have. I looked at her sharply, though it didn't require any great acuity to see what I saw there. "Are you okay?" I asked. She tried to give us the brave face but I saw.

"Let's get inside," I said, for the March chill even in mid-afternoon was something I had to consider. They followed me into the deserted dining room, and we didn't even sit down, but stood in a loose triangle just inside the door. "Give," I said. And a part of me wondered how I had suddenly become so bossy. Yet, it was as though I had the right, somehow, and she responded in kind.

"I didn't go on the tour this afternoon because I wanted to call my doctor and see if she had the results of the tests we did last week."

We waited.

"My bone cancer has come back – and my daughter is only nine years old!"

The two halves of the sentence didn't seem to belong together – and then they did. Jeff and I glanced at each other in dismay. We stood there immobile.

Jeff cleared his throat. "How sure is your doctor, Claire?"

She took a long, deep breath. "Very sure. This set of tests were a check on the results we got two months ago."

She looked like she was shaking inside. Awkwardly, tentatively, as self-conscious as I have ever been in my life, I reached out and put my arms around her. Without hesitation she returned my embrace and held on fierce-ly. "I wouldn't mind so much for myself," she said, almost whispering, "but little girls need their mother. She has all her teen years ahead of her, and I can't be there with her."

Jeff said, "You're not assuming that it's all over, are you?"

She let go of me, so I let go of her and we moved apart. "I signed up for Open Door when we got the first test results, so I could do Bridging Over. I wanted to be ready."

That was clear enough!

"Wait a minute," I said. "It can't be all that cut and dried. I've talked to plenty of doctors, researching medical stories. One of them told me he stopped telling people 'you've got six months to live' when he realized that his patients believed him and were dying when they were 'supposed to.' He told me, he finally realized that nobody knows how long *anybody* has, with *anything*."

"That's right," she admitted, "they're not saying 'you've got six months to live.' But, you know, they give you a range. They know the average length of time somebody lasts after diagnosis."

"But it's not absolute."

"Oh no, it depends on so many things – how healthy you are when you start, how young, how vigorous, what your mental attitude is, a whole raft of factors."

"So in a way, it's all guesswork. You're not just giving up, are you?"

"Well – I'm trying to be prepared."

Jeff said, "Listen, Claire, what about stacking the deck?"

We looked our question at him.

He shrugged. "Mainstream medicine doesn't have anything that works, or we'd all know about it. So you're going to have to go beat the bushes looking for some other technique that does work. Have you looked into alternative therapies?" He read her expression, and said, "I'm sorry. I'm trying to fix things, aren't I?"

"You are, but I know why, and I do appreciate it. And I *have* looked at some alternative therapies, it's just that it's so hard to tell what might be real from what is phony. But there's a healer in Spain who is supposed to do miracles, I may go there. But I don't have a lot of hope."

"Seems to me you need some kind of magic."

"I sure do."

"Well?"

Again we looked at him.

"Well, I mean, what better place to look than right here? The institute isn't exactly the beaten path."

I said, "You think they've got a cure for *cancer* here?"

"No," he said, drawing out the word, "not exactly. But I'll bet they know a hell of a lot that they'd never say in public but might be willing to say in private. I mean, who'd know more about practical ways to affect the body-mind connection?"

The body-mind connection again. "Somebody was talking about that on Sunday," I said. *The trouble is, I figure it's mostly wishful thinking.*

"I can't say it's not possible," Claire said. "And that's a good idea. I'll ask Annette. But at the same time, I have to be practical. I can't count on magic. I have to be as ready as I can be. That's what I'm doing here."

"I'm amazed that you can even do the tape exercises," I said.

"But don't you see, this may be my only chance! If I don't 'get it' here, how can I 'get it' in Bridging Over? So it doesn't make a lot of sense for me to quit preparing just because I've learned that it's really coming, what I was preparing for."

I could see the logic, but it seemed to me a frail reed. But was I going to say something to discourage her?

"And besides," smiling through her unshed tears, "it's interesting. New people, new ideas, new things to try. It gives me something to think about, instead of endlessly going over the same old territory that I'm so *tired* of."

We three ate supper together, along with Helene and Toni. "I'd just as soon it didn't become public knowledge," Claire had said. We'd said sure, and then didn't know what to do with ourselves. It was all I could do to meet the eyes of anybody else at the table. I picked at my chicken, wondering if my churning stomach was going to bring me to throw up.

❖ 19 ❖

"Well, since this is Monday evening, I assume you guys are all psychic superstars by now, right?" *Charlie had said, "probably they'll be a little pompous."* Not quite. Jim Bowen was shaking his head ruefully. "Psychic superstar. Do you believe that sh – stuff? But that's the news media for you; they're always either fawning on you to get an interview or they're attacking you for not being something you never said you were. Like they say, always at your feet or at your throat."

Edwin Carter Hall. The tables were arrayed in rows again, and we sat two to a table facing the front of the room where Bowen slowly paced back and forth. In the wake of Claire's news, I wanted to stay with her, regardless of whatever might be on the program, and so because she wanted to listen to Bowen, I went with her, sitting next to her. If she had wanted to talk, instead, I'd have skipped him in a heartbeat. But she wanted to hear, so there I was, and it didn't take long before I was as captivated as everybody else.

(*"And see what you can find out about Bowen, particularly. After all, he's Merriman's son-in-law. If he's phony probably the whole place is phony. If he's real, maybe not."*

(*"Charlie! How hard is it? If somebody says he's done something that can't be done, what's the point of proving that he hasn't done it?"*

(*"Just go see, Angelo, and* then *decide."*)

"I guess you haven't seen the TV, come to think of it. A couple of months ago, I was contacted by these television producers. They wanted to do a show about psychic abilities, and wanted to know would I be interested in helping them. I said sure, how much were they willing to pay me for my time." He gave a wolf's grin. "They *hate* that. They think you ought to be honored. You're lucky if they pay your expenses. Of course I knew that, and I knew I didn't have a chance in hell that they'd pay anything, but I thought I'd point out to them that it was them asking a favor and me maybe granting it, not the other way around." He savored his memory. "The guy couldn't believe it. 'We're talking about nationwide television,' he says, and I say, 'Yeah, and you want me as unpaid talent. Are *you* getting paid for *your* time?'" He laughed out loud, and people laughed with him. You couldn't help it.

"Well, of course I wound up doing the show, because even when you know something is a waste of time, still you think that every drop of water serves to wear down the stone, but I knew ahead of time how it was going to be, and sure enough, it was. It's like, while I'm still on the phone with this guy, he asks me to tell him something that's going to happen next week. I tell him it doesn't exactly work that way, but he says he heard that I can tell him things if I want to. So I say, 'Gee, you know, it's a shame, but my turban got dirty and I had to send it out for cleaning.'" Again the wolf's grin.

"So they fly me up to New York, and put me in a hotel overnight, and it's the same thing: Do it this way, because it makes for better video, that kind of thing. 'You can predict the future, can't you? If you're a real psychic, you can tell us tomorrow's winning lottery number, can't you? You know who's going to be the next president, because you're a psychic, aren't you?' See, they don't *really* believe that any of this is real, so they figure you've got to be either a flake or a con man. So they try to butter you up and get you pretending to do things nobody could do, just so they can put you on camera and make you look like an idiot.

"So I keep saying no, that isn't the way psychic abilities work. I tell them, 'There are things that work and things that don't, and you don't understand what you're asking. It's like you want me to swim across the river by flapping my wings, and just to be sure I'm not cheating, you want to tie a couple of hundred pounds of weights around my waist.'

"So finally the producer says – he's sneering at me – he says, so maybe you're not a physic superstar after all.' I was ticked! I said, 'Listen, I agreed to give up two days of my life because you people came calling on the phone, begging me. *I* didn't call *you*, *you* called *me*. I'm not getting paid a damn thing to help you put on your show. I thought maybe, just once, somebody in the media might actually listen to somebody who knows what he's talking about. But you don't want to do that. You just want to say 'psychic' and giggle like a teenage girl. Now, I'll tell you what. I took your round trip ticket and I'm staying at the hotel on your tab, so I'm giving you the day. You can use me or you can tell me to get lost, but what you *can't* do is make me into something that I'm not." Bowen smiled. "That got his attention. That's the way you have to talk to them, or they think they're important because they can get you on camera."

Bobby asked, "So did you do the show?"

"Oh yeah, that's what I meant, it was on last night. Naturally they cut out the important stuff and twisted the rest of it. The thing you've got to understand about media types is, the first and most important thing is to make themselves look good. That means, among other things, never look like you believe something that isn't the approved party line. So even if they do something on psychic abilities, they're careful to cover their bases by bringing in some idiot from CSICOP or something. That's what they call objectivity. The only reason I do the shows is that I figure that there's got to be a few people out there who don't believe everything they see, and maybe hearing about psychics will get them wondering whether there's more there than meets the eye."

He slowly rubbed his hands together. "But forget all that. I really didn't come down here to talk about TV twits. I want to talk about something else altogether, something you couldn't ever get somebody to talk about on TV, because they don't know what they're talking about. What I want to talk about is, *what does it mean?*

"Everybody here, or nearly everybody, already knows from personal experience that psychic abilities exist. *You* know, because you've experienced it. All right. That puts you beyond all the arguments about is it possible, is it fake, all that. You *know* they exist. But – for you and me and society and the human race – what does it *mean*, that psychic abilities exist? What does it mean for us in our personal lives, and what does it mean for society at large?"

He stood there, slowly, thoughtfully, rubbing his hands against each other. "You know, I didn't get involved in all of this voluntarily. When I was a kid, I never dreamed that any of this was possible, and I certainly never dreamed that it would become important to me. But as you probably know, when I was 35 I had a near-death experience, just like C.T. except that he was in the Caribbean skin diving when he had his, and I was in Vietnam getting shot at. But no matter how you have your NDE, it's the kind of thing that tends to change your life." He smiled as the nervous little ripple of laughter passed through the room. "When I came back to the land of the living, I learned very quickly that if I didn't want to be treated as if I was a halfwit, or crazy, I'd better keep my mouth shut. Needless to say, I wasn't the only one in that predicament, by far. I suspect the Army is riddled with closet psychics, like the rest of society. I know a few of them.

"I don't want to generalize about what happens to people after they have an NDE, I'll just stick to my own experience. In my case, I woke up being able to see people's thoughts. I don't mean see them with my physical vision of course, but I only had to look at people to know what they were thinking – especially when what they were thinking was different from what they were saying. This ability faded after a while but" – smiling – "it sure was useful to my career while it was going on."

"I'll bet you were sorry when it faded," Andrew said.

"No, actually I was just as glad to be rid of it," Bowen said. "You get tired, you know? You see what people are really thinking but it's like you're supposed to pretend that they mean what they say, and *don't* mean what you can plainly see that they *do* mean. It tended to make me really grouchy.

"Anyway, there was that, for a while. And then there were other things, the kinds of things you've probably started experiencing. And every single thing that happened was two-edged, a gift and a curse at the same time. It was new knowledge, yes, but every damn single thing raised more questions than it answered. And the farther I have gone along the path, the more I am convinced that not only do we *not* know very much, it's possible that there isn't any way we ever *can* know very much.

"Let me explain what I mean by that. For thousands of years people have been making predictions, seeing the future, knowing what was going to happen before they possibly *could* know. In earlier times people said that this was the voice of God, or maybe evil spirits, but whatever they thought, they never doubted that it was possible. After the Renaissance, as people started turning away from superstition, they went way too far, the way people always do, and they threw away the knowledge of what had been done. It's one thing to not know how something is done, but it's another thing, and not a helpful one, to say it *can't* be done therefore it *wasn't* done. But that's what society has been doing these past few hundred years."

("Go read about the Wright Brothers and the newspapers for three years after Kitty Hawk," Charlie had told me.)

"Well, if you start to become able to see things in the future, the first thing that happens is that you realize that mainstream opinion doesn't know what it's talking about. It says it can't be done, but you are doing it, and even though society thinks you must be cheating, *you* know you *aren't.*" The wolf's grin again. "Unless you are, I mean. But you *shouldn't* be cheating. You won't cheat if you want to keep whatever abilities you've re-discovered.

"But then after a while you start to question yourself. Sometimes it works, sometimes it doesn't. Why not all the time? And besides that, how can it work at all? I mean, if you look at it, how can we ever see the future when it hasn't even been created yet? The future couldn't possibly be specifically predicted, because it depends upon the free will of billions of individuals. And if you want to say that individuals don't have free will, then what are *you* doing when you're trying to see the future? Are you just a puppet? We don't *feel like* puppets.

"There's a million questions that start suggesting themselves the more you look at it. The one advantage that you have, though, because it *has* happened to you, is that you *do* know that it *does* happen. That puts you miles ahead of the philosophers and the skeptics and the debunkers and even the legitimate inquiring scientists. But it still doesn't tell you what you're doing! It still doesn't tell you what it means! It still doesn't tell you how it's possible, it doesn't tell you where the limits are, it doesn't tell you why some people can do it and some people can't do it. Now, as it happens, I'm convinced that anybody can do it who's willing to do the work necessary to learn how to do it. But the point is, it all leads to questions and more questions, and no answers. Some people find that kind of thing frustrating."

He was looking out at us earnestly, his eyes moving from one participant to another. "Once you start thinking about what this means, your old life is dead. You're going to be living a different life than you did when you took the world for granted."

❖ 20 ❖

"Look, the best way I can answer your question is to put it this way. You've got to understand that you and your family don't live in the same world any more. I mean that literally. All the rules of life that they take for granted, and that everybody around them takes for granted, aren't really rules. They aren't real the way people think they are, and you're beginning to see that. But suppose you and I had met last Saturday at the airport, and I told you what the world looks like to me. Suppose I told you some of the things I do, and things that happened to me, things I now know that I can count on. Even if you had believed me – which you wouldn't have – it wouldn't have been real to you because you hadn't experienced it. This is one area where there is no substitute for experience.

"So when you go home to your family and friends and the people you work with, the short answer is that you *can't* explain what you've been doing. You might as well get used to the idea now. Some people it will frighten, some will just assume that you're lying, and some will want to believe you but what you are telling them is really more than they can believe just on somebody's word for it. Even if they see it happen, they won't believe it means anything.

"Let me give you an example. Most people after they leave Open Door, go through a period of several days, or a few weeks, or months, or the rest of their lives, where when they need a parking place, they find one. I don't care how long it goes on, I'll guarantee you that nine out of ten of their friends and relatives – maybe ten out of ten – will call it luck. They know it isn't faked but they don't have any explanation for it, so it's luck. After a while they may even get used to saying 'well, Jim's always able to find a parking place, he's lucky that way.' And that's just a trivial example.

❖ 21 ❖

"Well, what's this, Monday? So tomorrow you'll be spending the day with the Time Choice tapes?" He glanced over at Annette, who nodded. "Well, Time Choice is a big obstacle for some people and for others it's a big 'Aha!' And I don't know for sure what makes the difference between the way people react, but I *suspect* that ultimately it's a question of how much fear the process induces in a given individual. If they're not afraid of it, they're the kid in the candy store. If it scares them, they don't experience anything at all if they can help it. And like most things, most people are in the middle somewhere.

"Do you understand what I'm talking about here? When you set out to do a Time Choice tape, you're opening yourself up to the possibility that time isn't what it seems to be – which means that *the world* isn't what it seems to be, and *reality* isn't what it seems to be. Some people, this doesn't bother them, they just shrug their shoulders and go play. They're the lucky ones, I sometimes think. They're the guy who comes down to the debrief room and says 'well, hell, that was easy,' and the rest of you want to throw things at him. Other people, they start to play and they realize 'holy cow, it works!' – and then they start to ask themselves how *could* it work, and what does it mean that it works, and all that. These folks often wind up getting wrapped around the axle.

"But guess what! They're the ones that are the most likely to keep picking at it until they understand it a little. That's how I reacted myself. I said, 'It works but it shouldn't work. Since it works, there's something wrong with my picture of what drives what.' And to my way of thinking, that's the scientific method. You investigate, you think about what happened, you investigate some more and you think some more. If it can't happen but it does happen – there's something wrong with your model! I mean, how hard is that to understand? But you'd be amazed, how hard it is to get such a simple concept across to some people."

"There's no guarantee that at any given time you are going to have an explanation of anything. You may not have any conclusions you feel confident enough to share. All you have is a technique, a way of acquiring first-hand knowledge."

He paused, and looked at Edith. "Does that answer your question? It really isn't about passing on what you learned, because probably it can't be done. It's like educating TV hosts. The best you can do is pass on your attitude, your confidence, your example. Maybe you will inspire somebody to do some thinking, maybe you won't. Either way, it isn't really your task to change others. Your task – especially from here on in – is changing *you*."

❖ **22** ❖

Jim had left, and David was sitting in the chair that Jim would have used had he not elected to pace. David was answering something somebody said while I was mentally elsewhere. "Yeah, well, he's really something." Broad smile. "Was anybody bored? Thought not."

He listened to a couple comments, and then swung into action once more. "Okay, it's getting late. Here's the plan. We'll take a few minutes' break and then when you hear us ring the bell, go on up to your rooms and we'll do our last tape for the day, Five Questions. Just like last night, when the tape is over, we won't debrief. You can go on to sleep if you want or you can come downstairs for snacks and conversation."

I didn't really feel like doing another tape, any more than I had felt like listening to Jim Bowen. But what was I supposed to do? Claire had eaten supper, and those who didn't know would not have guessed from her appearance. She had sat through Jim's talk, apparently interested. If *she* could do it, shouldn't *I* be able to do it?

"This exercise is a little like the one we did earlier, where you asked three questions while in a state of Wider Vision, only this time, instead of you posing the questions, C.T. will do it for you. In other words, you listen to C.T.'s question and, staying in a state of Wider Vision, you listen for an answer. I think after the results you got earlier, you'll agree that it isn't unreasonable to expect that there really will be one!"

He looked around. "Okay? Anybody have any problems? All right, let's take a little break, stretch, maybe have some juice or something, and when you hear the bell head off to your rooms by way of the bathrooms, and we'll see you at breakfast if not before."

❖ 23 ❖

"I don't know what else to do but keep right on, Angelo," she said. "I knew it might come to this. Well, it has. I thought, if I'm going to die young, I want to be prepared, and that's what I'm doing here. That's why I'm going to do Bridging Over, so I don't lose my way when I die. They say that can happen. That's why C.T. created Bridging Over, you know."

"No, I don't know. The research I did before coming down to do the program consisted of reading his book and wondering how anybody could take it seriously."

She smiled. "Surprise."

"Surprise is right! And I don't even *believe* in past lives! But – " I choked up, looked around to be sure nobody was paying any attention to us, standing in a corner of the room. " – but now, what, we're going to do it again? You're going to have to leave when I've just found you?"

"But it wouldn't have been the same anyway, my love. That was a different time, different people. We're married, and not to each other."

"You keep saying that. You know it's only half true."

She looked away. "Maybe. But even then it isn't that simple. Jeff and I have an old connection too. He told me he got a clear sense of it in that last tape, but of course he didn't want to talk about it in front of everybody. I haven't experienced it yet, but something tells me he's right. There's *some* tie between us. So there's a part of myself that belongs with him, as well as a part that belongs with you. Suppose my tie to him turns out to be as strong as the tie you and I are discovering? Then what do we do? And besides, nobody would understand what we're talking about, and they wouldn't allow for it. Not my husband, certainly. Not my daughter. And what about my ties to *them*? I can't be tearing up my life. I don't have that much time left."

"No, I know. And I don't want to make anything harder than it already is. But what are we going to *do*?"

"I guess we're going to do the program. And then you'll go back to New Jersey and I'll go back to Texas and maybe we'll see each other again and maybe not."

Annette rang the bell. "We've got to go," Claire said.

"I'll see you after the tape? You'll come down?"

"I'll come down. We can talk."

❖ 24 ❖

Lying in darkness, tears in my eyes, listening to the hissing, crackling pink noise.

C.T.'s voice, bringing us through the preparation process.

Instead of lying here figuring nothing's going to happen, now I'm afraid it will!

Whose agenda were we following here? The previous tape had led me to feel an even stronger connection to Claire than before – and then I find out that she's got cancer. And now we're going to ask some more questions? *Where is this leading?* It's funny how you can go from disbelieving in something to dreading it, practically without transition.

"Here is your first question," C.T. said. "'Who am I?' Holding yourself firmly in the state of Wider Vision, a state of expanded awareness, ask the question. Ask it firmly, with full expectation that you will receive an answer, the proper answer for *you*. Ask the universe your question. 'Who am I?' Ask it now."

All right, I'll play. Sort of bracing myself, I formed the question in my mind. *Who am I?*

Right away, the word "translator" formed clearly in my mind, and I waited for more. But time passed, among the pink noise, and nothing else came.

C.T.'s voice returned. "You will remember the answer. When you return to normal waking consciousness, you will remember the answer that you got to your question, 'Who am I?' Now rest for a moment."

I lay there, resting. *Translator? Maybe this tape isn't going to measure up to the one where I ask my own questions.*

"Now here is your second question. 'Who was I before I entered this physical body?' Again, holding yourself in a state of expanded awareness, ask the question. 'Who was I before I entered this physical body?'"

Well, that's crazy! Despite myself, I had to smile. According to whoever is on the other end of the line here, I was John Denver! I had gotten an image of a man sitting in a lumber yard, and his name was John Denver.

I tried to alter the name, feeling for another name, but it wouldn't alter. John Denver? *All right, a metaphor, fine: What are you trying to tell me?* But nothing came. There was just this man sitting amid a pile of felled timber. John Denver.

"When you return to normal waking consciousness, you will remember the answer that you got to your question, 'Who was I before I entered this physical body?' Now rest for a moment."

Again I lay there, resting. *John Denver??*

"Here is your third question. 'What is the purpose for my existence in physical-matter reality?'"

An image of myself as priest, performing a marriage ceremony. *Huh! Wonder what* that *means!* Again, I waited for more, and no more came.

"You will remember the answer that you received. Rest now."

What does that make, three? Okay. I lay there neutrally. *Amazing how calming this is, this process.* I wondered what answers Claire was getting.

"Now ask, 'What action can I now take to best serve the purpose?' Ask the question, 'What action can I now take to best serve the purpose?' Ask it now."

"Just do it."

That's it*? Just do it?* But that's all that came. I waited for more, but there was only blankness. I reviewed the message I'd gotten. Translator, John

Denver (!), priest, "Just do it." Again I thought, *maybe I'd be better off asking my own questions.*

"You will remember the answer to your question, 'What action can I now take to best serve the purpose?'"

Another pause, another period of floating, mind and emotions in neutral.

"And now here is your final question. Holding yourself firmly in the state of Wider Vision, a state of expanded awareness, ask the question firmly, with full expectation that you will receive the proper answer for *you*. Ask the universe, 'What is the content of the most important message I can receive and understand at this point?' Ask it now."

I ask, and immediately I see an image. It's a very clear image, no ambiguity or fuzziness. It's a very tight close-up picture of a man's head and shoulders, and it is as though I hear a voice (but I don't *hear* a voice; it is *as though* I hear a voice) saying "You are not alone."

The image expands a bit, and I can see that he is in a boat, rowing steadily. "You are not alone," that voice that is not a voice says.

The image expands a bit more, as if we were watching a long-distance camera shot retreating from the scene. *Like that close-up of the wounded in Atlanta in* Gone with the Wind. The camera pulls back, and I can see that he is rowing in a lake. "You are not alone," I hear.

The image keeps expanding, and I see from a larger and larger focus, as if the camera were pulling back, rising farther and farther into the air. I see that the lake is surrounded by wooded hills, and the voiceless voice says, "you are not alone." The camera keeps pulling back, and the rowboat is too small to be seen. Soon the lake itself is too small to be seen, and all that is in sight is a vast expanse of trees and hills, and the voice continues to repeat, "you are not alone." I know that in the middle of the picture the man is still rowing, unseen. Yet the voice continues to insist, with no one in sight, "you are not alone, you are not alone, you are not alone, you are not alone, you are not alone, you are not alone." How many times do the words repeat? Twenty? Thirty? Fifty?

"When you return to normal waking consciousness, you will remember the answer. You will return now to normal waking consciousness. You will return to normal waking consciousness, as I guide you." And back I came, moved. But I looked over at Bobby and I could see that I shouldn't ask if he'd had a good experience. Bobby was struggling, and I would have helped him if I could have, but I had no words that would have helped.

❖ 25 ❖

If I'd been in her situation, I don't know if I would have been much concerned about someone else's tape experience, but she took one look at me and saw something, and wanted to know. "Give," she said mischievously. Turnabout. So I told her the answers I'd gotten.

"A translator," she said. "What's a translator, Angelo?"

"Well anybody knows what a translator is!"

She smiled at me. "Allow me to remind you that I am a trained psychotherapist. What do you suppose we do for a living?"

"I don't know. Mess up people's minds, I suppose, to keep the cash flowing in."

She didn't laugh out loud but I saw it. "Maybe, but when we're not doing that, we help people interpret messages they get from within. The unconscious speaks in symbols, and if we want to know what it has to tell us, we need to learn its language. So whenever a symbol comes up, whether in a dream or a vision or even a fantasy, we ask what that symbol means. And how they answer the question tells us a lot."

"You mean it's a trick question, like?"

"No it's not a trick question! It's perfectly straightforward."

"Then how can it tell you anything? I mean, if I see a telephone or somebody else sees a telephone, that's what it is, regardless."

"You might think so, my friend, but you'd be wrong. What's a telephone to you?"

"It's a way to talk to people."

"To you, maybe. But to somebody else, it might be how they stay in contact with their family in another country. And to somebody else, maybe it's connected with bad news they got once."

"And maybe it's a bookie!"

"Maybe it is. Don't you suppose that a bookie's unconscious mind would use the telephone to tell him something different from what it would tell a CIA agent, say, or a roofing contractor?"

"Yeah, but – "

"There isn't any room here for 'yeah but.' That's how it works. You'll see. What's a translator?"

"It's somebody who listens to something and turns it into another language."

"All right, and why does he do that?"

"So that people who can't speak the first language can understand what the other person is saying."

"Yes, and?"

"And what?"

"When something gets translated people understand something they couldn't understand before. And what else happens?"

I shrugged. "And I don't know what."

"The speaker is able to make himself understood to those others. It's a two-way process, a two-way benefit, don't you see?"

"I do now that you tell me, yes."

"So how are you a translator?"

"I translate news events into something people can read?" It felt like a stretch, but I was trying.

"Perhaps. But do you think it could have a wider application than that, perhaps?"

"No, but clearly *you* do. What?"

She was smiling at me again. "That's not the way it works."

"What, am I going to get I-don't-know-what-do-you-think from you, too?"

"More or less. What *I* think doesn't much matter here, it's what *you* think. I have a hunch what it means – I've interpreted probably thousands of dreams – but *you're* the expert on you."

"Then God help us," I said. "Maybe it means more than that, but if so I don't know what."

"Well, let's go on to the second answer. Who is John Denver? To *you*, I mean."

I pondered. "John Denver? Well, I guess I see him as a spiritual man who enjoys his life and tries to wake people up with his singing."

"*Very* good! Do you care to draw any analogies?"

"Claire, speaking here to your very best interests – you have to trust me on this – you *don't* want to hear me sing."

"All right, it's not my job to smoke you out. You'll get it or you won't. What's a lumber yard?"

"I wondered about that myself. It's just a place where they stack up dead trees to put them to other uses, I suppose."

"And dead trees?"

I shrugged. "I don't know. Something that was alive, and grew, and got chopped down so people could make something out of them."

"Mm-hmm. And the reason that symbol is connected in your mind with John Denver when you asked who you were before?"

This was hard work! Perhaps hardest was not throwing up my hands in impatience and saying maybe it didn't have to mean anything special. But I knew that would hurt her, somehow. So I gave it some earnest thought. "Well, I don't know. Maybe it's saying I was a spiritual man who worked at recycling things."

"Maybe. Can you think of a more symbolic meaning?"

"Actually, no, I can't."

"How about being a priest, marrying people? How does that answer the question about why you're here in this life?"

It had me frowning. "Actually, that's sort of a form of translating, isn't it? Or transforming, say."

"Yes! Yes, it is! See, you can do this."

"Joining people together, taking two individuals and making them part of a team. Although, I can't see that that's what I'm doing, particularly."

"Maybe that doesn't refer to the past. Maybe it's a hint for you, another way your life may be moving."

"Huh! That's a thought. I assume it doesn't literally mean I'm going to become a priest, because I'm not going to."

"Nobody can tell you what it means, Angelo. Sit with it. True messages always come clear, sooner or later, if you honor them and sincerely want to hear whatever they have to say. So what about 'Just do it'?"

I laughed and shook my head. "Sounds to me like a formula for getting into trouble."

"Maybe it is. Is that *all* it is? Why did you get that phrase when you asked what you can do to serve the purpose of marrying people?"

"Well – " slowly, as I thought it through – "I suppose it *might* mean, when I figure out what I'm supposed to be doing, don't spend a lot of time trying to figure out where it would bring me – and more to the point where it would *leave* me – but just experience it and find out first hand. But that's just me guessing."

"Who better than you, since it's your answer? And then that wonderful final message, Angelo. What a gift. I don't suppose it gave you a lot of trouble, figuring that one out."

"No," I said, "and I find it very comforting."

"You notice, you couldn't *see* anybody else there, but you knew they *were* there?"

"Oh yes. And even I got it when they said 'you are not alone' about 150 times."

"That's one of the things that makes our lives hard, that sense of being alone. Secular people don't have the sense of connection to another being that cares for them that religious people have. It sounds to me that you're being told, it's really true."

"Maybe, but that doesn't mean the connection is the way the religious people say it is."

"No. But it does say that there's *something*." She was silent for a long moment. "It's very comforting, really, that thought. It may be the most comforting thing I've heard so far. We're not alone." She shivered. "I think I needed to hear that. Thank you. We're not alone, even when we feel alone. I'm going to hold on to that."

I cleared my throat. "Hate to sound melodramatic," I said. "But you know if there's anything I can do to help, count me in. Right?"

"I know. I don't know what it could be, but I do know that if I ask you, you'll be there."

"You got that right. In fact, I'll be there whether you ask or not, if you're not careful."

She smiled at me. "Well, you know, careful is one of my problems. Every once in a while I'm prone to absolute recklessness."

"Good," I said. "Let's try for that."

She smiled again. "But for now, let's go help decimate the snacks." She didn't say it, but I distinctly got the impression she was saying, *I need to be among a lot of people, preferably people laughing.*

❖ 26 ❖

Somebody had found a chessboard, and apparently Francois and Andrew had been at it a while. A few minutes after Claire and I sat down at one of the tables, Andrew turned down his king and got up from his chair.

"Angelo," Tony said. "You're a sophisticated man of the world, dweller among the Eastern establishment, acknowledged Ace Reporter, and all that. Maybe *you* can take on Francois. Aha, Andrew, look at his eyes light up!"

"Do I take it that you yokels want a demonstration of how the game is really played?" I raised an eyebrow at Francois, who gestured toward the chair Andrew had been sitting in.

"You've just been nominated as the Great English Hope," Bobby said.

"Good, except I'm Italian."

"Yeah, but you *speak* English, more or less," Jeff said.

"Oh, like *you'd* know." I glanced at Claire, and she nodded, smiling. "Okay, Francois, let me get some coffee and some goodies, and you're on." I picked the fist that held the white pawn, and so we began a long, intricate game. Francois was experienced, and he was subtle, and perhaps it had been as long for him since he'd had a good opponent as it had for me, so we were soon playing mostly in silence, with Klaus and Bobby and Andrew following intently. Jeff watched for a while, then drifted over to sit next to Claire at the next table. It was no trouble to divide my attention between calculating moves and listening to the other conversations going on, and I found it all equally interesting. So it went something like this.

Moved the white bishop instead of the knight. Hmm.

"And Edith, I owe you a debt of gratitude," Elizabeth said. "Our little conversation after lunch helped me immensely." (It's funny how you can tell when somebody changes who they're talking to even if you're not looking at them.) "I had had a tape experience that upset me, and Edith showed me another way to look at it." A pause. Embarrassment, maybe? I looked over to see, but she was mostly facing away from me. I could see only the smallest part of her face. "I won't go into how it went but it amounted to this. I realized that I don't know *anything*."

That sounded fairly anguished – but, again, I couldn't see her expression, and besides, Francois was looking like he was making a move.

Huh! I could get tired of that bishop. If I don't find a way to take the initiative soon, I'm going to get clobbered.

"That's being a little hard on yourself, isn't it?" Jane, I think.

"No, really, that's the literal truth. I've looked for so many years, through so many books, and done so many programs." *Aha! I knew she was a seminar hopper!* "And when we were doing the questions tape I asked if I would ever find the truth – and the answer was very clearly no."

"That *would* be upsetting," Jane said.

"The worst thing was, I knew it was true. All these years, all those books! And I don't *really* know *anything*!" I heard her voice soften. "And Edith, bless her, when I told her that, said when we realize we don't know anything, then we can begin to learn, but as long as we think we already know, there's no real opening for us."

"Good work," somebody said.

"I was drawing on personal experience, believe me," Edith said.

Well, this *could be a crashing blunder, if he can counter it. But it sure ought to throw him off.* I took Francois' king's bishop's pawn with my bishop, and had the satisfaction of hearing Bobby gasp. "Why'd you do *that?*"

"It's a sacrifice," Andrew said with artistic appreciation. "Stop the king from castling, break up his formation."

"Yeah, but a bishop for a pawn?"

"Watch."

"I'm beginning to think that maybe the most important part of the program isn't the tape experiences but the other people." I looked up in surprise. It was Roberta Harrison Sellers, answering something I hadn't noticed. "Just as Edith helped Elizabeth, I want to acknowledge you, Helene. I am not ready to talk about it in public, but as you know I too had a very upsetting thing happen today – and talking to you helped me so much. You have so much wisdom, I can't tell you."

Helene's voice was dry and intellectual as always, but I could hear that she was pleased. "You overestimate me. I merely pointed out what was there to be seen. It is my profession, after all." A pause. Perhaps she had to overcome something before she could say the next bit. "Just – well, remember that I'm working on my own 'stuff,' just like everybody else. I'm not any farther on the path than you are, and maybe not as far. Besides, helping you helped me, and perhaps by the end of the week I'll find it in me to tell you how, and how much."

Watch, now! You're down two points, you can't afford to be careless. But on the other hand you've got to keep him on the defensive or you're dead.

I looked up and noticed that Jeff and Claire had moved to another table and were deep into a quiet intense conversation. You'd think that might have bothered me, but it didn't. It felt good, like she was being cared for while I was otherwise occupied.

Did he just make a mistake, or is it a trap?

Sort of how we must feel in the next world if we see some former love happily engaged with someone. "If I'm not there for you, my love, I'm glad you have someone, and you're not alone."

Klaus was closely watching the game, but he turned aside at something somebody said. "Yes, I learned this many years ago, but today's tape wrote the line under it for me too. We are here to help each other. This is the part of my practice that I love. When someone walks away and I know that I have helped him, this feels very good."

There. That evens the field, at least.

Francois looked up from the board. "Man was made to love and cherish and assist, and those who look for happiness in things or pleasures or power are very foolish."

Klaus nodded. "Yes. This is true. My entire life tells me this – when I forget, as well as when I remember."

And, after quite a while, when most of the others had gone to bed –

Francois smiled and tipped over his king. "Excellent, my friend. Very engaging."

"Yes, that was great. Best game I've played in ages. Tomorrow night, another game, maybe?"

"It would be a pleasure."

"While we were in the thick of things there, in a way I didn't care who won, just so the game went on."

"Like life, a bit, perhaps, eh?"

CHAPTER FOUR

Tuesday
March 21, 1995

"I know what everybody'd say I'm supposed to *do*, and what I'm supposed to *feel*, and what I'm supposed to turn my back on. What I *don't* know is how I'm supposed to do it."

"Be a pretty good time to get drunk, sounds like."

"Boy would it. The only trouble is, getting drunk is like having sex. It doesn't solve anything and it doesn't last and afterwards you're that much farther behind."

Jeff smiled. "Well, yeah, but other than that."

I laughed despite myself. "Other than that, a primo solution."

"Except they also don't allow hooch on premises." A pause while we drank coffee and looked out at the mountains.

It was too much. In the first place, not to put too fine a point on it, I was in love with her. I loved everything I knew about her. Infatuation? Maybe, but I didn't think so. It wasn't sexual excitement – I knew more or less what *that* was worth in the long run! It was more like living with a sound like a dentist's drill incessantly whining, and then having it stop. She soothed me, somehow, just by her presence. Which would be great if she and I were single.

Which led to "in the second place." My being in love with her didn't have anything to do with anything. There was no future in it, for either of us. She wasn't going to leave her husband and I wasn't going to leave my wife. My home life was terrible, but I couldn't imagine leaving the kids without their father. And even in practical terms, I didn't make enough money to be able to afford child support and alimony and a place for myself. Besides, she wasn't about to break up her home.

And in the third place, she was going to die, and she was going to do it hundreds of miles from me, married to another man, concentrating on her soon-to-be orphaned child.

I thought of thirty years of marriage. Thirty years without rest, without comfort in each other, without easy understanding and mutual support. Thirty years without peace or contentment. Her fault? Hardly. Not mine either, really. We'd picked the wrong partners. My fault more than ours, probably: I'd been so *eager*, so hot-blooded. It hadn't occurred to me that marriage should be between two people who could *share* their lives, rather than silently endure incompatibles. Our life together – supposedly together – had turned into one in which what I loved she feared or hated, what I instinctively understood left her baffled, what she deeply believed in, I silently scoffed at. We tried marriage counseling; we gritted our teeth and endured for the sake of the children we loved, and the years went by, and ahead I saw only the prospect of more of the same.

"So how are you going to handle it, do you think?"

"I guess I'm going to do the program and spend as much time with her as I can, unless it starts to bother her, and then after that – " A sudden surge of anger caught me by surprise. "After that I suppose she'll go her way and I'll go mine and we'll never see each other again and that'll be everybody's happy ending. No family disruptions, no tragedies, just some careful memories. Think that's how I should play it?"

He put up a hand. "Hey, don't aim it at me. I'm not telling you what to do: I don't have the slightest *idea* what you ought to do, and if I did you wouldn't listen, and why should you?" He saw that my anger had abated. "And I care for her too."

I breathed out, a long breath. "Yeah, Jeff, I know you do. Sorry."

"Nothing to be sorry about, I'm just sorry you're hurting."

What kind of trick is this, God? Finally show me a sympathetic feminine ear, let me scarcely get used to the idea – and take it away. Not only take it away 1000 miles, but take it out of the world entirely!

I was holding my coffee in my left hand. My right hand was gripping the wooden railing hard enough to make the tendons stand out against the back of my hand. "It's just, there ought to be *something* somebody could do!"

"Oh, man, you don't want to get into that, it's the oldest story in the world. Every day people die, and every day the people they leave behind are asking, why them, why now, why this way. There's never an answer and there's never going to be. It's just the way it is."

"Maybe it's the way it is, but it sucks."

Jeff shrugged, finished his coffee. "Nobody's going to give you any argument on that." He saw me pull out my inhaler. "You need to go inside?"

"No, it's a little too cold out here, but at home I never get to see early morning in the mountains. I don't want to miss it." I sprayed the stuff into the back of my mouth while inhaling, held the breath as long as I could, gulping once in an attempt to bring down as much of the spray as I could. "Goddamn thing," I said. "It didn't feel like I got anything that time. I shook it again, tried a second time." *Side effects – but on the other hand it's nice to be able to breathe, too.* "God *damn* the goddamn thing! I think it's empty."

"That a problem, or do you have a refill?"

"I ought to have a refill upstairs. I'll get it before we go to breakfast."

"What do you do when you're caught somewhere without the inhaler?"

I shook my head. "*That* is a situation I don't let myself get into."

❖ 2 ❖

I hadn't expected her to discuss it, and perhaps she wouldn't have if the conversation hadn't turned to health problems, which it wouldn't have done, or anyway might not have done, if I hadn't been wheezing slightly as I brought my tray to the table. Claire heard it, looked up at me, and I saw that she was concerned. *Isn't that just like her? How important is my wheezing, next to what she's faced with, but she's concerned about me wheezing.* I put down my tray and went over to the machine to get a mug of coffee. Annette was there, filling her mug. She heard it too, and looked at me, and asked if

I was okay. I nodded and let her fill my mug. "It'll go away in a bit," I said, hoping it was true.

Claire was sitting next to Toni Shaw, who was sitting next to Dottie whatever-her-name-was. As I sat down, Klaus Bishof and Sam Andover joined us. Claire already knew me well enough to know I didn't like to talk about my asthma, but the others didn't. Sam said, "What's with your breathing this morning? Been running?"

"No," I said shortly, saving my breath. "It's just like this sometimes."

Toni Shaw said, "Asthma?" When I nodded she said, "Thought so. I had it for years." When Claire asked her what happened, she said she finally outgrew it, and I said, "I'm a little too old for that, I'm afraid."

I was breathing in a steady rhythm, eating slowly and keeping my lungs as calm as I could. *How could I forget to pack the refill?*

Then I remembered, *There isn't any refill! I forgot about getting to the pharmacy! I never gave it a thought!*

That was unbelievable. Yes, I'd been busy getting ready for a week at Open Door, and yes there had been that Barnes story and the follow-up, but how could I forget to get a refill? It's the kind of thing that I just wouldn't let happen. (*And,* I would think later, such *a coincidence, that it would happen in time for Open Door.*)

Klaus was sitting opposite me. "I wonder, perhaps it was your health situation I saw Saturday night, the thing I saw that I thought I must talk about for someone there."

"Remind me," I said.

"I remember," Claire said. "You saw a skull superimposed on your body, extending from your breast to your navel."

"Yes. This is it, exactly."

"You were embarrassed to talk about it, but you thought you should because it might concern somebody in the group. I meant to thank you for doing that. I don't think it concerned Angelo, I think it meant me. I've had breast cancer, and I'm doing Open Door so I can do Bridging Over, just in case I need it."

For a moment nobody knew what to say. Then Toni said, "You think Klaus' vision is warning you that it will come back?"

I held my breath (metaphorically) but Claire merely said, "It could, of course. That's always a possibility. I took it as a confirmation that I was doing the right thing, being here. I'm sorry I forgot to thank you for carrying the message, Klaus."

He made a gesture with his hands, embarrassed. "Today I do not know why it was so great an effort, to tell people. But it seemed then a big step."

"Yeah, since then we've all gotten jaded," Sam said. "'Say, I had a vision.' 'Did you? Thank you for sharing, and who cares?'" We laughed – even I laughed, though it made me cough. "It's old stuff, now. You want to get our attention today, you're going to have to bi-locate or something. No, actually, Angelo's already done that. It's going to take more than that. Levitate, I suppose."

True enough, I thought.

Toni put what I was thinking into words. "We've only been doing this a couple of days, and we've raised the bar that far. I hate to think what we'll think is normal by tomorrow morning, let alone Thursday, or Friday."

(I was *thinking* the same thing, but I wasn't really *feeling* it yet, and I hadn't yet had enough experience to know how thinking, alone, differs from thinking combined with feeling.)

"Yep," Sam said, "by Friday, logic will be out the window completely."

"Hope not!" That was Claire. "What good would it do to sharpen our intuition and abandon logic?"

"Isn't that the ideal of the New Age movement? Connect directly to other realms and everything else be damned?"

Claire gave him a skeptical look. "You're in a feisty mood today, aren't you? You know that nobody here thinks that." *Oh yeah? Selena's at the next table, Claire!*

Klaus was smiling and serious. "I think of it this way. We have two parts to our being. We have an upper level that communes with spirits and a lower level that lives in the world. If the two levels do not communicate, we live all in this world or we live – with some difficulty, I would say – primarily in the other world."

"Upstairs and downstairs, eh? Sounds like English television to me." I was pretty clear that Klaus didn't understand the reference, but the rest of us at the table laughed, so he smiled. "This is how it seems to me," he said.

"I like that idea," I said. "It does make sense of what we're doing here: We are establishing diplomatic relations with other parts of ourselves."

Toni said, "That's a very interesting idea. Yesterday we were asking three questions, remember? I asked, 'What am I here at Open Door to learn? What new paths might it open up?' I got an answer that I thought was pretty hopeful. I was looking at my canvasses, and thinking how dirty and smeary they were, and I changed them just by thinking about them, and then they were new and bright and very attractive. And then I saw some pots I had made, and they were cracked, and crumbly, and the glazing was deeply flawed. I was almost embarrassed, except that I somehow knew that it wasn't my carelessness that made them that way. Again, I *thought about* them, I *looked* at them a certain way, and the cracks were healed, and the crumbled places were sound, and the glazing was perfect. Very encouraging, wouldn't you say?"

"Yes indeed," Dottie said.

"Yes, but now I'm starting to think, maybe it wasn't only about my art. I'm starting to wonder if it could be my life in general."

"In other words," Claire said, "your health."

"Yes. It doesn't make sense, in a way, but I wonder if it could be a promise. Maybe there's more possible than I have been thinking. I don't know about the rest of you, but every time I do a tape, it becomes clearer and clearer that I don't really know what's possible and what isn't."

❖ 3 ❖

"Tuesday is all about Time Choice," Annette said, smiling, "but first let's talk about last night's Wider Vision experiences. You were sent to ask five questions. Does anybody want to talk about their experience?"

A moment's pause, then Elizabeth from Elizabeth spoke, softly as always. "I think we are extraordinarily fortunate to have a psychiatrist and a psychotherapist among us – and you too, Annette, of course, but I mean among the participants. In response to the questions, I got images I couldn't make much sense of, but then Helene showed me that they could be looked at as symbols, and she helped me to see what those symbols meant to me, and all of a sudden the answers made sense."

I reached over to Claire, sitting next to me, and touched her hand in acknowledgement. She smiled, not taking her eyes off Elizabeth, and slipped her hand into mine, and I was very glad to sit there with us holding hands like school kids.

Elizabeth talked about her visions, and what she thought they amounted to. I had to admit, they seemed right: Basically they said that she was being too timid about life, that she needed to push rather than drift, and they told her *why* she was too timid, though the imagery she described wouldn't have told *me* anything. Then Dee West – who rarely spoke in debrief – said that she had had a somewhat similar set of images, and a somewhat similar message, though what she got out of them was that she would not be using her natural gifts for empathy correctly until she took more initiative with people. That isn't the way she put it, of course, but that's what it amounted to, and looking at her and her behavior I was ready to say that the message was right and she'd heard it right.

Then Roberta Harrison Sellers talked about the messages she'd been given and oddly I got the feeling that although she was relating what she'd seen, she hadn't really heard what she was being told. *Silly to think so, though. Surely she's better informed about her life than I am!* And after Roberta finished, several more people chimed in to talk about one or more of the answers they'd received. Most of us didn't, but it seemed clear enough to me that few if any of the participants had gone through the tape without receiving at least something.

"What *I* would like, what would help *me*," Tony said, "is something clear, something first-hand, something tangible, not something I have to take on faith."

"Good luck," Andrew laughed.

"No, seriously. If this stuff is real – and I'm sure it is – why should we have to be groping around in the dark like this? Why shouldn't it be clear as day?"

"It doesn't come that way," Selena said.

"But I am saying, why *doesn't* it?"

Annette said, "That's a good question, Tony, and it deserves an answer. Let me put on my psychotherapist's hat, for a moment. We're involved here in learning to translate between our conscious and unconscious minds. That's a skill that has to be learned. A few people seem to be born with the knack, but mostly it has to be learned. Here's why.

"You may not have heard this number, but they know now that the conscious mind can process about 42 bits of information a second. The subconscious processes 42 *million* bits in that same time. That's a one-million-to-one differential. If you imagine somebody trying to talk to you a million times slower than you, or a million times faster, you can imagine it might cause some problems!"

"Wow," Andrew said. "I *guess!*"

"I think that's why the two parts of our mind communicate in symbols – dreams from the unconscious side, meditation on images from the conscious side. But you can see, there's going to be slippage, particularly when we're just learning the process."

A million to one. We sat there absorbing it

"Let's take a short break," David said, all but looking at the watch he wasn't wearing, "and then we'll come back and talk about the morning's first tape."

❖ **4** ❖

"Okay. Time Choice." David looked over at Ellis Sinclair. "Remember Ellis, I said to you yesterday I thought you were on the next page?"

"Yes, I didn't understand what you meant by that."

"I'm not surprised. Give ear, and all shall be explained, because here we are. Sunday was devoted to Entry State, and yesterday was Wider Vision. Today, we play with Time Choice. And if past experience is any guide, some of you are going to say, 'Well finally, something I can get my teeth into, instead of just sitting dead in the water listening to how everybody else had fun while I was trying to get my car started.' So to speak."

Annette laughed. "Somewhere amid those mixed metaphors, there's an important insight hiding, and it's simply that one man's meat is another man's poison. Different people thrive on different mental states. Just as some people would never in a million years go out of their way to experience altered states of consciousness, so others love one kind of altered state – Entry State, for instance – and don't have any use for another kind, like Wider Vision."

"So an engineer, say – and Ellis, I think you probably still have an engineer's mind-set – might find himself at sea while we're exploring Entry State, and suddenly have profound and meaningful experiences in Wider Vision."

"That certainly was true for me," Ellis said. "In fact, somebody pointed out to me that I seemed to gravitate toward Wider Vision. Angelo, I think it was."

"Well," Annette said, "today we move into an area that some people are going to think is the Twilight Zone, but others will probably take to like ducks to water."

"I don't think your metaphors are anything to write home about either, Annette." They both laughed. "In any case, Ellis, yesterday you experienced an intuitive sense of an ongoing connection between past and present, though perhaps you weren't thinking of it that way. You thought you were continuing to pay the price of getting caught stealing horses, if I remember rightly." He smiled through the little laugh he got.

"Let's talk about time. For the purposes of doing these tapes, we suggest that you consider that perhaps time isn't quite what we commonly think it to be, and neither is our own situation relative to time. Consider the possibility that past and present and future all exist – all the time, so to speak. Usually we think of the past ceasing to exist and the future not yet starting to exist, and the razor-thin present moment being the only thing that exists, always moving and always becoming the past. Just for now, consider what time and space would look like from a perspective *outside of* time and space. Obviously if you're not inside time, then one moment of time is going to be as real as another. In other words there won't be just one 'real' moment and all the others unreal. They'll all be real, in the same way that all places are real and don't cease to exist just because we in our bodies are elsewhere. And if all times always exist, perhaps other times can be accessed, if you know how to do it. We just happen to have a magic carpet available, for those who are so inclined. So, today's the day we give you your choice: Either you're crazy or we're crazy or we're all crazy together."

For some reason I started to think I had an idea of where they were going with this. I thought: *Crazy is right! If all times really continue to exist, rather than only the present. . . ..* But then Bobby weighed in with one of his technical questions that I never did get the meaning of, the kind of question that they always declined to answer, and the moment passed.

❖ 5 ❖

So for the first time we went up to experience Time Choice. First pink noise, of course. C.T.'s relaxation instructions. Moving to Entry State, then Wider Vision, then following to the new territory that he called Time Choice.

What did it feel like? Just as when we first experienced the other two states, at first nothing was clear. Was I feeling something definite, something different? Was I sliding into and out of that state? Was I moving at all? Was I letting my willingness turn into eagerness, and then into making it up? I tried to analyze it even as I tried to remain receptive, a delicate balance. The best I could do was to compare it to the place we go when we are lost in reverie.

And then there was the usual return to Entry State, and a pause, and a second run up to the new state, and a return, and a third run. Each time we made the moves, C.T.'s voice was advising us how to encode little memory keys that would enable us (hopefully) to return later, at will.

As I had expected, nothing very special happened. Fragments. Drifting. Half-seen, half-thought, half-imagined half experiences. Confusion, in other words, the confusion of first glimpses before you have any way to organize things.

I did think of various people I'd lost to death, starting long ago in my childhood with my grandparents, and for some reason the losses seemed particularly sharp and new. But whether that was a peculiarity of Time Choice or not, I couldn't say. Even at the time, I thought, *it could just as easily be emotional resonances from Claire's situation.*

❖ 6 ❖

"Anybody?"

"Annette?" Edith Fontaine, our massage therapist. "Is it typical that people get just, like, snapshots?"

"I'm not sure what you mean." *I-don't-know-what-do-you-think.*

"Well, I got this one really clear picture of some women eating around a table, a table like the serving-tables here, but there wasn't any action in it, and no follow-up or anything. And after C.T. talked us down and back up again, I asked to see the same scene, but it didn't come."

"Maybe you got what you need from that one snapshot, Edith. Have you thought about treating it like a dream?"

"I guess I don't really know how to do that."

"It isn't anything complicated. You take every element and consider that it is a meaningful symbol in itself, and is meaningful in the context of the rest of the picture, and ask what those symbols mean to you. So you have women, and eating, and a table that reminds you of our serving tables. Put all that together and see if you can intuit how your unconscious mind would use them to tell you something. If you want, I'll be glad to work with you during the break. In fact" – speaking to us all – "that's something I'll do with anybody who is interested. First try to figure it out on your own, but if you get stuck come talk to me and we'll see what we can do. And of course Helene and Claire know how it's done, and maybe they'll be willing to help."

"But in any case," David said, "to answer your primary question, yes, it's common enough for people to report single pictures like that – but it's just as common for people to see sequences, or to have several seemingly unconnected visions that actually tell a story or make a point once they're linked together."

Edith frowned, thinking. "Now that you mention it, there was another scene that I couldn't make anything of, something that gave me the sense that a funeral was involved, and when I think of the two scenes together, there is a sense of the women eating as you would after a funeral. But I don't have any idea whose funeral it might have been. It didn't seem to be set in our times, in any case. But I don't know anything else about it."

"Patience," David said. "That's why we make you do more than one tape in Time Choice!"

Annette said, "Anybody else?"

"Yeah, me I guess," Tony said. His voice was quite unusually subdued. "I saw myself after I drowned." That would have been a great opportunity for someone to make a wisecrack, if he hadn't seemed so somber. "I guess I had been paddling a canoe, alone, at nighttime, and the canoe overturned. I got a quite vivid impression of the panic and the sheer physical unpleasantness of drowning, with the lungs filling with water instead of air. The helplessness of it, you know? And I saw my body being carried, face upward, by some people I didn't know. I could see my naked upper body, glistening, covered with beads of water. Whoever were carrying me thought I was dead, but I could hear their thoughts loud and clear. It was still nighttime." He shook himself like a dog shaking off water. "Creepy, I can tell you that."

"Humph," Bobby said. "Could you see your surroundings?"

"I was heading south, I know that much, and I was paddling down some strange artificial waterway, very wide, very straight, very calm. As I think about it, it was like a ditch, but a ditch as wide as a four-lane highway."

"You think it was another life?"

"Well I don't remember drowning in this one!"

Andrew grinned and said, "Yes but maybe it wasn't a past-life experience. Maybe it was more like a dream, a metaphor."

"It didn't feel like a dream. It felt like a spontaneous recollection of drowning."

Lou said, "But how would you know?"

"Well, actually, in this life I did almost drown once, when I was a kid, so I know the feeling. I've been afraid of drowning ever since, actually. But I love canoeing and I don't have any fear of canoes. If this were a real memory of a past life, wouldn't you think there would be some fear of canoes left?"

"Or fear of big ditches, anyway," Lou said.

"Maybe it was a glimpse of your future," someone said.

"Don't know, but I hope not. It wasn't a very pleasant way to go."

We sat there in silence for a minute, then Andrew said, "Well, since we're talking about weird experiences, I was looking at a room, packed with people, and there was this woman standing under an archway, or in a doorway, or something. I tried to ask her where I was and what was going on, and I started to see pale images superimposed over her face. After a while I got the idea that I was watching her thoughts! I mean, every time she thought of something, I was seeing an image of it. Not that I could prove it, of course, but there was this great certainty. I can't understand what that was all about, and I wonder if you have any ideas about it."

David made a big deal of looking at him intently, and opening his mouth as if to say something, and pausing. Andrew said: "I don't know, what do you think?" and David nodded and smiled and closed his mouth and we all laughed. "But seriously," David said, "I *don't* know. That's why we say it so much, because it's true. We've been exploring these things for what, 20 years or so? What do we know? It's like asking Columbus what the New World is like when he just got back from his first voyage. Or maybe it's like asking him what Ohio was like, say, or California. We're only at the beginning of exploring all this. You guys are explorers, not tourists, and we're all exploring together."

"But you must have some ideas."

"Sure, and I'm willing to give them to you, as long as you keep firmly in mind that they're just my thoughts on the subject and *I don't know*. So if you ask me what it means that you saw a woman's thoughts – or rather, that you got this sudden conviction that that's what you were doing – I'd say that maybe the experience is a metaphor designed to show you that sometimes what we think are our own thoughts are actually promptings from off-stage. Seeing her thoughts as images may not be nearly as important as the realization that much of what you think is your property is actually on loan from others, so to speak. But that's just my horse-back guess as to what it means, Tony, and it comes to you not from expert to novice but from one explorer to another."

We all chewed on that for a bit.

"And speaking of exploring," Annette said, "let's do our next tape, which is a free-flow Time Choice. You know the routine by now, so we don't really need to discuss it. We're going to take a little break, and when we ring the bells, off to your rooms by way of you-know-what, and we'll see you downstairs afterwards."

I said to Claire, "Let's see if we can find a time when we were together. I mean, unless you have something else you'd rather use the tape for."

She said, "I don't feel like I have much control over what happens. If it were to happen, it would be fine with me. How's that?"

"I'll settle for that."

❖ 7 ❖

"Don't look so glum," I said to Bobby. "Maybe this tape will be the one."

"Maybe," he said. His voice was relatively lifeless, for him. It was a little hard to adjust to Bobby without exuberant optimism, and I had to admit, I liked the earlier version better.

Back on the bed, wearing earphones and sleep mask, listening to C.T. bring us up to Time Choice. "You are free," he said after a while. "Go, explore in the state of Time Choice. I will call you when it is time to return." And then I was lying there listening to hissing, crackling pink noise.

"I'd really like to see the basis of this connection I feel to Claire," I said. I said it aloud, but I muttered it, aware of Bobby's presence on the other side of the room. I was thinking that what I wanted didn't necessarily have a lot to do with what I'd get. It certainly hadn't up to now. Only later did it occur to me that this was the clearest intent I had brought to a tape experience.

What a difference clear intent (or something) makes! As soon as I made my request, it was as if I was watching a movie. Until this point I had had vague impressions and not much more. This time I saw a scene, and I watched and heard people interacting, and it made sense to me then and made no less sense later.

Was I dealing with an earlier incarnation? I don't know, because I don't know what I really think of the idea of reincarnation. Maybe we reincarnate, maybe we don't, but even if we do I suspect it isn't quite as simple and straightforward as most people seem to think. And maybe we don't reincarnate at all, but we somehow tap into memories of other people's lives and say "That was me!" For the time this experience was going on, I thought of the man I was watching as "me," and used the word "I" to describe him, but that was mostly for convenience. Our language isn't well designed to report this kind of thing.

It started with my looking at the outside of a house, and to my surprise I recognized it, for I had been there, in the flesh, more than once. It was Emerson's house in Concord, Massachusetts. As usual in altered states, I "knew" things that were not evident. Thus I *knew* that this was an image of the house not in the present day, but in the 1840s – more precisely, 1843. *How* did I *know* it was 1843? Have your own altered-state experiences and we'll talk.

"I" came to the front door and introduced myself to the maid. She went away, came back, let me in. Emerson met me inside the door. He repeated my name, as people do, and although I heard it clearly enough then, when I came to reconstruct the experience this was one of the things I couldn't recapture.

I heard "me" say, "Brattleboro," meaning, I take it, "from Brattleboro."

Emerson led me down the hall and introduced me – in the hallway, which I felt to be unusual – to Mrs. Emerson. She shook hands, expecting (I intuitively knew) that I would not really see her, being focused on her husband. A sort of hooded look in her eyes said, "Oh God, another one," meaning, another earnest young man come to sit at the feet of her husband, ignoring her. But I didn't do that. I was as interested in her as in her husband, concerned with her as a person. She was pleasantly surprised – gratified, in a guarded way. But she was even more surprised and gratified to hear that I had arranged to spend the night at the inn rather than quartering myself on them. Emerson, I somehow knew, frequently offered to let young admirers stay overnight – but it was she who would have had the work and the responsibility.

Then *(am I making this up?)* he introduced me to "Mr. Henry Thoreau, like yourself a scholar from Harvard." Thoreau and I shook hands across a sharp, instinctive guardedness between us, a sort of instant potential rivalry, a wariness. (Thoreau, like Emerson's wife, was used to people seeing him through Emerson, and was defensive and touchy about it, though he worked on it.)

Then there was a transition, as though I wandered for a second while someone shifted scenes (the same thing I have noticed often in dreams) and there was Emerson suggesting that he and Thoreau and I go for a walk down to Walden Pond, and asking "Lidian, my dear" if we will have time to walk to the pond and be back by dinner. There was something proprietorial, almost patronizing, about his attitude toward her which I disliked, not knowing why. She said yes, and suddenly I in the present (having *forgotten* what I had asked to experience in this tape!) looked at her through the eyes of her visitor in 1843 and saw something in her eyes and in the expression on her face that was familiar. I said (from the present), "Hold it. Freeze the film. I *know* that person." I started to really look at Lidian Emerson to see if I could figure out if I'd met her in this life – and at *exactly* that time, C.T.'s voice came over the headphones calling us out of Time Choice. But I knew. Lidian reminded me of Claire.

And then I remembered the intent with which I'd entered the tape experience. Lying there, I said to myself, "Hot Shit! It works!"

"But," I said to myself (silently) as C.T. talked us back to normal waking consciousness, "we're not there yet. There's got to be a lot more going on than one casual meeting at Emerson's."

As soon as the tape was over, I grabbed my journal and recorded as much as I could, as fast as I could. "I just wasn't ever in the right mental place before. It's just that simple," I wrote. "Till now I have been trying to be receptive to subtle perceptions – did I see it, did I invent it, did I this and that. And now that I have been there, it is *so clear* that I have never been there before." I had doubted whether altered states even existed, until I experienced them. Now I saw that it was just as Toni had said at breakfast – I didn't have any idea what was possible and what wasn't. I might have opinions, but I didn't really know, and couldn't know until I'd done some more exploring.

And suddenly I suspected that Jeff had been Henry Thoreau. It would fit, if he had been Thoreau and she Lidian Emerson, that she should naturally turn to him for support. Lidian Emerson leaned on Thoreau, and he in turn repaid her with platonic devotion. Of course, I was well aware that I had no objective reason for thinking Jeff was Thoreau; the guess was based on seeing the emotional tie between them, and reasoning that as she came to me in that context, perhaps he did too, but of course the tie between them could easily have been forged in a different lifetime. And later, as I will describe, we learned that the ties between them had nothing to do her Lidian Emerson lifetime. My "knowing" was wrong, something common enough in this kind of exploration.

I was sorry to see – no need for words – that Bobby had once again met only disappointment.

But I couldn't think of anything I could do to help.

She sat down next to me, and asked, "Before debrief begins, just tell me, did you get anything?"

"I got a lot! But I'm not going to talk about it here. Did you?"

"Yes, I think maybe I did. Why aren't you going to talk about it?"

"I don't want people thinking I'm making stuff up. When you start dragging famous names into things, people probably start looking at you sideways."

"Oh, you were somebody famous?"

"Hey, I'm not saying this guy I saw is me." She smiled. "Well, I'm not. I don't know *who* he is. It's just that I asked to see the basis for the connection between us, and this is what came up. But in any case, I don't think *he* was famous, he just met famous people. Emerson, for one." She didn't react to the name, as far as I could tell.

Annette looked around the room, counting heads. "Looks like we're all here. So before we head off for lunch, who has something they'd like to share?"

For a moment nobody said anything, so David added, "All this reticence isn't going to do you any good. We can't go to lunch until the kitchen ladies ring the bell for us."

Claire whispered to me, "You don't mind if I tell them something about us, do you?" I shook my head. "Whatever you want." So she raised her hand, a sort of gesture to the auctioneer that you'll meet the bid.

"Yes, Claire?"

"I have something, but let me know when I start holding up going to lunch." She got grins and some laughs. "You'll get the idea when you get trampled by the herd," David said.

"A while ago you told us that some of us might wind up finding ourselves connected to each other. I can't remember which one of you said it, or when – it seems like the week has been about ten days long already – but anyway one of you said it. That seems to be what Angelo and I are experiencing."

"We've noticed," Sam Andover said softly, and a couple of people laughed.

Claire looked as embarrassed as I felt, but no more. "Yes, well, Angelo said it's okay with him for me to talk about it. Before this last tape he suggested that we try to find out the source of what we're feeling, why we feel we know each other from other times. And there's another person involved, too, but I don't know – "

"It's all right with me," Jeff said.

"All right, so the three of us are feeling this connection, and if I'm not mistaken I think others in this room are feeling something similar among themselves." For some reason I thought of Regina and Emil, who seemed to be spending a lot of time together. "Well, Angelo said, 'Let's try to find out where it started.' So when we went into this tape I held that intent, and that seemed to help. At least, it was the strongest, clearest experience I've had so far, and if it wasn't a specific intent that strengthened it, I don't know what else it could have been."

"For what it's worth, I think so too," I put in. To Claire, "I interrupted you, sorry."

"Sometime recently, I forget when and where, but it was in one of our non-debriefing-room debriefs – you know, either at a meal or during the long break sometime – we were swapping stories and Angelo talked of seeing an old, old house that he thought was nearby somewhere, and he showed me a sketch he'd made. I thought, I know that place. So, when Angelo said 'let's use this tape to see what we can learn,' I thought, that old house is the place to start. I don't know why I had that thought, but I trusted it."

Here she paused, and I could *feel* her getting control of a surge of emotion that had taken her by surprise. Her voice when she resumed was flat, expressionless. "The story I got was that the house had been built in the 1760s as a father's wedding gift to a young man and his bride, providing the money and some of the hired labor to build it, you see. The young man – his name was John – worked on it too. They were young, and strong, just starting in life. This wasn't frontier country then, but it wasn't all that far from it. They were planning to raise their family in the new foothills country, comfortably removed from the tired old seacoast – that's how they saw it – but safe from the Indians on the other side of the mountains. I didn't get a sense of how long things went, because it wasn't really like watching a story, it was more like knowing this and seeing something else and knowing what it meant and seeing something after that. Anyway, it didn't last. She died, maybe in childbirth. But that was our connection. That's the story I got, anyway. I don't know if it's true, of course."

"It's true emotionally, though," Annette suggested.

"Yes. It's true emotionally."

Lou said, "But it could still be only somebody's overactive imagina-tion." Then, defensively: "Well, *couldn't* it? Nobody is saying that anybody is lying, but isn't this a lot to just take somebody's word for? Why can't it be that some part of Claire is making things up?"

Claire clearly had no intention of trying to defend her perceptions. After the briefest of pauses, David smoothly stepped in. "Lou, remember when I told you – Sunday night, I think it was – that the only time we experience our senses as if they were blended together is when we remember something or imagine something? That's why it's so hard to tell what's remembered and what's imagined. They feel the same, so to decide if they really hap-pened or not, we have to employ our judgment. But we don't always have enough data to make that judgment: What do we do then? Do we decide in advance what is possible, and throw out everything else? What if our initial judgment is wrong?"

"So what do you suggest? That we believe in anything and everything that comes our way?"

"Oh gracious no! That's what we call Psychic's Disease."

"Well, then, what?"

"Lou, I can't tell you how tempted I am to give you 'I don't know, what do you think?' but instead I'll just say, use your judgment! What else can you do? What can any of us do? Just – don't use it prematurely. Gather your data, have your experiences, let the evidence pile up on one side or the other, and sooner or later you'll find out what you really think and feel about it. That's what you do in the other parts of your life, why should this be dif-ferent just because the terrain is strange and maybe seems disreputable to you?"

There was a little silence, and then somebody said, "I don't see where Jeff comes in, in all this."

Claire looked at Jeff. "Jeff, do you have something?"

He cleared his throat, slowly, reluctantly. "I don't think I do," he said, "at least not yet, but who knows? You know how it is around this place, one minute you're lying in bed half asleep, the next minute you're watching yourself turn into a werewolf or something." *The laugh covered you, pal, but don't think I didn't hear it. You're not any more anxious to do a public strip-tease than I am.*

Debrief went off in unexpected directions, as though Claire's story had opened the way for others to reveal a little more of what was going on with them. Jane Mullen, for instance, who usually sat benignly and actively listening to other people's offerings, made one of her rare contributions. "I don't know what this means," she said hesitantly, "and so probably I wouldn't talk about this, but something says to share it. Maybe somebody needs to hear it. I was one of a group of students in a classroom, and the Dalai Lama was speaking to us. He walked up the aisle toward me, and said that perhaps Tibet's contribution is that it allowed people to speak their mind. I shook my head yes, emphatically, and this broadly smiling man saw it, and he smiled at me, and I couldn't meet his eyes, being in the presence of such greatness and love. I thought how stiff and formal by comparison photos of him are – and then there was a clap of great noise – and even then I knew it wasn't a physical noise, but a noise to make my mind remember the Dalai Lama's words. 'Tibet gives you the power to speak your mind,' he said." She spread her hands. "I don't know if that means anything to anybody."

Some others said things, too, but I didn't really hear them. *Yes*, I thought, *his name was John, and hers was Clara. But it wasn't childbirth, it was – it was – well, it was something else, something different.* My mouth was dry and I felt cold.

❖ 9 ❖

Perhaps if Jeff and Claire and I had been the only ones in the program experiencing dramatic changes, we'd have been the centers of attention at lunch, which would have been uncomfortable. But various others were going through upheavals of their own, so even at our table, after we were joined by Toni and Lou and Francois, *we* weren't the center of attention. Instead, the center of attention was what we were *experiencing*, and what we thought it might mean. Not just what Claire and Jeff and Angelo were experiencing, but, no less, what the others at the table were experiencing and thinking. As David had said, we were fellow explorers.

"I wonder about all the drama," Lou Hardin said. "You read about somebody experiencing past-life memories and it's always tragic deaths and romantic passions or some other Hollywood stuff. I don't mean to be doubting what you're experiencing *(No, Lou, of course you don't)* but I can't help wondering why it's always drama. I mean, why don't people come back remembering their life as a hired hand, or a street sweeper? I'm waiting for somebody to come back and say, 'well, I got in touch with a past life and absolutely nothing ever happened worth remembering, it was boring.' Why doesn't that ever happen?"

The questions were valid questions in and of themselves, but I didn't have any patience with his underlying attitude. I was used to meeting Lou's kind of guy all the time at work – though not usually in the context of psychic exploration! – and I didn't need the aggravation. When somebody's conviction of his own mental superiority is more important to him than anything else, you can't expect him to risk it by truly considering reports from others that might contradict what he already knows.

Besides, when you start defending the reality of what you're experiencing, you can't win. In effect you give the skeptic the right to judge your experience, regardless of if the skeptic knows the first thing about it or has any basis to judge other than his own certainty. Even if they were open-minded enough to be interested in judging fairly – which they rarely are – they don't have the data, and *can't* have it. Personal experience convinces the person who has had the experience, and perhaps those who have had similar experience. Others, no. So who needs it? I mentally shrugged and went on eating. Jeff and Claire, too, chose to give it a pass. It was Francois, our French-Canadian priest, who responded.

"I think that is easy enough to explain," Francois said. "Elementary psychology provides the answer."

"Oh?" I could see Lou getting ready to enjoy himself. Assuming that Francois, being a priest, would not take past-life memories seriously, but would explain them away, Lou could then tear into that point of view as well. *Pretty stupid game to be playing, Lou, instead of doing your own exploring!* But then I thought, *maybe he thinks that what he's doing is a valid part of the process. In fact, maybe it actually is.*

In any case, Francois surprised him, and me. "You have merely to consider what makes a lasting impression," he said. "Do you remember your home telephone number from 15 years ago? Do you remember your telephone number at work from that time? Do you remember every street address you have ever lived at, or the name of all your co-workers? Do you remember every automobile you have ever owned? And, if so, do you remember every license tag you have ever had? We remember what is important to us, and the things that are most important to us are the things that make the deepest emotional impression. So if your child dies, you do not forget it. If something happens that makes you suddenly very happy, you do not forget it."

Lou looked skeptical, but Claire nodded her agreement. "That's certainly true. If somebody insults you or hurts you in some way, you don't forget it. Years later it can still hurt. And if you love somebody, it marks you. Emotions are where we live."

"So any time something comes up that's got a lot of drama in it, we should assume it's real, because it's got drama?"

"No," Jeff put in. "But maybe if something dramatic comes up, we shouldn't assume that it's less likely just because it's dramatic. From what I hear Claire and Francois saying, if anything it's *more* likely."

To Francois: "Well, but surely you don't believe in reincarnation?"

Francois shrugged, a very French shrug I thought, though as a French Canadian he wasn't much more French than I was. "Perhaps these memories are true memories of other lifetimes, perhaps not. If not, perhaps they are psychological scenes dramatizing internal tendencies, in the way the unconscious sends us dreams to try to tell us things. And if they truly do describe other lives, that does not mean that Claire and Angelo and Jeff *lived* those lives. It means that for some reason they identify with them. How are we to know? Perhaps at some point we will form clearer ideas on these things, but I think it is a great mistake to decide these things before it is necessary."

"'It is a capital mistake to theorize in advance of your data,'" Jeff said in delight. When we looked our questions at him, he added, "That's a quote from that great French-Canadian priest Sherlock Holmes."

We laughed, but Lou said stubbornly, "But if I hear you right, Francois, you're saying that for all we know these things are just made up in our heads."

Francois regarded him gravely, and I wondered if he were wondering if it were worth his time to respond. Then he said, "I have heard many people say 'Perhaps I'm making this up.' I have had the same doubts myself, and, as I say, it is too early for us to be able to resolve these doubts. But perhaps it is more productive to ask ourselves a different kind of question. Perhaps we should be asking, 'If I am making this up, why am I making up this rather than something else?'"

❖ **10** ❖

Jeff very considerately pretended that he had things he wanted to do – or, maybe he really did – so Claire and I found a quiet spot in a corner of a little-used lounge. The lunch room had pretty nearly emptied out, except for Regina and Emil, quietly talking in one of the booths.

I told her about "my" visit to Emerson in the 1840s. "I knew you as soon as I saw you," I said. "Or – dammit, we need new language if we're going to talk about this stuff. What I mean is, that person, whoever he was, in the 1840s, looked at Lidian Emerson and recognized her as somebody he'd been connected to and cared about. I don't know if that made any more sense to him then than it does to us now, but that's what I felt him experience."

"Maybe we can find out," she said. "Are you willing to see?"

"You mean right here, right now?"

"Yes, right here, right now. Supposedly we don't need the tapes once we've learned how to get into an altered state. Let's just sit here and go to Time Choice." And so we began to deviate from the program – to explore the next page, David might have said – working together. Together (well, separately, but it had the *feel* of doing it together) we moved into Entry State, and then to Time Choice, and sat for a moment waiting for something to emerge.

"His father gave them the house as a wedding present," I said. I'd said this earlier, but perhaps she recognized it for what it was, a way of priming the pump. "His father lived in Scottsville, I think."

"Her parents were dead," she said suddenly.

"They were Quakers. Both families. Did Virginia *have* Quakers before the revolution? But that's what I get, they were Quakers."

"Did they have children?" She was asking herself and me at the same time. We pondered, trying to *feel* the answer. "I think they did," I said, "but did they maybe die as infants?"

"Tommy," she said.

"Did she die in childbirth? That's what I thought at first, but then I don't know."

"Not childbirth. She couldn't breathe. Couldn't breathe! Choking."

Chills swept my body. It was as if my body knew something before I did. "She couldn't breathe, that's right. But it wasn't asthma, or anything like that, it was something else."

"Couldn't breathe! Her throat swelled up."

"Yes!" I shuddered, and felt blood draining from my face. "Bee stings. Or, not bees, but – wasps or something."

"Bee stings. Everything was swelling up. Couldn't swallow, couldn't breathe."

"She was allergic to the stings, wasn't she?"

"Yes."

"Her throat swelled up, and she couldn't eat, and then after a while she couldn't drink and then finally she had to struggle even to breathe."

"Yes. And then delirium. She didn't know when she died."

I wasn't getting visions; wasn't watching a movie. I was being washed – drowned, nearly – in overwhelming waves of sorrow and regret and –

"Four days! It took four days." *How did I know that?* "He felt guilty about it for some reason. His fault."

"Not his fault, she was allergic to the bee stings. Or, whatever they were. We called them bees. They were in the chimbley."

"The chimney!" And another shattering chunk of feelings came, tightening my throat, bringing tears to my eyes, leaving me for many seconds unable to continue. "He meant to seal them in, to put mud over the chinks where they were nesting, but he didn't get around to it, and they stung her, and she died!"

"It wasn't anybody's fault, love. It was just one of those things that happen."

"She died! He didn't seal up the nest, and she died."

And from the twentieth century, Claire took my hand and said, "It wasn't his fault, Angelo. He has to give up taking responsibility for it. It happened and it's over and it's time for him to forgive himself."

From the twentieth century, I looked back at her. "It changed him. It colored his whole life. He wasn't the same person afterwards."

"I can see that," she said. "But that's the point of Time Choice, isn't it? It isn't too late to change things."

"John's dead."

"And Angelo's alive."

She surprised me, with that one. "What's that got to do with it?"

"Why, Angelo, what do you think this is all about? John and Clara had their time, and that's over. This is *our* time, and it's all about what we choose today, and from now on. But we have to learn to let things go."

I frowned, sitting next to her in the lounge, with her holding my hand in hers.

"You don't see? What John became is what *you* are, regardless of whether these are real memories or dramas from our unconscious minds."

"We're talking about *John's* life here."

"Yes, but then why did this story choke you up? Follow your *feelings*, Angelo. Your feelings will never lead you wrong. It's just a matter of finding out what they are, and what they mean. You responded – and I responded – because this all *means* something to us. It isn't just a mental game. It's real life. It's just that it's a part of real life that isn't usually this much in evidence."

"It seems to me that I can understand the story easily enough just by assuming that it's about what's happening to you here and now."

"You mean because the cancer is back."

"That's what I mean."

Those lovely brown eyes on me again. "Maybe it's as much about you as it is me, Angelo. You're sharing in the experience, after all."

"Here's an opportunity to deal with left-over guilt, you mean?"

"No. No! There wasn't any need for *John* to feel guilty, let alone *you*! That's not what I was thinking at all. I was thinking it's saying, suppose you were to die right now. So many things would be left forever undone, because there's no one to do them but you."

I shrugged. "There's always unfinished business, no matter when you die. That's basic economics: opportunity costs. Anything you do prevents you from doing something else at that time and with those resources. You have to choose."

"Yes, that's true. We always have more opportunities than we can tend to. But it's up to us to do what we can, while we're still alive, even knowing that it isn't all going to get done no matter what we do. Time is on the wing, my love. Are you going to let it fly away from you without your using it as best you can?"

I shrugged again. (I seemed to be doing that a lot recently, I noticed.) "You know how it is, Claire. We get all caught up in our worries about our family and our relationships and our careers and bills and all."

"Yes, but then you get a wake-up call and you say, 'what have I been doing with my life?' These past couple of years have been hard for me, but at least I knew I was alive. I knew what another day is worth, you know?"

"I do, actually. That's how I use Jesus, and Emerson, and Thoreau. You can't open the Gospels, or *Walden*, or Emerson's Journals, without being snapped back into yourself. You remember what's important and what isn't. You say to yourself, I may be a reporter, or a teacher, or whatever – I'm not Thoreau or Christ or St. Francis or anyone else who ever lived – but I'm here, living my life, and I ought to pay attention while I'm here."

"Yes, that's it exactly. It's a matter of paying attention."

"Of course, it would help if I had some faint idea of what I ought to be doing!"

"What *are* you doing?"

The answer came out with a bitterness that surprised me. "Living a lie, is what I'm doing now. I live in a suburb among neighbors I don't care about and don't have anything in common with. I'm in a marriage that was a mistake, with a wife who doesn't particularly like me and doesn't get much of my time and attention, and children that are in more or less the same position. I commute to work to do a job I lost interest in years ago. I'm so cut off from people, except my brothers and sisters, that you and Jeff are already closer to me than any friends I have on earth."

"That's a lot of unhappiness," she said quietly.

"Unhappiness is putting it mildly. My life doesn't seem to have anything at all to do with the real me." I was a little surprised I had said all that.

"So what are you going to do about it?"

I looked at her, wondering if she'd really heard what I hadn't quite said. "I don't know that there's anything I *can* do about it. More of the same, I suppose."

"Angelo," she said, almost impatiently, "didn't you hear what I just said? The bird is on the wing; time is moving, and your life is moving with it. Do you have to get cancer before you wake up to what your life is worth?"

❖ 11 ❖

"How would I *like* to live? I can't give you specifics, but I can outline it easily enough. As my man Henry Thoreau said long ago, simplify, simplify, simplify. But it isn't that easy to do."

"Why isn't it?"

"Well for one thing, that isn't the way the world pushes you. It's easy to forget the message, because you can't count on society, or other people, to remind you when you forget. Like, a couple of years ago I started playing at buying and selling mutual funds – "

"You didn't!"

"Sure, why not? I needed the money and I knew something about how markets move, and like anything else, it was interesting for a while, learning. I made some money at it. But if you're going to make money at something, you have to pay attention to it, and I got bored with it. Besides, I was amazed at how much more complicated it made my income tax return, and that was one more damn thing. It seems to me that most of the things needed in order to succeed in this world require more time and trouble than they're worth."

"And they lead away from Thoreau's simplicity."

"They do. And they don't make anybody any happier, you notice?"

"But you aren't happy in any case. What *would* make you happy?"

She got only yet another shrug. "Beats me. Nothing, maybe. It seems to me that the price of achievement is the day-in, day-out neglect of wife and family, and I don't feel justified in doing that."

"But you said that is just what you *are* doing, emotionally."

Guilty as charged. Funny that I hadn't seen that. I couldn't think of a thing to say in my own defense. And at the same time I felt no particular need to defend myself, not from Claire.

"You know what it sounds like to me, Angelo? I think you're trying to live your life without a set of rules that would give you something to lean on. You don't know who you are, when it comes to roles and relationships."

"I don't fit within the rules," I said. "None that I've ever found, anyway. I don't know what else to do but make up my own rules as I go along."

"Nothing necessarily wrong about living that way, if you can stand the strain. You are what you are, and imitation wouldn't change it. The question is, though, what do you want to do with whatever is left of your life?"

"I don't know! I don't know that I want to do anything! It isn't like I have these great unfulfilled interests."

"There isn't anything you'd like to do?"

"Well, nothing practical."

"How about impractical?"

"If we're talking impractical, sure I'd like to make the world a better place. But I've been a reporter a long time. I have a pretty good idea how hard it is to change anything."

"So" – she looked at me speculatively – "that means, give up? Make no effort to do anything?"

I squirmed, more or less.

"Lord Peter Wimsey says somewhere, it is astonishing how few people mean anything definite from one year to the next," she said. "Is that you, Angelo?"

"But I don't know what I have to offer," I said. "The only thing I really know is history – but what do I know that is worth anybody's time?"

"Do most people know whatever it is that you know?"

"Most people don't have a clue," I said. "But at the same time, I know how little I know. It isn't like I'm a Ph.D. in history, I just read a lot. That doesn't mean my opinions are worth anything."

"But don't you have a certain practical knowledge of the world from years of being a reporter? Isn't that worth something?"

"I don't know that the professors would think it was."

"By that logic, the only people who do anything are those who don't know how ignorant they are. Either that, or they don't let their ignorance bother them, or they get to work to master their incompetence. Maybe that's what work *is*: doing something badly until you are able to learn to do it better. You have heard the old saying that 'the best' is the enemy of 'the good'? Is it possible that your rather charming diffidence is really rooted in laziness?"

I frowned. "That doesn't sound so good, does it?"

"Well, no, my love, it doesn't."

I thought about it, sitting there, and felt my anxiety level rising. "The thing is, Claire, I think about getting out there in that lunatic asylum and I just cringe. It really doesn't seem possible to accomplish anything. I think maybe, instead of tilting at windmills, I'd be better off concentrating on my own growth."

"There wouldn't be anything wrong with that," she said gently, "if that's really what you were doing, instead of marking time. Maybe it's time for you to choose."

"'Make your option, which of two,' Emerson said."

"Well, what do you want to do? What *should* you do, to be true to yourself? There's nothing wrong with either choice, but sooner or later you do have to choose."

"I'm not even sure I can."

"Oh, you'll choose. One way or another you *will* choose, if only by default. That's what life is. And all paths are good, but they lead to different places by different routes."

"Well what do you think would be better for me?"

"If I told you, would it help you to know your heart any better? Or would it just confuse you? Listen to your inner voice. It knows."

"Let me put it this way: Do you *know* which way would be better for me?"

"I *think* I can see that one path is more in line with your inner being, and so it would be smoother, less stressful, in the immediate term. But long-term, who can say? It really is true that all paths are good."

I took a deep breath. "All right. But then I've got another question. Let's suppose I decide to do my bit to change the world. How am I to do that without losing myself in a lot of activity? Second question, come to think of it. What is my most productive way to influence the world?"

A big slow smile. "Is that your decision, then?"

"It has to be. It is what I am."

"It sure is, my dear. Now you can begin to know where you're going. Congratulations."

"Yeah, great. Still raises the question of where to start, though. So now what?"

"I don't think that's so hard. Start with whatever you know that has been systematically suppressed. Put the suppressed bits put back in, all the facts you can cite, and put them in their proper place so that people can see."

"I don't know if I really know enough – "

"I think you should stop talking about why you can't do it, and – and *do* it! If that's what you really want to do."

"Yes, but there are so many questions I can't answer – "

"Then put them to the reader and let them deal with them. At least they will know the questions exist. And maybe you'll start somebody else on this path. You don't have to do it all, you know, just your part."

"Whatever my part is."

"Whatever your part is. But I don't know who's going to find it if you don't."

❖ 12 ❖

We went for a walk down the unpaved gravel road past the cow pastures. We walked holding hands, more like survivors than lovers or even friends.

"I don't know that anybody ever said that dying is necessarily easy," she said. "It can be, but I don't think it always is. And it's like childbirth, once you're committed you can't stop in the middle of the process and decide not to go through with it. So in that sense I am afraid of dying, yes. I'm not afraid of the result, you understand, but the process. I wouldn't much care to do childbirth again, either. But people do it all the time, I notice."

"And how is your husband dealing with it?"

"Oh – mostly by looking the other way." I felt my anger, and to my surprise she felt it too. "It isn't that he doesn't care, Angelo. Maybe he cares *too* much: it's overwhelming. For me it's just death, and sooner or later we all have to face that. But for him, he's losing his friend, his lover, his wife, his daughter's mother – it's all that rolled into one. Plus he's feeling helpless, and he's angry because it seems unjust, and he's bewildered that he's feeling so much – and he won't get help with it. So it's all too much."

"But the end result is that you don't get any help from him."

She squeezed my hand. "Don't feel that way about it, Angelo, I don't. He's doing the best he can." She stopped walking, so I stopped. "Angelo, I suppose I can tell you this. Do you know why you're so angry at Gus?"

Because he's a jerk. "I'm not mad, I'm just – well, yeah, I'm mad. He's letting you down. You need him to be doing better."

She took my other hand and we stood in the deserted gravel road facing each other. Her eyes held something I didn't dare interpret. She leaned forward and kissed me on the cheek, then leaned back again. "Angelo, you're angry because you want to *do* something to help me, and there isn't anything to be done, and it's easier to lash out at something than to sit with those feelings."

"Oh – " *Bullshit! Worse, psychobabble.*

She smiled, a little lighter. "In a pig's eye, right Angelo? Everybody else, yes, but not you." Her words not only did not anger me, they immediately calmed me. *How does she do that?* She saw that something had happened. "A penny?"

"For my thoughts? I was thinking that somehow you've got me *feeling* things, and I don't know how you do it. Got me *thinking* about them, too."

She released my left hand and we resumed walking. "It isn't me, Angelo, it's you. You're starting to do the work. For you, Open Door is acting like intensive psychotherapy. You're off your accustomed turf, you can't fall back on your habits and routines, you're continually in unfamiliar territory – it's natural that things might change. It's good, too. You don't have to be afraid of it."

I pondered that as we walked. "If anybody else said that to me, I tell them they were full of it."

"Yes, you would – so, am I?"

I was having a little trouble breathing. Not asthma, and not just physical exertion. We were walking up a grade, true, but slowly, comfortably. *No reason, just your basic terror kicking in!* I glanced over at her, then away.

"No, you're not. I know that. In fact" – drawing in a deep breath and looking straight at her – "I can't imagine what you could say that I wouldn't believe."

The tears were back in her eyes. "Thank you, Angelo, I heard that." *Meaning, you heard what I didn't say, too. Well, I expect you always would.* "If we moved up to those trees over there, instead of standing in the middle of the road, you could put your arms around me for a minute."

My hand tightened on hers. "They took away my watch. It might be more than a minute."

"We'll just have to see how it goes."

❖ 13 ❖

Back to the debrief room after the long break. Another tape coming up, and not much inclination to do it. *Hard to keep my mind on the ball.* But Claire was keeping on, and surely I should. That's what I was here for, wasn't it?

Surprise, though. No tape. "It's time we took away your training wheels," David said, smiling broadly, as so often. "So this time, we're going to do a tape exercise without a tape."

Huh?

Annette said, "It wouldn't be much use to you in your everyday life if every time you wanted to move to an altered state you had to put on a tape player and listen to a CTMI tape. And it would be even less useful if you had to come back here and do a program. That's the exact opposite of what you want. So, since there's always a first time for everything, we're giving you your first time while you're still here, so we can help you get the hang of it, and so that the group energy can help you."

So up we went to do a tapeless tape, and it proved to be frustrating enough. I tried to return to the Emerson scene, but no luck. I tried imagining it, thinking I could somehow force my way into it, but got nothing. I tried various things that didn't work until finally I realized – sort of sheepishly – that it might make sense to ask whatever was guiding these experiences what the best purpose of the exercise would be.

I fully expected to get an answer connected to Claire, but I didn't. I didn't get anything, and finally there was Annette's voice telling us that it was time to return. *Nothing. Because it wasn't really a tape?*

Back to the debrief room. Apparently I wasn't the only one who had trouble getting something. Bobby had maintained his unbroken record of striking out. Katie was criticizing herself for what she said had been her own unrealistic expectations – which I took to mean that she was getting discouraged at her failure to contact her dead husband. It wasn't any easier to watch her struggling with it than it was to watch Bobby. However, there was an interesting bit of by-play between Dottie and Lou. Struggling to get people's attention, all but standing up, she said that she had used the exercise to try to find out why she was inaudible and invisible.

Annette said, "What do you mean by that, Dottie?"

"I mean just what I said. That's my whole life experience. I am inaudible and invisible. People just don't hear me or see me."

We waited a moment and no more was forthcoming. Then Lou said, "Well, we're working on the theory that our lives are under our control, right? So what are you doing that makes your life that way?"

She bristled a bit. "If it was something I was doing, I'd change it."

"So you're just an innocent victim here?"

David jumped in, smoothing the waters. "Many people find it true that our lives are more under our control than we commonly think, but that doesn't mean it's easy to find the key. We want to be careful not to suggest that if somebody is facing a problem, it's somehow their fault. We are all facing problems. Maybe that's what we're here on earth to do, for all we know."

"I don't see the value in assuming helplessness," Lou said.

"And I don't see the value in casting blame," Dottie shot back.

"You don't sound very inaudible to me," he said, grinning, "not at the moment." And I wondered if that wasn't his way of administering shock treatment. It made me reassess him, a bit.

After that, admonitions. Reminders that we couldn't expect uniform results while we were still learning. Encouragement. Go back and try again.

So back on the bed, lying with sleep mask on, hoping that the familiar feeling of the headphones (although no tape was playing) would help bring me to the states I had gotten used to attaining. Only, this time, since I hadn't had any luck doing things in the way they recommended, I decided to follow impulse and see what happened if I tried to contact Claire directly, mind to mind. (*How do you like* them *apples, Charlie? Quite a change from "I know there's nothing in it," huh?*)

I didn't know how to go about it.

All right, there's no pink noise, no instructions from C.T. Fine, you've done this before. First the systematic relaxation, muscle-group by muscle-group. Then, Entry State. Stabilize it, look around (so to speak) to see how you're feeling, then on to Wider Vision. Stabilize again, and Time Choice.

Let's assume you're in Time Choice. Try to go back to that house. (Nothing.) *Try working your way to Claire, linking up.* (More nothing.) *Try again.* (Still more nothing.) *Okay,* (very aware of time passing) *now what?*

"Emotions are where we live," she had said at the table. *She didn't say anything about willpower, and willpower certainly hasn't helped me so far. Maybe I'm on the wrong track.* "Emotions are where we live." *All right, how do you go about using emotions to find somebody else?*

Suddenly that didn't sound so hard. It made sense to me at a deeper level than intellect. I "remembered" (I don't know how else to put it) my feeling for her, and those feelings connected us. *"You don't do this stuff through the head, you do it through the heart!"* I said to myself, and instantly, it was obvious.

I *felt* connected to her. Nothing I could have demonstrated, certainly nothing I could have proved. There was no "objective" aspect to it at all. It's just, I felt her there, and I didn't doubt it and didn't wish to doubt it.

But now what?

"Maybe we can find out," she had said. "Are you willing to see?" *Suppose I try the same thing as if she were right here? Ask the question and listen for the answer, and see what happens.*

Did she die the way we got?

Yes, it was as you got. Wasp stings, and she was allergic to wasps, and that's how she died. She was 24.

Why?! But to this there was no answer.

All right, what happened to John after that?

I got the answer not in words but in a knowing, in a sort of image without an image. He became uprooted. He lost his sense of connection.

And the children? A sense that he had a sister, and she raised them, two of his as well as several of her own. Didn't get a name for her or even for the children.

And then? A sudden sense – not quite a visual, but an impression – of a tight-jawed, bitter, closed-off man.

He gave up on life!

None of this came with dramatic flourishes. It came with even less drama, if possible, than I am using to re-create it here. Yet it came with conviction. Then things took on a life of their own, and things happened that I don't intend to describe here, and I got an even fuller sense of how much Claire meant to me already.

A couple of small problems with that, of course. We had met Saturday, and it was Tuesday, nearly supper time. We were more than halfway through the course. We would go our separate ways on Friday and probably we would never see each other again.

❖ 15 ❖

The tapeless tape exercise ended. Without taking off my sleep mask, I reached over to the ready light and turned it off. I took off my earphones and let them drop beside my head. Then I lay there on my back, unmoving.

"Ready to go to supper, roomie?"

"Go on ahead, Bobby. I may skip it."

"Something happened, huh? You okay?"

"Yeah, I'm fine."

"You're staying with something you got I guess, right?"

"Something like that. Get yourself some supper, Bobby."

"Okay." I could hear a hesitation, "I'll see you after a while, maybe."

"Sure. You go on." I heard the door open and close, and I was alone. I pulled my handkerchief out of my back pocket, lifted the sleep mask onto my forehead, and wiped the remains of the tears from my eyes, and mopped the area between my eyes and ears where the tears had flowed. *This is crazy. You're married and she's married, and you're both way old enough to know better. And she's dying.* I reached up to the window and opened the blinds. The day was moving toward sunset. I lay there looking up at the darkening clouds.

It was very odd. *How can you have feelings without memories of whatever caused the feelings?*

There was no evidence whatever, not even a very good story. If someone were to ask me, "How do you know you aren't making it up?" I'd have to say, "I *don't* know." I didn't have enough tangible "facts" to make a short story. I had impressions, "knowings," feelings. Nothing substantive at all, really. But it didn't make any difference. I was sure. In other words, I was just as bad as all the true-believers I'd ever criticized.

The thing is, though – it's different when you experience *it.* Maybe it didn't make sense – hell, it *clearly* didn't make sense – but the fact that it didn't make sense didn't make any difference. I was just as certain as if I had reason to be.

We were one. We were as close as any two people could be. We were young, and in love, and we were a comfort and a support to each other. And then, one moment of carelessness, and she was gone.

I lay there while they went through debrief, and when I figured it would be about over, and Bobby would be coming back, I slipped on my shoes and put on my coat and hat and went off to Edwin Carter Hall, and stood leaning on the building on the far side, where nobody would happen to find me. It was cold, and it wasn't doing my lungs any good – it was getting harder to keep my breathing calm – but I didn't want to talk to anybody, especially Bobby. When they had to be at supper, I came back to my room, took off my coat and hat and shoes, and sat down on the chair by my desk. My breathing was too stirred up to let me be comfortable lying down on the bed.

The worst of it, in a way, is that when something's over, it's over. You don't get it back again just by wishing for it. And when something's over, it can be painful, remembering what you used to have. I suppose that's one reason we forget so much.

I sat on the chair, watching the sky change. The sun was down behind the mountains. The world got steadily darker.

❖ **16** ❖

I don't know if I would have gone over to Edwin Carter Hall for the program or not, but Bobby came back to the room looking for me. "Come on, roomie, they've rung the bell." I took that as a nudge from the universe, as Bobby would have put it. After all, what was I going to do, hide out till Friday morning?

"Looks like everybody's here," David said when he saw us enter. *Maybe they sent him after me. Or maybe it was Bobby just being Bobby, for he* is *kind.* I took the last available seat, at the back of the room. "Okay. Tonight you're going to get to hear something different."

"As opposed to the rest of the week?"

David laughed. "Yes, Andrew, this is different even for us. You're going to hear a tape that was made under very special circumstances, several years ago already. It was back when C.T. was experimenting a lot with his new frequencies. Anybody who claimed to have a far-out talent, he was willing to put the earphones on them and see what happened. If they looked like they were checking out all right, maybe he'd put the finger sensors on them so he could track what was going on as they progressed through their experience. And if it *really* looked like they had something special, he'd hook them up to the full monitoring equipment that Dave and Harry described to you yesterday. I don't know what you folks think of channelers, but that's what we're talking about here."

"David, what do you mean when you say channeler? There are about a million definitions out there and sometimes I think no two people mean the same thing by it."

"Good question, Sam. It's worth a little explaining." A pause for sorting mental notes. "In the first place, we can distinguish between trance channelers and those who can pass information from other sources through their waking consciousness. And then we can also divide them another way. Some of them bring forth information from a single source, a singular, named personality like Seth or Kryon – an individual, in other words – where others like Edgar Cayce have sources that are either anonymous or plural. So without going any farther we already have four variants: Channelers either go into trance or they don't, and they either bring in one or more personalities who are perceived as specific individuals, or they bring in information from indefinite or anonymous sources.

"Now, I don't know how many people here believe or disbelieve in channeling, and I don't want to know. What I would like you to do is bring to this subject the same attitude you've been bringing to altered states in general. Be willing to consider it as a possibility."

He cited scriptural references to apparent channels. "Whenever I read 'Thus saith the Lord,' that sounds to me like someone differentiating between what he as an individual was saying, on the one hand, and what he heard God say on the other." I saw Francois nod appreciatively, somewhat to my surprise.

"So, you might ask, what does this have to do with the price of beans? And the answer is, over time C.T. found a few channelers he liked and trusted, and used them to try to bring in information that would be helpful to us here on this side of the veil. One of these was a young man whose initials are R.K., which is how we refer to him. And one day, while C.T. was after something else, R.K. landed them in very deep waters, and the session had far-reaching consequences. Like all such sessions, C.T. was taping it, and we call it the 'Lost in Space and Time' tape. We have our own ideas about what is going on here, but no, we're not going to share them with you. You listen, and try to figure it out, and then maybe we can compare notes later."

He turned to where Annette was standing, at the console that played audiotapes or films or slides. "Annette?"

<h2 style="text-align:center">❖ 17 ❖</h2>

Now how do I describe the effect on me of the Lost in Space and Time tape?

It should be obvious that on the one hand I had gotten deeply involved in all this exploration-of-consciousness stuff, as soon as I began to have undeniable experiences. Like it or not – and I *did* like it, to my surprise – there's nothing like having something happen to you first-hand, so you don't have to take anybody's word for it. When you're having to take people's word for something, you're never on completely firm ground. It's not a question of fraud so much as general human unpredictability and unreliability. You may have heard that after you've heard two eyewitnesses describe an accident, you start to wonder about history. There's a reason for that, and nobody learns it more thoroughly than a reporter, unless maybe a cop.

But then in the middle of this massive readjustment of my beliefs there was this mysterious and undeniable connection with Claire, and to a degree with Jeff, but Claire was the critical factor. Thoughts of her were disturbing my mind, to the point that it was actually interfering with my participation in the various exercises. It hurt too much, and the fact that it *shouldn't* hurt, and that it made no sense for it to hurt, didn't have a thing to do with anything.

You don't have to be able to understand pain to feel it.

It hurt. It hurt enough that I couldn't face debrief, enough that I couldn't even face sitting with others at supper, but had had to skulk around to avoid a chance meeting.

I was listening to the Lost in Space and Time tape only because they sent Bobby to get me, and it was easier to go along than to make a big deal over it. So at first I sat passively, grateful for the protection of the darkness. Then – and not too far into it, either – I found myself gripped by the content. After a while, I was well beyond gripped, being awed by the implications. I'd read references to this kind of thing, but had always discounted it, like the Bridey Murphy stories of my youth. But this –

167

It is true that listening to a tape made years before is not the same thing as being there at the time. But it is also true that the very act of listening to the tape, under any circumstances whatever, constituted a first-hand experience of a different kind. Particularly when, at a certain point in the tape, an ice-cold chill runs through your entire body, and you gasp and those around you gasp at the same time, and for the same reason.

❖ 18 ❖

Annette turned a knob, or punched a button or flipped a switch or whatever she did – I was at the very back of the room and didn't see it, not that it matters anyway – and the speakers mounted at ceiling level in the front corners of the room suddenly came alive with the hissing noise you usually hear when old tapes are being played. This wasn't pink noise, just tape hiss, and there was a younger version of C.T.'s unmistakable voice, asking someone if he was comfortable and ready to go.

"Ready," the voice said. The voice was sort of muffled, in the way voices often sound when people are speaking from altered states.

We sat through four or five minutes of silence occasionally punctuated by comments by C.T. or responses by the voice of the man whose identity was protected by the initials R.K. I don't know what C.T. was after, but whatever it was, the session wasn't going that way, and finally he asked R.K. to see if he could contact someone of goodwill who was willing to interact with humans in bodies. He didn't get that either – or perhaps I should qualify it and say, he didn't get it directly, or obviously. But given what flowed from this contact, I think it's obvious that in fact it was set up by some intelligence who was indeed "willing to interact with humans in bodies."

However, as I say, it wasn't obvious right away.

C.T. was ready to get into a profound philosophical discussion with an intelligence from somewhere else, a Mr. Spock perhaps. That isn't what he got. He got a dead man. Took him a while to figure out even that much, in fact. At first he clearly didn't know *what* he was dealing with.

It went more or less like this, as I remember it. C.T. repeated his request to talk to someone who was willing to interact with humans in bodies. There was a moment's silence, and then R.K.'s voice changed, and he asked C.T., roughly, impatiently, what he wanted.

It was the first time I'd heard C.T. sounding unsure of himself, off-balance. He stuttered something like, he wanted to talk.

"What about?"

"Well, can you tell me who you are?"

"You don't know who I am?"

"No, but I'd like to."

"You've picked a hell of a time to come for a chat, man."

"Is this a bad time, then?" I don't know about the others who were listening, but I thought, *'Bad time??' How can it be a bad time to talk to a spirit?*

"Yes it's a bad time! What do you think?"

A pause, and we could all but hear C.T. wondering what he'd gotten himself into and how he was going to get himself out of it.

"Well, I'm new here," he said, and I and all the other participants cracked up. *Talk about desperate!*

The voice snorted. "You won't be new here very long, and you're liable to be here a good while, if you don't get out of here pretty quick. Don't you have any sense at all?"

"Listen, Mr. – I don't know your name. Would you tell me your name? My name is Christopher."

"John Anthony Cotter."

"Well, John, what is it that's going on? I know it's plain to you, but I can't see things very clearly."

"I suppose you can see *me*, can't you? You're standing here within a couple of feet of me, I judge."

"You judge? Can't you see either?"

"Does it look like I'd be in a position to see behind my back, man?"

"John, I'm sorry. What do you mean, behind your back?"

Another explosion of impatience. "Are you blind, then? How can you be wandering around where we've been fighting savages, and you not able to see?"

"It's a little hard to explain." A long pause, and I had the sense that it would have been longer if C.T. hadn't been afraid of losing contact with the man. *Some dilemma!* And in a way, we, hearing the tape, felt very acutely C.T.'s dilemma. We were hearing what he was hearing, and, like him, we were seeing nothing but our present-day physical surroundings. The rest was guesswork. Finally C.T. said, "John, can I help you in some way?" I would have liked to ask C.T. what made him think of that particular question, but by the time I saw him later I had forgotten the question, and anyway, I'm pretty sure I know the answer. He was being prompted by the same force that brought him into the scene in the first place. But it would take quite a while before I realized this, or realized even the most obvious implications of it. In any case, he asked it, and John Anthony Cotter's response was prompt, and so unexpected it made us gasp. At least, it made *me* gasp, and I could hear that I wasn't the only one. "You could stop your chatter and take the arrow out of my back, yes. That would help."

An arrow. So – wild west, or where? 1800s, or when? I could feel C.T. filling with new questions now that he had a place to stand.

"How did you get the arrow in your back, John?"

"Well how do you think? They caught us unawares and I was the first man down, or one of the first anyway. I never saw 'em."

"Then what happened?"

"Are you going to help me? I don't want to bleed to death here, and if you don't hurry up that's what's going to happen. I was already thinking it was too late."

"John – where are we?"

"*Will* you stop your questions and get working on getting that arrow out? We don't want to be still here after sundown. At least, I don't, and if you have any sense you don't either."

"No, I'm sure we don't."

"Don't try to pull the arrow through. Cut it off at both ends, so I can travel. It's best we don't pull it out till we get to a sawbones. I don't suppose *you're* a sawbones, are you?"

"No, I'm afraid not. Listen, John – "

They go back and forth like this for a while, C.T. trying to get information about who when where why and how, and John Anthony Cotter trying to get C.T. to get him into a condition to move before the Indians return. The more C.T. tries for information, the more upset John Anthony Cotter gets, that C.T. is concentrating on inessentials. All the while, the clock is ticking, and C.T. knows well that channeling takes it out of people. So finally he gives up trying to get information, and tries to provide it.

"John, I don't know how to tell you this. I guess I'd better just come out with it. Since you got hit with that arrow, have you seen any of your friends around?" Cotter admits that he hasn't. "You said you had about given up before I came. Do you have any sense how much time has passed since you got hit?" Cotter hesitates and then says it seems like it has been a while.

"John, don't you think enough time has passed that it ought to be dark?"

Silence. Eloquent silence.

"John, I think you died when that arrow hit you. If you didn't die right away, I think you bled to death."

Listening, I expected to hear a heated denial. Instead I heard more silence, more tape hiss over what seemed a long time but was probably less than a minute.

"It makes sense," Cotter admitted. "I knew there was something strange going on, but I couldn't figure it. I suppose you're an angel, come to fetch me? Or am I wrong about that too?"

C.T. made an inspired leap. Perhaps literally inspired. "Yes, John, you could say I'm an angel, come to fetch you home. Are you ready to go home, John?"

"Listen, you try lying on the ground with your back broke and you tell me how much you'd like to stay there!"

"All right, then, John, look around you. Somewhere you'll find a beam of light, or maybe it will just be a particularly bright spot, something much brighter than sunlight." A masterly pause. "Do you see it?"

"Yes. Yes, I do. How about that?"

"John, who did you love most in the world who's gone before you?"

"My mother, of course."

"Call her, John. Tell her you want to come home."

"All right." A pause, then, in a dubious tone of voice, "There's something coming out of the light, can you see it too? It's a person."

A pause, and then a wild joyous yell. ***"MOTHER!"***

I swear, I leaped like a fish.

❖ 18 ❖

Annette looked around at us. "Wow, huh?"

"Wow is right," Andrew said. "Just, wow."

John Anthony Cotter had screamed "mother!" and he was gone. C.T. had asked a couple of perfunctory questions to see if there was anyone left to talk to, and then had brought R. K. back to normal waking consciousness. Well, normal, if the word "normal" can be used to describe one returning to consciousness shaking with adrenaline, only half-aware of what had gone on immediately beforehand. And in present time, Annette had turned off the tape, David had turned up the lights, and they were watching us try to assimilate what we'd just heard.

"So – " Annette said. "Reactions?"

"So it was this experience that sparked the Bridging Over program?"

"That's right, Claire. C.T. had heard of people having an out-of-body being urged to go toward the light. He says that's what gave him the idea when he was talking to John Anthony Cotter. But he was a little shocked at how fast it worked, and how thoroughly. And the more he thought about it, the more he decided that it had happened for a purpose."

"Remember," David put in, "C.T. had asked to talk to someone interested in talking to humans in bodies, and he had gotten a dead man who didn't quite realize that he was dead. The more he thought about it, the more he got the sense that the incident had been orchestrated."

"Orchestrated by the dead man? John?"

"No, not at all. It seemed orchestrated *on behalf of* John Anthony Cotter. But in that case, who was doing the orchestrating, and why?"

"I should think it would be perfectly clear." *Selena Juras, naturally. Like editorial writers, often wrong, never in doubt.* "C.T. encountered someone on the astral plane and assisted him to the light. I've been doing it for years. Hundreds of people have been doing it. Thousands, maybe. It is a very well understood process."

"Well I don't know," Ellis Sinclair said. "I am not well versed in the subject, so for all I know it may be as well understood as you say, but it seems to me that this experience does raise several important questions. As David just said, who was doing the orchestrating, and why?"

"It was his higher self."

"I don't see how we can know that," Toni Shaw said. She said it tentatively, but she said it.

"Years of experience, is how we can know it," Selena Juras said flatly.

But Toni didn't back off, and I was proud of her. "Experience is one thing, but surely interpretation is another. We can know how to use something and still not have any idea what makes it work. Maybe it's the same with this."

"It isn't."

"Wait," David said. "We're now in danger of straying into theory, and theory isn't what we're about, here. Here, we're dedicated to doing real work, and getting real results. We don't want to let theory get in the way."

"But there's a difference between truth and error," Selena Juras said angrily. "What's the benefit of pretending that we don't know what we do know?"

"*You* may know it," Toni said. "*I* don't. And if I understood C.T. right Sunday night, he was saying go find out for yourself, not take somebody else's word for it." *What's gotten into Toni? I didn't have any idea she could be so feisty. Good for her, though.*

Selena Juras tossed her head in irritation.

"There's an important implication here that we should look at," Annette said after a tactful pause. "Think of it. John Anthony Cotter had been lying on the forest floor for decades – from sometime in the nineteenth century, anyway, if not earlier. We never did find out just when and where C.T. met him. In all that time, he had been thinking he was still alive. Now, what does that mean?"

Stated that way, it was suddenly obvious that we didn't necessarily know.

"I can't get this," Lou said. "I mean, he's dead. We're all agreed on that? Assuming it's not just a figment of R.K's imagination – assuming it really is the spirit of the guy – "

"The soul, not the spirit," Selena said.

"Whatever. Assuming it's real – how can he be talking to somebody in the twentieth century when he's been dead so long? That would be like talking to the future, for him."

Andrew said, "So?"

"So what kind of sense does that make? He doesn't know anything about the twentieth century, and I don't imagine he is much on time travel." He got a laugh.

David said, "Those are good questions Lou, and the short answer is, we *don't* know for sure what's happening. But I'll give you my personal take on the situation, for what it may be worth to you. To me, it shows that the dead, having no bodies, live outside of time. Living always in the present tense, with no body to drag his awareness into new circumstances, John Anthony Cotter had lived inside his own drama always in the present tense, thinking it a single long day. Only C.T.'s intervention interrupted his drama – and that's what freed him."

"Freed him to do what?" Helene asked. "What does it really mean, going off toward the light with somebody? I know what it means in psychology, but is that how you understand it, or do you see it differently?"

"Helene, again, I think we're better off staying away from theory. The important thing here is that in C.T.'s experience we got a sudden sense of possibilities. We realized that we can help the dead. At least, we can help those of the dead who need help. It's an awesome thought."

"It *is* a bit awesome, I suppose," Ellis said, "but it isn't quite clear to me how those of us who don't have our own personal channelers help them."

"Ah, but you see, Ellis, that's where the Bridging Over program comes in. If you can get into Interface, you have the tools to do just what C.T. did, without the channeler. The dead are not living in time, of course, so it doesn't matter how long they've been stuck in an illusion that they aren't dead, there is always the possibility of our contacting them and helping them. Depending on their willingness and our resourcefulness."

Since the dead are not confined by time, we can move through time to help them! I found the thought awe inspiring. And sitting in the debrief room shortly thereafter, waiting for our briefing on the last tape of the day, I suddenly realized what this meant to me in practice. There's more to life than romance, and more even than the death of new-found former lovers. I realized that here I was, in the midst of something huge – and I had been acting like a lovesick schoolboy. I thought of my skipping supper and hiding out from the others, and I burst out laughing. Jeff, sitting next to me, raised an eyebrow. "I really can be an idiot," I said. He smiled, and said, "Welcome to the club. I'm a founding member, myself."

❖ 20 ❖

Another tape, the fourth of the day, in the wake of the Lost in Space and Time tape. Lying in bed waiting for the tape to begin, I thought, *How do we top what we just heard?* They had given us only a short, sketchy briefing. This tape would help us deal with our fears. Okay with me, but next to what we'd just seen, it didn't sound too exciting.

Pink noise, and then C.T. bringing us through the relaxation process. *Claire knew that I'd been going though some emotional upheaval. She didn't buy it for a second, my saying I'd just been tired. And I think she knew more or less what it was all about, too.*

"Rest now," C.T. said, as we reached a plateau in the process. (*"John, it's okay," she had said. I said, "John?" and she just smiled at me and said maybe we could talk after the tape.*)

Pink noise, and then C.T. again. "Now, resting calmly in a state of Wider Vision, ask for an image of one of your fears that you are ready to let go. Ask for a vision of one of the things you fear. Experience that vision calmly, without emotion and with great understanding and compassion. Ask for a vision of an important fear, that you are ready to release. Do this now."

If the week had taught me nothing else it would have taught me to be ready for anything, or nothing, to appear. I *am* trainable! So I was surprised but not astonished to receive an image of snakes.

"Examine the image you have received," C.T. said, "and ask, 'Why am I seeing this image, and what deeper significance does it have for me?' Do this now."

Snakes. Well, doesn't nearly everybody fear snakes? Almost from outside myself – if that phrase still has any meaning – I heard "snakes in the grass." *Snakes in the grass. Treachery.* And I suddenly realized, yes, it's true, I do feel I live among hidden dangers. Maybe too much fear of the unknown tends to hold me back?

"Now ask yourself if you are ready to release this fear," C.T. said. "Ask if you are ready to release this fear, and if the answer is yes, just watch it dissolve. Release this fear and watch it fade away into nothingness."

Sheer suggestion, of course, nothing more complicated than that. I watched the image dissolve, smiling at myself for participating but knowing better than to allow the smile to override the participation.

"Rest comfortably now," C.T. said.

You have to hand it to him. He really knows how to use the tools. If that was anything more than a sort of hypnotic suggestion without the hypnotism, I'm a monkey's uncle. And yet – well, the image came to me on its own, I certainly wouldn't have chosen it. And the interpretation feels right, and that didn't feel like it came from me either. So who's to say the process won't do some good? It wouldn't be any weirder than anything else that's happened.

C.T.'s voice came back, and we went through the same process two more times. The first time, I saw a lamp in a window, and jumped to a sense of John's life after Clara died – a long vigil for someone who wasn't coming back. It was, I realized, a symbol for a fear of abandonment. I watched the image dissolve. The final image was of a paving machine, pressing down asphalt. That one stopped me for a second – *paving machine??* – until C.T. said to ask why I was seeing it and what it meant, and I realized it was symbolic of being run over. It was a fear of being run over roughshod, of not being accepted for who and what I really was. *If nothing else,* I thought, *whoever is putting up these images is pretty good at symbolism!* And then

C.T. told us to release the fear and watch it dissolve, and after a bit he brought us back to normal consciousness.

Interesting tape, I thought, taking off the phones and taking off the mask and reaching over and turning off the ready light. *I wonder if it will have any lasting effects.* I realized that I felt lighter somehow. But when I looked over at Bobby, doing the same things, I knew not to ask how it had gone.

❖ 21 ❖

"You know, this afternoon when we went upstairs to do the tapeless tape? I was so mad, I was ready to spit nails." (*What happened to being inaudible and invisible, Dottie?*) Dottie half turned around in her back-jack, facing Lou Hardin. "Lou, I thought you were the biggest jerk I'd ever met. I said to myself – well, I'm not going to tell you what I was saying. But your ears must have been burning. I thought, 'How the *hell* can he say it's *my* fault that people won't listen to me and don't even notice me?' Oh, I was mad! And all through the tape – or the non-tape – I kept going back to it, and the more I did, the madder I got. Even when we were listening to John Anthony Whatever with the arrow in his back, I couldn't stop thinking about it. Man, I was mad!"

She paused, and looked almost sheepish. "I guess I owe you a thank-you, Lou, and an apology. In the middle of the tape we just did I saw this huge fear of being out in the open – and I realized, that's why nobody ever heard me or saw me; I was always hiding out so I wouldn't be all exposed!" She turned back to Annette and David. "I don't think you even need to have tapes in this program. Just be sure you have enough people in it that they'll be needling each other at the right time."

"I'll mark it down on the evaluation form," David said, and we all laughed. "Anybody else? Claire?"

"That was a very valuable tape, and it came at a good time for me. I have a situation in my life that brings up certain very specific fears, and even though the tape didn't make them magically go away, it did help me get a handle on them, I think."

The trainers nodded.

"I agree, that was a good tape," Toni said. "I was able to release some fears about my health, and I hope that with the fear gone, it will be easier to see some positive changes." I heard Andrew say to himself, "*Count* on it!"

Roberta Harrison Sellers said, "A good while ago, I had a dream about an English teacher. He loved literature and more than anything else in the world, he wanted to write, and he spent his life writing. If he could have told himself that he had contributed even a paragraph that would live, he would have been satisfied, but at the end of his career he knew that even that ambition was more than he could fulfill. But he had one student who did succeed, a boy of great talent. The teacher told himself that perhaps he was partly to credit for his student's success, but in his heart he knew that the boy would have succeeded regardless, for he had come into the world to succeed.

"I have remembered that dream for years, but somehow it never seemed complete. This last tape seems to have completed it for me. When we were supposed to be finding our fears, instead I saw the teacher in his old age. He had gotten a letter from his successful student, and he knew that he had to answer it, but he didn't even have money enough for a stamp."

That fear seemed clear enough! We waited.

Helene asked, "Was that all of it?"

"No. The funny thing was, he knew that because he *had to have* a way to send the letter, it would materialize somehow."

"Ah," Andrew said. "So it was the living in faith that was the point."

"Perhaps. The puzzling thing is that after that I saw him with his student at the kind of place where students would eat. His former student ordered a pizza and shared it with his former teacher, who was glad to have whatever the student wanted to eat. He was remembering that at the beginning of his teaching career, he had very consciously decided to eat where the students liked to eat, and to be seen reading there. His reasoning was that they would see that reading was important to him and some would catch the infection."

It was interesting, but like so much about dreams, a bit puzzling and undefined. We sat with that until Annette said, "Ellis?"

Ellis was shaking his head gently, an introspective smile on his face. "I know the program isn't over," he said, "but if nothing else happens for the rest of the week it won't have been a disappointment. This has been a remarkable day."

Annette asked, "Are you referring specifically to the tape you just did, Ellis?"

"Particularly this last exercise, but the Lost in Space and Time tape, too, and the tapes we did earlier. You know, going into the tape, I thought, 'Well, I've dealt with a lot of my fears over the years. I don't know if I have any left to deal with.' But sure enough there were two more that I never would have thought of. Maybe we always have more, I don't know." He paused, in that deliberate way of his. "C.T. said visualize your fear and I was just lying there, not really expecting anything, and there was a wheelchair. Nobody in it, nothing happening around it, just a wheelchair. So I said to myself, 'Now what does this mean?' and I realized that deep inside, so deep that I haven't ever really been aware of it, I have always had a fear of losing my independence. And, you see? A wheelchair is a *perfect* symbol of dependence, at least it is for me. Now, I'm sure there are plenty of people in wheelchairs who are getting along just fine, but as a symbol, for me, it was perfect."

Andrew said, "And your other fear?"

"The other fear is one I'm not prepared to talk about just yet. Not because it is so private or even perhaps so unusual, but I prefer to think about it for a while. Maybe later I'll want to talk about it, I don't know. But even if I don't, I did want to say that this whole process is remarkable." I never did find out what the other fear had been. For that matter, *most* of what other people were going through, I never heard about. I had my hands full just trying to deal with my own stuff.

I said, "I agree with Ellis, remarkable is the word for it. I wonder, did anybody else feel physically different at the end of the tape? When I stood up I felt – well, I felt *lighter* somehow. Did anybody else feel something like that?"

To my surprise, several people indicated that they had. So then I had to ask myself, why did I feel surprised? Something had prompted me to ask the question, why should I be surprised to find that I had been prompted for a reason?

It occurred to me, I'd come a long way since Saturday night.

❖ 22 ❖

For a good while there, it looked like a very expensive mistake. Sometimes miracles come well wrapped, unrecognizable.

Debrief was over, and we were sitting around snacking, reluctant to let the day end. Somebody came in from outside and said the night sky was amazing and we should come look at it, and we did. And indeed, it was remarkable to those of us who lived our normal lives within the sky glow of reflected electric lights. We could see thousands of stars, pinpoint-bright against blackness and – for the first time in my life – the glow of the milky way. *Wow,* I thought, *think of that phenomenal background up there all the time, day and night, and us not noticing it.*

Then I started to wheeze. I went back inside and pulled out the inhaler – no longer self-conscious about using it in front of people, I noticed – and used it. Tried to use it. The little hiss it made as it expelled a charge wasn't a very large sound, and it might be that the conversations around me had masked it. But I hadn't felt the impact on my palate, either, hadn't tasted the indescribable but unmistakable taste of the spray. *Oh shit! That's right, the damn thing is empty!*

Not least among the remarkable things that had been happening to me in these few days was that I could forget something so basic. I had known it was empty, I had known there was no refill, and I hadn't even particularly worried about it. I'd had a little wheezing in the morning but it had settled down by itself, and I hadn't had any trouble for the rest of the day, even going out at sunset and standing around watching the sun go down. *I'd just forgotten about it!*

Now it was payback time, I guessed.

All right, this isn't the first time this has ever happened to you. You got through plenty of bad nights before you got the inhaler. You know what to do.

Nonetheless, speaking of fears...

I sat down at one of the tables and tried to smooth out my breathing, but I couldn't do it. Instead of relaxing, I could feel myself getting tenser. I knew where this was heading, and I had the entire night ahead of me. Nothing to look forward to. How often had I experienced it. . . .

Sitting at my kitchen table, a sweatshirt over my pajamas, a blanket over the sweatshirt. I wore a woolen cap like sailors wore, pulled down over my ears. I was holding my head in my hands, and I could feel the pull of skin under my fingers. The tips of my fingers were on my temples, the places where my fingers met my palms were caught under my cheekbones. I sat looking out the window, watching the sun lighting the sky, watching as the overhead electric light surrendered to the coming of the day.

Ironically – it always struck me as ironic, despite its predictability – ironically, as soon as I had seen that the sun was coming up, I could feel my lungs begin to ease. All night I had fought for breath, fighting my weariness and headache, fighting the muscle aches that came from tension and lack of sleep. All night I had fought to retain control, to soothe my own breaths, to provide a rhythm, to stop the wheezing from getting out of control – basically to no avail. But as soon as the sun came up, the battle was won – for the moment.

It was enough to make a man believe in astrology. Something *connected that sun to me – to my lungs, my psyche, my aching muscles, my head-ache, my bone-weariness, my stink of dried sweat and the general dirtiness one gets either by going for long periods of time without showering, or by spending a night fighting to breathe.*

I sat there a few minutes more, waiting as the iron band around my chest muscles eased, ever so slowly, as my diaphragm was ever so slowly able to open my lungs more easily, wider. I waited and observed as the muscles in my neck lost some of their rigidity.

At length, I closed my eyes to rest them, and when I felt myself give a long sigh of relief – a sigh having no catch in it, no raw spot halfway between the base of my neck and my nipples, I knew it was pretty much over. For the moment. More coming with nightfall, like as not.

Six-thirty. Time for an hour's nap on the couch. Two, if I was lucky. If it didn't come back. Then to work as usual, as if nothing had happened. If God had just asked me, I could have told him I didn't care, lungs or gills, just so they worked okay.

A long night like that never left me in the best shape the following morn-ing, and it got harder as I got older. Still, there was the day to be gotten through. I was in the Inquirer newsroom by 10.

❖ 23 ❖

I think Jeff sent her, or maybe not, but anyway there was Annette pull-ing up a chair next to where I sat at the table, hunched forward, leaning my hands on my thighs, pushing against them. "What's happening, Angelo?"

"Asthma," I said. No breath for further explanations.

"Is there anything you know to do that will help you stop it?"

I smiled at her. "New lungs," I said.

"Yes, but – practically. Hot tea? Something like that?"

Shook my head. Didn't have the breath to point out that if I had some-thing I could do that might help, I'd be doing it. It wouldn't be a question of too much trouble to move!

"Is there something I can get for you from your room? Medicine, some-thing?"

I shook my head. "All out," I said.

"Is this likely to go away by itself?"

"Dawn – probably," I said. I didn't know what time it was but I doubted we were as far along as midnight. Six hours, probably. More.

By now we had an audience, about the last thing I wanted.

Annette looked at me intently. "Angelo, are you all right with us doing some energy work on you?"

"Do I have to – do something?"

"Nothing physical. You won't have to move."

I nodded. "Okay with me," I said. "Don't go – near my chest." I knew from experience that someone touching my chest, however lightly, would make everything worse instantly. Not only would my muscles tighten ever more, my anxiety level would shoot up, which would tighten up everything – and knowing it in advance, my anxiety level would shoot up even higher. But I had no breath to explain this, and fortunately she asked for no explanations.

Annette looked around at the dozen or so people in the room. "This is where it gets practical," she said. "This is a little ahead of schedule – we don't usually teach this until Inner Voice – but if anyone wants to help me here, you'll get a glimpse of how much there is to learn."

All those people watching me? "You are not alone," the vision had said. "You are not alone, you are not alone, you are not alone." Well, alone is what I always have been, *especially during an asthma attack. At least it looked that way, but maybe not.*

"Angelo, are you okay with somebody holding your hand?"

I nodded, "Somebody – pretty, I hope."

She laughed. "You'll be telling jokes on your deathbed, I think. All right. Claire, sit there on Angelo's left and take his left hand, will you? I don't think he'll mind that." I'd have laughed with everybody else, if I'd had breath enough, but anyway I sort of grunted a laugh. "And Toni, will you sit here and hold his right hand with your left? Now the rest of you, anyone who wants to participate, form your chairs in a big circle and join hands so that Angelo is part of one big circle. I'm going to stand here behind him. Angelo, all right to touch your back?"

"Think so," I said. This was making me more tense, more nervous, if anything.

"First thing we're going to do is take a few nice deep long breaths – Angelo, I know that's just what you *can't* do right now, but I want you to sort of imagine doing it. You do what you have to do to breathe right now, but try at the same time to imagine what it's like to breathe deeply and easily. Everybody, deep slow breathing. Remember what it feels like when you're doing a tape and C.T. moves you into Entry State. Go for that feeling of relaxation."

Very quietly, she said, "Now, Angelo, I'm going to put my hands on your back, don't be startled." I felt the palms of her hands on my shoulder blades, her fingertips lightly resting on the back of my shoulders on either side of my neck. I don't think I could have borne to have her touch my chest, but her touch on my back and shoulders felt soothing.

"Now, from that state of relaxation, move into Entry State," Annette said, "just as if you were doing a tape. Everybody continue breathing long calming breaths, and move into Entry State."

"'Do this now,'" Jeff said, and everybody laughed. It didn't seem to disrupt anything, though.

After a few minutes, she said, "Angelo, follow along as best you can. Imagining is nearly as good as doing it. The rest of you, move on to Wider Vision. Keep breathing slowly, steadily, in a rhythm that is calming to you."

"All right, Angelo, your job is to form a picture of your lungs as they are when they are giving you trouble. Form a picture – a cartoon, really – of your lungs when you are having trouble with asthma. Visualize them in some way that's meaningful to you. Red and angry-looking, maybe, or tied up with cords around them. Some visual image that you can pass to your unconscious mind. It doesn't have to be anatomically correct; in fact, I think cartoons are better because they are more pointed, more obvious. Form a clear cartoon symbolizing your lungs during an asthma attack."

We could all hear the words "do this now" but this time no one said them.

"Now in a minute, you're going to take that image and change it, so be sure you have it clear in your mind. Do this while breathing as slowly and as deeply and as calmly as you can. Stay with that state of mind, even if you don't think you can do it very well."

A few minutes more, and she said, "All right, guys. What you did up till now is preparation; now it's the real thing. Go on to Time Choice, and, when you get there, staying in Time Choice, I want you all to close your eyes, and go back to remembering a time when you very intensely gave love or received love. Maybe a pet, maybe somebody in your family, maybe your first love – some time when you were intensely loved or when you loved someone intensely. Remember that moment, remember that *feeling*, and move into the feeling. *Become* love again. And when you are inside that feeling – not before – send that love to Angelo, and intend that he use that love energy to heal his body."

I was in no mood to criticize the technique or to question the logic. Besides, there was no need. I felt Claire squeeze my fingers, and I experienced an enormous surge of love for her, and from her. And it seemed to me I could feel the love being passed through her from Jeff, sitting to her left, and from Toni to my right, and from all those in the circle. More remarkably, I felt the heat of Annette's hands on my back, and felt her hands get hotter and hotter as the seconds passed.

"Absorb this energy, this love, that is being sent to you by your friends, Angelo. Absorb it and pass it on to your lungs. And as you do that, take that image, that cartoon, that you were holding, and let it morph into a vision of your lungs as they are normally. If you saw them as red and scratchy, now let that picture relax to something pink and smooth, or whatever represents normal to you. If you saw an iron band around your lungs, see that iron band cut off, or disappearing. Whatever, the specifics don't matter. What matters is that you receive this loving energy from your friends, and use it to transmute your physical condition. Go ahead. As our friend Jeff says, and I think C.T. has been known to say it too, 'Do this now.'" We all smiled at that, I think, and yet it didn't dilute the intensity of the experience. If anything, it accentuated it.

"Hold that loving energy, folks, this is very good work you are doing. Angelo, accept that energy. You're not alone in this. Accept it, use it, let your lungs return to normal." After a couple of long moments, she moved her hands onto my shoulders and gave me an affectionate squeeze. "How's that, tiger?" I am pretty sure she already knew.

"That's amazing," I said. My breathing was back to normal, or close to normal, and I knew that the attack was either over or close to over. I looked around at my friends who had done this for me, and suddenly they seemed like angels in bodies. *You are not alone*, I heard again, and I realized that I had tears in my eyes. Very embarrassing!

❖ 24 ❖

"I had to improvise as I went along," Annette told us, "because as far as I knew, none of you had done it before, but I trusted that it would work out all right, and it looks like it did."

"I've done it," Andrew said, "but I've never seen it done that way. Very impressive."

"Do you have a specific discipline, Andrew?"

"Oh, just various forms of energy work. Reiki, for one, but that isn't what I use most of the time. Most of the time, it's more free form."

I sat there sipping coffee, still deeply moved, lungs at rest, a normal night in prospect.

Edith asked, "So Annette, what actually happened there?"

Before she could say anything, I said "I-don't-know-what-do-you-think?"

They laughed. "Angelo's feeling better," Jeff said.

Annette said, "I'm afraid we had to get a little ahead of ourselves. As I told you, this isn't a part of the Open Door program. I only did it because we had to."

"I'm glad you did," I said. "And thanks again to all of you." I could feel myself getting all choked up again. Embarrassing. "You saved me a long night."

"You're welcome, and it was a pleasure. And, you know, when someone gives you a chance to help them, they are also giving you a great gift. So I'll speak for your fellow participants and thank you too. Believe it or not, not everyone is able to accept help when offered." *Don't I know that! If I'd had any choice at all, probably I wouldn't have, myself.*

"There's a reason we call the introductory program Open Door. It's the entryway, the first step on the road to higher consciousness. At least, it can be. But it's the basics, that's all, what my mother would call 'a lick and a promise.' There's only so much ground that can be covered in a week. Besides, these things tend to take time to work their way deeper into your fabric. Usually we find that you're more ready to go on after some time has passed, and you have assimilated what went before. Ideally, you'd leave at least a few weeks between Open Door and either Inner Voice or Bridging Over.

"You see? You are being exposed to a lot of new things here, and they take time to sink in. Each one of you will absorb these things at a different rate, so that some will be ready to do another program next week and others may not be ready for years to come. As David always says, individual mileage may vary. You all just participated in something that ordinarily we save for later programs, on the theory that you're more likely to be ready for it. So, I don't intend to tell you too much about what we just did. Let's let the Open Door process proceed at its usual pace, and perhaps later you'll have a better idea."

Francois interrupted, a rare thing for him. "I don't know, Annette," he said, and in his calm authority I saw his priesthood showing through. "It is well to follow accustomed procedure so as not to foster eccentricity, but in English you have a saying that 'circumstances alter cases.' In my world, we would say that providence brought us together to have this remarkable experience. Perhaps it was an opportunity for us to follow up exceptional experience, for reasons that are not yet apparent."

Annette frowned slightly, considering it. "We'd say 'the universe brought us to the experience'" she said. "That's about the same thing. Well, perhaps you're right. We'll look at it a little, with the understanding that at any point I may have to say 'enough's enough.' If I do, we drop the subject. Deal?" She looked around and saw no disagreement, then paused. "I just thought of another reason not to do this," she said. "You know how reluctant we are to tell you 'what something means.' And this is getting awfully close to that. But I'll give you my own personal opinion, as long as you understand that it's *my* opinion, and not necessarily David's, and not C.T.'s."

We waited, tacitly agreeing but sort of politely implacable.

"First off, realize that some things that are very effective aren't complicated and don't require special training. That visualizing and morphing exercise, for instance. It works well for specific localized problems, especially when you are working with the assistance of others. First you visualize the condition you want to address, then you morph the visualization to be the way you want it to be. That's all there is to it. It sounds too easy to be possible, doesn't it? It sounds like nothing. But you saw what happened."

Elizabeth said, "We saw what happened, but that isn't the same as understanding what we saw, Annette. It worked – but how did it work? Why *should* it work?"

"I don't *know* how it works, and really, I'm just happy that it does. How I *think* of it, is making a picture of the situation so that you can get the attention of the subconscious mind. The subconscious doesn't understand words nearly as well as it does pictures, so – draw it a picture. That's all you're trying to accomplish. Then, when you have that picture firmly in mind, visualize it changing, flowing gently into whatever your mental image is of a healthy situation. Once you have successfully communicated to the subconscious mind, it does the rest. At least, that's how I think of it. Scientists say that the unconscious mind processes information a million times faster than the conscious mind does. A million times. So, it no longer surprises me that we get cures seemingly immediately."

"Does it only work with group energy?"

"Well, it works *better* with group energy, faster. In my experience, everything does. But I think the most important limitation isn't whether you have help, or how well you can visualize, but how well you can bring yourself to overcome your own internal resistance to the idea. All your life, you've been taught things that may make visualizing and morphing seem silly to you. We don't find it easy to risk seeming foolish (even if only in our own eyes). But if you can't risk hoping that this technique will help you – then it won't be able to. If you *can* risk it, it *can* help. It's as simple as that. That's why this was a valuable gift to everybody here, Angelo. Seeing isn't quite believing, but it's a long step toward it."

"Made a believer out of *me*," I said.

"Me too, actually," Tony Giordano said thoughtfully. "Seeing's believing as far as I'm concerned, as long as you understand what it is you saw. I can see that there are more possibilities to this than I had reckoned with."

Bobby said, "I didn't understand what love has to do with helping Angelo's breathing."

Annette nodded. "All right, that's a good point to bring up, Bobby, thanks. It has been said that the ultimate polarity is between love and fear. This polarity could equally well be expressed as between love and despair, or between love and lack of love. 'Love' in this context is not about warm fuzzy feelings, or sentiment, or romance. We're talking about the binding energy, rather like gravity, that not only 'makes the world go 'round,' but *makes the world*. Love is the interpenetration of being, the fundamental oneness of everything. If we are to live in health, if we are to help others heal, we must live in love as best we can from day to day. Remember, now, this is how *I* see it; not necessarily how anybody else here at the institute sees it.

"We in bodies live in time and space, of course, but our minds and bodies extend *beyond* time and space. By definition, there can be no separation by space where there is no space, and no separation by time where there is no time. Although the part of us that is in space-time experiences separation, the part of us that isn't, doesn't. Thus part of us lives in a 'space' with different rules and fewer boundaries. When we connect with that part of ourselves, miracles happen.

"When you know that there is no distance to be overcome, you realize that distant healing is not a matter of overcoming distance, but of overcoming *the idea* of overcoming distance. Surely it's a lot easier to overcome an idea than a physical 'reality.' Healing, whether hands-on or at a distance, is the same thing. You hold yourself at a level of health and resonate with the person needing healing, and he or she revs up to that level, as if leaning upon the template of health that you are holding."

"Yes, this fits well with my tradition," Francois said. "Jesus said that the entire law and the prophets were contained in the command to do two things: Love God with your whole being, and love your fellows as yourself. You have said that to have health or to help others heal, we need to learn to trust the knowledge that 'comes to us,' and we need to come from the heart. Is that not what Jesus said? You must develop and use your intuition, and you must be love."

Annette said, "I would never try to discuss health and healing without acknowledging how much is to be learned from scriptures. I think that Jesus is the perfect model for us of bringing forth the higher self while still in the body."

"Or, as we would say, living by conforming our will to God's."

"I see what you're saying, but it wouldn't have occurred to me to put it that way."

"Everything we need to know is to be found in the world's scriptures," Francois said. "That's why they were put there. They are guidebooks to a fuller life, not texts to be memorized against an afterlife final examination, or legal manuals aimed at enforcing compliance."

"But we're always told that religion is a matter of belief!"

"Yes, but what does that mean? What someone thinks he believes is less important than how he lives. Our lives are our true beliefs, expressed in action. Many people who think they are religious believers live atheist lives, and many atheists unknowingly conform their lives to follow God's will as best they can."

Jeff said, "There's a joke that says that the churches are filled with Christians who want to go to heaven, but don't want to die to get there."

"Yes, they say 'Lord, Lord,' and they think this will let them enter the kingdom. But I think they are mistaken. Jesus said that 'the kingdom of God is within you.' That doesn't sound to me like 'wait till you're dead and hope you get to heaven.'"

Claire said, "Are you sure you're a priest?"

We all laughed, Francois included. "Occasionally my superiors ask the same question," he said, "but less often than you might think, because the mental world of the religious is not what the outside world thinks it is.

Because the secular world and the religious life speak different languages, we misunderstand each other. This is the tragedy of our civilization. But I believe that when Jesus said, 'I have come that you may have life and have it more abundantly,' he meant not merely *after we die,* but *now.* Few of my associates would disagree with that interpretation – but the world scarcely even understands the literal meaning of the words."

"Well for one thing," Bobby said, "not everybody believes in God. I don't, myself. And even those who believe in God don't necessarily believe in Christians!"

Again we laughed, and again Francois joined us. "As to belief in God, I have never tried to persuade someone to do so. I tell them, instead, look around you and see if it seems likely that all of this, that fits together so well, could have created itself. We may not understand what God is, or what God wants – we may have created God in the image of man, as someone said – but demonstrating that our ideas of God are inadequate is not the same thing as demonstrating that God does not exist."

"Science did that long ago," Bobby said.

"Did it?"

"Sure. The rise of science meant the beginning of the end for religion. I mean, I'm sorry, Francois, but – "

Francois good-naturedly waved away the apology. "So then, you think that science and religion are incompatibles? Opposites that never meet?"

"Well – sure. Don't you?"

"I do not. Good science and good theology are two aspects of the same body of inquiry. Science studies the world as revealed by sensory data; theology studies the world beyond the senses. They both ask: What is the reality of this world in which we find ourselves?"

"Except, science looks at the evidence. It *measures* things. It *investigates* and it changes its mind when its investigation changes its ideas. That's how it progresses. Religion just says it's so because God says it's so."

"I am aware of the mythology surrounding the scientific method, Bobby," Francois said, smiling. "However, in everyday life scientific practice diverges considerably from the theory of the scientific method. And in any case, theology too must square with the facts. Saying 'it's so because God says it's so' would be very bad theology."

"But doesn't that amount to agreeing that theology must follow science?"

"No, not at all. Think how often science changes its mind. Theologians would be stupid indeed to put themselves in a position where their theology had to change every time science changed. That would merely concede to science the position of ultimate arbiter of reality, in spheres that are not really susceptible to scientific investigation. The problem arises, you see, because in our day scientists have arrogated to themselves the exclusive right to decide what the facts are. Theology shouldn't change because of scientific opinions, anymore than science should change because of theological opinions."

"So you're saying it doesn't matter what science discovers, theology is going to keep believing whatever it believes regardless."

"No, I am saying that theology has its own ways of pursuing truth, and it should stick to them, regardless of whatever view is fashionable in the scientific world. However, there is all the difference in the world between truth – even revealed truth – and logic. Logic is only as strong as its weakest premise. So I see no excuse for maintaining any theological tenets that were based on obsolete scientific theory."

"It doesn't seem to me that theology is *ever* based in science, obsolete or otherwise!"

Francois smiled broadly, and I got a sudden sense that he enjoyed disputation as he enjoyed chess, for more or less the same reasons: the clash of arms, the exercise of skill, the mustering of resources, the sheer aesthetic enjoyment of it all. "Consider time," he said. "At one point our society knew, or thought it knew, that time was what it seems to be. The theology of those days was based in what society thought it knew about reality. It is always that way. Probably it must be. Theologians are a part of the world around them, after all. But now look what John Calvin constructed on the idea that time was what it appeared to be!"

"Calvin?"

"A Frenchman from Picardy, a man of the sixteenth century who spent most of his adult life in Geneva. He was a Protestant, best known for his doctrines of predestination and election. He wasn't the only one teaching those views, but they are mostly associated with his name. Predestination argues that we are all born predestined to go to heaven or hell after we die, because if God knows everything, then he knows ahead of time who will live as a sinner and who will not. Can you see that this theological idea is rooted in a certain idea of time? If his ideas about time fall, then so do his ideas about causality, and therefore so do his ideas about omniscience."

"No, I don't get it. Say some more about it."

"Calvin thought, if God knows everything, he knows who is going to sin and go to hell, and he knows this *before he creates them!* This is a necessary consequence of the fact that God knows everything ahead of time. But if time and space are not what they seem to be, and science proves it, surely theology must take that into account. And chaos theory now says that prediction beyond a certain point is impossible, regardless of how good your instruments or how extensive your data."

"Yes it does," Andrew said with satisfaction. "And the impossibility lies in the nature of reality, not in the inadequacy of our instruments. Just as Heisenberg's uncertainty principle stated."

"So if time is not what we thought it was, the world is not what we thought it was, and when we realize that, it becomes time to revisit our theological conclusions." He shrugged. "Of course, Calvin's theology was mistaken on other grounds in any case, but he serves as an example, you see. Advances in science can not be relied upon to advance theology, but they can sometimes help theology disentangle itself from past errors based on previous science. Theology could return the favor, if science were open to it."

"But you said that science and theology investigate different things, different kinds of things. How can theology help science?"

"Theology could give science advance knowledge of which doors lead to dead ends, and which doors that look like dead ends may lead to unsuspected treasures. We religious could never prove anything in scientific terms, you understand, but still we *know* things that we cannot *prove*. If scientists would pay more attention to what we say we know, and would attempt to prove or disprove them, surely this would be more efficient than stumbling around in the dark looking for new theories to make sense of puzzling data. It would also be more scientific than refusing to examine entire categories of experience because they cannot be investigated by means appropriate to the physical sciences."

Bobby said, "You think *science* ignores *data*?"

Francois wasn't the only one to smile! It was hard to remember, sometimes, how very young Bobby was, much younger than his years.

Andrew jumped in. "Bobby, sure they do. Let me pose a theoretical example. Suppose you are a scientist, and your scientific beliefs predispose you to 'know' that vapor could not possibly arise from the surface of a liquid. If you then came across a steaming hot cup of coffee, you'd have to disbelieve your eyes, or call it an optical illusion, or suspect a trick. It would be either that, or give up your belief, and giving up beliefs is hard. It's much easier to say: fraud!"

"Oh come on – "

"No, really, that's what scientists do, especially if they are committed rationalist materialists. I've seen them do it. Either they refuse to investigate, or they investigate while operating out of their own belief-system, in such a way as to invalidate their experiment in advance, like trying to reproduce the phenomenon of vapor coming from a liquid by using a cup of *cold* water, and saying that water is water, and if it doesn't work cold there's no reason to think it would work hot."

"That's a ridiculous example."

"Is it? How do you think they'd react to reports of half the things we're experienced right here, these past couple of days? You think they'd say, 'that's very interesting, we'll get right on it'?"

"Well, they might."

"The hell they would. If their beliefs say that something can't exist, they refuse to see it, so after that it would be 'unscientific' to investigate. Look at all the things they won't look at: Near death experiences, psychic healing, precognition, second sight, telepathy . . . a huge list of things. They dismiss the whole subject as myth, legend, superstition, and fraud. And yet, these kind of things have been recorded for as long as people have been on the earth. And we haven't even been at this a week and some of us are starting to experience them. How hard would it be to investigate, if they were really as open-minded and committed to seeking the truth as they think they are?"

Francois said, quietly, "It cannot be accurate to draw conclusions about human nature – about the nature of reality – about God – while you are deliberately disregarding so much evidence."

"But these things are outside the realm of science," Bobby said.

Quick as thought, Andrew shot back, "Bring them *inside*! Either that, or admit that you are building monuments of logic on foundations that are hopelessly flawed by the selective omission or rejection of evidence. You can't leave out whole classes of facts, you can't systematically ignore or deny phenomena, just because they make you uncomfortable. If you want comfort instead of truth, all right, that's a choice, but don't call it science."

I said, "If you want to see what my idea of science would look like, try reading Emerson while keeping in mind what we have learned about the left brain and the right brain. I think you'd be in for a shock." I grinned. "Be good for you." But this met no response. Nobody there knew Emerson.

"What we need," Andrew said, "in order to remove all this stuff from the realm of old wives tales and fraud and hysteria and inexperience, is an overarching theory. It will need to be more inclusive, truer, then any theory we have now. The first guy to come up with that theory will shake the kaleidoscope of our society and we will be different people living in a different world. It's happened often enough before."

"I don't see where this new theory is going to come from," Bobby said stubbornly.

"I don't either. We're waiting for our Kepler, or our Newton, who will perceive a relationship between what seem to us like disconnected phenomena. We haven't had that yet. But we have parts of it. Right here, in fact."

"Such as?"

"Well, it seems clear enough that the brain is a tuning device. Where we tune the brain determines what reality-program we pick up. Once we learn to set the dial by intention instead of having it set for us by circumstance, we will be able to verify or disprove reports of unusual states of consciousness, such as what we are experiencing here. For the first time, we will all be living in the same universe. Right now, we are all living in different universes because what we *can* perceive depends on what we are *prepared* to perceive. Thus, we can have no new perceptions unless we deliberately decide to risk making a fool of ourselves by tentatively believing something that part of us knows full well can't be true."

"Hmm," Bobby said. "Well, I don't know that I'm prepared to abandon science and pursue theology."

"It isn't a matter of choosing sides," Andrew said. "It's a matter of transcending opposites."

"Deep waters tonight," I said. "If only I had a watch, I'd know how late it is, and I'd probably tell myself it's time for bed."

"Well," Annette said, "we trainers don't wear watches, but we usually *do* have a pretty good idea what time it is, and my body says you're right. You are all welcome to stay up as long as you want, just be sure to turn out the lights and put away any food that's left. I'm going to bed and I'll see you in the morning."

CHAPTER FIVE

Wednesday
March 22, 1995

Jeff came downstairs and saw me at the table, drinking coffee and writing in my journal. Coffee first for him too, of course (you have to admire character when you find it), then he dropped into a chair across the table from me.

"Figured I'd find you outside," he said.

"Not this morning. Got to be a little careful."

"Colder, this morning?"

"Yes, but mainly I don't want to take chances." In fact, my breathing was a little rough, had been all night. I felt like I was just on the edge of having trouble. "I don't want Annette to start charging for her services."

"Boy, that was something, wasn't it?"

"You have no idea."

"Actually, I think I do, a little. I never asked you last night, what did you *feel* when we were working on sending you energy?"

I hesitated, partly to give myself time to find what I would say, partly because others were coming down the stairs, and I didn't know that I wanted to have my health be the center of attention again. *On the other hand,* I thought, *I guess I do owe them.*

Claire had said something to me, the night before, and I had heard her, though I might not have listened to anybody else. "It isn't a sign of weakness, Angelo, and it's nothing to be ashamed of. Or should I be ashamed that the cancer has come back?"

"No, of course not, but – "

"There isn't any 'but.' There just isn't. I know it's painful for you to talk about it, but that's only because you let it be. Start to talk about it the way you would a broken arm, or an ear infection, and you'll feel entirely differently about it."

"Well, I don't know about that," I'd said, but finally – more to avoid disappointing her than for any other reason, and because she seemed so sure – I'd promised, and then we'd joined the last stragglers headed up to bed. So – what was I feeling while the circle was working to send me love?

"When you're having an asthma attack," I said slowly, "you can't really forget about your breathing. Whether you're reading or trying to sleep or listening to music or whatever, what's really front and center is trying to get your next breath."

"Sure, makes sense."

"It hadn't really occurred to me until now, but I've never been very much in touch with my body. I'm beginning to see that it's gotten me into trouble over the years, not being in touch."

"Being your basic couch potato?"

"Not that so much as actively ignoring it for hours at a time, whenever I've been having an asthma attack. You know, waiting for enough time to pass that I could breathe again. I think it sort of built up a habit of putting my mind elsewhere until the trouble is over." I could see Jeff get it. "So to answer your question, I was too involved in my immediate problem to notice the process. I was worried about having a full-fledged asthma attack, and I was just hoping that whatever Annette was doing would have *some* effect. *Any* effect. I didn't have any idea it could stop an attack in its tracks."

Klaus was among those who were sitting down with us. "What you say about ignoring your body does not surprise me," he said. "I see this often in my work. I say to people, you do not need to have an out-of-body experience. First you should have an in-the-body experience. You should become acquainted with the environment in which you live, this complicated organism."

"I understand *that*," Ellis Sinclair said. "When you're young, you take your body for granted. After a while you start to realize that a little timely maintenance can save you from a lot of problems."

"Yes, maintenance, but more than a matter of maintenance," Klaus said. "In a more complete sense, it is a matter of how you see yourself and the world. It is my experience that a large part of the problem comes from our western *zeitgeist* – maybe you would call it world-view, or the way the world looks to us?"

"The spirit of the times, I think you might say," Ellis said.

"All right. Well, the *zeitgeist* for a long time has been materialism, the idea that the material world is what is real, and the non-material world does not exist, or is not important. This is what makes it difficult for the individual to control his own health. Or hers."

"And everything costs too much. Doctors, hospitals, prescription drugs, all of it."

"I mean something much more fundamental, because these things are not the same in Europe, where I live. But perhaps it is too long a subject to discuss before breakfast."

"As long as we have coffee, we're good to go," Jeff said.

"Ah, but I drink tea, you see."

"That's *your* problem. Nobody's making you drink leaves instead of beans. Go ahead." Jeff looked around. "I think we're all interested, right?"

"All right. I am a reflexologist, you know, and we are not considered to be in the mainstream of modern medicine, but we have our own experiences. This is how it seems to me. In the first place, there is the idea that things sometimes 'just happen' – that things happen for no reason."

"Out of left field," Jeff said. Receiving a blank look, he added, "Something that's unexpected and apparently uncaused."

"Yes. People believe that they may become ill for reasons beyond their control, reasons that have nothing to do with who they are and how they live their lives."

"I take it that you aren't talking about sensible diet, exercise, and all that," Claire said. She was sitting next to me, and I was glad to have her there. I thought of the cancer that had come back to her.

"That is correct. I mean to say, people believe that illness comes because they *do* something wrong, but it does not occur to them that they may be *being* something wrong. Can you say that in English?"

We reassured him that it was okay to say that in English.

"And other beliefs make it difficult for people to regulate their health. One is that what happens to the body is not related to what is happening in your emotional life, or your mental life. And not related to your *spiritual* life."

"In many ways our society silently assumes that there *is* no spiritual life," Ellis said.

"Yes. As I said. And so it considers the physical body a mechanical system, that may be effectively treated as though it were a machine. In my view, and in my experience of many years, not one of these beliefs is true."

"Well, they're not universal beliefs anymore," Andrew said. "Plenty of people right around this table know better, just from the evidence in our own lives."

"But these are the conscious beliefs of individuals. The beliefs of our society – of the *zeitgeist* – are held unconsciously, which means that most people have no control over them. Anything that remains unconscious affects our behavior without our even knowing about it."

"Madison Avenue wouldn't give you an argument on that," Ellis said. "That's how they make their living, manipulating people's subconscious behavior."

"Of course, and the combined effect is to make the individual feel helpless. If things just happen, then we are always living on the break – at the break?"

"On the edge? On the brink?"

"Yes, thank you. Anything might happen to anyone for no reason. And if illness may come for reasons beyond your control, you are even more on the edge. And if your body is a machine – how can you tend the machine except in mechanical ways?"

Claire said, quietly, "But what of someone like Angelo, who has had asthma all his life? What of someone who contracts cancer, or had a heart condition? Is it their fault that they are sick, then?"

"No, no, no. I know that some people say things like that, but no one *deserves* illness because it's somehow their fault, and no one would *choose* illness."

"We can't just *desire* ourselves well, in other words," Ellis said, perhaps a bit dryly.

"If it were so simple, would we not all be well and happy, and would we not all perhaps live for as long as we wished to? It is true that if we knew how to consistently create health – *choose* health – we would be always healthy. But in my experience, what we create consciously often contradicts our unconscious creation. And so we struggle against the assumptions of helplessness that we absorb from society. But we are not helpless, and we are not necessarily dependent upon medicines, as we saw our friend Angelo discover last night."

"I'm not quite ready to sign off on that, though," I said. "I've still got to get through the rest of the week without medicine if I can, and I have to say, I'm not looking forward to it."

"No, I am sure not. I have many patients who suffer from asthma and emphysema and other lung problems. I have an idea of what you suffer in an attack. The prolonged uncertainty in itself constitutes a strain."

It certainly does! And so does talking about it!

Ellis looked up as Bobby came downstairs. "Bobby, do you have a minute? I had a thought overnight that you might be interested in."

"Sure," Bobby said.

"Perhaps we should step out on the porch for a moment."

Bobby raised his eyebrows but nodded, and followed Ellis out the door. When they came back in, a few minutes later, he seemed to be lost in thought. He got some coffee *(I didn't know Bobby drank coffee!)* and sat listening to the conversation while we all waited for the breakfast bell to be rung, but he didn't volunteer and we didn't ask.

❖ 2 ❖

I guess I'm going to furnish the topic of conversation all through breakfast, too. I sure hope something happens today to divert people's attention!

"It seems to me that people ought to pay more attention to the placebo effect," Toni said. "Everybody recognizes the phrase, so they think they know what it is."

"I don't," Bobby said. "And pass the salt and pepper, please."

"If you give people a sugar pill or some other harmless but neutral substance, but they believe that it is a medicine, a certain percentage of them will get well with no other treatment."

"Oh sure, there's one born every minute."

"Well, I think maybe it isn't that simple. What's the difference between people's reactions to placebos and their reactions to patent medicines – or to prescription medicines, for that matter? In each case, they are putting their faith in a physical substance to correct a health problem. Yet the placebo effect demonstrates that sometimes it's the belief that cures, not the physical substance. By rights, it ought to be called 'the miracle effect.' And maybe those who got better after taking medicine also got better not because of the medicine but because of their belief?"

"Interesting idea," Ellis said.

"Energy healing doesn't work 100 percent of the time, but neither do religious rites, or prescription medicines. I wonder how many medical procedures work mostly because people believe in them."

"That must be at least somewhat true," Edith said. "You look at what past generations took as medicine and you wonder that anybody survived long enough to produce another generation. We don't believe in the medicines they believed in. What makes us think that our grandchildren won't laugh at what we believe in?"

"If it doesn't *always* work, what's going on when it *does* work? It's a fair question about energy healing and it's a fair question about conventional medicine. But you don't often hear people posing the question. They tend to believe in one or the other, and they mostly settle for sneering at the people on the other side of the issue."

God! I've heard more about health and illness this morning than the whole rest of my life put together, and we haven't even gotten through breakfast!

"Well," Toni said, "I think that the key to healing is to remove the illusion of separation, and the way to remove the illusion of separation is to love. There will come a day when we will live our lives *knowing*, not believing, that we're all connected, *knowing* that we are individuals and that we are *not* individuals. It is the perception of separation that creates the perception of lack of control, which creates fear. Eliminate the perception of separation and fear goes out the window. This is what love does. That's what we should be working on."

"I think I can give an example of that," Andrew said. "Sympathy pains."

"What are sympathy pains?" Bobby asked.

"That's when a woman is suffering labor pains and the baby's pro-spective father experiences pains just like hers, obviously for no physical reason. They're called sympathy pains."

"Yes," Helene said tartly. "He's looking for sympathy."

"No, I don't think that's it. Once I might have agreed with you. Now I don't think so. I don't have personal experience of *that* kind of sympathy pain, but in the years since I began helping others to heal, I have often ex-perienced a different form of sympathy pains. When I connect with people, I often feel pain in the places where they feel pain, and I feel it (so far as I can tell) with the same intensity and 'flavor' as they do. I find it enormously helpful. It tells me where to focus our efforts. It occurred to me one day that a prospective father's sympathy pains may be exactly the same thing. Being in close sympathy with the prospective mother of his child, perhaps the prospective father feels what she is feeling."

"I've always heard that we should never take on another's pain."

"No, that's right, Toni, but I don't think that's what I'm doing here, and in any case I certainly don't hold onto it afterward. I'm just saying, my experience gives me a different slant on sympathy pains."

I thought, *I wish somebody would have sympathy with me for the pain this endless medical talk is causing!* But I smiled as I thought it.

❖ 3 ❖

Debrief room again, ready to start the day. I felt like we'd already been going for hours.

"So I want to know what happened last night," Sam said. "We've been hearing about it but it's hard to know what to make of it. For once, could we get something other than 'I-don't-know-what-do-you-think'?" *If I hadn't had an attack and Annette hadn't showed us how to stop it, I wonder what we would have been talking about today!*

"As long as you realize that this isn't on the regular agenda. We had a situation and we had to deal with it, and as Francois pointed out, we might as well assume that it happened for a reason. But we don't want to take our eye off the ball, either. This is still Wednesday morning of your Open Door, and we have a few things lined up for you."

"And as far as I am concerned," I said, "we can start doing tapes any time."

People laughed, recognizing my reluctance, but that didn't make them any less interested. I should have shared that interest. After all, I had been on the inside of a miracle! At least, that's what it felt like. But I never did like talking about my lung problems, and I liked others talking about them even less.

"I heard people talking about it at breakfast, and I gather you were discussing it earlier, as well. Does anybody here *not* know what we're talking about?"

Selena Juras raised her hand. *I'll bet that kills her, everybody else knowing something she doesn't,* I thought. But in this I did her an injustice. "I heard people say that you did hands-on healing last night after the Lost in Space and Time tape. I would have participated if I had been told you were going to do it."

"Nobody knew, Selena," Annette said. "Angelo was having trouble breathing and his medicine had run out, so we had to do whatever we could. I asked the people who were there at the table, and they very nicely volunteered. You'd have been welcome, of course – all of you would have been – but we worked with those who were already gathered."

"I'm still wanting to know how serious the situation was really," Sam said.

Annette looked over at me, so reluctantly I said, "I wouldn't have gotten any sleep last night." *I would have spent hours waiting for the sun.*

"And what *I* want to know," Tony said, "is whether this would have worked just as well for anybody as it did for Angelo. If not, why not. But if so, why isn't everybody doing it?"

"Ah," Annette said, "that's the $64,000 dollar question. In the first place, it *might have* worked as well for anybody, but on the other hand it *might not* have worked for Angelo either. In this kind of work, a tremendous amount depends on the attitude of the person being worked on."

"I don't understand. Either it works or it doesn't work, right? What does somebody's attitude have to do with it?"

Annette looked at David, who shrugged as if to say, "In for a penny, in for a pound."

"Okay. Short course in healing as I understand it, with the usual *caveat* that what I'm saying doesn't necessarily reflect anybody's belief but mine, so please don't go off and quote me and then say this is what C.T. believes, or that CTMI teaches. Are we straight about that?" She paused, as if arranging her thoughts.

"First thing, it seems to me that our health is a balance between our physical states and our mental states. The ratio changes when you change either the physical or mental side of the equation, and thus you can change your health by affecting either side, but which side you change determines whether you get a quicker change or a more permanent change."

She looked around. "With me? Physical states change only slowly, over time. Changing your physical state will take time, but the change will tend to endure. Mental states fluctuate all the time – in fact, fluctuating mental states is practically a definition of normal consciousness – so when you change your mental state, the change will come quickly, sometimes instantly, but will be harder to hold."

Sam said, "How can you say that?"

"Experience, but I'm not going to defend it. In the regular program, we send you to experience things and – you may have noticed – we let you discover for yourself what they might mean."

"I-don't-know-what-do-you-think?" Jeff said.

"Exactly. But we're not here to teach you how to do healing. So I'm just telling you what I have found to be true, and we're going to leave it at that. You have other fish to fry today. There's no point wasting time arguing, which is what usually happens in the absence of experience."

"Or even in the presence of experience," David said.

"True. Okay, Sam? There's nothing wrong with your question, but we don't have time enough to show you, and it's useless to try to persuade anybody of anything. I'm trying to say why it worked with Angelo this time but might not work another time, and why it might or might not have worked with someone else. The short answer is, he was willing to change mental states, and we lent him enough energy to make the change. If he had resisted, it would have been harder, or impossible, depending on how much he resisted."

"Why would he have resisted something that was going to make him feel better?" *Why indeed? But the funny thing is, I did resist it for a moment there.*

"People do, for a lot of reasons, and no we're not going to go into them here. The only thing I'll say about it is that you can't benefit from these techniques while actively disbelieving in them. You don't have to *believe*, but you do need to *suspend disbelief,* or nothing can happen. You cannot be open to new possibilities and at the same time be closed to them. It is that simple."

"Angelo, what do you think about it?"

"Well, I wouldn't *have* thought about it, but I can see that whatever happened might have involved my mental states as much as my physical condition, or my health wouldn't have fluctuated so radically, so quickly. I was very glad it did, of course!"

"So were you cured last night?"

"Not as far as I know. Oh, you mean, did we stop an attack? Oh yes. But it wasn't a cure."

"So what are you going to do?"

"At this point I figure if something happens I'm going to make a run for Annette's apron strings and hope for the best."

That got a laugh, and Annette used it to make a further point. "We forget, sometimes, that illness is a gift as well as an affliction. The ability to suppress or remove symptoms can make things worse if it leads the sufferer to become dependent on something or someone external to himself or herself, or if it leads them to neglect dealing with the illness's underlying cause. Nonetheless, I think you'll agree that if miracles are possible, and *we* can grow to be able to perform them, it's very good news."

David said, "It can be hard to remember, but removing illness is not always appropriate. So much depends on what the individual needs. Some people *need* illness, for reasons we are definitely not going to go into here, or we'll never get started on today's program. If you are interested in obtaining healing abilities, it can be done. Inner Voice is one way; but there are lots of other paths. We can talk about it privately during breaks if you wish."

"This has led us off into places we don't usually visit during Open Door, but sometimes you have to go with the flow. Let's take a *short* break – don't go far, this is just to stretch our legs – and when you come back we'll tell you what's going to happen this morning."

"Or, at least our fantasy of what's going to happen," David said. "Subject to correction from reality, as you've just seen."

❖ 4 ❖

"If a picture is worth a thousand words," Annette said, "what is silence worth? A lot more, we think. This morning we're going to explore the power of silence to deepen our experience."

"Until this point in the process, we've depended heavily on the sharing of experience," David said. "Although the altered-state experience is intensely personal, each tape has been framed by group activity – discussion beforehand, then debriefing. There is good reason for this. Group activity, whether meals or snacks or just sitting around shooting the bull, serves to ground these experiences in ordinary consciousness. This helps assure that you won't wall off these new experiences and later lose access to them."

"But there is also great concentrating power in silence," Annette said, "and so this morning we add silence to our tool kit."

"We are going to explore various aspects of the state we call Interface, but we're going to do it in a manner totally different from the way we explored Entry State, Wider Vision, or Time Choice. This time we're going to do three tapes in a row, with a short break between each, but with no briefing or debriefing around them, and with you maintaining silence in the intervals between them."

"When we finish describing what we're going to do this morning, we're going to break for a few minutes and then, when you hear us ring the bell, you'll know to go to your rooms and do the first tape. At the end of that tape, we will *not* meet to debrief. Instead, there'll be a short break as usual. After the second tape, another short break, and then the third tape. After the third tape we'll break for lunch, and you can rejoin the world of verbal communication."

"During all this time, we ask that you preserve silence, both for your own sake and for the sake of the other participants. If you go downstairs for a snack or a smoke, please respect the process and preserve your silence."

"Everybody understand what we're doing this morning? Three tapes in a row, in silence, then for those of you who may wish to preserve their silence a bit longer – and usually one or two people do – we'll mark one of the tables as a silent table."

"Perhaps because our society is so continually inundated by noise, many people find this silent Wednesday morning to be among their favorite memories of Open Door," David said. "Please, don't cheat on this, and you may open yourself up to the most surprising and satisfying experiences."

"All right? Everybody set? Then let's take a break, and when you hear the bell, off to your rooms by way of the bathrooms, and we'll see you at lunch after your silent morning."

❖ 5 ❖

Lying in bed, waiting for the tape to begin, I thought, *A whole morning of silence? This is going to* kill *Bobby.* I couldn't help imagining him finally having a significant experience and then having to live through several hours before he could talk to someone about it. I was laughing to myself, imagining it.

Breathing fine so far. But then, during tapes, it always has been. I felt intensely grateful to Annette. *I'd have been in a mess without her!* Who would have thought it? All this time I had at my disposal such simple and powerful tools, and never suspected the fact. I wondered, *will it work in the real world? Well, without group support, maybe not. But even if doesn't I'll know that it* did, *and that tells me that the rules of the game aren't what I thought they were. Which is what Thoreau said.*

The pink noise began. I was thinking of Henry Thoreau, saying in the final chapter of *Walden* that our intuition can lead us toward a new life with unsuspected possibilities.

(A couple of weeks after I returned from Open Door, I thought to look up the passage, which goes like this: "I learned this, at least, by my experiment: that if one advances confidently in the direction of his dreams, and endeavors to live the life which he has imagined, he will meet with a success unexpected in common hours. He will put some things behind, will pass an invisible boundary; new, universal, and more liberal laws will begin to establish themselves around and within him; or the old laws be expanded, and interpreted in his favor in a more liberal sense, and he will live with the license of a higher order of beings. In proportion as he simplifies his life, the laws of the universe will appear less complex, and solitude will not be solitude, nor poverty poverty, nor weakness weakness. "

He wasn't talking merely about living economically.)

C.T.'s voice guided us though Entry State, Wider Vision, and Time Choice – familiar clearings in the forest as we moved deeper into the woods – and introduced us to Interface, the altered state in which, he said, we may encounter and interact with other life forms.

As I lay there, my feelings of gratitude broadened, from Annette to Thoreau. I gradually realized that I was feeling love, and as I became aware of that, the feeling strengthened and applied to more and more people in my life. It included my wife and children, and the family I was born into. It included Charlie Reilly – an intense shot of gratitude in his direction, as I realized that it was only his insistence that got me here. It included David and all the people who had spoken to us, or given us glimpses of the inner world of CTMI. Certainly it included C.T. himself, and my fellow participants, even those like Lou Hardin and Selena Juras who irritated me. Irritation, I suddenly realized, has nothing either way to do with love.

Naturally, it included Claire. To my surprise I found that it included, as well, Clara that was, and John and their children, and then it naturally broadened to include Lidian Emerson, and Waldo Emerson, and back to Thoreau again.

Where could you draw the line? I thought. *In a way, we're all one thing, connected by millions of unseen threads.*

C.T. established us in a state of Interface, and then bade us to "expand and prepare to meet alien life forms." I wondered what he had in mind, but knew enough by now to go along. I envisioned myself in the depths of outer space and tried to be prepared for anything, but nothing happened. Perhaps the intense love I was feeling was as close as I needed to come to experiencing an alien presence. Perhaps *I* was the alien presence that morning, at least alien to what I had been till then. No, that isn't the way to put it. Perhaps until that week I had been living a lie, and conceiving of myself, in a way that was alien to who and what I truly was.

❖ 6 ❖

In the second tape, C.T. directed us to retrieve "the five most important messages we can understand at the moment." *Well, if the messages stack up to the answers I got the other day, I won't have any complaints.* "Receive the fifth most important message that you can understand at this time," C.T. said. "Receive the *fifth* most important message. Do this now."

To my surprise, I saw a distinct image, a sketch of a figure turned to stone, like those found in the streets of Pompeii. Then I saw a table with many chairs, all empty. People appeared. I was at the head of the table, the host. More people appeared and the table and chairs expanded as more people arrived, so that there was always room for them.

"When you return to full waking consciousness, you will recall the content of the message you have received," C.T.'s voice said. "You will recall the content of the message you received."

As I lay there in the darkness, listening to the pink noise, waiting for the next instruction, I thought, *I have been living as if turned to stone, but I don't have to; my life can be filled with people, and with joy.*

"Now, receive the fourth most important message that you can understand at this time. Receive the *fourth* most important message. Do this now."

I saw a set of stairs, seen from above, descending into a room below. I was sitting on the second floor, listening to the party going on below, feeling sad and left out. The stairs became a ramp down into the room. I descended, barefoot. They welcomed me not as one coming from above, not as one who wasn't or was properly dressed, but as me.

"You will recall the content of the message you received," C.T.'s voice said, and again I was listening to the pink noise, reflecting on the message. *I descend from cerebral, disembodied heights into the warmth of life among humans.*

"Now, receive the third most important message that you can understand at this time. Receive the *third* most important message." And again I lay there in a receptive state, ready for anything.

I saw something mysterious floating in the water. It swam up to where I was standing on the dock. It was a mechanical dolphin, with a handle. I tried to pull it out of the water, but it was far too heavy. So I got into the water, and took the handle and it began moving with me. It was phenomenally powerful, and moved swiftly and easily. I wondered, why a *mechanical* dolphin, rather than a living one? The answer came: *I* am the *living* part. If the dolphin had a life of its own, I would in justice have to consider its desires and needs. As things are, I need think only of what I want.

"You will recall the content of the message you received." *Pretty self-evident. I am in touch with phenomenal, non-human power that will bring me wherever I want to go.*

"Receive the second most important message that you can understand at this time."

I seemed to be looking out at the universe, but I noticed it had a transverse wrinkle down the middle – so it wasn't the universe at all, but a *picture,* painted on a fabric. Some people rolled it up for me, and I saw that it was a hanging backdrop on a wall of our meeting room in Edwin Carter Hall. But the wall behind it, and the other walls, and the ceiling and floors were all of very heavy wood, very solid, with no doors or windows. No way out. I saw this not as something sinister, but as a fact of life. As soon as the fact registered, "they" rolled the universe backdrop back into place.

Again, "You will recall the content of the message you received," and I was thinking, *I get the message: There's no way you can see or get beyond this universe, this reality system, at this point. Play* here *for now. That's okay with me.*

Finally, C.T. bade us to receive the most important message that we could understand. It came in the form of a great beating heart, floating in mid-air. I grew larger, to absorb it. For the first time, I got a spoken message:

"Wear it inside and outside." And even before C.T. reminded us that we would remember the content of the message we had received, I knew what it meant, and why it had come in that form. *Dad used to tell me not to wear my heart on my sleeve, but this message says wear it on the inside* and *the outside. Okay, I can hear that.*

Some tape. Wonderful messages, not only in the analysis of where I was at the time, but in the clear portrayal of where I could come to. I don't see how any psychiatrist or counselor could have improved on them, either in effectiveness or clarity. As I lay there listening to pink noise, and then C.T. bringing us back to normal consciousness, I was very much aware of my surprise that I had received such distinct images and words. *The surprise is the difference between believing and knowing,* I thought. I was glad to have a few minutes to make notes in my journal before the third tape. I certainly didn't want to lose those messages! And on the other side of the room, Bobby was scribbling madly, holding on to magical messages. *So,* I thought, *the dam broke. He got something.*

❖ 7 ❖

A fast trip to the bathroom *(I wonder if we're building up an association of ideas between doing a tape and having to go to the bathroom first!)* and then I was lying down ready for the third tape of this very full morning. Pink noise and then C.T.'s voice bringing us back to Interface, and then instructions. We are going to practice changing our vibrations, starting from a lower state and moving up successively.

Again, very clear visual descriptions. First, I am staring out the window in boredom as someone talks. *In my own world, not really relating to others particularly.* I squirm a bit, mentally, as I think of my daily life among so many others in the newsroom who I don't really know or care to know or make any effort to know. I squirm more as I realize that in fact that's more or less how I relate – or fail to relate – to everybody. *No wonder I'm so bored!* I'm on friendly terms with lots of people, but it's only skin deep. *The problem is, my world is different from theirs, and nobody wants to step into mine. They're interested in sports and politics and celebrities and television and I don't give a goddamn about any of that. And they don't want to hear about Emerson and Thoreau and all the historical stuff that is so real to me.*

True enough. But the vision of my staring out the window persists.

C.T. tells us to move our vibrations upward, as the tones guide us, and I am walking across a wooden platform over a room, noting people relating. I see David kissing one of his children. *I wonder if David really has children.* I think of my own children, and the coldness that has grown between them and me, and it hurts. *What happened? Where did they go, or where did I go?* I remember them as babies, and as little children, and tears form in my eyes as I remember how we were. *I guess in those days I could still remember being a child, then. Or maybe I just responded naturally to their openness. Or maybe* – startling thought! – *only that kind of openness could get through to me.* We had had fun together. I well remembered that. They liked my silliness and we could make up games to play. *Maybe the separation is as painful for them as it is for me.* In any case, it's clear enough what this is showing me. *The wooden platform must mean something, I suppose. Something organic, maybe. I'll have to remember to ask Claire.*

Again C.T. moves us upward, and a third image forms, me staring at a part of a wooden beam, seeing more and more deeply into the nature of the wood. *More wood. The more awake we are, the more we see, I suppose.*

And finally, one more move, and I feel my concern for Claire. I want her to know that she is loved not just by me but by others. *"And the highest of these is love."* I all but heard it. And then C.T. is bringing us back to normal consciousness, and the long wonderful silent morning is over.

❖ 8 ❖

I ate lunch at the silent table, along with Francois. I don't know what his motivation was. I didn't want to lose the place the silence had brought me to.

Around us the other participants engaged in animated conversations about whatever strange places their morning had brought them to.

Clearly Dottie, our "invisible and inaudible" participant, had found her voice. Funny that she would find her voice via silence. Maybe it was from Lou's needling, before we began the tapes? She was talking with animation, and although I would have had to concentrate to make out what she was saying – an effort I very much *didn't* want to make – it was clear that she was being listened to.

I heard Andrew: "Basically I was told, get used to it. What is going on is an intensification of effort, a multiplication of cause and effect. Things move more quickly now. You have wanted involvement and have expected it. More consciousness is possible now, with more service. Don't resist, but serve, and grow. Work hard on every facet of existence now. Grow like weeds."

And I heard Jeff. "I was letting the images flow, trying hard not to block them off, and at one point it was like I was talking to a fireman in a firehouse. He was standing by a yellow fire truck, and I was up in the air and he was looking up at me. And he was saying 'you and I' to me, thinking I was part of him – and suddenly I got the sense of him being real and me being just a vision to him. And I realized, we don't *know*. Are our visions in our minds, or are we visions in the minds of others? Or both? Or neither!"

"I don't have a lot of patience for this kind of mind game," Lou said. "It's like the Chinese philosopher thinking he was maybe a butterfly, because he had dreamed he was a butterfly."

"I don't know about the Chinese philosopher, but this is not mind games for me, it was just a sudden sharp change in perspective."

"So if we are visions in someone else's mind, why do we feel real to ourselves?"

"I don't have the slightest idea which is real. I'm not as sure of anything as I used to be. For all I know, maybe our visions are as real as we are, and we alternate back and forth, which is why our visions don't always seem to make sense."

I thought that was interesting, but I neither felt left out of the various conversations nor had any urge to join in. Silence suited me just fine. In fact, in a strange way it seemed that Francois and I were carrying on our own conversation, without words, without exchanging glances, without even particularly thinking about each other. I sat at the table, eating, writing in my journal, drinking coffee, looking out the window, feeling far away from wherever I had spent my life, feeling myself being pulled, unresisting, toward a new way of being.

❖ 9 ❖

I was still sitting at the silent table, alone, writing, after Francois had left and the room had pretty well cleared out. She walked over with a mug of tea, and smiled, and lifted an eyebrow.

I said "Hi," and closed my journal, and gestured for her to sit down.

"Hi," she said. "I don't want to disturb your silence if you want to maintain it, but if not, may I join you?"

"I was praying that you would. Let me get some more coffee." When I sat down again, she said, without preamble, "So how was your morning?"

We were the only ones left in the room. I looked at her, and for one last self-protective moment I did not speak, and then I said, "I spent the morning learning how rich my life has always been, and how little I have appreciated it. I learned that the only thing that really counts is fullness of life, which really means fullness of our ability to love. I was told to wear my heart on the outside *and* the inside, and I have been trying to imagine how it will be if I start doing that."

"Angelo, that sounds wonderful!"

"Yeah? Does it also sound a little scary? Because, if it doesn't, it ought to!"

"Of course it's scary. It's the opposite of everything that's familiar to you. I think you were raised to protect yourself, and now you're being told that you have to lay that protection down. Who wouldn't be scared? But it's wonderful, all the same."

"Well, we'll see. Claire, how will you respond, I wonder, to my telling you that I love you? And how will Jeff respond if I tell him the same thing? And how will the rest of the group respond if I tell them that after our last tape they all seem to me like angels? Even the ones that irritate me seem like angels. And how are people going to respond if my eyes keep filling up with tears like this all the time?"

"Maybe they'll respond with envy. Maybe with thanks. Maybe with incomprehension, or amusement. Probably they'll respond as many different ways as there are people. Why do you care how they respond? What's important is what's happening inside *you*."

"Yes. That's true."

"And by the way, I love you too, and I want to tell you how much I admire what you're doing."

"What *I'm* doing?"

"You know those movies they produce using time-lapse photography, where everything is all speeded up and in about a minute a bud develops into a fully developed flower? That's what it's like watching you this week."

"Seems to me C.T. ought to get the credit for that, not me. It's his program. C.T., and Annette and David."

"I'm not going to accept that, Angelo. It's like Annette said about sending you energy to overcome your asthma attack. It wouldn't do any good sending it, if you weren't able to accept it."

I struggled with that. "All right," I said finally, "I accept that. It's really another aspect of taking responsibility for our own lives, isn't it? If we accept responsibility for what we've done wrong, or what we've failed to do, we should also accept responsibility for what we've done right, and what we have accomplished."

"We have to own our gifts as well as our limitations, our strengths as well as our frailties, yes."

"It's a funny way of thinking, really. It's going to take some getting used to." I took a long breath. "Speaking of which, we need to talk about your health. If I'm going to wear my heart on my sleeve I guess one aspect of that is horning in on other people's business when I care about them. What are we going to do about your health situation?"

She sat looking at the mug of tea on the table before her, and for a long moment she didn't answer. I realized as she spoke that she had been looking for an answer that would balance several things that needed to be addressed at the same time.

She reached across the table and took my hand. "I have some things to say, my love, and it will help me to say them if you know that I do love you, because some of these things aren't easy to say."

I thought, *Oh-oh, that doesn't sound too good!* "What'd I do? Did I do something to upset you? I didn't mean to."

"No, I'm not upset, I'm afraid *you'll* be upset."

"Why should I be upset?"

"Because, Angelo, I know you want to help me, and I'm grateful that you feel that way, but – I think we're up against a boundary issue here. You know what a boundary issue is? It's a term we use to talk about the ways that are or aren't proper for one person to relate to another."

"Such as?"

"Oh, it might be a mother who didn't allow her children any autonomy in choosing what to wear or what to eat, or spouses who were too controlling, or who allowed themselves to be controlled. It's any situation where one person takes on too much responsibility for someone else's life, or, the other way round, where one person gives too much authority over his own life to someone else. It isn't healthy, and in the long term it doesn't work."

That puzzled me entirely. "And you think that's what I'm trying to do with you? Take over your life? I'm just trying to help."

"I know. That's what I said. And I'm scared, Angelo. I'm so frightened I can hardly breathe sometimes. But there are some things that others just can't do for you. When you said 'What are *we* going to do about my health situation,' I thought, *we* probably can't do anything. This is *my* problem."

"I don't get it. You don't *want* me to try to help? You *want* to deal with it by yourself?"

"It isn't that, it's that really we don't have any choice. That's the way it is."

"But you saw what happened last night! You were *part* of it! I needed help and Annette knew what to do, and you all helped. Why shouldn't we be able to do something like that for you? God knows you need it more than I did. I was in for a rough night, but you're looking at dying, here."

"I know, but the two situations aren't comparable."

"Yours is way more serious, but how do we know that we can't help you too? Why shouldn't we assume that we can until it's proved otherwise? Don't you think it's possible?"

She sighed. "Anything is possible, I know that much. But energy medicine wasn't discovered just yesterday, you know. If it were a universal cure-all, don't you suppose that everybody would be using it?"

"Everybody doesn't know about it."

"But even those who do know don't necessarily enjoy perfect health, Angelo. And they all die, you know, sooner or later."

"Yeah, sure, but still – "

"Angelo, there's a concept you may not have heard of, called 'the healer out of control.' That's your temptation right now, to be the healer out of control. You've found this wonderful new tool and you can't wait to use it on everybody in sight."

"You bet, and you first, because I care about you and I want to help you."

"Yes, but – this is brutal, but I don't know how to say it better – Angelo, you don't know what you're doing yet. You just discovered it and you think it's a cure-all, but it isn't. You think it's the key to magical powers, and in a way it is, but not the way you're thinking of. You can't just *wish* things away."

I didn't know what to say. I felt misunderstood, and hurt. After all, I just wanted to help! "I don't think that's what I'm doing. I'm saying we could at least try this technique. We know it works at least on *some* things!"

"I know what you want to do, and I am very grateful that you are trying to help me. But it's like, sometimes people say, 'you can be well if you wish,' and to the sick person, it sounds like they are being told: 'if you are sick, it's your own fault.' That just isn't helpful, because while it may be true that our health is under our own control, that doesn't mean that it's

necessarily under our *conscious* control. In fact, I would say that by definition we get sick for reasons *beyond* our conscious control. Other layers of
consciousness introduce or allow illness, for reasons that seem good and
sufficient to them. Well, obviously, if an illness is unconsciously caused,
we have to find the key to it – and that means we have to bring the cause to
consciousness and deal with it. We have to move our health problems from
the realm of the unconscious, where we can't much affect it, to the realm of
consciousness, where we can make whatever change is needed."

"Well, sure! But – "

"The problem is that you've just discovered that healing energies can
be transmitted, and you're elated, and you're jumping to the conclusion that
anyone could and should be healed of anything, regardless."

"What's so wrong with that? Wouldn't it be a good thing if we could?"

"Not necessarily. Illness isn't always by definition bad, and removing
illness isn't always good."

"I don't understand how you can say that."

"I sometimes think we ought to start thinking of illness as a messenger,
rather than as an enemy. Illness isn't some irrelevant interruption of our
lives – and healing isn't necessarily a return to the life we were leading
beforehand."

"You don't care if you get better or not?"

"Of course I *want* to get well. If I didn't have any other reason, my
daughter would be reason enough. But it isn't up to me."

"You think it's a mistake to fight for your life, any way you can?"

"No. But it's a mistake to be attached to outcomes. It's a delusion, because for one thing, we can't know what kind of healing we need ourselves,
let alone what someone else needs. We can't judge the cause, we can't judge
the process, we can't judge the outcome. To be able to do it, we'd have to
be able to judge the entire pattern of someone else's life. Maybe the healing
they need is enough energy to obtain their release from life."

"Are you saying you think you need to die?"

"*I* don't know what I need, how can I? I know what I *want*, but that may
not have much to do with anything. I do know that we don't necessarily
know what's best for us."

"I'm going to have to think about all that. But you're not going to
convince me that it isn't right to want to help."

"It's always good to offer love and healing energy, regardless of whether
your action in itself is on the beam or way off target. But health and whole-

ness and life and death are out of our hands, really, and it's just as well for us to recognize it."

"But you do believe that miracles are possible?"

"I do, but I don't believe they come on schedule, or in response to specific activities. That's a different kind of magic, a kind I don't believe in."

❖ 10 ❖

Bobby was among the others in the break room, and he was grinning from ear to ear. "I take it something went right this morning," I said. I couldn't help smiling.

"You bet it did," he said happily. "Finally!"

"Well, I could see that you've been having a hard time. Does this have something to do with whatever Ellis said to you this morning?"

"Yes indeed! I owe him a big one. He gave me the word."

"Did he. And the word was?"

"He said he'd suddenly figured out what I was doing wrong, because he was an engineer and his mind worked the same way mine does. I was asking for technical data so that I could proceed logically, and that wasn't the way to go about this."

"Well, Jesus, Bobby, you haven't been told that in debrief more than about 150 times!"

"Yes, but they didn't say it so I could hear it!"

I had to laugh. "That's going to be devastating to Annette and David. How did Ellis put it that you were able to hear it, finally?"

"Well, you know, everybody's been telling me, use your heart, not your head, trust, just go with it, and that doesn't do me any good at all. Why don't they tell me to become left-handed all of a sudden, or have different color eyes? It isn't *me!* Ellis didn't do that, he just said gather the data first without judging the source or the nature of it, and examine it later."

Jeff, sitting near him, laughed out loud. "That's the exact same thing."

"It doesn't sound like the same thing to me!"

"Well, maybe it has been translated out of liberal-arts-speak and into geek-speak."

"I resemble that remark," Bobby said. It was nice to see him in high spirits again.

I turned to Ellis. "Maybe you should get a job at the UN as a translator."

Ellis looked as pleased as Bobby did. "I don't know why it didn't occur to me earlier, but when I woke up this morning, there it was, plain as day, and it was just a matter of telling him. He got it right away."

"Boy, *didn't* I! And it unlocked *everything!*"

Jeff said, "Ellis, do you spend a *lot* of time dreaming about Bobby?" Ellis laughed too. He was very pleased with what he had facilitated. "Seriously, though, like Ace Reporter here says, you done good."

"Yes, you did," Katie said. "And what you did for Bobby, Francois did for me last night." (I glanced over at Francois, and saw, with surprise, that he looked troubled. *Maybe I'm misinterpreting?* But a second glance confirmed the first. I wondered what was going on with him.) "Perhaps you remember, I came here hoping to contact my husband. I thought, if I just had one clear contact, one thing I could put my finger on, I'd be satisfied even if I didn't get anything else out of the week. But last night, it was Tuesday night and nothing had happened and it looked like nothing was going to happen. It was – distressing. So last night I'm afraid I pulled Francois aside and bent his ear about it."

"You were perfectly welcome to do so, dear lady," Francois said. "As I told you, such signs of confidence are an honor, not a burden."

That may be, but you've got something *on your mind!*

"Yes, but it was so helpful. I hadn't any idea." Katie colored, slightly. To the rest of us, "We get taught all these things and we accept them and they don't have any basis in fact. I'm embarrassed at some of the things I've assumed about Catholics, and especially Catholic priests. I never would have dreamed I'd have a conversation like I did with Francois. I would have assumed he'd never be able to understand even if he tried to understand. I would have expected him to lay down the law according to Catholic doctrine, and that would be the end of it."

"At that, it would be easy enough for you to meet such priests," Francois said, the corners of his mouth curled ever so slightly upward. "I could arrange introductions."

She laughed. "No thank you, I'll stick with beginner's luck."

"Yeah, yeah," Andrew said lightly. "So what was the magic word?"

"He told me I was being too literal. Said I was trying to dictate how the contact would come, and that doesn't work. He said it's like the Bible says, the spirit goes where it wants to, and how it wants to. I wouldn't have thought about it that way."

"That's certainly how dreams work," Claire said. "You can't dictate to a dream; you have to sit down before it like a child and listen to what it wants to tell you, in the way it wants to say it."

Andrew said, "Edgar Cayce always said that dreams are the purest form of psychic input, because the conscious mind doesn't have any part in shaping them."

"So," Bobby said, "it worked?"

"Not last night, but this morning, yes it did. The most important message for me was my husband telling me he's okay where he is."

"In so many words?"

"No, but the meaning was clear." Equally clear was that she wasn't going to share so precious a moment.

"Francois gave you the same message Ellis gave Bobby," I said.

It seemed to surprise people. "Why yes, I guess it is the same," Katie said. "If you look at it that way."

"So you done good, too, Francois," Jeff said. "That's two of us today."

"Three," Roberta Harrison Sellers said. "Tony helped me a great deal, just a few minutes ago."

"I did?"

"Yes, you did, and it's just like I thought, you didn't even know it. Tony asked to see my artwork that I have in my room, and I could see that he really liked it, he wasn't just being polite. And, Tony, you don't have any idea why that meant so much to me. Ever since we did that tape on Monday – the one where we asked questions of the universe – I've been having a very hard time. I made the mistake of asking something about my artwork, and the answer I got I interpreted to mean that I didn't have any real talent, and what I was doing didn't have any real value."

"Oh, Roberta," Toni said, "how horrible! And you've been carrying that around for two days?"

"Silly of me, I suppose, especially with so many talented people all around me to talk to about it. But maybe I was afraid to know. Then dear Tony asked to see it, and I thought, 'Oh well, I suppose I might as well *really* see what people think of it,' – and he *liked* it!"

Tony laughed. "But maybe I'm a lousy judge of art, have you stopped to think of that?"

"No because it doesn't matter. When I saw you actually appreciating it, I realized, *that's* not what the answer was saying, at all! It was saying something entirely different." I think she would have stopped there, but the weight of our collective interest was too much for her. "I'd assumed, you see, that I was being told that my artwork was of no value and that I was fooling myself. Suddenly I realized that I had been told that artwork *in and of itself* doesn't have the value I was putting on it; it's only when it connects with other people."

"What about art for art's sake?" Toni asked.

"I can't explain it any better, dear. But I got the message and it's just marvelous, and if it hadn't been for Tony maybe I wouldn't have gotten it at all, and I am just so happy, and so grateful."

Tony was shaking his head, smiling. "This is so weird," he said. "I probably wasn't going to tell anybody, but it's so weird the way it's working out. I was *told* to look at Roberta's stuff. That was one of my important messages, believe it or not. I thought, 'Well, *there's* a wrong number,' and I was going to ignore it, but it just so happened that we met in the hall and I remembered and I said could I see it. To tell you the truth, Roberta, I sort of thought, 'Well, I'll say something polite and get out.' I thought I was doing you a favor."

"And so you were."

"Yeah, but listen. I've been dealing with my own stuff, and I've been having as hard a time as you have. It wasn't until last night when we did that 'fears' tape that I realized that I have this huge fear of failure, and all the stuff that gets on my nerves – my family life, my job, the commute, the whole works – is all tied in with the fact that I'm doing stuff I don't want to do because I think I *have* to do it or I'll be a failure. You know? No career, no money, no future, nothing. Back where I was when I got out of college. So, last night this all comes front and center for the first time and I realized it was a major fear, and blew it away, and I thought, 'Okay, let's see if anything really changes now.' So then we have this morning's tapes, and they're important, but then I'm standing in your room looking at your artwork and it hits me. This stuff is *great!* I don't know if it belongs in museums or if it's going to make you famous or even if it's very good technically. I don't know, it's not my field. But" – looking around at the rest of us – "what I *did* get is 'Roberta has been doing this because she loves doing it.' You can't look at it without seeing that. And she sells it basically to get enough money to buy more supplies and get enough money to live so she can do more of it. Am I right, Roberta? Yeah, well, then it *hit* me! I mean, it really *hit* me: She's doing it out of *love*, and that's where her creativity is coming from. That's her *link*. She isn't doing it trying to be a success – which is the same thing as saying, she isn't doing it trying to avoid having to consider herself a failure. And I thought, great leaping lizards and donkeys with mustaches, what in the world is wrong with me that I never understood that?" Shaking his head again. "I can't believe it has taken all these years to understand something that simple."

"So it's off to Antarctica next week, Tony?"

"Andrew, the way I feel now, if I could figure out how, I'd be on my way."

"Meanwhile you can at least buy something from Roberta."

We laughed, but Tony didn't. "I intend to. And whenever I am in danger of forgetting what I just realized, all I'll have to do is look at it and remember."

"I think maybe you won't buy something, Tony," Roberta said. "You pick what you want and I'll give it to you, and then I'll be able to remember you having it, the way you're going to remember seeing it."

"If you want, Tony, you can pay *me*," Jeff said.

But even that wasn't the end of it. "I thought *I* was having a big day, and I am." Helene said quietly. "I am glad to see that others are too, that I'm not alone in this sense of being blessed."

I was a little surprised at the source, but I knew where she was coming from. I said, "When people were working on me last night, I got the sense of everybody here being angels for each other, Helene. Is that what you mean?"

I could all but see her overcoming internal resistance. "Angelo, all week I have been struggling with a realization that came to me in a very early exercise." Another pause and a struggle. "Ever since I was a little girl I was aware that I have a powerful, accurate mental apparatus, and I have been proud of the fact."

"And why not?" Andrew said.

"Why not indeed. And I *am* proud of it. After all, I could not have become a physician and a psychiatrist without having something on the ball, as people say. But in some ways this has been a painful week for me, because first a tape experience showed me how chilly and intellectual my life has been, and then being blessed by the presence of so much warmth around me, watching you helping each other and caring about each other – it has been wonderful, and it has also underlined my sense of loss. So many years in which I could have functioned differently!"

"Nobody here doubts that you've done your patients a world of good," Claire said.

"Thank you. But I see now that I might have helped them so much more by giving them my heart as well as my head."

Nobody seemed to know what to say until Selena opened her mouth. *Here comes the law*, I thought, and the thought was both unjust and incorrect, which ought to have been a lesson to me.

"My guides said much the same thing to me this morning," she said in a subdued tone I hadn't before heard from her. "They told me that I have been underrating all of you, merely because I have developed a talent that you haven't yet developed. You, Angelo, in particular."

"Me?"

"You *move*. You don't remain stuck. That's not as common as you might think, and they asked me specifically to tell you that, to encourage you."

!! Physically, my mouth was closed in a firm and manly fashion. Metaphorically, it was lying on the floor where it had dropped.

❖ **11** ❖

Back in the debrief room, talking about our morning's experiences. I noticed that although people were willing enough to speak about what had happened to them, few people volunteered to tell us the content of the messages they had received. Some things are destroyed if examined in the light of day, and nobody seemed inclined to take the chance. Besides, we were all somewhat subdued anyway. Not depressed or lethargic or even particularly pensive, just somewhat inward, somewhat half in another world. I don't remember much of what went on in that short session.

"Okay," David said, before very long, "we're going to move into our fourth tape of the day." *Fourth? Well, sure, we did three in a row this morning.* "We're not going to brief you for it. You aren't newbies anymore, so there's no need to spoon-feed you." *Besides, how many ways can you remind people to use the bathroom before doing a tape?* "You shouldn't need to be reminded, by now, to stay open to whatever new experience comes your way, and not judge too soon. Ready for your briefing? Here it is. This is a free-flow Interface tape. If you have an intent, probably it will help. If not, you might ask to be given whatever would be most useful for you to receive. Have a good trip, go to your rooms by way of the bathroom, and we'll see you down here afterwards." He turned to Annette, feigning concern. "Do you think I went into too much detail?"

So, back on the bed, my eyes covered by the sleep mask and my head framed by the earphones. Was it only this morning that I lay down here for the first of three silent tapes? *Never did see an alien life form. Sure got messages, though.* I thought of the words I had gotten, "And the highest of these is love."

Again the pink noise, again C.T.'s voice leading us through the preparation process. *Healer out of control. Is that really how I'm reacting?* "Proceed now to Wider Vision," C.T. said. *An intent. We're supposed to have an intent. What should I intend?* "Move now to Time Choice." *Time Choice. Of course: I want to see more of John and Clara, or maybe go back to that scene at Emerson's.* "Next, proceed to the Interface state that you have learned. Proceed now to Interface." *No, I don't think so. I'm going to stay in Time Choice.* After a moment, C.T.'s voice instructs us that we are free to explore Interface. "I will call you when it is time to return." For the first time, I decide to do my own thing rather than going with the flow, so to speak. *Doing my own thing. How appropriate, given that it was Emerson who said it first!*

Easier said than done, however. Maybe doing your own thing always is. For quite a while I tried to get back to the scene at Emerson's. Prior to that, I tried to recapture at least the feeling of being John. In both cases, nothing. After a while I gave up and just lay there passively. *What's the problem here? Am I trying too hard?*

I tried again, and a third time, but still got nothing, and felt bitterly disappointed. *Maybe I should have tried Interface after all. I wonder if too much time has gone by and it's too late.* So, I told myself to relax into Interface, and I guess that's what I should have been doing in the first place, because as soon as I gave myself up to the idea, something clicked (metaphorically) and there I was. I was sitting on nothing, riding down the road, and laughing to myself because I could remember the feeling, how well!

When I was a boy (maybe 17?) I would occasionally wake up elated from a particular kind of dream. Those dreams were always experienced particularly vividly. They had an intensity and an innate joy that I cannot remember being matched by anything else in my life. Yet I realized only when I experienced it again during Open Door that for many, many years – for decades – I had forgotten that they had ever happened.

I was driving down a particular street in my hometown, moving east to west. I was in a sitting position as one would be, behind the wheel, except I was sitting on nothing!

*I was driving down the road, in the sense that I was proceeding at a
steady pace, faster than one could walk, and was doing so in the position
one would be in if behind the wheel, only there was no seat beneath me,
no car around me. I was in a seated position, a few feet above street level,
"driving" west on Chestnut Avenue.*

*I had no awareness of being in a dream. It seemed real to me, as dreams
do, and logical and commonplace. Only when it ended and I was back in
the everyday world did I realize "that couldn't have happened, it was only
a dream." And yet, there was an aura of reality around it that couldn't be
shaken by logic or daylight.*

I think I had such experiences, such dreams, every so often, but I can't
remember how young I was when the dreams started, or how often they
came. In any case, it had been a long time. Lying on the bed in Interface on
this Wednesday evening in March, I thought, *I wonder if they were out-of-
body experiences, instead of the dreams I always assumed they were!*

All right, I thought, *maybe* this *is an out-of-body experience too! And
yet, how can it be? I know full well that even while I am "sitting on nothing"
I am also lying on the bed. I thought that in an out-of-body you lost awareness of your ordinary body. Well, whatever it is, let's push it.*

I realized, *I am free, finally.* But – unexpected problem – I hadn't any
idea what to *do* with freedom. For a while I was – somewhere – doing –
something. Whatever it was, wherever I went, I came back without any
memories of it. I hope I had a good time.

Finally, it was as if I refocused somehow. I thought, *maybe I don't have
a lot of time left. What do I want to do while I still have the chance?*

I went into Claire's room and reached my spectral hand to her, willing
her to wake up (if she were asleep) and know that I loved her.

❖ **12** ❖

A few days earlier, I wouldn't have believed it. But then, that was getting to be my theme song!

We were sitting in debrief. Claire was among the last ones down, and so
I hadn't had a chance to talk to her. She sat at one of the few vacant places,
on the other side of the room from me, so I still couldn't compare notes.
Had she experienced my presence? I sure wasn't going to be the one to
bring it up in debrief, in front of everybody!

Somebody was talking about something – I can't remember who, or
what – and suddenly I had this terrific pain in my teeth. It was as if the

molars on the right side of my mouth had all spontaneously abscessed. The pain was incredible! Stunning, in a way, too great to be dealt with. *I'm going to have to get some aspirin somewhere*, I thought – and then, as instantly as it had come, the pain was gone.

What was that all about?

A few minutes later, it was my back muscles, spasming for no reason at all. I didn't react in any way that anyone would notice – at least I don't think I did, and I had had long practice in not showing physical discomfort – but it certainly got my attention! After a minute or two, the pain went away as suddenly and as completely as had the pain in my teeth.

Then Claire was addressing the group. "I don't know how much of this actually happened," she said hesitantly, "and how much might be just me, making it up."

Andrew gave a great snort of laughter. "We've heard *that* before!" Annette's right hand made a shushing motion at him, perhaps unconsciously, but Claire hadn't seemed to notice his interruption.

"Most of the way through the tape, I was drifting in and out. I may have had some minor experiences, nothing worth talking about, but I was thinking that the tape must be nearly over, and suddenly I got the sense that I wasn't alone in the room." She colored slightly. "And I'm not talking about Marta." I don't know if everybody else had a guess as to the person she would imagine being there with her, but I suppose they did. Nobody was rude enough to make a joke about it, though. "It isn't the first time I've thought there might be somebody else around, but it *is* the first time I thought it was one of *us*, someone alive, in a body, rather than maybe a spirit of something unexplained."

Annette said, "Claire, you say, 'in a body,' but you don't mean that someone actually came into your room during the tape, do you?"

"Oh no, that's why I say, I don't know for sure that it wasn't me making it up." She hesitated. "I haven't asked the person if it's okay for me to mention their name. I don't want to embarrass anybody."

There was a moment's hesitation, and since nobody else said anything (not that I expected that anyone would) I said, "Well, I don't know if it was me you experienced being there, but that's what *I* experienced." And as I said that, suddenly my back muscles spasmed again.

"Yes," she said, "it was you. So you knew you had done it?"

"I had an OBE, I think, and I went to see you." If my back hadn't been hurting so much, maybe I would have been doing a little blushing myself.

"It wasn't an accident, it was a decision. I thought if I could contact you and you remembered, we'd both know that it really happened and we hadn't made it up." The rest of my agenda, I could tell her in private. I wasn't about to advertise.

Bobby cleared his throat, and between his clearing his throat and his first words, my back stopped hurting. *What in the world?* "Well," Bobby said, "I wasn't sure I was going to talk about this." He cleared his throat again, and I thought, *Bobby's getting shy all of a sudden?* "I don't remember what was happening in most of the exercise, but then all of a sudden I had a vision of myself in one of the bathrooms upstairs. It was very specific, I could show you which one it was. I – uh, I saw Claire taking the last of her clothes off and stepping into the shower, and I knew that Angelo was inside the shower waiting for her." *He's more embarrassed than I am!*

"We ought to point out," Annette said quickly, "that these are still initial explorations; you're still learning the terrain, and part of the learning process is learning to interpret symbols. I know you know better than to think that you're getting a straight visual feed. You're seeing symbols, not movies. While we're just learning, we have to expect that lots of what we bring back is going to be severely misinterpreted."

Nice blocking, and I appreciate it, but they've been doing this a long time, both of them. They have *to know. Misinterpretation, my ass!*

You know what sex is like. Speaking only of the physical aspects, we could describe it as the intense build-up of tension and excitement in the body, culminating in a joining of the sex organs and then the sudden intense release of accumulated tension and excitement. That's the physical side of it, right? Now imagine that instead of only the sex organs joining, you could interpenetrate your entire bodies. Imagine an explosion of sensation not relatively localized, as it is in the physical body, but everywhere at once, leaving you drained, exhausted, and gloriously glowing. Then imagine increasing the level of excitement and ecstasy (literally ecstasy, being out of the body) proportionally to the love and longing you feel for the other person. Bridegroom jokes don't express the half of it.

Yet – maybe they don't *know. Maybe* Claire *doesn't! Maybe it didn't actually happen! Maybe the skeptic who got on the plane in Philadelphia has moved so far so fast that he's now imagining astral sex!*

David said, "But even though the symbolism may be skewed, surely everybody will agree that something significant just happened here, that has implications for all of us. One of us sent his astral body out to see another one; she perceived it and reported it, and then a third person reported seeing the two of them together in a way that implied a meaningful connection. In other words, for those of you who think that maybe all these experiences are 'all in your head,' evidence suggests that no, they're not."

"That's right," Annette said. "We may not know just what we're dealing with, but it's something, it isn't nothing."

And maybe the skeptic didn't just make it all up. Maybe what he experienced was real, on what they always call the astral plane, that I always called the half-astral plane, not believing in it for a minute. One more thing to change my mind about, I guess.

Again that terrific pain in my teeth, and again, after a few minutes, complete instant relief from pain.

❖ 13 ❖

"Let's go, partner," Jeff said. "Time for what I do best. It's supper time. Want a hand up?"

"Yeah, thanks," I said, and I pulled myself up slowly, carefully. "I need to talk to Annette for a minute, though. I'll catch up with you."

I waited a few seconds while she finished some housekeeping chore with her papers, and then she said, "Yes, Angelo?"

"I don't want to hold up your going to supper, but I've got a fast question. At least, I hope it's a fast question. While I was sitting there in debrief, suddenly I was experiencing this incredible pain in my teeth. There wasn't any reason for it at all, as far as I can tell. I mean, it was *incredibly* painful. Then it went away, and things were fine again, and then it was like my back muscles spasmed, and that hurt just as much as my teeth had. And that went away and my teeth started hurting again. Back and forth, two or three times."

"Are your teeth hurting now? Or your back?"

"No, they're fine. Neither one hurts now, and it's okay with me if they stay that way. But – do you have any idea what that was all about?"

"Maybe I do. I think maybe you blew out a blockage. If so, that's a big deal, and it will probably get bigger, but it's nothing you need to worry about."

"You mean, it's going to hurt more regardless, so don't worry about it?"

"I didn't say it's going to hurt more, I said it's probably going to be a bigger deal. There's a world of difference. What I mean is that if you really did blow out a block, you're going to keep experiencing larger and larger consequences, as you change. Probably it won't hurt at all, physically."

"Hmm. I don't really understand what you're saying. Can you say anything more about it?"

She shook her head. "Not if I know what's good for me – and I do. I can't really say any more, we're not supposed to. Just don't worry about it."

I didn't understand why she couldn't talk about it, but it had been many a long year since I'd first heard someone say 'no comment.' One of my old newsroom buddies used to quote Canadian humorist Stephen Leacock, who wrote somewhere, "'Shut up,' he explained." That's 'no comment,' in a nutshell.

❖ **14** ❖

"She's talking about chakras," Selena said with her customary self-assurance, putting butter on the dinner roll in front of her. "She's saying you blew out a block in one of your chakras. It sounds to me like it might be your fourth chakra."

Selena Juras and I hadn't had anything to do with each other. If I affected her the way she affected me, I quietly rubbed her the wrong way without meaning to, less by what I did than by what I was. We hadn't butted heads, but we hadn't gone out of our way to seek out each other's company, either. I thought it was interesting that she and I had wound up at the same table, apparently without either of us particularly intending it. And what was even more interesting was that I was moved to tell Claire what Annette had said – and not said – even with the others there at the table. *Wear your heart on the inside and the outside.* Edith and Klaus I didn't mind, or even Bobby, but ordinarily I wouldn't have opened up in front of Selena or Lou Hardin.

"I don't know anything about chakras," I said. "I know the word, and that's about it."

"Yes, I gather that C.T. doesn't want them discussed within the framework of this program," she said. "It's very annoying, and it means that people don't get to make some connections that would otherwise be very obvious."

"Well, I don't suppose he can stop one participant from talking to another about them. What are we talking about?"

To give her due credit, she really did know her stuff, and presumably she'd been explaining these things for years, because she had the material at her fingertips. "Our physical bodies are connected to our energy bodies primarily through seven specialized centers that are part physical matter, part energy. At least, that's how *I* visualize them. Reading from lowest to highest, we have chakras at the base of the spine, then the sex organs, the solar plexus, the heart, the throat, the brow or face, and the crown of our head. Each chakra is associated with a color. From bottom to top, they're red, orange, yellow, green, indigo, violet, and clear, or white."

"Colors?" I said. To me a color was an accidental quality, not an essential one.

"Yes, color. This might make more sense to you if you remember that colors are actually just divisions of the unbroken band of light. So, as you move up the scale of frequencies, you move up the band of colors, just as in the rainbow."

It did make a certain amount of sense – as long as you were willing to assume that things we couldn't see emitted color.

"Each chakra is also associated with specific functions, and this is what Annette was hinting at, even though she didn't feel that she could come out and say so." I was uncomfortably aware that Annette was eating her supper only a couple of tables away from us, and Selena was never very concerned with modulating her voice. But I decided that it was Annette's problem, if anybody's, not mine. "The root chakra involves our grounding in this world. The second chakra deals with creativity in all its aspects. The third is will-power, the fourth is connection – love, of course – the fifth is communication, the sixth, awareness, or psychic functioning, and the seventh might be said to be higher awareness, or spiritual functioning. Clear so far?"

"Very," I said.

"The energy in our lives should flow through our bodies so that we can function normally. But if one of the chakras is constricted, or is closed off, we experience problems, not only in that particular set of issues, but in general, because the smooth flow of energy is disrupted. People can live their whole lives in an unbalanced state and never suspect it."

I didn't know if I bought what she was saying, but for the moment I was in reporter mode. "Why do they get closed off?"

"The chakras open and close to match the needs of the moment. At least, ideally they do. In some situations you don't want your chakras wide open, because you would be flooded with harmful influences. You shut down to protect yourself, you know? But other times being shut down is the last thing you want, it's like being in solitary confinement. So, ideally, your spirit adjusts your chakras to let you get the most of the circumstances you are in, and sometimes you want them open, and sometimes only a little bit open, and sometimes you want them open as wide as they'll go. It depends on what is going on around you and within you. The problems only arise if the chakras get stuck, and don't open or close properly. Of course, this explanation is vastly oversimplified; different chakras open or close at any given time for different reasons. But perhaps you get the idea."

"I do," I said. "You're a good teacher." *That isn't something I would have said, ordinarily, to someone who irritates me. But – good for me!*

"Thank you. So you see, when you told Annette that you were experiencing what I would call energy-body pains – pains that move around and come and go without any real reason – she assumed that you had experienced a sudden change in your energy body."

"And you agree?"

"Oh yes." She looked not *at* me, but sort of *past* me, a little to the side of me. "Yes, definitely your heart chakra. It's popped way open – more than you'll be comfortable with, probably, but it will readjust and you'll feel at ease with it. It may be uncomfortable for a little while, but it's better than being stuck, as you were."

"So you can see these chakras?" It was fascinating, if she was telling the truth.

"There's nothing particularly difficult about it," she said. "I imagine that they teach you how in one of their other programs. Meanwhile, you should learn how to check on them every so often, to be sure they're functioning properly."

I was impressed, but I was also amused. I said, "How do I do that, given that I can't seem to experience them first-hand the way you do?"

She thought for a moment. "Do this. Every so often, maybe when you get up in the morning, visualize the base chakra and say this. 'The red chakra is healthy. It is open as wide as my life's purpose calls for at any given time, and the power flows through freely.' Then move to the next. 'The orange chakra is healthy. It is open as wide as my life's purpose calls for at any given time, and the power flows through freely.' You see? And go right on up the scale to the clear light, or white, however you want to think of it, at the seventh chakra. That ought to help you stay balanced while you're learning to perceive them."

❖ 15 ❖

Edwin Carter Hall, once again.

David said, "Tonight you're going to meet one of the living legends around here. She hasn't written any books and she hasn't been interviewed by the press and – to put it mildly – she hasn't any interest in either thing happening, so unless you've heard about her from somebody around here, probably you haven't heard about her at all. And yet she's probably done as much to give the institute direction as anybody but C.T."

Annette picked it up, smoothly as always between these two. "Mary Jane Torrance hasn't had anything to do with developing programs like Open Door, and she doesn't concern herself with fund-raising or adminis- trivia or even with liaison with academics and scholars, though that's where her background lies. Instead, she's the head and the heart of our black-box exploration program. When you took the lab tour, you talked to Dave and Harry and Rudy, and together they should have given you an understanding of the physical basis for our black-box sessions. But what they *didn't* give you, because they *couldn't* give it to you, was the human side of a program that has given us so many valuable insights and promises to give us much more. So we're going to give you the briefest of outlines of Mary Jane's career, and then we'll give you the chance to have her talk to you directly. I promise you, you won't be bored."

"That hasn't been a major problem so far!"

"Thank you, Andrew. Let us know when you start getting sleepy," David shot back.

"Mary Jane Torrance did one of the earliest Open Door programs, more to support a friend who wanted to do it than from any interest in the program itself. But Open Door did to her what it is doing to some of you, and within a year she had taken early retirement, cutting short a distinguished academic career, and had moved down here. C.T. recognized the value of having a Ph.D. psychologist on staff, and it wasn't long before she was up to her neck in work, with the added advantage of being unpaid."

She met our laugh with her usual smile. "Anyway, she wasn't here very long before C.T. asked her to create a program that would use the black box to bring back something of value. He told her he didn't care how she struc- tured it, because he didn't have the slightest idea how to do it, and with her background she probably did. That was a good number of years ago and in the meantime she has retired again, although she still does the occasional session monitoring somebody in the black box. That's all I'm going to say. You're better off listening to her than to me. Mary Jane Torrance."

A vigorous, trim, white-haired woman stood up from her chair against the wall and walked to where Annette and David were standing, front and center. She gave them each a hug, and as they made their way to take seats at the back of the hall, she sat in the chair placed in the center, where C.T. had sat – was it only three nights ago? – when he had talked to us.

"They always pin this portable microphone on me, and I always find myself hoping against hope that it will work, because if it doesn't, those of you in the back won't hear a thing. Is it working? Good." She looked around. "Wednesday night. I remember the Wednesday night of my own Open Door program very well. I won't ever forget it, and I don't suppose you will either. As I look out on you, I envy you that fact that most of you have discovered this program at such a younger age than I did. It must be so marvelous to be so young, and still have all of this ahead of you." *Not all of us*, I thought. *How much does Claire have ahead of her?*

"Now, every Open Door they ask me to give a talk to the participants, and every year I wonder what I'm going to say. You can't do something for 20 years without learning something about the process, but that doesn't mean that whatever happens to interest me at the moment is going to interest you. However, you'll just have to take your chances, same as I will.

"As Annette has reported, I did an early version of Open Door with a friend who had read about C.T.'s work in his book, *Extraordinary Potential*, and was eager to participate in a program. She asked me to accompany her, and fortunately I did. My whole world changed in that week. I had thought of myself as a rather stodgy university professor, but during Open Door I found that my life actually had been full of color and amazing adventures. I hadn't planned to retire from teaching for another ten years or so, but I couldn't resist the lure of this new adventure. I moved down here, and, as Annette told you, C.T. turned his black-box program over to me shortly after his lab was opened. Being unpaid does have the advantages that you can set your own hours and you aren't likely to be fired. On the other hand, I was very much aware that I didn't have the slightest idea how we should proceed! However, no one else did either, and somebody had to do it, so I set my mind to thinking what we knew and how it was safe to proceed.

"Well, there was the subject in the black box, that was obvious. And it was clear that somebody would need to watch the instruments, both to be sure the proper signals were fed into the box and to keep a sense of the subject's condition as the session went on. So we figured, okay, one to watch the instruments, one to talk to the subject. We'd get it all onto tape, and if we came up with something that seemed likely to be of value to humanity, we would share it with the rest of the establishment. Because that was the emphasis, you see: C.T. asked us to 'ask questions that would result in information that would be of value to all mankind.' So, for months that became years, that's what we did. I ask you to remember, I was still a fairly conventional person, from a very conventional, respectable academic background. And now here I was, charged with talking with disembodied entities! I would characterize that as a fairly significant change in self-definition."

She laughed along with us.

"I have often asked myself what is really happening during these sessions, and I will tell you frankly that after all these years I still do not know. We put words around experiences and sometimes we fool ourselves into thinking that we know what the words mean, but in our more reflective moments we remember that we don't know, really.

"Hundreds of people volunteered for one or more sessions over the years, and all of them got questions from us, questions on topics such as consciousness, health and healing, environment and earth changes, the nature of the universe, and various spiritual and philosophical questions. Usually the individual in the booth received questions from the monitor, proceeded to search for this information from whatever source they contacted, then reported it. Over time, they often began to let the information flow in directly, cutting out the middle man, so to speak. I have dealt with subjects who are in connection with entities who often begin to respond to my question or comment before I have completed making it. Let me tell you, it can be disconcerting to be dealing with someone who appears to be reading your mind.

"But the issue of awareness during the process of reporting information from contacts with non-embodied energies is not as simple as whether the recipient was or was not conscious. The degree of awareness varies, not only between recipients, but also over a session, and between the sessions of one person. The person reporting the experience may feel as though the words are coming unbidden through his or her vocal cords, or they may be hearing the words as though they are sitting in a lecture hall. In either case, the words may be fully recorded in their memory, or totally forgotten, or vaguely or partially remembered. In other cases, the subject continues over many sessions to feel that he is present but that he is neither the source of the information nor the director of the flow. At the end of a session, he may remember very little but will recognize the material when it is called to his attention. I think you will agree that these variables present certain obstacles to the researcher."

She paused, apparently shuffling through her mental notes.

"Now, how do people report communicating with these presences? As you may know, such communication comes in one of several forms – hearing, seeing, feeling, or 'knowing' – or in combinations of these. Each of these modes of perception offers specific advantages and disadvantages, and some call for particular strategies of interpretation.

"The most direct, and often the most underrated, is direct knowledge that comes without visual or auditory content. I have had people in the black box apologize for this form of perception, which seems to them to be mere unfounded assertion. This form of perception, experiencing a 'knowing,' requires them to attempt to express in words something that did not come to them in words. Those whose language skills are good are often able to accomplish this by using analogies and metaphors. Others apparently 'know' something they are unable to communicate, which I assure you is as frustrating to the monitor as to the experiencer.

"Perhaps the most common and among the most useful modes of experience are messages in visual form, something that many of you probably have experienced this week. Even here, however, reporting the visual content is not enough to convey the content of the communication. The experiencer must also describe what that visual image means to him or to her, a process akin to dream interpretation.

"Some will seem to hear words, though it is not always clear from their description whether they are hearing what we would term an auditory illusion or are merely employing a metaphor. Are they really hearing something, or are they acquiring information somehow and expressing it *as if* they were hearing it? That often is not at all clear, and often we would be able to clarify the ambiguity only at the cost of interfering with the process itself, which we are usually unwilling to do. Again, this has the potential to produce widespread frustration!

BABE IN THE WOODS

"Finally there is the category I call 'feeling' the message. This at least has the advantage of being more frustrating for the experiencer than for the monitor."

She smiled through our sympathetic laughter.

"Perhaps you can imagine having a strong feeling, and being absolutely confident that the feeling represents some worthwhile content, without your having any idea why you are experiencing that feeling, or what it means or where it came from. Then have a monitor asking you in some impatience to explain what you mean, and see how well you like it. Communicating with other realms is not all beer and skittles, as my father would say."

❖ 16 ❖

Without watches, there was no way to know how late it was getting. The only light was coming from the room next door, where the people who weren't watching the movie were snacking and talking, carefully leaving us alone.

I'd thought, *a movie? They never stop surprising you here, do they?* But when I'd queried it, David had said that we'd all been working hard and we needed the time off. So some had stayed in Edwin Carter Hall to watch a movie and others had wandered off to snack and chat and play chess and just generally pass the time. We were all becoming uncomfortably aware that our remaining time together was short. Another full day, and then we would go our separate ways. It was hard to grasp, and a little painful.

Claire and I were in the debrief room, together on the little couch, my arm around her, her head resting on my shoulder. She held my left hand in her hands, and every so often I left a kiss on her forehead, or in her hair. For minutes at a time we sat saying nothing, and when one or the other spoke, it was as though continuing a conversation that was being conducted mostly in the silence.

"What do you think you'll do after the program, Angelo?"

I shook my head. "Same as before, I expect. Not a lot of choice."

"Back to the newspaper, then?"

"I owe Charlie the story, anyway. He's the only reason I'm here." *The paper, and commuting across the bridge, and –* "No use talking about it."

"You made promises," she said. "So did I, and it's too late for us anyway. Nothing to be done about it. But Angelo, what about the rest of your life? It has to change now, doesn't it?"

Tears were blurring my eyes. "Has to? Sure. The only problem is, it can't."

She twisted to see me more closely. "If it *must*, it *will*, my love. Trust me on that, I know what I'm talking about. Everything I've learned professionally and everything I've learned from gett – these past couple of years – tells me that. You changed internally. If you want to hold on to those changes, you have to change externally, or you will be working against yourself. You'll tear yourself to pieces."

"Most of my life, I've been one person inside and another person outside. I expect it's that way for just about everybody, it's why you don't get to see very far inside people. Maybe that's the way it has to be if we're going to live with one another."

"Maybe the old rules don't fit now."

"Maybe they never did fit very well."

"Maybe not, and maybe it doesn't make any difference either way. You came here thinking you were here to research a newspaper exposé. Are you going to go home and write a story and pretend that everything inside you isn't changed? It would be like Columbus going back to Spain and trying to keep his discoveries to himself. Instead, he returned from the New World and he told everyone he knew, and he *hugely* changed the history of the world."

"Yeah, and after he became governor of the New World he wound up being sent home in chains."

"But in the meantime he had made his impact. And who says you can't be Columbus without making his self-aggrandizing mistakes?"

I smiled at the thought.

"And you know we're not talking about physical exploration here, so there's no point in your pretending that we are. We've *got* maps of *this* world. Now we're talking about mapping the other world, or I guess I mean the other aspects of this world."

"Well then, in that case your analogy is skewed. If we're talking about Columbus, that would be C.T."

"Do you see how much energy you use, avoiding uncomfortable realizations? You have a responsibility here, Angelo. It's not a coincidence that you have access to the pages of a major daily newspaper in a big city. You could make an impact. Potentially you could have a positive impact on the lives of millions of people."

"You vastly exaggerate the *Inquirer's* circulation, not to mention my readership."

"Will you stop? That's just the fallacy of insignificance, and you know what I mean. You write something and it changes people's minds and years later they do things that have an effect and nobody can say where it ends. You can't measure such things in advance, you can only do your best."

"Well, maybe."

"There isn't any 'maybe' about it. But even more important than the impact on others is the impact on *you*. It's *you* I'm concerned about. You've opened up all this wonderful territory inside yourself. You can't wall it off again because it's too uncomfortable to change, or too much effort."

"I don't know, Claire. I've been a reporter a long time. My family is used to me being who I am. You understand what I'm saying? My life's pretty set."

"And the way it is set, you have been happy with that?" We both knew the answer. "Does it seem as set to you tonight as it did last week at this time?"

I sighed. "Point. It's just – I hadn't planned to come here for a week and go home a different person."

"No, nobody does, I'm sure. We make our plans, but when life says go another way, we have to go."

"Predestination?"

"No, that's not what I mean."

"They can't make you do it but they can make you wish you had?"

"No, not that either. It's more like – if *you* change, you don't fit into the life that was built around what you were before."

"I never *did* fit all that well."

"I know. But you might have come here and moved in one direction and fitted in better with your life, or you might have stayed where you were, and you wouldn't be any better off or any worse off. That isn't what happened."

I gave her a self-mocking smile. "Doesn't seem like it. The week's not even up and I've started to turn into a weirdo."

She settled back against my shoulder. "That's your old life talking. You know better than that."

Wear your heart on the inside and the outside. "Yeah, I suppose I do."

"So, do you want to go back to what you were when you were flying in here on Saturday?"

I kissed her hair again. "You know I couldn't do that, love."

"Then you're going to have to try to figure out where your life wants you to go."

"Meaning that somewhere it's been decided, and it's hopeless to fight it?"

"Angelo, maybe it's a mistake, fighting it. Maybe it's better to follow life where it leads."

✦ 17 ✦

The movie ended and Jeff poked his head in the door, started to back out again, but Claire called him in. She wasted no time. "Jeff, have you told Angelo about your vision?"

"No, not yet. I haven't even started counseling him about taking care of his health. I figure, now it's part of my job to nag him."

"And besides, it's embarrassing?"

"Well, that, yeah."

"I think it's time, if you're going to do it at all."

"Because tomorrow's the last day?"

She moved her head sort of sideways. (If she'd been Italian, she'd have said, "meh?" Basically, "who knows?") "It's always a good idea to leave time for people to process things, and maybe it would be easier in person than trying to do it later over the phone or by email."

I said, "What am I, the doorpost?"

"Uh – no," Jeff said. He came farther into the room.

"Give," I said.

"I gave at the office."

"Maybe I made a mistake, Jeff, I'm sorry. I should have let you choose your time."

He cleared his throat. "No, that's fine. I agreed we ought to talk about it, and you're right, this is maybe as good a time as we're going to get today. Only, I was thinking, what if somebody comes in? I'd hate to be interrupted in the middle of it."

"I wouldn't worry about that. If this is the time, it will work out. If it isn't, we'll find another time."

"Yes, okay." He sat down on a chair facing us, and took a breath. "Big things have been happening on the reservation this week, Kemo Sabe, and it's given me a lot to work through. I don't know if you remember yesterday in debrief, Tuesday, when Claire was talking about how the three of us were connected – "

"You knew something you weren't talking about, I know that."

"Yeah. And I certainly wasn't going to tell the group before I told you and Claire. I was going to tell you at dinner, but you disappeared, so I told Claire instead, and then came the Lost in Space and Time tape, and the excitement about your breathing, and there didn't seem to be a good time after that. And this morning I was going to tell you, but we got involved in a big discussion of healing, and then it was all morning in silence, and after lunch everybody sort of wanted to talk, and somehow the right time never came."

"*Was* kind of a full day, wasn't it?"

"You bet."

"But now you've run out of excuses and besides, Claire has run you into a corner."

He grinned. "Exactly."

"She has a way of doing that, I've noticed." She nudged me with an elbow. "Okay, I'll shut up. So what did you see yesterday?"

"It wasn't yesterday that I saw it, actually, it was Monday, but it took me a while to process it. You remember that tape where Ellis remembered being hanged? Well, I got some flashes too, but I couldn't make too much out of them. I didn't know what I was seeing but it looked a lot like home, actually. I mean, it might not have been Wyoming, but it was definitely out west somewhere, all prairies and maybe some mountains in the distance, though I'm not sure. Could have been anywhere from someplace in Alberta down to, I don't know, Texas, maybe. But somewhere on the plains, and probably in the States."

"Okay."

"And I knew somehow that it wasn't in the present. It was in the late 1800s sometime, or maybe the very early 1900s. That time period. Anyway, I had the sense that that's when the three of us knew each other. You know, you two got that you were connected in the late 1700s around here somewhere, but none of us had the sense that I was involved."

"But there was never any question that *something* connected the three of us," Claire said.

"That's right. And I got that it was this time in the west."

"Huh," I said. "So you think – "

"Hold on. That's what I got on *that* tape, but then we did that 'asking questions of the universe' tape, and I asked what that vision had meant, and did it have to do with us being connected and all." *Sure, I asked basically the same question, only just about Claire.* "And this time I got that we were a family."

"Huh," I said again. "You mean like brothers and sisters? Or like parents and child?"

"Parents and their child."

"So which one was the baby, you or me?"

"Uh – Claire, actually."

"How – ?" (*"First there was darkness, then came the dawn."*) "Oh, you mean one of us was a woman?"

"Yeah. Me."

"Huh. Gives me a funny feeling! I hope you didn't have that mustache when you were my wife!"

"Hey, you're Italian, you should be used to wives with mustaches."

"And," Claire said, "after the two of you get finished dancing around your discomfort, the question is, what does this mean for us here and now?"

"Damn kids," I said to Jeff. "Can't you keep her under control?"

"Don't look at me, she's your child too."

"Oh God," she said.

I said, "It does explain some things. I remember the very first day we were out here – "

"Which was all of four days ago!"

"Yeah, unbelievable. But even then, when we barely knew each other's names, it felt so natural, the three of us."

"Yes it did," she said, "and thank God you were both here. When I got the news from my doctor, I was standing here wondering how I was going to get through the day, not to mention next week, and the two of you came back from your lab tour exactly at the right time, and you did, and said, exactly the right things. And it was like that yesterday, too. Whenever I needed support, one of you was there. I don't know what I would have done without you both."

"What are you going to do next week, I wonder? Not that you can't do it on your own, I realize. But it would be easer if you had somebody."

"Angelo, the universe sent me the two of you, and Toni Shaw, and Jane Mullen. I am confident it can send some more people to cover next week."

"Well, maybe. Anyway I'm glad you had Jeff at suppertime Tuesday when I was having my little snit. I was thinking about myself instead of thinking that you might need support."

She turned to face me. "I was very glad to have Jeff, but there's no reason for you to beat yourself up about having your own feelings and being your own first priority."

"I've never thought selfishness was a very attractive quality, even when I was manifesting it."

"It isn't, and it's always good work to care for others and help them. But it's like your wanting me to be well; it's not your responsibility, and anyway you don't have the power to fix my life. Nobody does."

"A good thing, too," Jeff said, and for a second I thought he was joking. "It's like the government, if it had the power to fix everything it would have the power to break everything. If somebody could fix our lives, they'd have the ability to run them for us, instead of our doing it for ourselves."

"I hadn't thought of that. It's true. Well, my love, you know I'd fix your life if I could, and I'll do anything I can to help you."

"I know."

"Me too," Jeff said.

"I know, and I thank you both." She turned from one of us to the other. "And you'll help each other, the same way, right?"

(Something very serious was said just then, and it wasn't primarily about Jeff and me. If I didn't get it then, perhaps it is because I didn't want to get it.)

"Of course," Jeff and I agreed. Indeed, I had been taking it for granted, and I assume that he had been as well. I had a thought. "Say, wasn't Tuesday the day you had that weird OBE?"

"Yeah, right after the 'questions to the universe' tape."

"Why do you suppose you experienced that, in the context of the rest of this?"

He shook his head. "I don't have a clue. Maybe they don't have anything to do with each other. Seems to me we're being given little bits of this and that, like teasers, so we can connect the dots ourselves later. I'm beginning to think it's just barely possible that the changes don't stop when the program ends."

"Y' think?"

❖ 18 ❖

They'd finished talking about the movie while Jeff, Claire, and I were still in the other room. As usual they had formed an irregular circle centering on the snacks on the table. We pulled up our chairs in time to hear Selena and Sam, at it again as so often.

"I identify with the divine side of me, not the human," she said.

"Oh? So you're only half here. Or only half real. Which is it?"

"That's insulting, and I see no reason to respond to it!"

"I don't mean it as an insult, but I think you're making a big mistake. Helene, you're a psychiatrist, what do you say? Isn't it dangerous, what Selena is doing?"

Helene looked about as anxious to be pulled into this on-going dogfight as you might expect, but she never shirked giving a direct response to a direct question. "Anything dealing with the spirit has its dangers, Sam," she said.

"And trying to live by ignoring the spirit has even greater dangers," Selena snapped.

"Yes indeed. But it's a matter of balance. As you yourself said, Selena, we have our human side, not just our divine side. Each aspect of ourselves had its needs, and we neglect them at our peril. Our bodies have valid claims on us, after all. Our conscious everyday dimension requires expression no less than does our more extended self."

"Our *everyday* selves are continually reinforced by everything around us," Selena said. "Society makes sure of that."

"Well, yes, but it is important nonetheless to remember that anything can be carried too far. Or perhaps I should say, anything can be pursued in the right way or the wrong way – in a safe and balanced way or a way that isn't so safe."

"Maybe safety isn't everything," Selena said. "I experience things every day first-hand that have no part of ordinary life. I will not disown them or live as if they did not exist."

"You couldn't," Helene said. "To do so would do violence to your very being." (Selena wasn't expecting agreement; clearly, it disconcerted her far more than Sam's comment had.) "As a psychiatrist and as an individual having experiences of my own, it would be impossible for me to believe that life is not vastly more than appears on the surface. The only people who can hold that opinion are those who are ignorant of the evidence, not only in psychical research but in depth psychology. No Jungian psychiatrist could think so for one moment, certainly. However, if you think you can relate to archetypes as if you were at their level – as if you were as big, as significant, as transcendent, as they are – you are just playing with dynamite. With the fuse burning. You are not a god, and that's the level of the energies you're dealing with. If at any time you are not in proper relation to them, it is impossible for you to do meaningful work. Besides that, you are putting your sanity and maybe your life in danger, and for no good reason."

"I have not experienced any difficulty," Selena said stiffly, "and I have been doing this work for more than a decade."

"That's well and good, but the pitcher can go to the well too often. Many talented, sincere, intelligent people have become inflated by contact with larger-than-life internal symbols. For some, it happens the first time, but for others, not till the hundred-and-first. One can always fall off the path. Jung always stressed the necessity of protecting oneself from psychic inflation. The dangers are real."

Edith said, "So how do we protect ourselves?"

"The best preventive I know is to keep going down into yourself and *seeing* everything there is to see, like it or not. Make conscious what is unconscious. It isn't much fun, a lot of times, but it is vital if you are going to stay in touch with who you really are, down below the level of your human personality. That kind of exploration becomes a matter of integrity, because our first task is not to *change,* but to *recognize.* First we must admit what we are, *then* we can think about changing to become all of a piece. The first step, the absolutely essential step, is integrity, oneness of being. That means integration of conscious and subconscious elements, willingness to open the portals and see what happens and adjust to that. This is why we must also live an ordinary life, to purge the inflationary effects of encounters with archetypes. As a corrective to talking to the gods, there's nothing like washing the dishes and taking out the garbage."

"However," Selena said, "what is an ordinary life to one person may not be what it is to someone else."

"No, of course not."

"It is important to dethrone the ego. But try convincing it that it isn't the center of our being!"

"That's true. But the pitfall here is that the ego is so good at sneaking in the back door. If you want to change residence, so to speak, from living in the ego to identifying with your full self, it means discovering everything about your present self and the world, and all the other parts of you that are in other places. You are after *wholeness*, and that means the human side too, not just the divine side."

Klaus said: "I will give it to you in a sentence. Treat yourself as a supreme artist, and every moment as your masterpiece."

"Yes," Helene said. "That's very good. This work requires just that sort of perpetual soul-searching, to find out what is unconscious within ourselves."

"And," Francois said, "to make it conscious while we still have time. All religious traditions, whether they teach reincarnation or single judgment, are unanimous in saying that once we are out of the body it is much harder, if not impossible, to change who and what we are. The time to do that work is while we are in bodies."

We sat munching chips or popcorn, or dipping raw vegetables in the tubs of cheese or whatever.

"You know," Edith said after a while, "I sometimes think the hardest thing about pursuing non-ordinary experience is the suspicion that it is all wasted energy, that there was never anything to pursue in the first place, or that even if there is, we could never find it."

Andrew said, "I don't think we *could* find it, if we were working by ourselves. Ideally we should have a mystery school, but we don't, so we have to make it up as we go along."

Then Sam said, "What if there's nothing to find?"

Selena looked at him with renewed distaste. "You don't think that, do you? *Could* you think that? That everyday reality is all that exists?"

"Surely it's possible that here and now is all there is, and things are just as we experience them, and nothing more."

"I for one cannot believe that the world has no meaning beyond what is apparent to common sense, and if it did, I wouldn't want to live in it."

"I agree," Andrew said. "Things are what they are, but they are what they are also in a deeper, more meaningful way."

"Sure, I can see that people here are pretty invested in that belief. I'm just saying, what if it's wrong? What if we're wasting our time chasing shadows instead of working to fix the problems of the real world?"

"I don't see how there can be any work that's more important than working on yourself," Helene said. "I have seen many a person run away from this work, telling himself he was going to try to save the world."

"Henry Thoreau said it long ago," I said. "He talked about cowards who run away and enlist."

"You think it's that simple? There is always evil in the world. I know that first hand." (This was as close as he ever came to saying what it was that he was doing at this stage in his career. Supposedly he was retired from the military. Only the very naïve among us took that for granted.) "It resolves itself into a simple question: Whose side are you on? The people who put people into the ovens at Auschwitz, or those who opposed them, or those who stayed neutral? As long as you are here in the physical, you must choose, like it or not. And even not-choosing is still a form of choosing."

"Not-choosing is the worst way to choose, in fact," Ellis said.

"I agree with you. And you know, I'm not against what we're doing here. I just wonder if maybe it amounts to sticking our heads in the sand."

"Maybe evil isn't an active force," Edith said. "Maybe it is only ignorance."

"And maybe not. Maybe evil is an active principle that opposes good. Either way we have to ask what our personal responsibility is. It seems to me we have to balance between our private and social development. Sometimes we have to sacrifice for the common good."

"I don't know about *that*," I said, "Emerson, when he was just 25 years old, said: 'If you think you came into being for the purpose of taking an important part in the administration of events, to guard a province of the moral creation from ruin, and that its salvation hangs on the success of your single arm, you have wholly mistaken your business.'"

Jeff leaned over and said, "How do you keep all that stuff in your head?" I grinned. "I liked hanging out with Emerson and Thoreau even before I started hanging out with them, so to speak."

"Perhaps more to the point," Helene said, "when Carl Jung was asked if the world could still be saved from destruction, he said it depended on if enough people would do the necessary work on themselves. He didn't say, if enough people would join together to form political or cultural movements. He said the physical salvation of the world depended on if enough people work on themselves. How do you overrate the importance of saving the world?"

"Maybe this is a false choice," Andrew said. "I think that in some ways, every form of individual violence, from vandalism up, stems from the fact that some individual feels powerless to register his presence in the world except through an act of destruction. If we could demonstrate to people that each of us, as individuals, as we are and where we are, can do powerful good, I think we could change the world. And what better way to demonstrate it than by giving them access to their personal power?"

"Just as this program is doing for us," Edith said.

"I don't know, though, Andrew," Jeff said. "If you give people the power to do good, you give them power to do evil."

"Yes, that's called free will. But if a sense of powerlessness really is at the root of evil, maybe the only way to root out evil is to risk what happens when people's power to choose is enhanced."

Francois was shaking his head, but more in thought than in negation. "The church has always said that it is too dangerous to give that kind of power indiscriminately. Any esoteric society with even the slightest wisdom and knowledge of the world knows better than to confer such gifts without first testing the character of the recipient."

"Well, maybe so," Andrew said, "but that gives a tremendous amount of power to those who run the church or societies, doesn't it? And who is to test *their* character? I understand that they will have been tested before they reach positions of power, but we all know that power corrupts. Anyway, it hardly matters. The cat is out of the bag, and I can't imagine it getting put back in again."

❖ 19 ❖

It was very late, had to be, but I was not tired. *I wonder if my sleep patterns will go back to normal when I'm home. I've never needed so little sleep.* The others had gone off to bed, leaving Francois and me locked in a long slow game. If we hadn't been alone? If it hadn't been so late? If our attention hadn't been sort of fixed on something between ourselves rather than on each other?

Anyway, we *were* alone, and gradually Francois began to tell me what had been going on within him all the long day. He would tell me a bit, and make a move, and tell me some more, and absorb what I had just done, and make a move. And I was honored to receive the confidence, and surprised, and troubled, and even humbled, by the nature of it.

He was eyeing his king-side knight, clearly measuring the pros and cons of setting off what might be a series of exchanges. "You are not a Catholic any more, I believe you said. You left when you were in your teens. Do you remember why you left?"

It is perhaps not the least remarkable thing about that week that I should be able to speak to him calmly about what might have been so touchy a subject. *He's still thinking about taking with that knight*, I said to myself. *If he were a little more devious, I'd suspect him of trying to distract me.* "I heard about the Index of Forbidden Books," I said, "and I didn't like the idea of somebody telling me what I was or wasn't allowed to read."

He moved, and suggested that there must have been more to it than that. A couple of moves later, he said, "For me it is not a matter of resenting authority. And if I have my doubts about the infallibility of the Pope, I have had none about the infallibility of the church at large, not on important issues. Given enough time, given enough thought, given good intent, so large a body will find its way to the truth, however many errors it commits on the way."

"I can't say I agree with you, thinking of Congress," I said.

He smiled, and he moved, and I contemplated and I moved, before he spoke again. Looking over at me, rather than at the chessboard, he said, "I do not know how you imagine the life of a priest. Perhaps, having left the church, your memories of the clergy are unhappy ones."

"Not particularly," I said. "My issues with the church didn't have anything to do with the priests and nuns I knew. I could see that they tried hard, and I never supposed that a priest's life is particularly easy. Between the rules and the faithful, I imagine it can be quite a struggle. And celibacy, if that's an issue for you."

"At my age, you mean? I assure you, it remains an issue." He moved. "However it is a very old struggle by now, and nothing to compare with what it was when I was in my twenties. As to the rules and the faithful? One can always find a way around rules, if only occasional convenient forgetfulness. And in whatever one's walk of life, always there are people to be dealt with. None of that matters, if one is doing what he should be doing." He sighed. "However, to have put one's life into a path and to see the path disappear – Perhaps one comes to wonder what use is it to anyone. What use it ever was. I said to Selena tonight, I wonder if she does not do more good than I can do."

I had been considering pushing the king's bishop's pawn, but I looked up in surprise, losing my train of thought entirely. "Than *you* do? That's all you've been doing all week, as far as I can tell, helping anybody and everybody." All week, I'd seen him informally counseling one person after another. He was a good listener, non-judgmental, with professional training in counseling. He was sympathetic and understanding and helpful. People found themselves drawn to him. And so his Open Door had become an extension of his ordinary life, not that he seemed to mind.

"Thank you, but that expresses only *willingness* to help, not *ability* to help. I have begun to think that I have no answers that will serve."

"Seems to me you've been *a lot* of help." I was dumbfounded, really I was.

"Selena speaks in the language these people can hear. I have to work at translating what I know into something they may listen to. It gives her a great advantage in effectiveness. And in this, unfortunately, I may be representative of the church. This week, here, shows me what I already knew in the abstract – perhaps there is no future for the church, unless it moves itself out of the corner it has backed into. Faith alone in today's world does not suffice. People require direct experience, and they will seek it out and find it, escorted and protected or not. And it is right that they should do so."

"Do you intend to say so, to your superiors?"

"Of course. But I fear that they will not be persuaded, any more than the church fathers in general."

"So what do you think is going to happen?"

"If the church fathers do not adjust to the times, so that the church is able to answer the spiritual hunger in the form it presents itself in our times, they are going to bring it down around our heads."

I didn't know what to say, so I went back to considering the ramifications of my proposed pawn move.

"As you may imagine, my life's efforts begin to appear – futile, at best."

I looked up again. "Francois, you're working from your heart, right? How wrong can you go, doing that?"

He nodded acknowledgement, a slow smile beginning in the corners of his mouth, as I had seen so often. "Yes, I know, and this is true. But it is also true that one must speak the language of the times, or find oneself unable to communicate. And it is also true that the church must move with the times, or find itself irrelevant. Carl Jung once said that the gods never return to the houses they once abandon. I am very much afraid that God may have abandoned the church, and we scarcely know that it has happened." He looked so troubled! "I feel the loss more strongly here, where his presence can be felt in so much sincere searching among unsuspected or forgotten things, than I did in my everyday life, serving the church he has fled."

We had played out the rest of the game more or less in silence. Whatever words we used had mostly to do with chess.

CHAPTER SIX

Thursday
March 23, 1995

SNOW! We woke up to snow, and it transformed the day.

Jeff found me on the side deck as usual, drinking coffee as usual. "Um, excuse me, Mr. Chiari," he said, "but you *have* noticed that even though it is March in Virginia, it's snowing?"

I gave him a big grin. "The thought did cross my mind, Mr. Richards, yes. Either that, or God's got a really bad case of dandruff. Ain't it beautiful?"

"You're not worrying about your lungs?"

"Not at the moment."

"That's great." Cautiously: "People do get colds still, probably."

"Let 'em! Not me!"

Claire came out. Instantly she said, "Isn't it *pretty!*"

"You're just in time," Jeff said, "Superman here just declared war on the common cold."

Her face lit up as she saw my mood. "A very good idea, too," she said. "The common cold has had its own way for far too long."

"Yeah," I said, "and you know what? Let's take a walk! We've got time and we'll hear the cowbell when they're serving breakfast and even if we're a little late who cares? I can't *remember* the last time I took a walk in the snow!"

Claire beamed. "What a good idea! You know how often we get snow in my part of Texas?"

Jeff said, "See, unlike you two, I see snow all the time. I know all about it. Snow falls from the sky and it gets pushed into little hills on either side of the street, and it gets painted black by car exhaust, and it sits there until Spring. Also, it makes icy spots for you to get stuck in when you're driving so you have to get pulled out of it, assuming your car starts in the first place. Snow's a *lot* of fun! I've got to admit, though, it's been a while since I actually *walked* in it. Let's do it."

And so – after we finished our mugs of coffee, a little quicker than usual – we did. It was easy, not very deep. We headed down the little road toward the lake.

"Stuff's pretty wet," Jeff said after a bit. "You can see it isn't going to be around very long. Probably be gone by tomorrow morning."

Tomorrow morning. The thought cast a shadow.

We came to a row of trees, and Claire stopped in her tracks and said, under her breath, "Look!" and pointed, sort of surreptitiously, scarcely moving her arm. It was a hawk of some kind, sitting in a tree watching us. We stood there and watched it back.

After a while, I said, quietly, "What do you suppose it's doing, sitting there watching us?"

"I think it's sitting there watching us," Jeff said.

"It's like an omen," I said, "if you believed in such things."

"I don't know about you," Claire said, "but I do."

"Well," I said, "I've always assumed that omens are superstition, but I guess after this week, I'm not so sure. It's getting hard to know where I stand on anything any more."

"Maybe that's good," Jeff said. "Maybe that's one of the benefits."

"Yeah, maybe. Going to make my life interesting."

The hawk sat unmoving, and we stood there watching it.

Claire said, "The ancients believed in omens."

"Sure did," I said. "The Romans, the Greeks, all of them. The Roman army wouldn't make a move without consulting the gods."

"Maybe there's something to it."

"Maybe so – but it seems to me the devil's in the details. What do you suppose that hawk is telling us?"

"I think he's telling us that if we don't get moving again, we're going to freeze out here!"

"Sensible bird. I think we'd better listen." We resumed walking, and the hawk didn't move even as we came nearer, then suddenly it spread its wings and rose into the air. We watched as it flew a short distance and descended to some tree that was out of our line of sight.

Abruptly, Jeff asked if either of us had seen a film called *Witness*.

"Yes, I've seen it," Claire said. "It's a classic."

"Harrison Ford," I said. "Great actor."

"Yes he is. You remember the plot? John Book is a Philadelphia cop and he winds up living in an Amish community for a while?" Jeff paused. "I'm sort of feeling that way."

Claire got it, I think, but I didn't, at first.

"For just that little while, John Book was a member of a real community, you see. It didn't last long, but it was long enough to remind him that in his normal life, he didn't *have* a community."

"And you don't either," Claire said softly.

"That's how I'm feeling, yes."

"Story of your life," I said.

"Yeah. From time to time I touch hands with somebody, but mostly, I'm on my own."

"And your family isn't any help?"

He shook his head. "Different worlds. Even when I was a kid I was alone. I figured, that's just the way it is in life, it doesn't seem to be a matter of choice."

"But this week has been different."

He nodded, and for a moment none of us said anything, or needed to say anything.

"It's like I've been living in solitary confinement all my life, and here for the first time I've found my real family."

"And tomorrow it's gone, and back to solitary," I said.

"Yep."

"You don't give off that impression," I said. "Always a joke up your sleeve, always a funny way of looking at this planetary lunatic asylum."

He smiled and shook his head.

"I mean, it's not your fault if your jokes aren't funny, you're doing the best you can."

Claire said, "And of course Angelo doesn't have any idea what it would be like to be laughing on the outside and hurting on the inside. You'd never catch him joking about feelings." She did it without leaving a sting, though, leading me to wonder once again how she did it. "It's a cold and lonely life sometimes, Jeff, right? Probably for everybody"

He nodded. "I feel like when I was a kid, even though I was alone, there was a kind of euphoria about it, you know? Every day was going to be something great, and even if I had to go to school, something good could happen, any time. I'd forgotten what it was like to live like that."

"Me too," I said.

"Wouldn't it be great if we could live this way *all* the time?"

I trudged along in the snow, doing my second-best pair of shoes no good. "I don't know about you," I said, "but feel like I've been *starved* for something all my life, and I've just now found it, or anyway a promise of it."

"And life is just so *dull* without it," he said.

"It's hard, sometimes, to balance inner and outer at the same time," Claire said.

"Yeah. It's like I have to choose between them, and you know which one the world wants you to choose!"

"Maybe you shouldn't think of it as an either/or situation, Jeff. It seems to me that life is mostly a matter of reconciling opposites."

"Compromising."

"No, not compromising; reconciling."

For a couple of moments we walked through the thin snow in silence, Jeff and I thinking about it.

"I suppose a lot of program participants get these spells," Jeff said finally.

"The Germans call it *weltsmertz*," I said, "which I've seen described as nostalgia for a place you've never been."

"That doesn't make it meaningless."

"No, not at all. Just the opposite. Something that universal must mean something."

Back at the center, somebody rang the outside cowbell, and sure enough we heard it loud and clear.

Claire said, "That *sounds like* morning, somehow, doesn't it?"

"Yeah," I said. "It makes you think of peasants out in a field somewhere, stopping to say their morning prayers."

"Out in Wyoming, we'd be more inclined to associate it with cowpokes being called to come eat."

"Well, that's what it's doing."

We turned around, and on the way back, Claire said, "Jeff, you know you've been through a lot of changes this week, we all have. Every change has left you a little bit different than you were when you came here."

"Don't I know it!"

"Yes, but those changes have to percolate through many levels, and that takes time, so if you feel a bit disoriented, it's certainly understandable. I sometimes think, instead of talking about resonances from other lives, we ought to be thinking about the past-live resonances we get from *this* life! We change, but parts of us are still geared to the person we were when we arrived here."

"When you put it that way," Jeff said, "of course it's disorienting."

"Yes. Or, you might just as well say it is *orienting*! You are finding your new location."

"Well that's a hopeful way of looking at it."

"You aren't anywhere near finished, you know. What you're going through now is something you're going to have to go through again and again, every time you change."

"Good lord!"

"It's not so bad. It just takes some getting used to. It's mostly a matter of continual reality checks. Not only is it not a *problem*, it's a *good* sign. The first step is the hardest, always."

"Besides," I said, "we're not alone any more. Just because the program ends doesn't mean we have to lose touch with each other. I certainly don't intend to."

But there was that doubt, sitting in the back of my mind like a hawk in a tree, comparing friendships based on extraordinary shared experiences to shipboard romances, wondering how our lives would look after a week back in what we called the real world.

Breakfast. Almost our last breakfast together.

"*Love* pancakes," Jeff said in contentment. "This is almost like a real breakfast."

"*Real* men eat pancakes," I said. "And sausage. And they drink plenty of coffee with them."

"You'd better believe it. And real men live where snow in March isn't any big deal."

"Real men, with real low IQs," I said.

"It's amazing," Claire said ostensibly to Toni. "Neither one of them has let up all week, and neither one has gotten any better."

"Natural talent," Jeff said.

"Real men don't *need* natural talent," I said.

Nonetheless, beneath my exuberance I could feel a sadness, or at least a sense of impending loss, and before we even finished breakfast, it became clear that others were feeling it too. It wasn't said in so many words, more in the pauses between words, in the silences that came as if on their own schedule. Our time was running out, and we could all feel the sand spilling down the hourglass. As I stood up to get another mug of coffee, my glance happened to land on Francois, and it reminded me of our conversation the night before. Very curious. Who'd have thought? I got my coffee and sat down again, and Andrew said out of the blue, "Toni, I was thinking, would you like it if we tried a healing session on you?"

"Here?"

"No, this afternoon sometime, during the long break. I thought maybe we could do you some good, the way people did Angelo some good the other night."

A long hesitation, and I thought I understood why. "Who did you have in mind?"

"Me, for one. I have done energy work for years at home, and sometimes I get lucky. And anybody else you wanted."

Another hesitation, then an acceptance, and I thought I understood that too. "How can I say no? If there were ever a place where miracles happen, it seems to be here. I believe I heard someone say that at some point. Claire, would you want to participate?"

"If you'd like me to, I'd be glad to. I don't have any experience with energy work, though."

"You helped me a lot, yesterday and the other day, and I'd like you to be there if you're willing."

"I agree with Toni," Andrew said. "Your energy will be great. I'll show you what to do, but mainly it's a matter of furnishing heart power."

"And I trust your heart, absolutely," Toni said to her.

"Anybody else who wants to is welcome, as far as I'm concerned," Andrew said, looking around the table at us. "The more the merrier, right, Angelo?"

"Well, I was only on the receiving end. But I'd be glad to try, Toni." *No idea what I'm getting into, here, but what else is new this week?*

"Me too," Jeff said.

"I'll be glad to help, if I can," Edith said.

"All right," Andrew said, pleased. "Let's call it a date. In the debrief room, maybe, right after lunch?"

❖ 3 ❖

"Okay, here we are again," Annette said. She paused a moment, and as she held the pause the group's attention tightened. She waited until she judged that we were properly focused before she continued. "This being Thursday morning, it's natural that you should be very aware that the program is nearly over. Tomorrow after breakfast, this group will scatter, forever. Some of you will stay in touch, some won't. Of those who do, some will stay in touch only a short time, others perhaps as long as you live. But the group *as a group* dissolves tomorrow, and can never be brought back together. It's natural that you should be aware of that, and it's appropriate that at some point you should regret the necessity. Even a certain amount of mourning is not out of place, perhaps. However – "

Another pause while she again gathered our emotional attention.

"However, I want to say two things about that. The first is, yes, you're leaving tomorrow. But be *here* now. When Friday morning rolls around, it's appropriate that you hold your attention on Friday. But it's equally appropriate that you hold your attention here, now. While you're here, *be* here. Don't let half your attention wander because you wish this moment could last forever."

"Remember," David said, "that was the bargain the devil made with Faust. He could have Faust's soul if Faust even once said to the passing moment, 'Stay, you're so fair.'"

"Don't make that mistake. Let the passing moment pass. The present moment is where you experience life." Another pause. "Besides, Thursday is culmination day. For many of you, Thursday is the day you will remember when you think about Open Door."

"And," David said, "just to keep you on edge, we're not going to say anything more. That's just a teaser, to keep you looking. But it's also true, so be prepared for everything to happen, or nothing, or anywhere in between. As always, try to stay in a state of expectation, without specific expectations."

"So," Annette said, "now that you're all really here again, on to the day's first exercise."

"This one is simple," David said. "Yesterday we had you do a tapeless tape, just so you'd realize that you don't need to spend the rest of your life plugged into earphones. Today, we carry it one step farther. When we finish here, we want you to put on your shoes, and your coats and hats, I guess, and walk around until you hear the bell. Wander around wherever you want to on the grounds, just stay close enough to hear the bell."

"The purpose of the tape is twofold," Annette said. "Now you will be walking around – you won't be lying passively listening to a tape, and won't even be lying passively recreating the mental states you associate with the tapes. Instead, you will be learning to move to those mental states while your body's surface attention is concentrated on other things. And at the same time, you will be practicing moving from one state to another."

"Yes, all the time you're walking around, practice moving between Entry State and Wider Vision and Time Choice and Interface. You don't have to move between them in that order. In fact, it would be good practice to go from state to state in a different order each time, as if you were using 'random shuffle' on a CD changer. But keep moving from one to another, and concentrate on how each one feels. If you're going to actually *use* these states in your everyday life, you need to know how to access them and change them as casually and automatically as you use your memory, say, or as you focus your attention on a crossword puzzle."

Annette said. "Any questions? Bobby?"

"You want us to maintain silence, I suppose."

"Absolutely, thanks for bringing that up. Silence, for two reasons. You don't want to break into the other person's space, and you don't want to distract your own concentration. Other questions? No? All right then, off you go. Since experiencing it while moving around is the point of the exercise, for once we don't care whether you go by way of the bathroom or not."

Andrew, standing up, mock-grumbled, "Where's Sergeant Preston when you need him?"

"Time Choice, maybe," David said. "Or you might try Interface. If they don't work, try Sled Dog. He has to be around here somewhere."

❖ 4 ❖

I stepped out into a cold gusty day. Instinctively, I monitored the effect of the first breath. *So far, so good. We'll see how it goes.* My coat was warm enough, but not any *too* warm. It would just about do the job, with luck.

I saw my fellow participants scattering in all directions, looking like a slow-motion explosion. Those I could see were wearing a somewhat abstracted expression. *We'd make a comical picture, I guess, wandering around in silence, apparently in deep thought.* On the other hand, who cared what we looked like?

Okay, Entry State. I felt for the state, tried to determine if I was really in Entry State or if I just hoped to be, or thought I was, or was pretending to be. *Odd, how different it is, doing it on my feet.* I decided that I was in Entry State, or as close to it as I was going to be, and so I tried Wider Vision. *If this is truly Wider Vision, I ought to be able to notice details I wouldn't have seen.* Well, maybe I was fooling myself, but as I walked around the corner of the building I did find myself really looking at the pattern of the needles in the fir tree I was passing, feeling the green, trying to imagine life rooted deep into the ground.

Time Choice? I walked around toward the back of the building, wandering where for some reason I hadn't gone before. My walks with people had tended to be toward the west, or toward the lake, or down the roads. For some reason the side of the building that backed into a grove of trees had not yet attracted me. *Time Choice?* Hard to tell if anything was happening. I saw that Jeff had preceded me. He was walking among the trees, reaching out to touch the branches as though petting an animal.

There's a thought. I came to a fir tree just as a prolonged burst of wind began tossing it back and forth. I moved to Interface, and instantly thought, *this is another life form, after all, as alien to us as anything else, but no more so. Why shouldn't I be able to communicate with it?*

I watched it tossing back and forth in the wind, looking like a great green cat getting its fur ruffled by a loving friend. *It's calling to me,* I thought, and for the moment I set logic aside and acted as if the thought were the truth. I stepped into the tree, pushing between its branches, and stood there engulfed in it.

It is difficult to speak or write truly of these things, because you can't get the right emphasis, or the right *lack of* emphasis. Some things that come with a lot of flash and bang turn out to be superficial, while things that have very profound effects tend to occur in a very matter-of-fact way, and merely talking about them distorts them in a sense, by giving them too much direct attention. Some things, like faint distant stars, are best seen in the side of the eye, and can't really be seen by looking straight at them. "All" that really happened as I interfaced with that tree was that I was sent back to my early childhood on the farm, and I remembered with great vividness how very much I had loved the patch of woods we'd had behind the field that was behind the house. Fifty years earlier, in those years right after the war finished, in an America long vanished now, no one had thought anything about my disappearing in those woods for hours at a time, at a time when I wasn't even ten years old.

I'd forgotten that before I had books in my life, I had the woods! And before I absorbed our society's notion of what is real or unreal, I lived in a world that I experienced directly.

Staying in Interface, I was again *so* aware of the essence of the tree, after so many years.

I used to know that the energy of woods was not the same as the energy of fields, and fields were not the same as cities or suburbs. How could I have forgotten that where trees are, the land is different? Standing there, my mental and emotional energy entangled in the tree, I was experiencing again a form of communication without words, a form of communication natural to children, lost somewhere in the difficulties of adolescence. I knew even then, standing there, that the experience itself was beyond words and would remain beyond words. Words could hint at it, perhaps.

I thought, unexpectedly, of Clifford Simak. Years ago, when I was a kid, I had read one of his science-fiction stories in which a man interfaced with a plant. I had always remembered Simak saying, How do you communicate with a plant? You don't exchange algebraic equations, or deep thoughts – you exchange emotions. *I wonder how he knew that.* The thought gave me my cue, and I set my intent to give the tree love. In return I felt this tremendous outpouring of joy at being alive. *I must remember this!*

Later I would consider this moment as the beginning of my life as a conscious being. Conscious life involves a lot more than human beings, or even humans and animals, or even – as I would come to realize some time later – human beings and animals and plants. The great chain of being, I would find, extended farther down the scale than I had realized, and farther up.

❖ **5** ❖

"According to my count, we're all here physically. Anybody still mentally lost in the great beyond? No? Okay. How was it?"

How was it? Well, debrief was – brief. Nobody seemed to have much interest in reporting. I wondered, maybe others were having experiences as difficult to express as I was. Or maybe they – we – were not much interested in talking, which was definitely a normal-consciousness activity. Much more comfortable, luxurious even, to remain as we were, half in other states. Probably this, because our trainers seemed neither surprised by nor concerned about our non-communicative state. They were smiling at us, fondly I thought, as if to say "right on schedule."

Finally Tony said, "It reminded me of one time I was in the Desolation Wilderness, out by Lake Tahoe. After you climb up Mount Tallac a ways, you find yourself wandering around in this immense field of rocks and boulders, stone everywhere – desolation is the word for it – and you can't imagine how it got that way. But with a little chemical assistance (he coughed, comically) my friends and I could see, all of a sudden, that we were looking at the results of a huge flood – some unbelievable water-driven catastrophe. We could see – once our eyes were opened to it – the patterns that had washed these massive boulders down into this jumble. That didn't tell us a thing about where that force of water came from or how it manifested in other ways, but it was certainly clear enough what had placed this jumble of stone where we found it. Perhaps someone with enough scientific or geological training might have seen the same thing, but my point is that we had no such training and saw it anyway – once we soared high enough, so to speak. Doing these tapes is like that, only without the chemical weirdness to deal with."

The rest of our debriefing didn't last long, and neither did our briefing for the final exercise of the morning.

"Okay," David said, "let's go do it again. This time, concentrate on Time Choice. Lying down, standing up, sitting, walking around inside or outside – whatever you want, but try to stay in Time Choice, and experience what it feels like to be physically functioning in the real world outside while functioning in Time Choice inside."

"Now, understand, what David just said isn't exactly what's happening; it's just shorthand. Even when you are lying in bed listening with the earphones, you are functioning in the world. There's only one way to avoid functioning in the world, as far as we know, which involves obituaries. But for training purposes you were radically reducing your physical activity so that you could concentrate on the inner world, and to that extent it was as if you weren't functioning. Now you're readjusting the balance again, as you did last tape."

"So, off you go to experience Time Choice as background while you remember that you are functioning in the real world. See you a few minutes after we ring the bell."

❖ 6 ❖

My first thought was, That *doesn't make any sense!* And my second thought was, *Experience first, judge later. Let's see what happens.*

We think of them as Hessians, but the Revolutionary War generation of Americans called them Germans. At least, that's what came to me. John was sent to guard the captured Germans!

No, no, his family were Quakers. At least, I think they were; that's the idea I got. Quakers wouldn't have been serving in the army, would they? Or maybe they weren't Quakers, or maybe he was a kind of renegade Quaker, like a lapsed Catholic, or a Jack Mormon. He had something to do with the army.

Where was this coming from? Outwardly I was just walking around the grounds. But inwardly, I was trying to stay in Time Choice even at the same time I was trying to analyze the feelings and intuitions coming in. Hard balance to strike.

I'd gone looking for John, to see what had happened to him after Clara died. And the sense I'd gotten was of him guarding prisoners of war. *But – where was any sense of John in the army? None.* Even as a guard, I got no sense of him as a military man. How did that make sense?

My knowledge of the Revolutionary War eventually came to my rescue. Could these be the British troops from Cornwallis' army that Gates and Arnold captured at Saratoga? They were held for quite some time, out west somewhere away from sea-based British troops, I remembered that. In

Charlottesville, maybe, or near there? It seemed to me that I remembered Thomas Jefferson having something to do with them.

But *memory* isn't the same thing as Time Choice. I could figure out the meaning later. What was I actually experiencing? I tried to reach backward to those times, tried to *feel* John's existence. *Trying too hard*, I muttered to myself, almost slipping on a patch of ice. *You find it in that in-between state.* I tried to hold myself there, an odd state of active passivity, or expectant non-expectation.

I got an image, a sort of picture of a man dressed as a farmer – rather than as a soldier – talking to a man at least half a generation older. For a second I could see them in my mind's eye, shivering as they walked up and down on a cold day, talking partly to take their mind off the cold. I hadn't any idea what they were talking about, then I got a strong surge of affection and gratitude, and then the excitement of getting something had pulled me out of the state.

What was that all about? We called them Germans, not Hessians. He was a Sergeant. What was his name? Sergeant something. An older man, from Darmstadt, wherever that is.

Yes, he was one of the prisoners from Saratoga and – suddenly I knew – John was in the militia, not the army, which is why I had the sense of him being not quite army but not quite a civilian either. *As to being a Quaker, was he still a Quaker, after Clara died?* It was pretty murky. A very sudden certainty about the militia, though, and about that sergeant.

Convention troops! That's what we called them, for reasons that escaped me at the moment. Convention troops, and Sergeant Schultz – *was it Schultz?* That's the name that comes to me. Old Sergeant Schultz (Old! He probably wasn't much more than 40 or 45) sort of took the younger man under his wing. The younger man was the guard and the older man the prisoner, but when it was man to man, the equation was reversed. Maybe it was friendship, maybe it was boredom, maybe it was nothing more complicated than good-heartedness. Over a few months the older man learned what had happened and perhaps he set himself the task of healing the younger man.

The remembered lesson leaped out at me as I walked through a similarly cold day, so many decades in their future. *You can't just give up on life, you can't let life's hardships and tragedies turn you sour. You have to accept what happens, and move along. You can't just give up.*

I thought of Claire, and of so many blind-alleys my life has led me to. For a moment the old German seemed very near again. Much later it occurred to me that John and the old German, themselves, must have had history that brought them together for that interchange.

I didn't talk about any of this in debrief. Too many uncertainties, too much reticence about discussing something that involved Claire as well as me. Too much disclosure, maybe, in the past few days? Maybe I had reached saturation point?

About the only thing I remember is Andrew saying, in response to something I don't remember, "The roads are somewhat cleared now, more than they have been in many centuries. That's good and bad. A road smoothes the way, and helps travelers move more quickly and easily, but smoothing the ground facilitates contradictory or discordant motion as well. So we may expect more friction, more jostling, and we must learn to watch every little thing." Don't know why that stuck with me, but it did.

That, and the lesson that had come to me, possibly from another lifetime, from an old soldier named Sergeant Schultz. You can't just give up. You have to take what life hands you and go on. You can't just give up. You can't give up.

❖ 7 ❖

And so to lunch, our last lunch as a group. Tomorrow at this time (whatever time it actually was, but lunchtime, anyway) we would have scattered to the winds. But we ate cheerfully, talking about our experiences of the morning – talking more around the lunch tables, it struck me, than we had in debrief.

"'You can't give up on life,'" Claire said, echoing me echoing the sergeant's message. "No matter what happens, you don't give up. That's very true."

"That's what John *had* done, though," I said. "At least, I think so. He had thought he had his life planned out. They had the house, they had a farm, I think, or maybe he was raising animals, I don't know, but whatever the details, he had what he wanted. They must have been very much in love. And they were young. They had a couple of children, I think. Then she got stung by wasps or whatever they were, and she was allergic to them, and she died – and he just never got his balance back. He knew what he'd lost, and he'd lost the ability to value what he still had."

She pondered that. Edith said, "The funny thing is, her being dead wasn't necessarily a tragedy for *her*. Presumably she built that possibility into her life plan."

I waggled my hand in that rocking gesture that means maybe, maybe not. "If we *have* life plans. Maybe we just come in as we are and what happens, happens, and we adjust as we go."

"He never accepted her death," Claire said. "Life hurt him, so he gave up on life. Is that it?"

"Until the old German took him in hand, yes. And I get the feeling that was quite a few years down the road."

Looking straight at me – "So, not to put too fine a point on it, how is that you, today?"

"Man," I said to Edith (and the rest of the table), "I'm glad she's not *my* psychotherapist!" Claire smiled, but she waited, and I didn't feel I should refuse her. "Yeah, it's me somewhat. I mean, probably I can have that tendency in certain circumstances, but it's only one tendency among others. I have plenty of contradictory qualities that keep it in check." *Except when I'm feeling sorry for myself because I'm losing you as soon as I found you!* "Remember, I'm *after* the old German talked to John, not before." I could see by the affectionate amusement in her eyes that she wasn't taking that entirely at face value, but she let it drop.

Helene, though, didn't. "John might have done things differently, but you don't necessarily know if things would have turned out better or worse. In a sense, it doesn't matter. You might say that taking one choice or another amounts to driving down one block instead of another. Perhaps it costs you or saves you a few minutes: What's a few minutes?"

"I'd have expected that you as a psychotherapist would think it made a difference," I said. "If it doesn't matter, why do you care what choices people make? Why do you care professionally, I mean."

"The important thing is to begin to express what you have learned. What is currently formless inside you will become more structured as you work with it. And as it becomes more structured, it becomes more available to you. You grow."

"Grow weirder, you mean."

She made a motion with her head that was the equivalent of a shrug. "If that's what you really are, deep down inside, you do, yes."

"Oh well," I said, "I've had enough of trying to be normal, this lifetime. I'm ready to try weird, thank you very much."

Jane made one of her rare interjections. "I just try to work as hard as I can at being actively aware. It seems to me that our work is here in front of us, and the work will bring its own rewards, and that's the way to be happy – working and growing."

Helene smiled, a wintry smile that was yet somehow warm. "Jane, as a mental-health professional, I have to say how much I admire your simple goodness. And that word 'simple' is not meant as an insult, believe me, but as a great compliment. Were you born this way, or did you come to it by working on yourself?"

Jane hesitated, and I thought, *Here's one person who is not used to talking about herself.* "It was a deliberate decision, some years ago. I won't go into what had happened, but I said to myself, 'For the rest of my life, I will serve others, thinking not of my needs but of theirs, so that perhaps I can become free to experience universal love.'"

It was one of those quiet statements that are stunning.

"That's beautiful," Claire said after a moment. Jane smiled. "Yes, and like most things that are beautiful, it's easier to say than to do. But I keep trying."

"It shows," Edith said.

Again the hesitation before talking about herself – or maybe she was just a quiet, thoughtful person by nature, accustomed to examining her thought before speaking it. "I have never thought owning things important. And I don't seem to have a taste for fame or money. I don't have any particular talents, so achievement perhaps was never a realistic possibility for me in any case, but none of those things seem to me to really matter. What is important to human life is love, the ability to love and receive love."

Again, the simple words produced an impact. Francois said, "Sartre to the contrary, it is the sleep of *love*, not reason, that breeds monsters."

"Yes," Jane said.

"Sometimes I wonder what happened to my ability to love," I said. I didn't mean to say it. I wouldn't have, if I'd known I was going to, but it slipped out. It left a silence much like the ones Jane had caused.

"Maybe it has been in the deep freeze," Helene said finally. "Circumstances can do that. Or, maybe nothing happened to it, but now you are waking up, and growing and stretching, and what used to be comfortable is no longer enough for you. You experience the difference as an absence, perhaps."

"That would be a nice thought," I said, to fill the silence. Fortunately, at another table Sam Andover and Selena Juras got into it, and the whole room must have registered the words, for there fell one of those little hushes that left their words front and center. He'd said something about enjoying the danger that came with his work, and she'd said, "That's just like a man!"

"You say that like it's an insult," Sam said. "I happen to *be* a man, why *shouldn't* I be just like one?" I looked over at her. Her every line expressed exasperation, but Sam pushed on, where angels fear to tread. Sensible male angels, anyway.

"I think it's a basic difference between men and women. Women seek safety, men seek danger. Isn't life usually a mixture of the two? Isn't it just as well that one half of the human race is not only able to handle danger, but thrives on it?"

"I just think it would be better if men grew up and didn't need such things."

"Yes, you think that now, and you call it growing up. But if we were in a war, you'd be glad enough to have soldiers protecting you and your children."

"If women ruled the world, we wouldn't have wars."

"Oh sure. We've all seen how peaceful women are when they get crossed. But forget about war, you're glad enough to have men who thrive on danger when your house is on fire, or there are criminals on the loose. Or do you think that if women ruled the world houses wouldn't catch fire, and there wouldn't be any criminals?"

"There's still something childish about looking for trouble."

"It doesn't have anything to do with looking for trouble. It has to do with a sense of being equal to the occasion. It has to do with being a man, and if you don't think that men should be men, that isn't men's problem, it's yours. What would you say if somebody said women should be more like men? Never mind, I know what you'd say. You'd say: 'just like a man,' and you'd think that covered it."

Edith and Claire and Helene and Jane and Francois and I looked around at each other and perhaps we each silently said, "whew!" and were glad that Sam and Selena were at another table.

I thought, *Even here!* At the same time, I was glad to get off the hook I'd just impaled myself on.

❖ 8 ❖

Until now, I hadn't seen Andrew in his healing mode. When they'd worked on me, Annette had taken the lead and in any case I hadn't had much attention to spare. But this time he took front and center, and did so by right of knowledge, experience, and confidence. This was an Andrew new to me. As though dropping a mask, he dropped the jokes and witticisms, and something fine within him showed through.

We were in the assembly room at Edwin Carter Hall, lunch over, gathered around Toni. Andrew had her seated comfortably in a chair – a real chair, not a back-jack – with us seated around her, also in real chairs. "Us" means, besides me, Andrew, Edith, Claire, and Jeff.

"We could have asked more people in," Andrew explained, "but this many is fine. With more people, we'd have more energy to draw from, but also more chance of distraction. Energy work isn't a matter of adding one person's energy to another, it has to do with drawing in the energy of the universe and helping the person receive it and absorb it. So once you have a few people, you have all you need. Two or three would do."

He stood in front of Toni, talking to her.

"The way I do healing is that we don't even try to figure out what's wrong or what caused it. Instead, we energize the subconscious mind so that it gets on the job. After all, as Annette said the other night, your subconscious mind runs your body moment to moment. What do we consciously know about producing adrenaline, or processing sugar, or regulating our heart-beats to match our level of activity, right? We don't know anything about how to digest food or replace injured tissues or anything. Right? It's all automatic, like the way our bodies change as we grow up. First there's a growth spurt, then a consolidation, then another spurt." He smiled at her. "Let alone what happens when we change from being children to being teenagers! Well, all of that is obviously under some kind of central intelligence that plans and reacts to things. So we count on our bodies to grow according to plan, and maintain themselves, and repair themselves, all without our having anything much to do with it on a conscious level. And that's just as well, because *we* couldn't do it, any more than we could regulate our breathing while we are asleep. Make sense so far?"

It did, of course. This was not far ground for anyone who'd been through the week we'd just been through.

"And I take it we're all on the same page about energy? Everybody here recognizes that we are continually supported by energy from the other side – or, anyway, energy that is transmitted by some means other than food and drink? Well, just as we did the other night for Angelo, we're going to have several people bringing the energy through and holding the space, and Toni, you're going to be visualizing some readjustment as I guide you."

"Do this now," Jeff said.

"Right," he said, and hardly cracked a smile. An Andrew very much in a different mode, very intent, a one-pointed beam focused tightly on Toni. "Now, I don't know if you've had other people work on you – ?"

"Some, from time to time."

"Everybody does things differently. My way is to start by seeing where you are. And since you – conscious-you – doesn't know the answer to that question, we're going to have to talk to the part of you that does. Toni, I want you to close your eyes and go into Entry State, and tell me when you're there."

"All right," she said after a pause. "At least, I think so."

"Now move to Wider Vision."

Another pause. "All right."

"Now we want to deal with your subconscious mind as if it were a different person. So I'm going to ask a couple of questions, and you're going to pose them to this other person, and tell me what you get in response, okay? Just like tape exercises, your answer might come in words, or in pictures, or in a knowing, or in feelings. However it comes, you're the translator. Okay?"

"Okay."

"Then bring up an image of your subconscious mind, the part of you that controls the parts of your life that are not under your conscious control." Not taking his eyes off her, he said, "The rest of you will get your chance to join in, in a bit. It helps if you move to Entry State and stay there while we work."

I moved into Entry State, keeping my eyes open. *Amazing the things you can get used to!*

"Now, Toni, have you got the image?"

"Well – I think so. More or less."

"That's fine, it doesn't have to be like a movie. Now, Toni, ask this person, 'How do these illnesses serve me?'"

We waited for what seemed a long time. Perhaps it was only two or three minutes.

Slowly, reluctantly, Toni said, "I don't know if it's my imagination or what, but I do have a sort of an answer. I get an image of somebody beating a hunk of clay to center it on a potter's wheel. You know, hitting it on this side and that until it's centered enough that you can start the wheel and begin shaping it."

"So these illnesses have been getting you ready to be shaped?"

She frowned. "It's like I'm the clay and I'm the one hitting the clay, at the same time."

"Yes, and – ?"

Silence. Delay. "That's all I get."

"That's fine. Then ask, are you ready to be rid of the diseases, or are they still useful to you?"

Again the intense, inward frown. "I don't know, I'm sort of resisting this. I don't much like the idea that all this, everything I've been fighting with all this time, was somehow necessary. I don't see why it should be necessary for me when it obviously isn't necessary for everybody else! That sounds whiny, I know, but – "

"No, no. Follow that. Ask. Why should it have been necessary for you? And, is it still?"

Another long pause, then she gave a little laugh. "It's like, some clay is more resistant than others!" Then I *saw* her get another aspect of the message, and she said, "Some clay is harder, sturdier, and if you use the harder clay you get a sturdier product. I don't know that that's true in real life, but it's what I get."

"Go with what you get. And is it still necessary to you?"

A smaller pause. "At some point either you get the clay centered or you're never going to. What I get" – she smiled – "is that we're as ready as we're ever going to be."

"That's great. Makes sense, of course, or we wouldn't be here. Okay. Hold on to that realization. It was needed, it wasn't wasted, and you're as ready to be done with it as you'll ever be." He straightened up, and it was only then that I realized that he had been bending over, a little, concentrating on her as she sat in front of where he stood. "Time to bring in the Greek chorus," he said.

"The peanut gallery," Jeff said. Something in his voice, some difference in cadence, said that he wasn't in normal consciousness. I thought, *So, he jokes in Entry State, too.*

"That too," Andrew said. "Now Toni, we have Edith, Claire, Angelo, and Jeff here to help us. They're going to close their eyes and concentrate on sending you energy. Open up to their energy. And you all, open up to Toni. Feel your way toward the love you share with each other. Create whatever image you like of your being a channel of love. Bring in love and support from the other side, funnel it through you, and let it extend to Toni.

Toni, this energy is coming *through* them, not *from* them. The energy that supports our lives pours in, there is an endless supply of it, and nobody could possibly take more than their share, there is so much. You guys, open up to that endless supply, and become a conduit for Toni. Toni, concentrate on receiving. Be sure that you don't close off from it. We do close off from it all the time, thinking ourselves unworthy of it, or unable to receive it, or too independent to want to rely on it. Don't do that. Open yourself to the love and concern and support of your friends and receive this healing, rejuvenating energy."

I found myself with tears in my eyes as I listened to him and felt the energy flowing through me, and listened to him some more. *Never had so many tears in my life*, I thought.

"Envision that energy pouring through your body. See it carrying away obstructions to health, repairing what needs repair, strengthening everything as it passes. Maybe see it coming in through the top of your head and passing through your body and out the soles of your feet, or whatever feels comfortable and right to you. The content of the visualization isn't important; it's the connecting with the energy. Open yourself to the healing energy your friends are gladly providing you access to, and intend that it go wherever it is needed."

I don't know how long the whole session lasted. Half an hour? Three-quarters? Less? However long it was, finally Andrew brought it to a natural end, and reminded us to return from our altered state. As usual (*It's gotten to be "as usual"!*), on opening my eyes after coming out of the altered state, the world seemed unnaturally bright.

"Some stuff, huh?" Andrew stretched, looking at her benignly.

"That was fantastic, Andrew," Toni said. "Thank you so much." Looking around, "And thank all of you. I can't tell you how much I appreciate it."

Edith said, "So how do you feel, Toni?"

Toni concentrated. "A little tired, I think. But good tired."

"Yes, that's not surprising. Be sure to drink a lot of water. Any other reactions?"

"Well, you know, I do feel a little better. I feel lazy and sleepy now, not tense and on edge the way I often do. But maybe the biggest change is that I realize, I have been too *passive* about it. I mean, I have been to plenty of doctors, and I've done plenty of my own research, looking for information and trying new things – but I've been treating my body as if it were a *thing*, instead of thinking of it as a person. I think that's going to make a big difference."

"Sure. That'll make all the difference in the world. It gives you a feedback mechanism, if nothing else."

"Also, in the middle of all that, I had a curious experience. I got the sense that I could now get any information I wanted about any of my past lives. It was a sense that some barrier had come down."

"Hmm. Interesting. Leaving you feeling – ?"

"Vaguely uneasy, if you want to know the truth. As if maybe I really don't want to know too much."

"If you aren't ready – "

"But isn't the truth always better than a lie?"

Claire said, "Yes it is, but it's sometimes worse than ignorance, if you're not prepared for it. Ask any psychotherapist."

Andrew looked around. "Anyone else? You guys feel like doing a little more?"

Jeff asked, "Are you still up for doing more? Aren't you tired?"

"Nah. Well, a little, but it passes."

"Well, how about Claire?" *Good move, pal! And about half a step ahead of me.*

Andrew looked at Claire. "Interested?"

"Very much so."

"Okay! Why don't you exchange chairs with Toni, here. Toni, I'm sure you'd like to help, but why don't you sit this one out? In fact, this would be a good time to drink some water, and maybe lie down for a while, take a nap. Okay? Now, Claire – "

❖ 9 ❖

So that was our last long break. We worked on Claire, and then we sat around and talked about what we'd done, and after a while David rang the cowbell and we all reassembled for the introduction to our third tape of the day. I tried to count back, see how many tapes we'd done all told, but couldn't.

"All right, people, this is our last tape coming up. It's an Interface tape, a free-flow, no commentary by C.T. Because it *is* a tape, you'll be doing it in your rooms, one last time. And, because you're going to be doing it in your rooms, you'll be going there by way of the bathrooms. That's about all the briefing I propose to give you. You want to add something, Annette?"

More of their prepared routines. Or maybe they've just worked together so long they do it automatically.

"Yes, I do, thanks. I will add just one thing. Since this is your final tape exercise, perhaps it would be appropriate for you to ask your internal guidance what you should be learning from this week, what lessons you may have missed, what new directions may be open to you. It's a free-flow tape, it's Interface, so the sky's the limit."

"And so," David said, dismissing us, "we'll see you back here after the tape."

So, back to the bathrooms, back to the bedroom, and there I was again, lying down with sleep mask and earphones, listening to pink noise. I lay there without any particular expectations, knowing that I had experienced enough this week to turn my world upside down. In fact, as I lay there quietly waiting for C.T. to bring us back to Interface via the other altered states we had learned in the past few days, that's what I was thinking of: how my world had been turned upside down.

The session with Claire had gone about the same as the session with Toni, except that when it came time for us to send energy – to send love – I had been astonished and almost frightened by the eagerness with which I had responded, and by the depth of love that had poured out of me like (I thought, absurdly) a ripped-open sack of grain. I had held nothing back, even while in a sense scaring myself with my willingness to sacrifice. I had poured out love, and hadn't counted the cost, and although something told me that I couldn't injure myself by giving so freely, still I didn't *know* that, but I gladly took whatever risk there might be. And in a moment of revelation – a little late in life, but better late than never – I'd thought, *So that's what love is!*

C.T. came in and we began the relaxation process. I went through the familiar routine consciously, but automatically, still thinking of other things.

My dad used to say, when he found something new that he really liked, "How long has *this* been going on?" That's how I was feeling. *How could I get this old and still not know what love is?* Anything true or false that could be said of love had been said long ago. You couldn't live in twentieth century America without hearing it every day. Only – nobody was offering any clues as to how to tell truth from falsehood. You had to figure it out for yourself, and that made for some expensive trial and error! *Except*, my cynical inner voice said, *you ought to know that anything that's used as a way to sell things probably isn't true.* Well, maybe. Or maybe the most effective sales tools rely on staying as close to the truth as possible, bending it to their own purposes.

C.T. moved us into Entry State, and I flowed along without effort, remembering suddenly that it had once been difficult to recognize. "Once" – as in, four or five days ago!

It doesn't have anything to do with *owning* somebody, or *possessing* them, and it certainly doesn't have anything to do with bending them to your will, or in fact manipulating them in any way. I thought of the outpouring of joy that had accompanied that willing gift of love. *I would have died for her, at that moment, and it would have been all right.*

"Wider Vision," said C.T.'s voice, and we moved onward as usual.

Not that simple, of course. Well, it was and it wasn't. *Was*, in that it was only a matter of choosing to open yourself. It wasn't a matter of learning how. Yet – *wasn't*, in that we don't deal with only one important person in our life, with everybody else being part of a cast of thousands. Suppose I had died for Claire – what of my children? What of my brothers and sisters? What of Julie, for that matter – for after all she and I had been together, if one could call it "together" – for many long years. *It's not as simple as "give everything to one other person."* No. Especially if that led to your giving others so much the less.

C.T. invited us to move to Time Choice.

No, if it's going to transform your world, it's going to have to transform how you relate to everybody. You can't be open to just one person and closed to everybody else. I thought immediately of Selena. Irritating, cutting, knowledgeable Selena. Would it be even *safe* to open up to her? Or, say, Lou Hardin? It certainly didn't seem so. But then, just as C.T. brought us to Interface, I thought, *Maybe it isn't about 'safe.' Maybe safe is the opposite of open.*

Jane Mullen – sweet, unassuming, placid, *good* Jane Mullen – said sometime during the week that all the emotions in human life boil down to either love or fear – either expansion or contraction. "Of course," Selena had said, dismissing it even while acknowledging it, "in a world of duality everything has its opposite. The important thing is to choose love over fear."

"Now you are free," C.T.'s voice said. "I will call you when it is time to return."

Yes, important to choose love over fear, but just because we say *we do, and* think *we do, doesn't mean fear doesn't sneak in through the back door.* Besides, it occurred to me, in a world of duality, is it desirable, it is even possible, to always sit at one extreme? Was seeking to be entirely expanded any more possible, any better, than seeking to be entirely contracted? "Boundary issue," Claire had said. For that matter, Selena had said the chakras expanded sometimes, contracted other times, and needed to.

Well, the question was beyond my ability to untangle at the moment. "Above my pay grade," as my brother George used to say when he was in the military. To business. Here I was in Interface. Last tape. Maybe I should have been giving thought to what I wanted to do with my last opportunity.

"There's no reason for it to be your last opportunity. Think of it as your *first* opportunity."

What was that? And where did it come from??

This is a little harder to convey without distortion, because our language is not designed to convey any but an ordinary experience of reality. Either we have to invent our own specialized language – a sort of initiates' jargon – or use words like "heard" and "sensed" and "saw" when we mean something between "just knew" and "intuited" and "received." So when I say I heard a voice, or saw an image, you will have to make allowances for the language that is being used to do what it was not designed to do. In the same way, "just knowing" is not the same thing as guessing, nor is "intuiting" blindly grasping at random, nor "receiving" making it up.

So, when I "heard" this new and previously unsuspected inner voice, I didn't hear it with my physical ear, obviously, and I didn't have what they call an auditory hallucination – "hearing voices" – where what you perceive mentally is identical to what you perceive from external sound, and so is indistinguishable from real sound except that there is no one around to make it. Nor did I consistently experience – "just know" – words in sentences. Sometimes, yes. Sometimes I "just knew" the *sense* of what was being conveyed.

As you should know by this time, I was accustomed to talking to myself, the habit of a lifetime of being alone among others. But that's just *me* talking to *me*. (Usually. But sometimes I say something that surprises myself. How should that be possible?) And I was accustomed to that "you" voice that I think is our internalized voice of our parents and other authority figures: "You sure screwed that up!" or "Is that the best you can do?" or "You'd better get moving if you're going to get done on time!" We all live with that one, I imagine. My life got easier when I stopped identifying with what I now call the you-voice and started identifying only with the I-voice.

(The I-voice – "I'd better get going, here!" – never carries the critical tone that the you-voice so often does.)

But this voice – and remember, it wasn't a voice – was not me, or at least it wasn't any part of me that I was familiar with. I experienced it as "other" and it was a big surprise! Being in Interface, however – being at Open Door in general – "surprised" didn't mean shocked. I rolled with it, automatically, as if it were just one more thing. Which it was.

Still, my automatic reaction was, *What was that?*

"Did you think you were alone in your life?"

I flashed back to the message from the silent morning – only yesterday. *Well, no, I guess I've been getting the message that I'm not alone, but I didn't think it meant – Wait! Are these messages and visions and all coming from you?*

"From where else?"

I've got to be imagining this!

"No, this is not a sign of psychic inflation. You aren't someone special, different from everyone else. You are beginning to experience us directly because you wanted improved access. Here it is."

(How do you go off by yourself to think about something when the other person is inside your head? *Them old dreams . . .*)

"Not literally inside your head, but as close to you as your skin. Closer, in a way."

Well, whoever you are, you're still speaking in riddles.

"Not by choice. We are happy to be as plain as you allow us to be, now that we have gotten your attention."

Okay. Who are you?

"We are you."

Yeah, that's a great start on not talking in riddles.

"We are you, literally. But you are a much larger being than you suspect. You have begun to see that you are part of other lives in other times. You are on the very verge of suspecting that you are a part of other lives in your own time, as well. But beyond these, you are also part of something that extends beyond time and space, and that is what you have been dealing with, this week. That is what you are dealing with right now, as you lie listening to the pink noise on the tape, wondering if you are making this up."

(I scarcely dared to think, lest I be overheard.)

"Angelo, how do you suppose that Angelo connects with John and with other lives? Do you suppose you are a trapeze artist, jumping from one moving perch to the next, with or without a net? Do you think that one personality winks out of physical existence at his death and another winks into physical existence at his birth, with no bridge from one to the other?"

Hadn't thought about it, I guess.

"You may wish to think about it now, while the tape runs. We will give you a capsule summation, if you wish."

All right.

"Until this week you have been living your life as though you were alone among strangers and some few affection-bound acquaintances. Some of these – your families – you loved to the extent that you were able. You felt affection, you were willing to sacrifice for them, and you could communicate better with them than with others. Still, you were enduring life as a long hard solitary slog, without much interest and with only the most transitory or abstract of pleasures."

The summary was true enough, if depressing.

"Now you have realized that your life has been self-imposed exile. You don't *need* to live that way. You are not one of a kind, and you are not separated from others by invisible but impassible limits. Claire and Jeff, in particular, came to you as angels, angels for Angelo, bearing the message that you do know how to love, and who you are can inspire love, as well. Now we say to you, what you are calling 'past lives' are as real and as alive and as present-tense to themselves as you are to you. *Therefore*, you, as you exist in the eternal present-tense, may be said to exist as many individuals in many times and places – but you might equally well choose to see Angelo as one small aspect of one huge being. A small aspect, but as important as any other to the larger being, and incomparably important to yourself considered as if independent, for who you are and what you choose to become is solely your opportunity and responsibility. We are the non-material aspects of that larger being of which you are a part. Hence, as we say, we are you."

This larger being. God, I suppose?

"No, not God. To regard the creator as an aspect of the creation, one would see God perhaps as the largest being, comprising in that being all lesser beings. However, this is not the time to lose ourselves in abstraction. We are introducing ourselves, and providing you context, because you have work to do."

Oh Lord! Go see Pharaoh, I suppose, and say let my people go.

"If you will substitute for Pharaoh the dead-end materialist worldview, yes, more or less."

[A pause.]

"What, no wisecracks?"

What would you like me to say? You can read my thoughts and feelings, you know where I am.

"Yes, we do. Stunned, somewhat. First, that you are 'imagining' this conversation at all. Second, that it is nonetheless telling you things you find surprising. Third, the thing that is tightening your chest in apprehension, that you may have a task that is yours, specifically and alone."

That's about it. Starting with "why me?" I didn't even believe in any of this!

"Neither does Charlie Reilly, but he found himself inclined to send you – against your inclinations – to have a look."

You mean he doesn't know why he sent me?

"He has reasons – you always have reasons for what you do or don't do – but no, on the level of individual consciousness, he does not. He thinks you'll bring home a good story and he hopes it will break you out of the state of dispirited discontent that has been growing on you."

Lying on the bed, I gave a huge sigh, surprising myself. *Okay, what is it you want from me specifically?*

"Not so much. We want you to be fully *you*. We want you to choose to expand to the greatest degree possible. We want you to come into your own."

While single-handedly defeating our materialist civilization, right.

"Well, if you can't defeat it single-handed, fight it anyway, preferably unarmed. You might consider giving it a handicap."

It startled me. *That was a joke?*

"Why shouldn't we make jokes? Where do you think *you* get it?"

Lord, lord. Who'd have thought?

"Angelo, look at your life before this week. Do you want to return to living that way?"

No!

"Then you must change, and remain changed, even if your surroundings do not."

Can I?

"You can if you maintain and develop this contact."

Do tapes all the time, you mean?

"You know what we mean. More access is always possible; it is a matter of your not blocking it. If you live day by day in a state of not blocking it, then you live in a state of continuous access."

Wow! But then, second thought: *It's going to make things difficult from time to time! People are going to think I'm nuts.*

"You will need to exercise discretion, yes, lest the fearful and the single-visioned see you as demented, or as doing the work of the devil. But for you the alternative to continual access is probably a return to the life you have been leading until now."

No. I'm not going back to that prison!

I startled myself with the vehemence of my feelings.

A long pause which they did not break. Then:

So what do I need to do, to function in the world without losing what I have gained this week?

"You are doing it. Learn to connect with all levels of your own being. Learn to love, truly love, with all your strength. Learn to master the new and overwhelming emotions and forces in your life. The rest will follow in sequence. Master one step and the next step will be the thing nearest to hand. It is always a safe thing to do, the thing nearest at hand. Only keep in mind that you have a real task to do and that you need to keep yourself as focused, as hard working, and as altruistic as you can be. Lack of grounding does not enable you to fly; it cripples you. You know it. Live it."

Well, all right, that sounds like good advice, wherever it came from.

I drifted, and refocused, and returned with a knowing that could be put this way: "The message is simple. Love and persevere. With perseverance comes success."

I asked if there was something I could do to improve my ability to communicate with other parts of myself, perhaps unsuspected parts of myself. The answer, put into words, would go something like this:

"The more you love, the deeper you will be in touch with your own emotions. The deeper you are in touch with emotions, the easier to get to other layers of being, which are more or less the same thing. A closed-off person cannot access other lives because he cannot even access his own life. If you can't examine your own life because it is too painful, how can you go to other lives previous or future?"

A pause, and then C.T. was saying it was time to return.

❖ 10 ❖

Again, nobody had much to say. Maybe the messages were too personal. Maybe some people were disappointed that they hadn't gotten any messages, or maybe they didn't like what they got. Most likely, though, the others were reacting much as I did, with weariness. We were to the point of almost too much of a good thing. We had stretched, and stretched, and stretched ourselves, and we didn't have much stretch left in us.

Besides, we knew we weren't anywhere near being able to summarize what we'd learned, or put it into a system. We had fragments, and preliminary fragments at that. It was going to take a while, probably a long while, before we could begin to find our footing in this new terrain.

None of this seemed to surprise our trainers. No reason why it should. They handled the few questions and comments they received, and came quickly to the point where they asked if anybody had anything else they wanted to say about the exercise. No one did.

"So there we are," Annette said. "I think we can all see that this is about as far as we're going to go this week. I suppose we hardly need to say that this can be only the beginning? You've got the tools, from now on it's up to you."

"Of course," David said, "if these exercises have done anything at all, they ought to have showed you that it always *has* been up to you."

"That's right." Annette paused, timing her warning. "Can I leave us with one cautionary note? One of the things this week has been about is developing your intuition, learning to use non-rational ways of knowing things and functioning. That's well and good, provided you don't go off the deep end. There is such a thing as Psychic's Disease – you've heard us talk about it – which means trying to live as if every stray thought was an inspiration, and every hunch a certainty. Don't do it. Or anyway, if you catch yourself doing it, stop. There isn't any benefit to being one-sided either way." (I happened to notice Bobby getting startled, and I wondered what she had just sparked, but I didn't find out until he spoke his piece during closing circle.)

I raised my hand.

"Annette? I think maybe I have an example of what you're talking about. You know that Claire and Jeff and I have been getting a sense of our having been connected in other lives? The other day I had a real clear sense of something with Claire and me, and I sort of invented Jeff into the scene, figuring it made sense for him to be there – but then we got something else and I realized that I'd sort of jumped to a conclusion, and it wasn't right. Is that what you mean?"

"Well, perhaps. It all depends. You got a clear perception, so you knew something – but then your logical mind tried to make sense of it by building a story around it. That happens a lot."

"So it's always going to be a problem."

"Once you recognize the process, you start to look out for it. It's a matter of experience."

"So, not fatal, huh?"

"Think of it as the measles. It's just something you go through."

"Got it," I said.

"Okay, we'll take a brief break – just a few minutes so don't go far – and then we'll do one more exercise before supper. Something different. You'll like it, and you'll find it will be useful."

❖ 11 ❖

"Something different, again," I said to Jeff. "As many tapes as we've done, what can they do different? A tape that leaves us where we are, maybe?"

"One that brings us back to normal consciousness, after a week's vacation," he said, and as it turned out he was closer than he knew.

"All right," David said, "I promised you before break that this was going to be something different, and it is. For one thing, we're going to do it together, right here in this room. For another, we'll put a little Entry State music on the speakers, pretty low, like background-music, to help you stay focused. And the third thing that's different, it isn't recorded. Instead, Annette is going to talk us through it." He gestured toward her with his hand, like introducing a speaker, and stood up and turned on the sound system.

"Let's consider what we've done, these past few days," she said softly. Behind her, the pink noise that I associated with tapes began, not intrusive but not unnoticed. It seemed strange to hear it while listening to someone talking. "It's like we've been on a long journey, exploring various islands. First came Entry State, and that was all about being centered and receptive. Then, Wider Vision, which was concentration and intense focus. After that came Time Choice, which for some of you is where it got weird. And then Interface, which should have opened up new worlds for future exploration. But now it's time to be sure you're ready to return to the other world."

She smiled, that warm smile we'd seen so often. "After all, we couldn't just plop you back into your old life without preparation. Your present mental state may seem normal to you, but whether you realize it or not, what you feel as normal has changed quite a bit since the last time you checked. So we're going to do a little meditation. Your part in it is simple, just be attentive and receptive, and I'll do the rest. Okay?"

David turned up the speakers just a bit.

"All right, let's begin. Probably you will find this works best if you close your eyes, but it doesn't matter, just do whatever is comfortable. Let's sit quietly, listening to the sound of the tape, just like the free-flow tapes you've been listening to this week."

I closed my eyes, content to be at ease, and the pink noise filled the spaces. Annette spoke slowly, and continued speaking slowly, often with long pauses between her sentences that I will not attempt to reproduce. You'll just have to – imagine them.

"We are sitting together in this room. So imagine the room. Remember what it looks like. See us sitting in it. Imagine what it looks like, seen from the ceiling. Look down on the room from the ceiling." *Do this now.* "Now pretend that your body is on the ceiling, looking down, and go *through* the ceiling to the next floor. What does the room just above us look like, if you look at it from the ceiling? Call up the memory of the entry hall and one of the rooms next to it, and imagine what they would look like if you were looking down on them. We're not trying to induce an out-of-body experience here, we're just imagining. Make it up, but try to make up an image.

"Now go through the ceiling again, and imagine that you are on the roof. What does the building look like, from the roof? Look around. What could you see, from the roof? Look to the west, and remember what Edwin Carter Hall looks like. What would it look like from the roof of this building? Look south, over the trees to the hills a few miles away. What do they look like, late in the afternoon on this day in March? Look east. What do you see? Can you remember the trees? What do they look like, from the roof? Look to the north, across the road. You have seen that view every day all week. What would it look like from the roof?

"Now hold all that together. Hold an image of this room, and the rooms above us, and the roof of the building. *Feel* the building as a whole, as a unit. Then remember the views you just recreated. Hold an image of this building as it exists within that landscape."

The pink noise crackled and hissed in the background, and I sat there quietly, peacefully, holding an image of the buildings as part of the landscape, and us as part of the buildings.

"Now imagine that you could rise up into the air and see a larger and larger circle of terrain. Rise up until you can see Charlottesville in one direction and Lynchburg in the other. You may not have any idea what Lynchburg looks like, but don't worry about it, it's only your imagination."

Them old dreams is only in your head!

"Now broaden the circle, until it encompasses the whole state of Virginia, with us in the middle of the circle.

"Now make it broader still. Imagine it encompassing the whole country. Now, North America.

"Broaden the circle now until it includes the whole world. Think of us as the center of the whole world, related to every part of it, part of the undivided whole. Retain that thought, that image. Remember that wherever we go, we are always the center of the world *for ourselves*, and this is as it should be. Everyone else is the center of the world *for themselves*, and this is as it should be, and as it must be. We are here in time and space, so the time is always now, the space is always here, and we are always at the center of our own circle. There's nothing wrong with it, and even if there were, there would be nothing to be done about it. It is the way it is, and it is the only way it can be.

"Now, you have an image of this immense area of which we are the center. Take that area, take the whole world, and compress it. Compress it, until it fits inside you. We are the whole world; the whole world is us, even though we seem separate. Carry the world within you as you go.

"Now, notice how you feel. *Holding* that feeling, slowly and carefully open your eyes. Opening your eyes will tend to bring you closer to your accustomed mental state, the state from which you normally function. Open your eyes, hold the feeling, and you will blend this expanded, connected state with your normal, focused state. Taking your time, holding the state you have come to, open your eyes."

I did, and I have no way to tell you how strange the familiar room seemed.

As so often, she was smiling at us. "Welcome back. Probably it feels strange, sort of float-y. So we're going to do one thing more. Slowly, carefully, holding on to your mental state, trying not to snap back into ordinary consciousness, stand up. Do it slowly. Watch your balance. But watch your mental balance too."

I leaned forward to get leverage to stand. It seemed extraordinarily difficult to move, and just as difficult to move without (I feared) snapping back into "normal" mode. I noticed that Claire was able to rise smoothly and gracefully, while I felt like a camel unfolding itself.

"Now, moving slowly, put your arms above your head," she said, and we did. "Slowly rotate your wrists. And you can put them down again. Can you feel how much more *in* your body you feel than before you moved?" *Yes indeed.* "Can you still feel that sense of connection to the rest of the world?" *Well, maybe. I feel* something *different.* "That's how you can go through life, with a little bit of time, a little bit of attention."

Interesting. Interesting indeed. *And how do I write* that *up?*

Ellis said, quietly, "I got the most distinct feeling of actual connection to the physical universe, the physical solar system. A real feeling of oneness with it."

Andrew asked, "What do you think it means, that you got that just at this time?"

"I don't know what it means. Maybe it doesn't mean *anything.* Maybe it's just a sign that things are changing inside me, that I am extending farther than I used to. I don't know."

After a long quiet moment, David said, "And so to supper."

❖ 12 ❖

You might think it would be a morose occasion, but you'd be wrong. We were grounded, we were centered, and we were filled with the week's cumulated energy. For many of us, the week had been a life-changer, and nearly everybody, even if their lives hadn't been turned upside down, had had at least one major experience, connected either to the tape exercises or to other participants, or both. Where was there room for depression? So we ate, drank (non-alcoholic liquids), and were merry, for tomorrow we would return to the world.

At the end of the meal, David stood up with a sheet of paper in his hand. "I want to run through our arrangements for getting you out of here tomorrow. If I have it right, Klaus, Claire, and Marta are staying on for Bridging Over, right?" I touched Claire on the arm. "There you go. Already you'll know people. You won't be starting from scratch." She nodded.

"And the following people are driving and don't need arrangements: Sam, Lou, Helene, Elizabeth, and Dee. That right? Good. We're sort of counting on you being able to find your car and making your own way home." He grinned.

"Now for those of you who are flying, here's the schedule I have for getting you to the airport. Let's be sure we're on the same page. It looks like Mick is making three runs with the van tomorrow morning, at 4:30, 7:30, and 11.

"Leaving on the van at 4:30 in the morning, the following poor victims: Francois, Regina, Emil, and Ellis. That should get you to the airport by 5:30 or quarter of six, allowing for the unexpected, and gives you plenty of time to check in and go through security before your flight out to Dulles at 6:30. Agreed?

"Okay, 7:30. I have Bobby, Dottie, Katie, and Roberta. Also right? Flights at 10 and 10:30, roughly. Yes? Good.

"And finally, at 11, a full boat, looks like you're going to be sitting on each other's laps. Good thing the van has three rows of seats. I have Edith, Tony Giordano, Selena, and Jane on the 2:00 United to Dulles. I have Jeff, Andrew, and Toni Shaw on Northwest to Detroit leaving at 2:45. And I have Angelo on the 3:30 USAir to Philadelphia. Everybody checked out on to-morrow's schedule? Anybody unsure of anything, anybody has a problem, talk to me. Nobody? Good.

"So I think I've earned my dessert, and after a while, when we ring the bell, we're going to assemble at Edwin Carter Hall for tonight's program."

❖ 13 ❖

Back in the assembly room of Edwin Carter Hall for the last time, strag-gling in, carrying our mugs of coffee or tea. *Not even a week – five days – since I sat in this room for the first time. Bobby and Roberta and me trailing David after our rush-rush supper. They were all strangers.*

I was holding hands with Claire as we walked. She leaned slightly toward me. "Doesn't it seem strange that a week ago none of us knew each other?" I nodded, not trusting myself to speak. I knew she knew what was in the nod. *How could we not have known each other, sure – but, now, how are we – ?* I squelched the thought. She squeezed my hand, and took a chair. They were arranged in a circle this time, the desks pushed against the walls. I sat next to her. Jeff came in and sat on her other side and took her hand, and I felt no emotion more complicated than love for both my friends.

The room filled, and after a while Annette said, "So here we are, gang. Journey's almost over. Four of you are leaving at 4:30 to catch an early flight, so there'll be empty chairs at breakfast. That means we've had our last meal together. In a very real sense, *this is it*, right here, right now." The room was intensely quiet. "Tomorrow, back to the real world, right? Family responsibilities and commuting and job and taking out the garbage and all the *stuff*, you know?" We did. It was accompanying us, had been, increas-ingly, all day.

"It's okay to be sad about it, but there's no use wallowing in it either. And so we come to our guest of honor here." She lightly patted the hand of the woman sitting next to her. "Some of you know Sandy. For those who don't, Sandy Merriman Bowen is the institute's managing director, and, incidentally, C.T.'s middle daughter and Jim Bowen's wife. If that doesn't qualify as life experience, I don't know what would. Sandy's going to talk to us a bit about what comes next. Sandy?"

"Thanks, Annette." Sandy's voice was low and mellow, with just the slightest trace of southern. I guessed her to be in her early 40s. "'What comes next' sounds like it's going to be a sales pitch for our other two programs, but it isn't. You probably already know that we have two graduate programs. The first one, Inner Voice, helps you to get into closer contact with your internal guidance system. Bridging Over, our newest program, teaches how to contact those on the other side of the veil." *Man, what I would have thought of that last Saturday!* "They are good programs, and once you've finished Open Door, you can take either one. All right, enough about that. I'll be glad to talk to anybody about them, but not here and now. Here and now, the question is, where do you go from here?"

I chewed on my lip. *Sure is.*

"Okay, let's talk about this week. It's been quite a week, hasn't it?" She moved from face to face, meeting people's eyes. "For nearly all of you, something changed this week. You all took the same tapes and participated in the same discussions, but I'm willing to bet that no two of you had the same experience internally, for the plain and simple reason that no two of you are alike. The fact that you had different experiences doesn't matter. It isn't what specifically happened, it's that *something* happened.

"If this group is like most groups, one or two of you are leaving here totally blown away, one or two are thinking that this week has been a total bust, and the rest of you have seen enough, these past few days, to realize that you are a well of unsuspected possibilities. I'm going to speak to those of you who feel like you've been utterly transformed, and then to the ones who are sitting here disappointed. But first I'm going to speak to the majority of you who aren't sitting there feeling utterly changed, but aren't feeling totally unchanged either. Probably you feel that you had a good experience and learned some things that will come in handy, and you're already filing it away like 'it was a good experience.'" She smiled and got her chuckle.

"Be a little slow to judge.

"I'm sure that at some time or other David or Annette told you that after you've learned to direct your mind, you can't go back to being what you were. It's true, you can't – and why would you want to? Why spend the time and money to come here if all you want is to remain where you were? But change doesn't come free – and I'm not talking about the money you paid. Change requires readjustment, and as it says in one of my favorite movies, feelings don't necessarily tickle." *Tell me something I don't know!*

"Here's my prediction. Before very much time goes by, you're going to have to decide what this experience has meant to you and how you're going to deal with it. How are you going to relate to your friends and family? You'll find that some people you will be able to tell everything to. Others, not much. Others nothing at all. And that's only if you decide to be more or less open about it. Some of you – many of you perhaps – won't feel it's safe to talk about any of it to anybody, for fear they'll call the guys with the lab coats and butterfly nets and put you in a padded cell.

"How are you going to handle it?

"Has it occurred to you that although you have seen some unsuspected possibilities, most of them are unsuspected still? Has it occurred to you that although you have already felt changes within you, whether or not they lead to something solid, these changes are only the beginning? And most of all, has it occurred to you that an increase in abilities may mean an increase in problems?

"Well, if it hasn't, let it occur to you right now. *Your life is going to change.* Some of it will be delightful, some of it won't. But if your life gets hard – and it may, it really may – remember that your ability to deal with problems has also increased. It is my personal belief, again based on everything I've seen, and what I've learned from C.T. and Jim, and what we've heard from so many people in so many programs, that we never get anything that we can't handle." She laughed. "That's not the same as saying that we *want to* handle it, or that we wouldn't prefer to get roses without thorns. But we *can* handle it, or it wouldn't have been placed in front of us. I'm sorry if that sounds all mystical and woo-woo, but it's what I have come to believe.

"Now, those of you who have already experienced and recognized your miracle. You are the luckiest people here, in some ways, but at the same time perhaps you're going to be the most challenged. I won't say definitely that you *will*, because there's no point in programming that kind of belief. Nothing about what's going to happen to you from here on in is set in stone: But let's just say that it seems to be a law of life that of those who have received much, much is expected. Another way of looking at it is, if you couldn't handle it, you wouldn't have received it. If you are sitting here knowing that you have been transformed, that new possibilities have revealed themselves, accept my deepest congratulations – and hear this warning. Don't confuse the gift with the recipient – and above all, don't confuse the gift with the giver.

"What do I mean by that? I mean, the fact that you suddenly receive a huge gift doesn't mean that you *deserved* that gift. It doesn't mean that you are superior to others, or on the fast-track to enlightenment. It just means that maybe you can handle it. And it doesn't mean that you are suddenly superman because the gift came. Gifts come from wherever they come from, for whatever reason they come, and come to whoever they come to, for reasons that we never can figure out, no matter how elaborate the fairy tales we tell ourselves. Our religions would say 'the spirit blows where it wants to'; Carl Jung would say that the Self has its own reasons that may or may not be apparent to the ego-self. It amounts to the same thing. If you are one of those who have been given a great gift this week, listen to me: Beware of psychic inflation. You're just as good as anybody else, and they're just as good as you. Nobody knows enough to judge other people, no matter how much we do it anyway. If you've been given great gifts, let me tell you, you'd better start practicing humility, or you're in for a rough ride.

"And finally, I want to say something to any of you who may be sitting here thinking, 'I didn't get *anything* out of this. It has been a complete failure and a waste of time.' If any of you are feeling that – and usually, one or two of you are – I offer you this advice: Wait a bit before you decide. Be open to the possibility that more has happened than you realize, or that it is *yet* to happen. More than once we've gotten a call from somebody who left feeling quite downcast – even angry – who realized only weeks or months later that what happened here prepared them for something that couldn't occur until later. So if you're feeling a little left out, a little down, I encourage you to live in hope, instead.

"Yogi Berra said, 'It ain't over until it's over,' and we've found over all these years that we don't even *know* when it's over. In fact, 'over' in this context is pretty much meaningless. Where there's life there's hope – but you have to be willing to *hold* that hope, to *tend* it, to keep it alive especially when there isn't any good reason to believe in it. There isn't anything I can say to you tonight more important than, *don't ever give up hope*. My experience tells me that sooner or later we always get what we want the most. We may not get it when we want it or where we expect it – and we certainly don't get it by stamping our feet and *demanding* it right here and now or else – but if we persist in wanting the same thing, we do get it. Of course, sometimes we get it and don't recognize it. Please, if you're still waiting, *don't give up.* Miracles happen whether we're expecting them or not, but they have a much harder time manifesting if we're closed to them. Don't be closed to them.

"All right. I've said my piece, and I'm going to go. This is no time to add another person's energy to the group energy you have built together since Saturday night. On behalf of C.T., and of the institute staff, we thank you for coming, and we remind you that we're here whenever we can be of assistance." And with that, accompanied by our applause, she walked across the room, climbed the stairs, and was gone, and we participants refocused on Annette and David.

❖ 14 ❖

They had us get up and stand in a circle. Hokey, I would have thought it, before.

"Okay, gang," David said, "this is it. This is actually the last part of the formal program. If you have anything you want to say to the group, this is your time.

"We've come a good way together in a short time. You've had challenges and you've had opportunities. Some of you have broken into brand new territory, and maybe some of that territory is scary. But you've had an experience *together.* You've been part of each other's experience, and this is the time to acknowledge that."

He moved his eyes around the circle, connecting with us one by one as he spoke. "You know, I like to think of an Open Door as being like a wagon train in the 1800s. We were strangers, and we travel together and at the end of the trip we go off in different directions. Many of us – perhaps most of us – will never see each other again. But for this short time, we've been a community, and we've looked out for each other, and we've gone into new territory together. This is the time to acknowledge that, in whatever way you wish to." He held up a wooden rod, maybe two feet long, embellished with paint and tied with ribbons and feathers. "This is a talking stick, made by one of the participants in a previous Open Door. I'm going to hand it to Edith, and while she holds it, she has the floor. When she's finished, she will pass it to Francois, and so on until it comes around again." He started to hand it to her, then added a last-minute thought. "If you choose not to say anything, of course that's perfectly all right, just pass the stick to the person next to you. The point is to say what you're moved to say, whether much or little, or nothing at all." He gave the talking stick to Edith Fontaine.

"No doubt everyone here is going to express their gratitude to our trainers," Edith said, "so I might as well be the first. David, Annette, you did a magnificent job, and you helped make it a wonderful week. If all the trainers are as good as you two, the institute is very fortunate. This week has been eye-opening for me. I thought of myself as average, and I still think so, but I look around at all you other average people and I realize, the difference between average and extraordinary is mostly how much you apply yourself, how well you learn, how much you let yourself express love and receive love. Plus, it's easy to see, now, that we don't have a clue as to how much more we can grow into. Sometime this week I had a tape experience that at first I interpreted as saying that I could expand my massage practice but as I have thought about it, I think it was really saying that I can still expand my life, in many directions. This week certainly shows how much more there is to life! So I'm very pleased and very encouraged, and I hope if any of you are ever out my way you'll give me a call so we can get together." She turned to Francois Arouet and handed him the talking stick.

Francois said, "Thank you, Edith," and paused. "I am a priest, and so I am accustomed to taking part in what you might call spiritual self-help seminars. Usually, though, I am the one giving them! It has been very interesting to experience this seminar as a participant, and to see how well these exercises serve our spiritual natures. I know that not everyone here considers that we have a spiritual nature, but" – humorously – "as I have the talking stick, this once I will say it. In my view, it is the tragedy of our times that our society ignores and starves our spiritual nature. Many people feel this in their bones, I think, they feel that something is wrong, but they have no sense of what we can do to bring it right. I would wish that people could find what they need in the church, for it is there, and has been there for centuries. But perhaps this new time that we are coming into will require new institutions. No one can know for sure. The Age Of Faith being over, and The Age Of Materialism perhaps coming to an end, perhaps we are entering The Age Of Personal Experience, and perhaps this institute is leading the way." He handed the talking stick to Selena Juras.

THURSDAY

Interesting interchange between those two! Who would have guessed? I thought back to what Francois had told me. *Sometimes we really never get a clue.*

"Do you know what I got out of this week?" Selena Juras asked. "I got a reminder that we all have different gifts, and that what matters is not what our gifts are, or how well we have developed them, or what our potential may be. What matters is that we *use* the gifts we have been given, and use them to help others. I am going to work to remember that whenever I think of this week that we have had together." *Well, that's still Selena, not much interested in what's been going on around her. Still, it's better than I would have predicted Saturday.* She handed the talking stick to Elizabeth Tyrone – Elizabeth from Elizabeth, as she would always be when I thought of her.

Elizabeth said, simply, "I came here looking for something. I didn't know exactly what I was looking for, and I didn't know how I was going to recognize it if I found it. But I did know that after years spent reading and studying and listening to other people, I had a lot of information, and I had opinions, but really it wouldn't be correct to say that I *knew* anything. So that's what I was hoping to get here, as I have looked in so many other places, and if I didn't find it here, then maybe the next seminar, or the one after that." *Well, at least she knows it.* "Really, I was running out of hope. But now I have experienced a few things first hand. I *know* what I experienced, even if I may not yet know what they mean, or what they'll lead to. So I'm very grateful. I feel like I've taken at least a first step."

Sam Andover took the talking stick, and held it for a couple of seconds. "I've had a good time this week, getting to know you all. I'm taking home some fond memories, and I wish you all well." He handed the talking stick to Dottie Blunt. *Baffling,* I thought. *He never experienced anything, as far as I can tell. He just watched everybody else go through the program. He never moved, and apparently that's fine with him. It's – well, it's baffling.*

"Since I'm holding the talking stick, I guess you *have to* listen to me for a minute." Dottie smiled along with the smiles and laughs she had gotten. "This has been a big week for me. I have felt like I was inaudible and invisible my whole life. Before I came here I thought, 'Oh God, if only that would change, I'd be so grateful!' But I didn't really think it could happen. And then Lou here challenged me. He put it right in my face, and made me see that I could either keep thinking it was everybody else's fault, or I could see that I was the common denominator. So I particularly want to acknowledge Lou for doing that, and I want to say, Lou, you can be a real pain in the butt! But I needed that, and I'm very grateful that you said what you did, when you did. I'm not going to be silent any more."

Lou Hardin took the stick. "I don't know, I think maybe I liked it better when you were silent. But you're welcome, and thank you for saying it." He paused. "I want to say, I've never been around such high spirits for so long a time! That's been a treat in itself. I can see that for some of you – many of you – this week has been full of surprises. I can't say that I've had a lot of surprises, unless you count Angelo deliberately trading a bishop for a pawn. I've had what seemed to be messages, or visions, like most everybody here, but I think in my case I have to put them down to an overactive imagination. Nonetheless, I'm glad I came, and I wish you all pleasant journeys." He handed the stick to Dee West.

I thought, *Well, if you're determined that you won't experience anything, you'll get what you want. But if that's where you are, why spend the time and money to come here?* Then it occurred to me: This way he could go home telling himself that he'd examined it for himself but was too realistic to fool himself the way the others had.

Dee said, "I have had a very pleasant week and it's been fun meeting all of you. Having read *Extraordinary Potential*, I was curious about C.T. Merriman, and it was very interesting to hear him speak. My friends are waiting for me to get home and give them a full report, and I'll be able to tell them it's quite worthwhile." She handed the stick to Bobby Durant. *Hmm,* I thought, *another one who didn't move. Well, maybe she is happy where she is.*

Bobby held the stick in both hands, thoughtfully. I had a sudden image of him as an American Indian, I don't know where that came from. "I have to say, this week wasn't at all like I thought it was going to be. I didn't have any idea it was going to be so frustrating, so long! But I finally got it, with the particular help of Ellis Sinclair, who gave me the right way to approach it. Ellis, thanks again. And thanks Annette and David for giving me the same answer to all my technical questions, so that I finally had to give up the left-brain approach." A pause. "In one of yesterday's tapes, I got an image I kind of like, and I thought I'd share it here. I saw myself riding a bicycle the way kids do when they're first trying to learn, wobbling first to one side and then the other. And what I got was this, the way to do this stuff is like riding a bicycle, you've got to keep re-balancing. If you let yourself lean too far in either direction, you're going to crash. You can't go about it just with logic, and you can't do it just with intuition; you've got to balance the two. So from now on I'm going to be practicing riding the bicycle."

Katie van Osten took the stick. Just like Katie, simple, sincere, short and to the point. "You all know what *I* hoped to get out this program, and I got it, and I am so grateful. But I got more than that. I got support from so many of you, and I learned so much listening to other people's lives and problems and hopes and wishes. I don't have any real words of wisdom to share with you – I wish I did. All I can recommend is that you do what I try to do – live in hope, and love your friends, and thank God for both."

Ellis Sinclair took the talking stick and looked around the circle. "Everybody in this room is an angel. I realize that now. You may know, or you may not, that in the Bible angels are messengers. I have realized, this week, at a deeper level than ever before, that we are all angels, all messengers. And if you think about some of the remarkable things we have seen this week, things between different people, things that one person may have experienced that in turn influenced somebody else, who in turn influenced somebody else, I think you'll see what I mean.

"For me, this week has brought a challenge, and this surprised me, because I thought I had reached the age when I was beyond challenges, other than the challenge that comes from age itself. I had thought I was honorably retired, but in one of our exercises a few days ago I realized that I have one more job to do. I can do that job, or I can choose not to do it, but if I don't do it, it won't get done, and I have to tell you, I find that a *hell* of a responsibility.

"You know I was a businessman, an executive at the highest level of a very large company. And what I learned there, I have seen again here, this week. And that is, at the highest levels of business, and at the farthest edge of exploration, all decisions are made not on the basis of logic but of intuition. Other businessmen know this, of course, for the highest levels never see decisions that can be made on the basis of logic; those are made at some lower level. At the top we continue to apply logic, but we never dare to disregard intuition as an important tool. Well, reluctant as I am to do so, I seem to have received a message this week: I am to write a book, explaining to people who think of themselves as hard-headed practical people that intuition is as practical and as indispensable a tool as logic. I don't know the first thing about writing a book, but it seems I have to try. If it's really something I am supposed to do, I am confident that assistance will appear as needed. In any case, wish me luck. I thank you all for your work as angels this week, and perhaps we will see each other in future programs." He handed the stick to Toni Shaw.

"Like Edith," Toni said, "I got a message this week that may have meant more than I thought at first. I thought it was saying that I could be in for a period of renewed creativity, which as an artist is naturally very important to me. But now I think it was saying there's a whole new way of looking at life available to me. No, a new *life*. I'm counting my blessings tonight; thanking so many people who have helped me. At one level that means C.T. and all the people who keep the institute going; including the ones we haven't met. But mainly I mean our wonderful trainers, and all of you. I am leaving realizing that so much more is possible than I had dreamed. I'm overwhelmed with gratitude. There are three people I am particularly grateful to. You know who you are. I just want to say, I love you very much indeed." *That would be Claire and Andrew, I suppose. And – Jane, maybe?* She gave the stick to Klaus Bishof.

"This has been a very large time for me," Klaus said slowly. "It is difficult among so many things to choose the ones to talk about. I will mention one thing, because it taught me that sometimes it is right to follow promptings even if I do not understand them. On the very first day, I was compelled – no, I was – urged, I think you would say – from within, to tell people of a vision I had had of a skull. I did not want very much to do so, because to me it sounded like you would think me presumptuous. However, I did it, and days later I learned from Claire that the skull was meaningful to her. So I said to myself, I listened, and I was right to listen. I offer that to all of you. Sometimes – listen. So. I am glad that as I take myself back to Germany, I bring many good memories and new friends."

Jane Mullen took the talking stick. "Thank you, Klaus. For me, this week has not been full of revelations and wonders. And yet in a way it is a continuation and fulfillment of a path I have been on, as a Rosicrucian, for almost my entire adult life. It has given me great satisfaction to come to this place where I could put some of those teachings to the test, and see that they are not wrong. I have very much enjoyed and benefited from being in the presence of so much loving, supportive energy, and I thank you all for your part in the program." She handed the stick to Tony Giordano.

Tony said, "I was going to say this week has turned my life upside-down, but actually I think it would be closer to say, it has turned it upside-*up*. I'm leaving here with a whole different attitude than the one I came with. A *better* attitude. I'm going back home and I'm going to have fun again. I'd almost forgotten how. Hell, I'd almost forgotten that it was possible! So, thanks everybody who helped bring me to this point – and that's a lot of you, in a lot of conversations, and especially Roberta, who dropped the penny into the slot." With a little sketch of a bow, he handed her the stick.

Roberta Harrison Sellers said, "I too feel that this week has brought me to a huge revelation, and for that I very much need to thank Tony and Helene. Some of you have heard that I got a vision early on that seemed to tell me that my artwork has no value as artwork – that I'm just fooling myself. After a while, I had to tell someone, and I'm so grateful that Helene was available and was willing to listen to me. I think if she hadn't helped me with the fears this vision brought up – well, I don't know what would have happened, but I am very glad that it didn't. And then Tony, just by appreciating the things I brought with me, suddenly made it clear that I was misinterpreting the vision, and told me what I am doing and should be doing. And beyond that, I am grateful for the caring and the support and the interesting conversations and all the help that we got from our wonderful trainers. However, I must say, this is the first time in my life since I was toilet trained that I have had people concerned about whether I use the bathroom." That got her a nice laugh, and she handed me the talking stick.

My turn. "I didn't think, when I got on the plane to come down here, that I was coming all this way just to have an asthma attack! But I must say, it turned out to be worth it. Annette, you were an angel all right, and so were all the rest of you. I saw it then, and I remember it now.

"Now, I hope you won't be shocked to learn this, but even though I am a reporter by trade, I sometimes write poetry. I have been thinking about a poem I wrote a while ago, about Antarctica coming out from under the ice. Here's a part of it that I can remember:

"Ice melts,
hard-pinned rock recoils, and water flows.
From every interior gap, through every pass,
torrents spew outward to the sea,
sanding and battering ice mountains,
punching with bergs and floes, thundering
relentlessly toward the circling ocean.

"That's what this week has been about for me, coming out from under a huge burden of ice. I've seen new land emerging, and maybe it's going to take the rest of my life to figure out how to live on it. I'm very grateful for all the people who made it possible, which certainly includes everybody here." I gave the stick to Claire.

Claire said, "I want to express my gratitude for Open Door, and our trainers, and all the participants, especially my previous acquaintances, let's put it that way, Jeff and Angelo. I thought I was coming to Open Door primarily because this was the only way to get to Bridging Over, but I see that I was wrong. I have made some very close friends, in a very short time, and I am grateful for that. Whatever happens, I am glad, *very* glad, I was here this week among you all."

Jeff took the talking stick she handed him. "I don't have a lot to say. This week has been a succession of shocks. Good ones, but just one after another. It started Sunday morning, actually, with Angelo and Claire and me on the side porch. I certainly never expected to find myself so closely connected to two other people. I mean, we liked each other, but then to get the word that we knew each other in other times – as we all did, from various tape experiences – well, it certainly has given me new ideas of who I am, how far we must extend. I'm a little bit in shock, really."

He handed the talking stick to Marta Verdura y Rielo (whose surname I still hadn't learned. Fortunately it was on the list of participants that they handed out). She said, "I wish to thank Dee West especially. On Saturday night I went downstairs to be with the rest of the participants because I was tempted to hide in my room, and I did not want to do that. But everything was too new. Too many people, and I was in a new country, and I was the youngest person here, and I believed that everyone else would know much more than I did, and I would have to be silent all week. I think that Dee saw that, and from the goodness of her heart she put me under her wing until I could regain my feet under me. So thank you Dee, and thank you everyone for a wonderful program." She handed the stick to Emil Hoffman, our mystery man, still as much a mystery to me as he had been on Saturday night – that seemed months ago.

Emil toyed with the stick and looked up at us a little shyly. "I have not felt able to say this in our briefings, but quite early on I was given a new view of my life that I did not very much enjoy seeing. My life has been an intellectual one, centered on the pleasures of the mind. I thought I would come here and learn new approaches to understand life. Instead, it was explained to me that in some ways my life has been a prison." He paused. "This proved to be a great good fortune, however. When this happened, on Monday, I felt the need to talk to someone who might understand. Regina speaks French, and what I had to say came easier in French, which is my first language, than in English. Also – I am willing to believe that some part of me knew that it was important that I talk to her and not any other person. Before many words were spoken or many walks taken or many meals eaten, I had fallen in love with this beautiful person. It has made this week a lovely experience. I leave it not the same as I was when I came – and I believe that I have escaped my prison."

Regina de Plessis received the talking stick. "No more than Emil did I expect that this week would be what it has been. He and I do not know where it goes from here. We shall see. Like Emil, I feel a very different person than the one who arrived here, and I feel fortunate to have been here at the right time, with the right trainers and the right participants." She passed the stick to Andrew, almost abruptly, as though fearing to say too much, and again took Emil's hand.

Andrew St. George took the stick and held it in silence for a long moment that seemed neither theatrical nor contrived. When he finally spoke, he did so mostly looking at the carpet. "I have been trying to think what would be appropriate to say, to sum up such a week, and nothing that comes to mind is anywhere near adequate. I won't talk about the program itself, because what's the point? You all experienced it with me, and you all experienced the love and the care and the skill that Annette and David brought to our experience. When I try to find words for it, I find myself near tears and I don't want to do that." I watched him struggle to retain his composure. *Interesting. Yet another Andrew.* "You know, this isn't the first program like this that I've done. I've had some shamanistic training and I've done courses in energy healing and such like, so I thought I knew more or less what I could expect. And, I must admit, I thought that since I would be among a group of people who probably didn't have that level of experience, maybe I wouldn't learn so much. Well, it wasn't true.

"You often hear or read that true awakening comes not from the head but from the heart, and it's easy to agree in principle, abstractly. But it's another thing entirely to see it in action. This week – it doesn't matter how long I live, I'll never forget it. I learned a lot this week, but the thing I learned that was worth the most came from being with so many beautiful souls, coming from the heart, working on themselves, helping each other. I know that David is going to find this hard to believe, but I think that for me this week has been about finding true humility." He shot a glance at David, and they exchanged smiles that were something more than merely smiles.

Helene Porter took the talking stick and nodded. "I didn't know how I was going to find words to say what I am feeling, but Andrew put it quite nicely. More than anything else, even more than remarkable experiences with altered states, I think this week gave me first-hand knowledge of what it is like to live in love and community. That's a far cry from the solitary, somewhat removed life I had led until I came here, but that's my life from here on, as best I can learn to put it into practice. I am very grateful to each and every one of you for your part in setting me such an example."

And that brought us back to Annette, who took the talking stick respectfully and moved her gaze to each of us, one by one, meeting our eyes. "And I too want to thank you all. As we told you on Saturday night, I train a lot of these Open Door programs, nearly every other week, and one reason I do is that it is such a source of richness for me. Think what a gift you all are! You come here with your far-flung backgrounds and experiences and hopes and talents and even your hang-ups and problems, and you get mixed in the Merriman Institute blender and magical things happen, and I get to be part of it. And it is special for me because I do so many programs, I can see the things all the programs have in common – the emotional tendencies that are liable to surface on Tuesdays, for instance, or your probable reaction to this or that tape experience. But at the same time, every Open Door brings us into new territory. In fact, I often suspect that there is some sort of cumulating energy, for we notice that over time, each Open Door goes a little farther than previous programs did. We can do more. So, every new program, I look forward to what's in store for me, as well as for the participants. I feel so fortunate!

"So. Thank you, my friends, for what you have given me and what you have given each other. How about a group hug to mark an end and a beginning?"

Well, I thought, *I knew it would come to group hugs!* But I was smiling to myself, and at myself, because I was right there participating, and I didn't feel in any way separate from my fellow participants.

And after we broke up the huddle, David said. "Snack time. Party time. And as a symbol of your return to the outside world" – reaching down to the floor behind him, behind the flip chart – "I'm going to give you your watches back."

I would need my watch – couldn't function in my profession without one – but I didn't want it on my wrist, grabbing my attention all the time. I put it into my pocket, and that's where I carried it for weeks afterward.

❖ 14 ❖

So then it was party time. Annette and David came out from the kitchen, she with trays of cookies, fruit, potato chips, and nuts, he with a cooler packed with soft drinks in ice.

"Where's the beer?" Bobby asked.

David shook his head. "It wouldn't taste good now. It's a depressant, and it would kill that glow you're feeling. Trust us."

"My God," Andrew said. "Is this for life? Angelo has to go back to the *newsroom!*"

David grinned. "Give it a couple of days, you'll be back to normal."

"Gee, I was hoping for better than that," I said.

Jeff said, "Oh? I wouldn't have thought you'd admit the possibility."

I looked at Francois and he nodded and said, "Yes, my thought exactly. I will go find the chessboard."

"Oh boy," Bobby said, "here we go again. Are we going to get to see you sacrifice your bishop again?"

"Time will tell," I said. "But I wouldn't bet the ranch on it, if I were you." To Claire, I said, "We'll get to talk tonight before you go to bed? After things calm down a little? You're not going to bed early?"

"I don't have anything I need to do tomorrow. I can sleep all Friday and most of Saturday if I wish."

"And then Bridging Over."

"And then Bridging Over."

We left the rest unspoken.

Francois and I were well into the middle of the game, with three people watching and everybody else having animated conversations on all sides, when in walked C.T. Merriman. "I thought I'd see if we had any dissatisfied customers," he said with a twinkle.

Of course he was instantly the center of attention, and soon he'd gotten a mug of coffee and a few pretzels and had sat at one of the tables and lit up a cigarette. *Where did that ashtray come from? David got it out of the kitchen, I suppose.* Francois and I looked at each other and set the board aside for later, or never, whichever came first.

"So," C.T. said, "a reasonably satisfactory experience?"

Bobby: "Best week of my *life!*"

Jeff: "Eventually." We all laughed, Bobby included, and Bobby told C.T., "It took me a while to get the hang of things."

C.T. said, "Overwhelmed for a while by new perceptions?"

"No! Couldn't *get* any perceptions! *Nothing!* Drove me crazy. But finally Ellis told me what to do, and *Bam!*"

"It was merely a matter of suspending judgment," Ellis said.

C.T. nodded. "It's a balance. Before you can analyze a thing, you have to be able to experience it. But once you've experienced something, it's important to examine it, to try to understand it. I always tell groups – maybe I told this group – first wallow in the sensation, then bring in the worm of analysis. We've got a left brain for logic and a right brain for pattern-recognition; we do our best work when we use them together." He took a sip of coffee. "That's how we learn to discover who we really are. We go inside, we experience new things, and then we think about them and try to figure out what the new things mean. It isn't something anybody can do for you. We're a pretty hard-headed species, we have to see for ourselves."

"Which is where your book comes from, *Extraordinary Potential*," Klaus said. "You experienced, and you thought about what you experienced."

"Yes indeed. What we hear from others, or read, is only hearsay. What we experience, is ours." He took a drag on his cigarette. I had noticed, Sunday night, that he used his cigarette primarily as something to hold and gesture with. Long moments would go by between puffs. *He uses it for punctuation*, I thought. "For instance, sitting here, I can feel the difference in the energy of the group. Can you?" We could, and said so. "What good would it have done to *talk* about it?"

"Your writing about it in *Extraordinary Potential* is what got us here!" Andrew said.

"Well, it's true, that's what we use to whet your appetite, but you see what I mean. Until you experience it first-hand, it's only a promise."

"C.T.," Andrew said, "you told us Sunday night that we are in the middle of a big change. Some of us think you were talking about Earth changes. Were you?"

That called for a drag on the cigarette, and a pause as C.T. retreated into himself, absently staring at Andrew. Then there was an almost visible sense of him returning from wherever he had gone.

"Let's be sure we're using the same words to mean the same thing," he said. "By Earth changes, you mean prophecies that various places are going to fall into the sea, or rise out of the sea?"

"What Edgar Cayce predicted, that kind of thing," Andrew said. "Do you think that's what we're in for?"

C.T. was looking around at us, taking the temperature perhaps. "That's a difficult topic. It isn't something I address in public. You'll notice I didn't mention it in my book, and I assume that your trainers didn't mention it during the course, either. I'll talk about it here, because where you are right now should allow you to hear me. But people at an ordinary random level of perception couldn't possibly understand what I have to say. They would hear the words but the words wouldn't mean to them what they would to me."

"They who have ears to hear, let them hear," Francois said. C.T. smiled. "Exactly. It isn't enough to say it, there has to be somebody on the other end who can hear it."

A pause. "In the first place, there is a lot of nonsense spoken about prophecy, and it's because people are speaking without having experienced what they're talking about. I'll say it again, if you haven't experienced it, you really don't know. It's that simple. Edgar Cayce made a lot of prophecies about Earth changes that were going to happen between 1958 and 1998. Well, unless the next three years are going to be awfully crowded, they *didn't* happen. So what does it mean? That prophecy is impossible? That he was a bad prophet? That his prophecies were somehow only metaphors? You can find people who will tell you all those things. I just don't happen to believe any of them. You see, I *had* a prophetic vision, or what I took to be a prophetic vision. I shaped my life around it, and so I *know*. What I know may not be true for all such visions, and part of what I think I know is probably wrong – but still, I have had first-hand experience. I *know*, in a way people don't who only read about them.

"Think about it," he said. "What is prophecy? It isn't saying that something will happen regardless. If it were going to happen regardless, why bother telling us? Oh, to play favorites, I suppose, or get us out of harm's way, like Noah and the ark. But mostly that doesn't seem to me to be the purpose of prophecy. Instead, it is to say 'if you keep going the way you're going, this is where you will wind up.' Now surely it's obvious that the main reason to say that to somebody is that you hope they'll wake up and go some other direction! So, if Cayce's prophecies changed people and because they changed the future changed, then it looks like he was wrong, because he succeeded!"

"Like Jonah," Francois said, nodding.

C.T. looked over at him. "You mean like Jonah and the whale?"

"The point of the book of Jonah is that Jonah didn't want to deliver the message because he thought that the people would repent, and God would spare them, and then he – Jonah – would look foolish for having predicted something that didn't happen. This is why he fled. And it worked out just as he had foreseen."

C.T. chuckled. "Well, that's one of the risks of the prophecy business: If people don't listen to you, you wasted your time and effort. If they do listen, your prophecy is wrong." He took a drag. "Tough racket." He chuckled some more. "Besides that brings me to 'in the second place.' *There isn't just one future.*"

"Quantum physics," Andrew said.

"Very good. I should have guessed that someone here would anticipate that. Yes, even our scientists are catching on – but I got it the easy way, years ago. Well, 'easy way' if you consider a near-death experience easy. Easier than studying quantum physics, maybe." In a few words, he outlined the way quantum physicists had been brought by mathematical necessity to consider the world as one in which each decision by anyone splits the world into two, creating one reality that lands heads (so to speak), and one that lands tails.

"I don't see it quite that way," he said. "I think that all possible realities exist already, and we choose which ones we experience. But" – holding up his hand to forestall the argument he saw coming – "this isn't the time to get into the ins and outs of it. All I am going to say is that if all possible futures exist, you can see why prophecy sometimes works and sometimes doesn't: It's because sometimes we land in the future that was predicted and sometimes we don't. The prophecy was accurate, we just didn't go there." He smiled. "Pretty foolproof excuse for prophets, isn't it? 'I was right, but you took a wrong turn.' But anyway there's an 'in the third place,' and that is that what concerns me isn't the question of whether we are or aren't going to see what are called Earth changes, because it doesn't matter in a way. Whether we get Earth changes or not, we are entering into a period of intense *human* changes."

The last of the cigarette, and a careful stubbing out. "Our scientists don't seem to realize it, but there is an energy underlying events that can manifest either in physical terms or in mental and emotional terms. I'm not speaking in metaphors. The same energy manifests sometimes as a hurricane, say, or an earthquake, and at other times manifests as a war, or a widespread emotional contagion. It is the same energy, and if it doesn't find one outlet it finds the other." He paused, looking around at us. "I know that's hard to understand."

"Not at all," Francois said. "That is what you referred to a moment ago, the prophecies. That is what they say: If you do not change what you think and feel, this physical result will follow."

C.T. nodded. "I never thought of that. I guess whoever wrote the Bible knew a thing or two."

"So," Tony said, "maybe World War II drained off the energy that would have led to Earth changes?"

C.T. shrugged. "Could be. I wouldn't know. But what I do know is what I told you Sunday – this is the end of the adolescence of the human being, and we are experiencing all the growing pains that teenagers go through. Maybe we'll have to go through external stress like Earth changes, or maybe it will be more wars, or maybe not. It depends on which future we go to, doesn't it? And that isn't something that any of us can decide – at least, not consciously. All I really know for sure is that the story of our time is that what we are is changing, practically day by day. But it's the elephant in the living room that no one seems to notice. As I say, I wouldn't dare talk about some of this in public. The news media would jump on it and make me look ridiculous."

Tony said, "That right, Angelo?"

"Oh sure. Journalists are mostly herd animals, always on the bandwagon. They don't necessarily care who's driving, or where it's going, as long as they get to ride."

Jeff said. "Huh! It's like Claire asking Francois are you sure you're a priest. Are you sure you're a reporter, Angelo?"

I laughed. "I'm not as sure as I was last week, no. I think I'm becoming a sort of foreign correspondent."

❖ 15 ❖

We were ending as we had begun, three of us quietly talking. It was too late and too cold for the side porch, so Jeff and I were sitting next to each other, facing Claire, in a booth in the otherwise deserted dining room.

"You didn't finish the chess game," Jeff said. "I presume you were losing?"

"Not hardly. But I wasn't winning either. Francois had to go to bed; he's on that 4:30 van."

"Did I hear you wheezing, a little bit ago?"

"Yeah, but I stopped it, at least for now."

Claire said, "Are you going to be okay?"

"I know what you're asking, but the question is, are you?"

"I'm okay for the moment. That will have to do."

Not much to say to that.

Jeff cleared his throat. "We have each other's phone numbers. If we can still remember how to use telephones, back in the world, we can call each other."

"I would certainly hope so," she said. "I'll be counting on it."

"We'll expect a report on Bridging Over," I said. "Maybe – uh, maybe I'll call you next Sunday? Is that too soon? That'll give you Saturday at home first."

"Call me whenever you want, both of you. And let's agree right now, if one of us calls and it isn't a good time for the other, we'll just say so and talk another time. That way, we always feel free to call. Okay? But – call."

Jeff and I nodded.

A little silence.

"If you see John next week, say 'hi' for me," I said.

"I shall. But why don't you say hi for yourself?"

"Uh, yeah. That's a thought. But by this time next week, you'll have a whole bag of tricks at your disposal. You'll probably have call waiting."

"Teleconferencing," Jeff said. "You'll be putting them on speaker phones."

A pause.

"Say hi to John's wife for me, too," I said, but that brought another little silence.

Jeff cleared his throat again. "You know what strikes me as a good idea? I might come back in a few weeks and do Bridging Over." He left it hanging there, tentative.

"Good idea," I said. "Find out the times they're giving it and let me know, and maybe we can do it together." Another small silence. "And maybe the three of us can do Inner Voice together."

"That would be good," Jeff said.

"Yes, that would be a lot of fun," Claire said. Implied: *Let's not wait too long, though.*

Again we ground to a halt. Finally Claire smiled, that wan smile I'd gotten used to seeing. "To proceed to the elephant in the living room, I know I can count on it, but I want to ask you both anyway. When I go over, even if you haven't done Bridging Over yet, will you come check on me, be sure I'm all right?"

The elephant in the living room had its foot on my chest, and he was squeezing, hard. She looked at me, concerned. "Angelo, you know I'm going to die. *You're* going to die. We all are. It can't be avoided, and the timing isn't up to us, ever."

"I know."

"Yes, intellectually you know, but what are your emotions saying?"

"Claire, I don't think I can – "

She reached over and put a hand on mine. "This is the time to *use* what you've been given, Angelo. You've been given wonderful messages, especially today. They told you we're all part of something larger. They told you we go on forever. They told you – showed you – that we don't even have to lose touch with each other. If you don't believe what you were told, that's one thing. But if you *do*, this is how you start to integrate it, you know? You use it with the things that happen in your life, one by one."

It would have been easier to respond to that if the two of us had been alone, but she had chosen to say it in Jeff's presence. It altered my response, but perhaps not for the worse.

"I know," I said.

"You said that once. You *know*. But can you *feel*?"

Can't you see how much this hurts? It made me angry. "Can I *feel*?"

"There, Angelo! That's a feeling-level response, that's what I'm talking about. It's hard, but try not to stuff it all away. It's going to be there anyway, whether you let it be conscious or not. Please, *try* to let it be conscious. Unresolved feelings have no time. If you don't let this pain be conscious, you might have it for years and not even know it, and it will be a rock in the pit of your stomach."

"God!" I said. "How can you be so cold-blooded about it? We're talking about you dying, and you say, 'let it be conscious, so you can forget about me.'"

"That's not what it means, resolving your feelings. I don't want you to forget about me. I don't want either of you to forget about me. And I don't want to forget you, either, when I'm on the other side. But I don't want you petrifying your emotional life, thinking you're making a shrine for me. What kind of memory is it, when you shrink from remembering because it hurts all the time? And if you don't deal with it, it's going to hurt, *and it could hurt for the rest of your life.* Is that what you want? It isn't what *I* want. I want you to smile when you remember me, and I don't want you smiling through your tears. I want you to be glad to think about me, and if you haven't passed through the grieving process, how can you be glad again?"

I shook my head. "Your way of taking this is beyond me," I said.

"It wouldn't be, if you weren't caught between two ways of seeing things. That's your old way of living, hanging you up. You know, 'life is real, the afterlife is theoretical and vague and maybe it's real and maybe not.' But Angelo, the things you've been told this week, I *know* they're true. I *know* there's a part of me that existed before I was born and continues after I die. And I know – or anyway, I *feel*, I *trust* – that life makes sense. It isn't just a succession of accidents. It has a pattern, and it makes sense, regardless what we think of it. Knowing all that makes a big difference."

I didn't say anything. Couldn't, really. Nor did Jeff, for whatever his own reasons were.

"Do you think I *like* the idea of leaving my daughter to grow up without me? I *hate* it! Do you think I like leaving the world when I've just barely started to see how magical it can be? Do you think I want to leave the two of you?"

Didn't mention your husband, I notice.

"But it isn't up to me, and maybe it shouldn't be. I don't have the big picture – none of us do – because we're down here in one moment at a time, and it's always changing, and it's hard for us to get a true perspective on our lives. So when something happens, I have to trust that it's for the best because it's part of the pattern."

"'All is for the best in this best of all possible worlds,'" I said. "*Candide.*"

"Maybe the people who used to say that, whoever they were, knew a thing or two that Voltaire didn't."

"Maybe," I said.

"Well," Jeff said, "speaking as a representative of Little-Picture Land, when you go over, I'm going to miss you, and I know Angelo is going to miss you, and we're going to do our best to remember you smiling. But maybe you won't go over any time soon. We don't really know, right?"

"Nobody ever knows. Doctors think they do, sometimes, but no, I don't think we ever do. So maybe I'll still be here in 20 years and we'll all be sitting here talking about our operations and the meds we're on, and what the grandkids are doing."

"But if not, it's still fine," I said.

"It always is, Angelo. Try to believe it."

"The funny thing is, in a way I do believe it. I mean, what were the chances that the three of us would choose to take this program at the same time. And look at how *many* things have been happening to people all week long and people who weren't here would say, 'just coincidence.' But another part of me *doesn't* believe it, and it's yelling and screaming, saying bullshit. Like Yeats, you know? 'What is it but sleep? No, no, not sleep but death.' It's real, and it can't be talked away."

"That's right, and don't forget it. But accepting it isn't the same as talking it away. Coming to terms with what has happened isn't the same as saying that's what you wanted. Remember Sergeant Schultz, Angelo."

"Yes," I said, nodding. "I do. You can't give up on life. You have to keep on, regardless."

"You do. We do. It's the only sensible attitude to take."

"And as I get it," Jeff said, "it's not a matter of grim endurance, either, but something much more matter-of-fact. It's something between 'here comes the next transforming experience' and 'life is one damn thing after another.'"

We all laughed, a relief.

"For all you know," Claire said, "the only reason we met this time was so that you'd both *have to* integrate what you've learned this week. There's nothing like the prospect of death to really get you right down to essentials."

"That works out great for Jeff and me," I said, lightly ironic, "but what was in it for you?"

"Perhaps it was because I needed the love and support," she said quietly, and we were back in what Jeff would call Awkward-Pause Land.

"Perhaps," I said "if you do go over, you'll return the favor, and keep an eye on us." I don't know where that came from, but I was learning to just say whatever came to mind without examining it first, a trait that seemed likely to get me into a lot of trouble if I let it become a habit.

"I will," she said. "I will if I can."

"Bearing in mind that we still don't have any idea what we're doing," Jeff said, "here or there."

"Bearing that in mind," she said, smiling.

CHAPTER SEVEN

Friday
March 24, 1995

Outside it was still full dark.

Francois said, "You are up at this time of the morning just to say goodbye?"

"Well," I said, "I'm still wearing my pajamas under my coat. Unlike you, I'm going back to bed, and I just came to rub it in."

We stood there just inside the front door awkwardly. "You ever play chess by mail?" I asked Francois. He smiled broadly. "I intended to ask you last night, but then forgot." He promised to begin a game soon after he got home.

"Ellis? Good luck with your novel. If you need some exotic background set in a major metropolitan newsroom, give me a call."

He smiled. "Perhaps I shall. Meanwhile, you stay healthy."

I said I would.

Francois and Ellis I felt I had gotten to know very well. But it was different with Regina and Emil. I said, "You guys traveling together?"

"Only as far as Dulles," Regina said.

"In the short term," Emil said. "Later, who can say?" He had a twinkle in his eye. It startled me.

Mick came in from the van. "Let's be sure we've got all our luggage, everybody." They assured him that what he saw was everything they had brought. Emil, Francois, and Ellis carried their bags out to the van, and Mick rolled Regina's bag, and packed them all in the back of the van. I walked out with them. I noticed that almost all of yesterday's snow had gone. Only a few linings clung to the sides of the driveway and the foundation of the building.

I saw Mick glance at his watch. "Well, good journeys, both of you. Maybe we'll meet again. So long." We exchanged hugs, as people mostly did on leaving the institute, and I watched them all climb into the van and out of my life, at least for the time being, and maybe forever.

❖ 2 ❖

Bobby got up at six, so I got up again, got myself showered, dressed, and fully and finally packed. Then I went downstairs to hang out and say my good-byes to the four who were waiting for the 7:30 van. Bobby, Dottie, Katie, and Roberta were sitting at a table drinking juice or coffee. "No breakfast, huh? Brutal," I said.

"Could have had toast or some fruit," Bobby said, "but it's too much trouble."

I got a mug, took some coffee from a thermos. "That's not what's brutal. What's brutal is that you'll be eating breakfast at an airport in Cincinnati or somewhere."

"Better than on an airplane."

"Marginally." Looking at Roberta: "So did Tony get his picture?"

"Yes he did." She looked quite pleased. "He got a very nice one, too, one of my favorites."

"Did you think to get a photo of him with the picture?"

"Oh. No, I didn't. That would have been good, wouldn't it?"

"We have each other's addresses on the participants list, you could ask him to get somebody to take one and send it to you."

"That's a very good idea. I'll do that."

"If I remember I'll mention it to him this morning. But you can still write him. Bobby, it's been very interesting watching your process this week. Seems to me you came a long way in a short time."

"Yeah, that's how I feel too. I *knew* this would be a great week!" *Well, that's the note he started on, that's the note he's ending on.* "I'll shoot you a note when I get home."

"Do," I said. "I'd like that." *And that's the truth, too. I'm kind of going to miss him.*

And so to small talk, as we lived out the dwindling time. Others came down to say their goodbyes (and wait for breakfast) and then Mick arrived from the kitchen where he had been snacking, ready to pack them up and do a second trip to the airport. Last goodbyes all around, and then they and their luggage were being bundled out the door, and they too were gone.

❖ 3 ❖

Which left sixteen of us, and Annette and David. Three tables of six for our last breakfast. Sort of a quiet meal, all meaningful things having been said – or being incapable of being said – and trivial or casual things being disregarded. Mostly we talked about this or that thing that had come up during the week, or things we wondered about, or – things we faced on our return home.

Not a subject I cared to dwell on. Didn't quite see how that was going to play out. The Angelo who had left home was not coming back. Elvis had left the building, or maybe he had entered the building. Everybody would have to adjust and there was no reason to assume they'd like it. *Well, at least Charlie can't complain. Whose fault is it, if not his?* But actually, I suspected that he would be pleased. Maybe I'd stop in at the shop before I went home. Might be an interesting conversation.

I tried to envision going back to work on Monday. Couldn't. Didn't want to.

"Penny?" Claire said, and I realized that somebody must have asked me something, because everybody at the table was looking at me.

"Uh?"

Jeff said, "May we quote you on that, Mr. Chiari? 'Pressed for comment, Angelo Chiari said "uh," severely displeasing the prosecuting attorney and the judge presiding.'"

"Daydreaming," I said. "What did you ask, Claire?"

"It was me," Toni said. "I wanted to know if you're going to write a story about us."

"Umm, well, I am, actually. A couple of stories, maybe a series, if I can talk my editor into it. Coming to Open Door wasn't my idea at all, you see. I was sent on assignment."

Jeff: "Big exposé. 'Our man in Entry State: Massive fraud found in central Virginia, as people pay big bucks to lie in bed listening to pink noise.'"

"Yeah, that's pretty much the way I figure to approach it. A little sex and violence, some hints of high-level politics."

"Don't forget the Illuminati," Jeff said. (In my innocence I had never heard of the Illuminati at that time, and in his compassion he didn't try to fill me in.)

Toni said, "Did you think you *would* be writing an exposé?"

"Toni, when I came down here last week, I didn't necessarily think the place was a fraud, but I didn't have a doubt in my mind that people here were fooling themselves. I figured all it would take would be a hard-headed investigation."

"And you were right," Jeff said. "Nothing in it."

"Nothing whatsoever. Well, except stopping an asthma attack without medicine. And mind to mind communication. And visions. An out-of-body experience or two. Some psychological healing, I guess you'd call it. That kind of thing. Learning how to enter altered mental states on demand, just as they promised. Nothing, really."

"What are you going to say was the high point of the week, do you know yet?"

"What do you mean, do I know yet? I traded a bishop for a pawn on the tenth move and won the game decisively. What's going to top that? Probably be my lead."

❖ 4 ❖

She said, "May I ask what you were thinking about, at breakfast? Don't tell me if you don't want to."

Last coffee on the porch with Claire and Jeff. Breakfast over, bags packed, a couple of hours to kill, waiting for the van. Beneath the trees, in the most sheltered places, I could see remnants of yesterday's snow. It had greened the grass, added a little water to the water table, presumably. Otherwise, it was as if it had never been.

"I suppose I was thinking about returning to work, being back in the newsroom, all that."

"Tomorrow?"

"Monday. Soon enough. Not looking forward to it much."

"You and Tony Giordano," Jeff said.

"Oh, me and pretty nearly everybody, I suppose. But still – "

"Vacation's over."

"Vacation? More like a new start. A rebirth almost, if that's not too over the top. It's been a hell of a change."

"And you're wondering if you'll be able to hold onto it," Claire said softly.

I focused on her. "You too?" I hadn't thought about that, somehow. "I guess I assumed you had a firmer grip on it than I did. That *everybody* had a firmer grip on it than I did."

Jeff: "You think Sam does, or Lou?"

So, you saw it too. Well, why should that be surprising? It was there to be seen. "Well, no. But you know what I mean. This is all newer to me than it is to most of you."

She said, "Comparisons, my love. It will go easier if you can forget making comparisons."

"'Who's ahead?'" I said, agreeing with her. "Annette's field of stars."

"Exactly."

"I just hope I can hold it when I go back to my real life."

"Angelo," she said, almost fierce in her intensity, "*this* is your real life. Don't start walling this off as just some weird experience you went through, or you *will* lose it! What's so real about being unable to feel? What's so realistic about not knowing half the things you can do?"

"I know," I said, nodding. "I know."

"When you *know*, you won't say things like 'my real life.' Just remember what it was like when you couldn't breathe and then you could. Don't you suppose that was real?"

"I'd be an idiot to deny it."

"Yes," she said bluntly. "You would. And you aren't, so don't."

"Yessir," I said, but I was smiling.

"Hey Angelo," Jeff said, "I guess she told you. How'd you like to be married to *her*, huh?" But that was a bit of a distraction, for we all knew that I was thinking that I'd like it very much indeed, but it wasn't going to happen.

And then, in the course of the next hour or so, more good-byes as those who were driving departed, most with a long day's drive ahead of them. Well before 11 – by 10:30, anyway – David was gone, and so were Dee, Elizabeth, Helene, Lou, and Sam. When our van load left, Annette, Claire, Klaus, and Marta would have the place to themselves until suppertime when the new trainers arrived.

"You're going to find it pretty quiet here in an hour or so," I said to Klaus.

"Yes, it will be quiet, and perhaps it will seem even more quiet tomorrow."

"Well, I gather that participants for Bridging Over start arriving any time after noon, so if you sleep late you won't have that much time to kill."

"I was not thinking of time in quiet as a burden," he said. "It will be good reflective time. Do you say reflection time?"

"Either one, I'd think."

"Yes, a good time. I have much to think of."

"Don't we all."

I wished Marta a good program. She flashed a bright smile and said she would send me a postcard from whatever new altered states they introduced her to. It was as close to a joke as I had heard from her, and I realized how little I had learned about her in the week. *Too many barriers, too many differences between us*, I thought – but then I realized that no, that excuse was an echo of my previous life. Missed opportunities were missed opportunities. No need to feel guilty about them, or mourn them as irretrievable losses (though they were, in a way) but no need either to pretend that there was nothing behind the door not opened.

"Annette," I said, "I know you probably get mushy farewells from all your participants, but I don't know how to thank you, and not just for Tuesday night, but for all you did to make this program go so well. C.T.'s technology is great, and the program seems to be very well designed, but it was *you*, and David, that made it what it was. I saw from the very first day how careful you were that people feel safe being themselves." I heard what I had just said. "God, that sounds sappy! One week, and I'm becoming a New Ager! I'm going to buy beads, and sandals, and crystals! I'm going to walk into the newsroom chanting 'om'!"

Annette laughed and thanked me for the acknowledgement, and reminded me that I was only at the beginning.

"You mean it gets weirder?"

"I mean maybe your life *until* now was weird. Maybe now it starts becoming what it always should have been."

And goodbye to Claire, a very public goodbye, with so many people standing around. To say goodbye in another room would be so conspicuous as to be nearly theatrical. To say it in front of everybody else was to do so largely from within camouflage. What we had found words to say, we had said already. What was beyond words – well, somebody said, in a very different context, 'What can't be said, can't be said, and it can't be whistled, either.' So, a short, intense hug, and a kiss, among other goodbyes taking place around us. "You take care," I murmured. "I love you too," she whispered, and then I got into the van, and put on my seat belt, and cast my mind forward to the hour-long trip ahead.

❖ 6 ❖

It was a mostly silent ride, our thoughts mostly elsewhere. And then we were at the airport, just at noon, pulling our bags from the back of the van, saying goodbye to Mick, and going through the automatic doors to the check-in counters. Edith, Tony, Selena, and Jane, who were headed out to California by way of Dulles, queued up at the United counter. Jeff, Andrew, and Toni were going Northwest, via Detroit. I went up to the USAir counter, no one else in line so far ahead of departure time, and when I had checked my bag and gotten my boarding pass, I walked over to the other two counters and suggested we have lunch in the little coffee shop. "Otherwise, once we go through security, if we get hungry, we're out of luck," I said.

"Noon, it must be time to eat," Jeff said. "Back to clock and bell." I laughed, taking his point.

So we had coffee or soft drinks and sandwiches and what the English call push-conversation, and after a while we went through security. United boarded at 1:30, and we said our goodbyes to Edith, Tony, Selena, and Jane, and then we four trooped over to the Northwest lounge, and Jeff and Andrew and Toni checked in, and after a while the airline began the boarding process.

We had already talked about the remarkable healing ceremony we had participated in – was it only yesterday? I gave Toni a hug and wished her a full recovery and soon, and she wished the same for me, which actually was something of a startling thought. I thanked Andrew for letting me participate and he thanked me for participating, and oddly I realized that the tie between us was stronger than I had realized.

Jeff and Claire and I had said our real goodbyes on the porch after breakfast. He and I took leave of each other, as we had taken leave of Claire, from within deep cover. "Stay in touch, big guy," I said as we gave each other a farewell hug. "Yeah," he said. "I'll probably give you a call in a couple of days, see if you're still out of the loony bin." And then they got in line to board, their attention on the ticket taker and the flight ahead.

❖ 7 ❖

My plane wouldn't be boarding for another 45 minutes. I stood by the window in the Northwest lounge, watching them walk out onto the concrete and over to the plane and up the steps and out of sight.

I'll have to remember to get my prescription refilled. I thought of Annette, encouraging me to *imagine* drawing long deep breaths, directing my friends to send loving energy for me to use. *"Maybe your life until now was weird. Maybe now it starts becoming what it always should have been."*

I thought of Andrew, leading us through a healing session for Toni, and for Claire. *"We want to deal with your subconscious mind as if it were a different person."*

Toni saw herself as both the potter and the clay. Let's program for us both to make a full recovery.

What we create consciously may not agree with what we create unconsciously, Klaus said. I wondered if I could somehow overcome the asthma, get beyond the need for medicines.

I asked, "Will it work in real life?" and she said "This is your real life. Don't start walling this off as just some weird experience you went through." It called up an image of Lou Hardin, ruthlessly discarding whatever experience didn't fit his preconceptions. *"Probably I was just making it up."*

"Here's my prediction," Sandy Merriman Bowen had said. *"Before very much time goes by, you're going to have to decide what this experience has meant to you and how you're going to deal with it. How are you going to relate to your friends and family?"*

If I tell Julie half of what I've experienced, she's going to go ballistic. For years she's wanted me to get religion. Now she'll be sure I've joined a cult.

It's like there are two worlds, side by side, with no tolerance for each other. Three, maybe. The fundamentalists, the materialists, and – whatever this is.

Interpreter. Priest, marrying people. You are not alone.

Columbus, right. *How in the world am I going to meld them, when all of society holds them apart?*

There's got to be a way forward, something that doesn't involve blind faith one way or the other. I thought of Bobby's bicycle, and David's wagon train. *Maybe I'm just in one of the earlier trains and it's a matter of time. Maybe is just a matter of bringing enough wagon trains through.*

I thought of Francois, shrugging as he pondered his next move. *"The very word 'religion' means 'linking up again,' and one way or another, humans find it is painful, futile, to try to live without those links. Perhaps, as you say, Christianity no longer serves to link people up with the spiritual world. If this is true, then sooner or later it will be replaced by something that does. But, my friend, where do you see its replacement?"*

"Are you sure you're a priest?" Claire had asked.

I thought of Andrew, saying that awakening comes not from the head but from the heart. Andrew, who kept showing new unsuspected sides of himself.

Francois said it didn't sound to him like wait till you're dead and hope to get to heaven.

Well, what happened, happened. No use pretending that it didn't, and no use pretending that I don't know what I learned. Now it's a matter of learning to live it.

I had traveled for a while with the wagon train, pushing into an undiscovered world. What it would be like, living there, I had no idea. *"You're not alone in this,"* Annette had said.

I was a babe in the woods. Always had been, but now I was aware of it.

The funny thing is, what I mostly learned this week is that I don't know anything! It's all ahead of me!

The nose wheel on the jet turned, and the big airplane began to turn on its axis, moving toward the taxiway. I turned away from the window and went to check in for my own flight home.

EPILOGUE

Friday Night
March 24, 1995

"All right," Charlie said as we waited for the elevator, "sounds like we got our money's worth. Write it up and we'll see what we've got."

I hadn't told him everything, of course, or even hit all the highlights. That would have been some epic-length coffee break! But I had given him the sense of the framework around Merriman's process. "It's a new way of exploring, Charlie," I had said. "You don't have to be superman to do this. Anybody can do it. And it's safe!"

He'd given me the Reilly fish-eye. "One size fits all, money-back guarantee, but you must act now. Call 1-800 – "

"Is that what I sound like?"

"Let's say you sound a little bit short on the old journalistic objectivity. Luckily for you, you've got a good editor's blue-pencil to keep you straight."

"Like you've used a pencil in ten years!"

"You know what I mean. You're going to have to stop yourself from getting so carried away that you lose the reader. You're quiet about it, but I've never seen you so hopped up."

I smiled at him. "You sent me there, so whose fault is it?"

"I just hope I haven't created a monster. You've got to be careful you don't sound like you've joined a cult," he said. "No matter how carefully you write about the occult or the supernatural, some people are going to react with suspicion."

"Nothing occult or supernatural about it, Charlie," I said, but as it turned out, he was right as usual. My series provoked a flood of critical letters, some from self-styled Christians saying that I was playing with evil forces, others from self-styled proponents of a "rational" or "scientific" point of view, saying that I had deluded myself.

The elevator doors opened and we went in and he hit the button. The doors closed. On the way up, he said, "We'll do a six-part series, more if you've got enough to go long. And if you feel up to it, we can probably get you a slot in the magazine for an expanded version. Assuming the material is as good as it sounds like."

A piece in the magazine wasn't instant fame, but it was a big step upward. *Is this what he meant when he said this could be my ticket?*

Reading me without much trouble, as usual, he smiled. "Don't start signing autographs yet," he said as the doors opened and we got out. "But still, who knows? Maybe you'll get a book out of it."

That made me smile, but it was a wry smile. "Yeah, if I want a divorce. The series is going to be bad enough."

Charlie shrugged. "If you're going to admit that you're taking all this stuff seriously, you're going to admit it. If you're not, you're not. It's kind of hard to stay half-pregnant."

True enough.

We stood there at his desk. "So now go home," he said. Implied: "Good luck." I hadn't anything much to say to that, so I nodded and walked back to the elevator. *Okay, Charlie, I'll write the story specifically for you, and let the public read over our shoulders. If I acquire a public persona as a weirdo, too bad.*

I punched the button, and the doors opened right away and I got in. *As to my private life, well, I guess I'm going to find out.* I punched One and the doors closed, shutting out the newsroom. *Next step, home, if it's still home. Next step, whatever comes.*

The End?

The beginning?

About Hologram Books

For a complete list of titles available from Hologram Books,
go to our website: www.hologrambooks.com